IN THE KINGDOM OF DRAGONS:

DWARF AND DRAGON

Book Two

—— D. L. Burnett ——

"Whether you're a fantasy reader or not, this exploration of responsibility, of tolerance, of love, spiced up with danger, dragons, humor, and humanity, is a must-read. Hellestorm the baby dragon will tickle your senses, and Thorne the warrior mom will shake up your beliefs. But Strumgued the honorable Dwarf will steal your heart."

—Laurel Yourke, U.W. Madison, Emeritus

Praise for:

ROSE AND THORNE

Book One

"*In the Kingdom of Dragons* is a grand saga of high adventure, set in a vivid land of fables and magic, featuring a stalwart (albeit inexperienced) heroine. Highly recommended."

—The Midwest Book Review

Also by D. L. Burnett

IN THE KINGDOM OF DRAGONS:

ROSE AND THORNE

In The Kingdom

Of Dragons:

Dwarf And Dragon

In The Kingdom —— *of* —— Dragons:

Dwarf and Dragon

Book Two

D. L. Burnett

Effertrux Publishing
Sun Prairie, Wisconsin

Effertrux Publishing
P.O. Box 694
Sun Prairie, Wi 53590-9998
www.Effertrux.com

Copyright © 2014 by D. L. Burnett
www.DLBurnett.com

Library of Congress Control Number: 2013950574

ISBN: 978-1-940251-00-4 (pback)
ISBN: 978-1-940251-03-5 (ebook)

Cover Design by Ingrid Kallick

For My Father
Aaron Dan Hazen,
who always believed in me.

ACKNOWLEDGMENTS

Thank you to Bruce Burnett, John Strikwerda, and Ingrid Kallick. Very special thanks to Laurel Yourke and the past and present writers in Laurel's Monday Critique Group and Novel Critique Group.

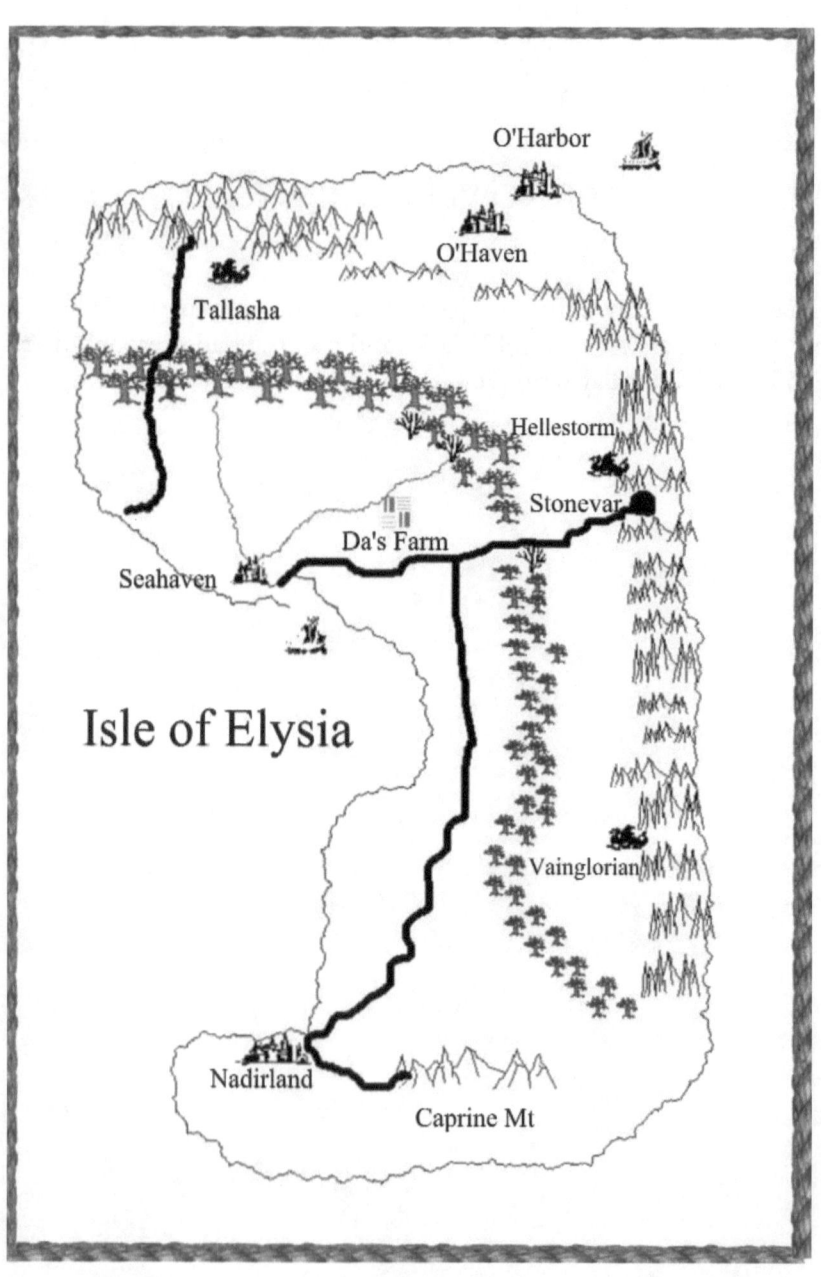

CHAPTER ONE

Thorne rushed along the battlement cut from the mountainside, dressed for war in black Dragon leathers, hand resting on her sword, Dracodurus. She gazed over the orchard to the other side of the river where the Dwarf invaders had almost finished building a raft bridge, their hammers echoing in the gray predawn. Now that Stonevar's Dragon was dead, they intended to reclaim their ancient homeland, which the Dragon stole from them millennia ago.

However, the formidable fortress, carved from within a mountain, was Thorne's home now, and she would never surrender it. She knew Stonevar was her destiny the first time she traversed its Great Hall, moving amongst carved columns and surging arched spans.

Now as she sought strength from the stone beneath her feet, the Dwarf Lord shouted orders. His warriors sang as they worked. To Thorne, their muffled words had the pestilent hum of locusts. She pictured shooting arrows into their hearts or fiery brands into their bridge. But the distance was too great.

Hearing clattering from behind, Thorne turned to look down into the bailey. Her soldiers rushed from the castle to the stable. Her mentor, Brutte, limped outside on his peg leg, holding the reins of Thorne's warhorse. Though Brutte had but a single eye, and one sound arm and leg, he would've saddled Thorne's horse himself, made sure the cinch was tight.

Brutte and his wife had taken seventeen-year-old Thorne in after her father, Da, cast her out three years before. Brutte trained her to use a sword, forging a bond between them stronger than blood. Then Brutte and his wife had given up everything to follow her here.

1

Without his advice, Stonevar would never have prospered, and she'd probably be dead. He taught her how to lead men and declared her a goddess, saying her legend would discourage brigands. But Dwarf warriors were far more dangerous.

Now he motioned to Thorne with his amputated arm. She dashed down the stairs to join him.

"How many?" Brutte whispered.

"A hundred or so."

His gray hair, usually tied back, stuck out in all directions. "A company."

"Should we ambush them?"

"Your lasses are no match for Dwarf warriors." He was all soldier now, his single eye sharp, his jaw set. "Takes five good fighters to drub a Dwarf."

She'd only seventeen: nine middle-aged men, six women, a Giantess, and a young Wanderling. These last eight had vowed to guard Stonevar's Dragon hatchling and confirmed their commitment by drinking Dragon blood, which heightened their senses and made them stronger. But would their uncommon strength be enough?

Thorne tongued a small copper coin, a soothing dragonish habit. "Should we wait them out?"

"Lass, you cannot defend the castle. Dwarfs know the passageways inside the mountain."

"Secret doors even in solid rock." She should've suspected that.

"Aye. That's the Dwarf way."

"Then what should we do?"

"You must meet the Dwarf Lord on the plain."

Bumps rose on Thorne's skin. "You said it takes five men to defeat one. There'll be five to each of us."

He put his arm around her. "Show them your courage. Fight till you cannot stand. Don't surrender even if wounded." He took a deep, chest-expanding breath. "If you fall, show no fear. Bare your breast and offer your heart to sheath his sword. Thank him for sending you an honorable death."

Thorne didn't have that kind of courage. She was only twenty, and didn't want to die on the Isle of Elysia, the same place where she'd been born. She wanted to travel the world. As if Brutte knew her thoughts, he squeezed her arm.

"We must safeguard Hellee," Thorne said. The orphaned

2

Dragon whelp, Hellestorm the Great, had hatched three months before. When he matured, he'd become their protector. Until then, those who had drunk Dragon blood—the Dragon Guards—must protect him.

"I'll defend the tunnel into the Dragon's cavern."

"But Brutte—"

"I'm still soldier enough." He clasped the knife strapped to his thigh. "Have no concern. I'll not let anyone harm the wee Dragon."

The "wee Dragon" was the size of a small horse. She hugged Brutte as if for the last time. "Thank you."

When Thorne released him, Brutte adjusted his eyepatch, using the back of his hand to wipe his good eye. Thorne pretended not to notice. Instead, she watched the men bring the horses outside, men she'd grown to love like brothers. They'd had enough of war and had followed her expecting to farm and raise their families.

"How can I lead them to their deaths?" Thorne asked.

"Do as I say. It's our only hope."

The nine men assembling in the bailey wore mismatched armor, but every shield had a Dragon profile. In full battle garb, Thorne hardly recognized them. They seemed different, as if they'd left the battlefield yestereve.

Amid the noise of clanking armor and children's questions, their families gathered around the men, wishing them well. More than one wife turned away to hide tears.

While Thorne offered encouragement, the Fairy, Raspberry-Frost, landed on Thorne's shoulder and folded its moth-like wings. As the Fairy combed its white head tuft with needle-sharp fingernails, Thorne stroked its bird-like leg. Raspberry-Frost was Thorne's first friend and had saved her life more than once.

The Fairy, who stood eight inches high, plucked a gnat from its silvery chest fuzz and ate it. "Foolish Humans confront Dwarfs."

"I have Stonevar because I'm foolish." With Raspberry-Frost's help, Thorne defeated the giant constrictor devouring Dragon eggs, and Stonevar's orange Dragon reluctantly let Thorne stay.

As if sensing her faltering courage, Raspberry-Frost nipped Thorne's ear.

Accustomed to this, she didn't even wince. "Find out what the Dwarfs are planning."

The Fairy flew off to spy.

Thorne had no more time. As she donned her breastplate, she sent the white-haired Wanderling, who was a willowy fourteen, with Brutte to defend the Dragon whelp. The other seven Dragon Guards joined Thorne. They wore red Dragon leathers with breastplates scavenged from Dragon treasure. Chestnut-colored horsetails crowned their helmets, giving them added height and the aspect of champions.

Thorne hadn't found her helmet but would count herself blessed if that were her only loss today.

Lott, the men's leader, limped to her on a leg speared in battle years before and handed her a helmet threaded with a white horse's tail. "For luck, Goddess. Saved it for you."

She wanted to rub the coarse hair from her first horse against her cheek, but a general wouldn't do that. Later—if there was one. "Thank you. This means more than I can say," she mumbled, before mounting her warhorse.

They didn't have enough proper mounts, so some rode workhorses, two on each animal, and others bunched in farm wagons. Under Thorne's command, the men seemed confident. If only they hadn't misplaced their faith. It seemed unlikely that all those leaving through the bailey gates would return. More likely, none would.

CHAPTER TWO

Strumgued the Dwarf Lord resisted urging his bay stallion to gallop, unwilling to leave behind the ninety-nine Dwarf warriors accompanying him. He'd see Stonevar Castle after they crossed the temporary bridge. Millennia ago, his forbearers had cut the castle from Ventamar Mountain so skillfully that a river traveler might pass it unaware. He and his warriors intended to not only reclaim their ancestral home but also salvage their clan pride for losing it to a foul Dragon.

Behind him, armor rattled on his warriors' broad backs. Their braided beards swung like pendulums across their chests as they sang:

> "We burrowed deep in our mountain keep,
> to mine for gold in tunnels cold.
> A beast most brazen destroyed our haven.
> Fleeing the drake made our hearts break.
> Now we march with pride to our home denied.
> Our wanderings cease. We'll sleep in peace."

From the direction of the castle, puffs of dust rose as riders approached, their silver helmets glittering in the morning sun. A war party, yet only the leader rode a proper warhorse.

Strumgued whistled and raised his arm with an open palm to halt his warriors.

Ahead, three wagons rattled to a stop. He'd never seen such a mongrel band of fighters. These fools challenged a Dwarf Lord? None would live to tell the tale.

As Lord Strumgued waited, the warhorse's rider dismounted

5

twenty paces away. Long white hair streamed down his back. The rider strode through hissing needlegrass, his gait smooth as a wole-lion's. Except for a frightened grouse who took flight, quiet gripped the meadow. Not even a horse neighed.

Strumgued slid off his saddle. When his horse danced, he crooned and patted its neck, calming the stallion. His son rode up, and Strumgued passed him the reins. He strapped on his breastplate, leaving his shield on the saddle, then donned his bronze helmet with the faceplate up.

Ten paces from his challenger, he stopped mid-stride. The leader was a woman. As a trained beholder—one who observes with all his senses—little escaped Strumgued's scrutiny, and the sight astonished him. With her helmet and heeled boots, she stood nearly as tall as a Giantess. Her rib cage was as large as a Dwarf's. Although she didn't have the pleasing features of Dwarf females—thick lips, bulbous nose, and round cheeks.

A Giantess rode with her. Another puzzle. They seldom left their mainland mountains, and he'd never known one to cross the sea. He rubbed his clean-shaven chin, still missing his beard after twenty years.

What manner of challengers were these? Less than a score, outfitted in dissimilar shields, breastplates, and helmets. Had they tamed the wild land behind them? Cattle grazed near the river. Fields were cultivated. Orchards planted. When had they taken Stonevar?

Had they cowed a Dragon when Dwarfs could not? Unthinkable. He'd heard rumors of a goddess commanding the beast. Surely Human exaggeration. His lips pressed together in a thin smile. Goddess or not—no matter. The castle belonged to the Dwarf Clan of Stonevar.

Three paces from him, she stopped. He bowed his head, giving respect to all wingless beings until they proved undeserving. He frowned at the hedge Fairy riding her shoulder. Fairy folk were tricksters and betrayers. Without their spying, no Dragon would have forced his clan from Stonevar.

"My forefathers carved Stonevar Castle from the mountain," Strumgued said.

"A fine job. Now it belongs to the Dragon."

His face twisted as if he'd tasted rotten meat. He hated Dragons for more reasons than stealing his family home. "The vile wyrm is dead."

She set her jaw. "The Dragon lives."

Since the adult Dragon breathed no more, she must have offspring. After dealing with this shabby troop, he'd dispatch the whelp. "Then a Dragon will also die this day."

Her eyes narrowed. "I've sworn to protect him."

"I've no quarrel with Human or Giant."

Her arm motion invited his departure. "Then pass us by."

"Lady Warrior, it's unwise to block the path of a Dwarf Lord."

"I defeated a giant serpent to earn the protection of Stonevar's Dragon."

Strumgued heard the snake had gone south. Legend said eating Dragon eggs made it grow enormous.

He sniffed. The breeze carried a silvery scent. "Are you a goddess of Dragons?"

"That's not for me to say. Judge me by my deeds."

He'd never met a goddess and doubted she was one. But even a goddess couldn't take his homeland. "Stonevar is my birthright."

She locked her gaze on his. "Stonevar is my home."

"A home to squatters." He motioned with a finger. "Step aside, Lady Warrior."

"I will not." The wind ruffled the white horse tail topping her helmet.

Strumgued smiled. Fifteen Humans and a Giantess facing a hundred Dwarf warriors. Hopeless. His warriors had more stamina than a Giant. He doubted anyone in this motley group would prove worthy of a Dwarf death stroke. Nevertheless, a sword fight with a goddess might prove diverting.

After retrieving his shield from his saddle, he whistled, extended his arm straight up, palm open, then motioned downward, signaling a single Dwarf fighter to engage each Human and to kill only on his signal. A battle would sweeten their homecoming. After centuries, a short delay was nothing.

The Humans and Giantess now flanked the Goddess. The cowardly Fairy flew off.

Sword still strapped to his back, Strumgued bowed from the waist. "The first strike is yours, Lady Warrior."

The Goddess raised her sword and swung at his neck.

He blocked with his shield. If she expected to defeat him, she must do better. He drew his sword, which was similar in length to hers, but wider and thicker.

"Die well!" He swung his blade over his head, hitting hard, but far from his strongest blow. Her knees buckled when she blocked with her shield, but she held her position.

Few could withstand that. He grinned. This might prove a worthy diversion.

Around them, swords clanged against shields. When he risked a glance at the fighting, he saw the shadow of her sword descend. He sidestepped, and her blade sliced air. He chopped at her side, which she stopped with her shield brim. Experience taught him that pain ripped her elbow, but she only gritted her teeth and grunted.

She upper cut. He batted her point aside, countering with a blow to her thigh that failed to cut leather. Only Dragon hide was that strong. Intriguing. She stumbled but regained her balance. A weaker swordswoman would have fallen.

"My name is Strumgued."

"Why tell me your name?" She sounded out of breath.

"So you can speak it in the Citadel of the Slain."

"Then you will speak the name Thorne, for you will precede me." Limping, she jabbed at his eye.

He laughed, a guttural sound from deep in his belly, while circling his blade to deflect her point. Strumgued couldn't remember enjoying a fight more.

A woman screamed and fell on his right. Thorne flinched. His Dwarf warriors circled their opponents and grunted when they wielded their swords, but no Dwarf would cry out, even if dying.

Strumgued's next strike had enough power to separate the head from a bull. Blocking pushed her back, though she remained upright. Her strength surprised him. Her height gave some advantage but didn't explain how she could withstand his blows.

Her blade whirred in a backhand sweep. No time to raise his shield, he took the blow on his brass breastplate and staggered. She appeared pleased, evidently thinking he suffered weariness. But his endurance was barely tested.

She lunged. He sidestepped and flicked her throat with his sword point. Her eyes widened. Her pupils had a diamond shape, like a Dragon's. Her blood clotted quickly.

"Are you a goddess in truth?"

She gasped. "Do you wish to surrender?"

He smiled wider and tongued the tip of his bloody blade, a dwarfish custom. Human blood with a hint of silver. His mouth tingled, and his stomach warmed as if he'd drunk ale. The warmth spread outward. Something strange was happening, and he loathed anything strange.

Thorne rushed him, thrusting her sword at his neck. He deflected it. For a moment they were arm to arm. Lightning zinged up his arm into his chest, stealing his breath. Then she pushed him off and resumed a fighter's stance, shield over her heart, sword raised. Clearly, she had a warrior's spirit.

His son whistled, requesting a kill order.

Strumgued's heart thrashed in an almost forgotten way. "Submit, Lady Warrior."

"Never." Her snarl showed pointed canine teeth. "Will you yield to me?"

He laughed. No opponent had ever made him so jovial. Though her life balanced on his sword edge, she'd never surrender. He admired her futile valor. For the first time since his wife's death, a female interested him. He'd never admit it, but he was lonely though never alone. He missed Lea-Lea warming his bed, tending his hearth, dumping ale on his head when he'd drunk too much.

The black Dragon had killed his beloved wife, and Strumgued would kill Stonevar's Dragon before the next sunrise.

While memories of his wife distracted Strumgued, Thorne rushed him, swinging at his knees. Off balance, he blocked, and she struck his face with her shield. He spit blood. No mere Human had ever penetrated his defense. He didn't believe in spells, but this Human must've enchanted him. Under other circumstances he would have mined Thorne's mysteries.

Now unless she surrendered, he must slay her. His warriors had disarmed their opponents and held them at sword point. Half-dozen surrounded the Giantess. They awaited his kill command.

But first he needed them to witness his final strike.

CHAPTER THREE

Thorne's aching arm could barely lift her sword. Her legs wobbled. A woman's scream chilled her blood. Who had fallen? She mustn't think about that. Be a warrior. Or she'd make a mistake and the Dwarf Lord would do more than prick her.

She needed a surprise attack. However, before she mustered strength to strike, Strumgued rushed her with a second blow at her neck. When she held up her shield, he swept a leg around hers. Thorne hit the ground hard, landing on her knee. Fire exploded in her joint. She tried to rise, but pain buckled her leg. Her breath came in ragged pants. On her knees, how long could she defend herself?

Power radiated from Strumgued, like heat waves shimmering over water on a blistering summer day. Their fight hadn't even winded him. He would kill her, and she'd never know why he had no beard. If she weren't so tired, she'd laugh. So near death, why wonder about something so irrelevant?

Lowering his shield, he stepped back, watching her with sharp green eyes that seemed to burrow inside her. Then he grinned at her as he'd done for most of their fight. Strumgued sheathed his sword, placed his fist over his heart, and extended his arm, saluting her.

While she panted, he left the battlefield, his mumbling Dwarf warriors following him toward the raft bridge.

She yanked off her helmet. Why hadn't Strumgued killed her? Willow-Bender the Giantess pulled Thorne to her feet and passed her a water skin. Thorne drank until her stomach ached.

"Why did he stop?" Thorne asked.

Willow-Bender shrugged. Sweat clung to the red anchor tattooed in the center of her forehead. "Your name Dwarfs will sing."

"What do you mean?"

"A long measure you fought."

Thorne wanted no Dwarfish songs, only the answer to her question.

With the back of her hand, Willow-Bender wiped her square face, smearing dirt. "Why kneel before him?"

"He swept my leg from beneath me."

"Appeared you yielded."

"I couldn't rise." Brutte had warned her against surrender. Would he be upset with her?

Around her, exhausted soldier-farmers collapsed on the ground. The albino healer fetched her medicine bag from a wagon and knelt beside the wounded. Thorne's breath caught. "Who's hurt?"

"Glitter took a cut." The Giantess wiped her round nose on her sleeve. "A sword slipped under her tunic."

Thorne cringed. Glitter's twin sister held her hand. In their late twenties, the twins had patrician features and deep red hair. They'd given up whoring for mucking Stonevar's barns, and found the change an improvement. Thorne doubted they expected battle.

She surveyed the plain. Everyone was on the ground. Who was resting and who was injured? "The soldier-farmers?"

"Minor cuts."

"Good." At least they'd all survived. More than most Dwarf adversaries could say. Still, Strumgued's retreat made no sense. Every Dragon Guard and soldier-farmer should be dead.

Why had the Dwarf Lord spared them?

#

When Thorne entered Redilik Cavern, Brutte collapsed on a stool beside the tunnel leading outside. "You lived." It took a moment for his breathing to even out. Clearly he'd been worried. "The others?"

"A few wounds. Glitter most serious. They've returned to the castle."

Emera the Wanderling dashed between the massive, carved pillars dividing the colossal cavern. At fourteen, Emera was the youngest Dragon Guard. From her father, a member of the legendary Wanderer race, she'd inherited her lank figure, honey-brown complexion, and round ears the size of her hand, which she could move at right angles to her head. From her mother Nella, Emera inherited upturned eyes.

From the blood of the ancient black Dragon, Gaspotine the Dark, Emera gained white hair like Thorne's. Two years ago, a red Dragon mortally wounded Emera. Though legend warned Dragon blood was poison, Thorne knew it facilitated healing. To save Emera's life, Thorne gave Gaspotine's blood to the Wanderling.

The year before that, Raspberry-Frost took Thorne to Gaspotine's cavern. She arrived weak with fever and near death. After a young Dragon killed Gaspotine, the Fairy insisted Thorne drink his blood, which cured her.

Now Thorne's sweaty shirt clung to her skin as Emera helped remove her armor.

The Wanderling hugged Thorne and said, "Tell us what happened."

Thorne pulled the damp cloth away from her chest. "I need wine first." Her throat was so dry that speaking hurt.

The three crossed the cavern to small living area beside the hearth. Emera poured wine for Thorne and Brutte.

"Thank you, lassie." He emptied the cup. "Couldn't see the fight from the Dragon Ledge."

"The Dwarf Lord tripped me." Thorne related the battle. "Willow-Bender said it appeared I surrendered."

Brutte's laughter surprised Thorne and woke Hellee from his nap. The whelp screeched happily and tottered to Thorne on spindly legs barely able to support his rotund belly. His pale bat-like wings flapped uselessly, and his oversized head bobbed on his thin neck as he bumbled into Thorne. He nudged her with his nose and mewed sorrowfully. He resembled a newly hatched bird, ugly and constantly needing food.

She wrapped an arm behind his head, reassuring him. "What did it mean when the Dwarf sheathed his weapon then saluted me?"

"Made you appear to yield."

"Why?"

"To avoid killing you while preserving his honor." He took his pipe from the pouch on his belt, and Emera lit it with a taper.

Thorne scratched behind Hellee's brow bone, and he licked her arm. She motioned for Emera to take Hellee away. Emera rolled a log through the center of the cavern, and Hellee bumbled after it, tripping over his own foot claws.

"But why didn't the Dwarf Lord kill me?" Thorne asked Brutte.

"You're a mystery to him, and Dwarfs cannot abide a mystery."

There had to be more. "Will they leave?"

Brutte shook his head. "They intend to take back Stonevar. He'll approach with his terms for your surrender."

"What terms?"

Brutte shrugged. "You're alive. That's what's important. Now we wait."

This was all too much. Thorne sat at Brutte's foot and leaned against his thigh, inhaling his musky scent. "At least no one lost a limb in battle."

Brutte lifted the stump of his left arm, gone halfway down the forearm. "I didn't lose mine fighting."

In the three years she'd known him, he'd never told her. "How then?" Thorne asked.

"I don't speak of it, because it upsets my Magda." His wife of thirty-nine years. "I was a spy."

"I thought you trained soldiers. And spies are small men who hide in trees, not big ones like you."

He gave her a wry smile. "Just what my captain hoped the other army would think. He sent me to the enemy camp. I hired on as a mercenary and passed back information till they caught me. Their captain ordered my arm and leg cut off, and my eye put out with an arrow." He puffed on his pipe until a cloud formed above his head.

Thorne shuddered. Brutte and Magda were her family. "You might have bled to death."

Brutte's mouth twisted into a forced grin. "In battle I would have, but they cauterized my wounds with a hot blade. Pain upon pain. Made sure I'd live. I prayed the gods would send me death but none were merciful. They seldom are." He held out his cup for Emera to refill. "They tied me to my horse and sent me back with a warning."

His ride must have been torture. She touched his arm. "At least they spared your life."

"A useless one until Magda brought you to me. Before then, I'd lost hope. Each day was longer than the one before. I'd nothing to do but wait for my Magda to come home from cooking at the inn. You gave me purpose." He set down his pipe.

She raised an eyebrow. "What would that be?"

Brutte chortled. "Curing Dragon hides and training a band of females." He took a honing stone from the pouch at his waist and gave it to her.

"I'm grateful for both. But most of all I'm grateful for knowing you."

"Don't get sentimental. Facing death makes even the meanest soldier get mawkish. My manner toward women was no better than the next man's before I lost my limbs."

She drew the stone along Dracodurus's blade. "And afterward?"

"My Magda clothed and fed me." He patted Thorne's shoulder. "I should've ignored you when you knocked on my door."

"You trained me to use a sword."

"An experiment."

Thorne scratched beneath her shirt. She needed to bathe. "You helped me buy land."

"Dragon land no one wanted."

And she smelled. "You treat me like a son."

"You won't let me treat you like a daughter. You're a difficult girl."

She laughed.

He shook his head. "Never thought we'd get this far."

"You chose the right men."

Brutte had carefully selected the retired soldiers who'd come to Stonevar, choosing men who would follow a woman's lead and wanted farmland. Their leader, Lott, was especially valuable. He set an example for the others, obeying Thorne without question. But Brutte had objected to some of the women who came seeking sanctuary. He warned they would be a burden.

Nevertheless, Thorne had insisted they stay. When she touched these women, she felt tingles, what Raspberry-Frost called Dragon-Fating. The Fairy had explained, "By Human deeds, a Dragon will flourish or perish." Thorne had felt the same tingles from the sea captain who killed Hellee's mother, Rustofona the Magnificent.

Thorne could only guess who intended to harm or to help a Dragon. But she believed that the women who had Dragon-Fating, those she called the Dragon Guards, were destined to raise Hellee.

Now Brutte squeezed her shoulder and said, "Those who follow you would die for Stonevar."

Thorne wanted to prevent that. "What should I do now?"

"Return to the castle and rest for the next challenge. Take this. I finished it while I waited." He passed her a buckler, a small shield thrice the size of her hand, made from black Dragon hide. When Thorne hugged Brutte, she felt powerful tingles; his Dragon-Fating was stronger, foretelling he would preserve the whelp's life.

#

Thorne rode to Stonevar Castle, planning to relieve Brutte after she ate and checked on everyone.

In her sleeping room, Thorne washed and discovered more bruises. Though none as large as the one on her thigh, which extended from knee to hip. Tomorrow it would hurt like a bone break. At least Strumgued's sword hadn't penetrated the Dragon hide.

After donning a clean shirt, she rested on her bed a moment, looking around. Her large room was sparsely furnished: mirror, clothes chest, table, two chairs, and a giant deer skull over the hearth. The trapdoor overhead led to a small room, where she sometimes went to think.

This room might be hers only a few hours longer. The battle today made it painfully clear that they couldn't defeat the Dwarfs in combat. What would Strumgued set as the terms of her surrender?

How would she protect everyone? The middle-aged soldier-farmers and their families. Hellee and the Dragon Guards. And her sister, Lily, who Thorne had rescued from a miserable marriage.

Thorne had chosen Stonevar, because Lily would be safe here. Lily's husband wouldn't dare come after her while Rustofona the Magnificent lived. When the orange Dragon patrolled her territory, she inadvertently protected Stonevar Castle. But Rustofona was dead. And Hellee wouldn't be grown for decades. Now they must protect themselves.

Zarra entered after knocking, but without waiting for an invitation. She was the first woman to follow Thorne to Stonevar, and the first to ask Thorne for Dragon blood. Sir-Sir, her wole-rat companion, sat on Zarra's shoulder. Reflexively, Thorne tucked her hands under her arms. Sir-Sir's wide jaws could easily bite off a finger. He eyed Thorne suspiciously as he wrapped his furry tail around Zarra's neck. He couldn't seem to forget that on their first encounter, she'd netted him, then tried to choke him. In her defense, she'd thought him an oversized common rat. Still his hoop earring should've clued her that he was special. Zarra called Sir-Sir smart and handsome. Thorne didn't know any other wole-rats and couldn't disagree.

Zarra narrowed her close-set eyes. "How we going to rid ourselves of those Dwarfs?"

"I don't know yet." Thorne sat up. "But I expect Brutte has some ideas by now."

She growled, showing crooked teeth. "I'm going to kill the one that hurt Glitter—as soon as I can tell one from another." When Zarra plopped on the bed, Sir-Sir scampered away from Thorne. The wole-rat sat on a bedpost, cleaning his chestnut-colored fur, which turned white in winter. "I wanted to stab the Dwarf Lord's eyes for the way he looked at you."

"What are you talking about?"

"After the he licked your blood from his sword, his eyes glazed."

"How could you see that while you were fighting?"

"A nanut of a Dwarf attacked me. He disarmed me quick, so I spent most of the battle watching." Flushing, Zarra punched a pillow. "That don't matter now."

Before coming to Stonevar, Zarra often watched from the shadows. When she was seven-years old, their landlord threw Zarra and her mother's dead body into the street. To survive, Zarra pretended to be a boy and stole to eat.

Zarra continued, "The point is the Dwarf Lord couldn't look away from you."

"Of course he couldn't. I was trying to kill him."

"He could've disarmed you. He played with you like Sir-Sir plays with a beetle."

"Maybe." After three years of practice, Thorne didn't want to believe she was a poor swordswoman.

"I've seen men ogle women. You interest him."

Thorne didn't want to interest anyone. "Brutte said I was mystery."

"That Dwarf wants to know too much."

Thorne had a feeling like someone was watching her. "Get some rest. I need you clear-eyed tomorrow.

Zarra nodded and left.

After pulling on her Dragon-leather trousers, Thorne carried her tunic and sword into the hallway.

Stonevar Castle had an uncommon design. No castle floor was directly above another; the upper floor was north of the Great Hall; the lower level, which contained the War Room, was to the south. Whether designed for defense or to track currents in the stone, she didn't know. She admired the dwarfish persistence that hollowed this castle from mountain rock as skillfully as men carved wood.

The Dwarf Lord could answer her questions about Stonevar, but Thorne hoped never to have the opportunity to ask. She limped down the curving passageway and descended the circular staircase to enter the Great Hall. At a trestle table, she ate bread and goat cheese, while the soldier-farmers related their battles. Their wives rubbed their shoulders. The children sat on their fathers' laps or on the bench beside them. Along the wall, rolled pallets and chests marked each family's sleeping area.

From angled openings in the arched ceiling three stories above them, sunlight descended the twelve columns, six on a side, which supported stone beams for chandeliers. Shorter pillars held oil for lighting. Thorne had wondered if Dwarfs liked living in immense spaces after burrowing in narrow tunnels. She no longer cared.

A child ran by Thorne, bare feet slapping stone. Someone banged a pot. Two snarling dogs fought over scraps. The sounds comforted.

Fehera the albino healer approached with a firm step. At forty-five, she was the eldest Dragon Guard. She had a pointed chin, and a thin body made of bony angles. Her poor eyesight made her to look past people rather than directly at them, which spooked some folks. When not with Hellee, she spent much of her time tending her herb garden or inside her drying hut preparing potions. Like most healers, she stayed calm in dire situations.

"How's Glitter?" Thorne asked.

"The sword went deep, but the wound felt cool after I stitched it."

Like the other Dragon Guards, Glitter had drunk Dragon blood, so her injury should heal instead of rot. But wounds were unpredictable; fevers often developed.

As soon as Thorne swallowed the last bite of cheese, Magda stopped waiting on everyone and said, "Brutte's with the Dragon," as if Thorne had forgotten. Clearly Magda was worried. Her normally tidy gray hair was mussed, and she hadn't changed the stained apron tied around her plump waist.

"I'll relieve him." Thorne would nap with Hellee, who spent most of his time sleeping.

Riding to the Dragon cave on the other side of the mountain, Thorne couldn't get comfortable. Her arms ached from battle, and her thighs burned as if she'd run miles. When she'd climbed halfway up the steps to the Dragon Ledge, Hellee screeched. She stumbled and landed on her sore knee. Pain speared upward into her eyeballs. When she could breathe, she struggled onto the ledge. The end of the tunnel was unusually bright. Though broken glass seemed to jab her knee with each step, she rushed down the passageway.

Before entering the main cavern, she drew Dracodurus and advanced until she met six Dwarf warriors with torches. They must've come through the mountain so they wouldn't be seen, intending to have their revenge by killing a helpless Dragon whelp. Thorne wouldn't let that happen.

Outside the hatching antechamber, seven more pointed swords at Emera, who appeared a decade older than fourteen. The gaunt-faced Wanderling faced the warriors, moving her sword in a slow half-circle. Glistening perspiration dotted her honey-colored skin. Dwarfs might hesitate to kill a Wanderer, but they could disarm Emera. Why hadn't they?

Behind her, Hellee clawed stone. No one had noticed Thorne yet. She sidled closer.

Brutte lay at Emera's feet. With a tortured cry, Thorne rushed to him. No Dwarf stopped her. She knelt beside Brutte, ignoring the pain shooting up her knee. Hellee howled, shoving past Emera to nuzzle Thorne. She pushed the whelp behind her.

"Brutte," Thorne whispered.

He groaned and opened his eye. Thorne fumbled at her throat for the vial of Dragon blood. She poured it into his mouth, but he coughed and spit it back.

"Thank you, lass."

Thorne could hardly speak. "Don't . . ."

"For taking an old soldier into battle." His hand pressed against his chest.

"Stay with me."

"My time, lass." His chest gurgled.

She'd never heard anything so terrifying—as if his chest held blood, not air.

"I wanted to see you once more," Brutte said.

"Please, Brutte, hang on. Dragon blood will heal you."

He gasped. "Tell Magda that I've left on my last campaign."

"Don't leave me."

"My boy's waiting for me."

Magda and Brutte's only son had died a decade ago in an unnamed war.

"Been poor all my life," Brutte said. "I've naught to leave you."

"You've given me everything." She put her hand over his. Brutte's blood oozed over her fingers.

"Take my knife."

She unsheathed it. The Dwarf nearest her grunted but maintained position.

Brutte struggled to speak. "The inscription."

"I yield to death alone."

Brutte murmured something she couldn't hear. "What?"

"I love you, lass." His hand relaxed, letting blood stream from the wound he'd held closed waiting for her. She tried to stop the bleeding with her hands, but each heartbeat gushed more. "Hold on. I'll send Emera for Fehera."

The bleeding slowed, then stopped flowing between her fingers. His eye closed. She'd never known such courage. She touched his neck. No pulse. Too late for Dragon blood. Too late to tell him that she'd loved him like a father, but he must have known. She kissed his forehead.

Thorne leapt to her feet, wiping her bloody hands on her tunic. Brandishing Dracodurus in one hand and Brutte's knife in the other, she bared her teeth and growled. "I will cut the heart from Brutte's killer and throw it to the hogs." She beckoned the Dwarfs, inviting their approach.

They ignored her. Evidently they'd been ordered not to kill her yet. Hellee tucked his head under her arm. When she pushed him back, his sulfurous snort made the nearest torch flare up, but the bearer stood steady. She lunged at a Dwarf marked by a scar over his eyebrow. With a reluctant snort, he retreated.

A dragonish fury coursed through her. Aware that only killing would satisfy, she fought to think clearly as cold sweat beaded her brow. She gritted her teeth. "Who has done this?"

The warriors parted and the Dwarf Lord stepped from the shadows. He seemed unafraid, though he should be terrified. She intended to bathe in his blood.

Lord Strumgued's voice held no compromise. "The wyrm must die."

"Never!" Thorne rushed him. She wouldn't rest until she sheathed Dracodurus inside his heart.

He parried and tried to prick her throat, but she anticipated this and deflected. After feinting toward his chest, she sliced open his sword arm at the wrist. Eyes wide with surprise, he stepped back.

"For Brutte." She licked her sword tip. The taste of Strumgued's blood spurred her fury into ecstasy. She swung.

He ducked, bellowed, and lunged at her stomach. Her awkward parry let his blade slice her wrist. Blood slicked her fingers. The Dwarf warriors smiled.

Behind her, Emera gasped. Hellee screeched, his breath heating Thorne's neck.

Without looking, she said, "Keep back."

Strumgued advanced. With a feint and point thrust, he sliced open her other wrist. She pressed her lips together, suppressing a cry. He could've severed her hand. "Why not kill me?"

"Yield."

What did he want? Her dragonish rage interfered with swordplay and clear thinking. "Never."

She thrust at his chest. His sword slammed Dracodurus from her grasp. His second flick sent Brutte's knife clattering to the floor. She could neither defeat him nor protect Hellee.

"Well done, Lord Strumgued," said a Dwarf with a long red beard.

Thorne crouched, yanked the dagger from her boot, and slid it up her sleeve. At the first opportunity, she'd cut out his eye. "What do you want of me?"

Strumgued pressed his sword grip to his forehead, saluting her. "A truce."

Her wrists had stopped bleeding but still burned. Without Dragon blood facilitating her healing, she might have bled to death. "Your terms?" She watched for a chance to throw her dagger.

He rubbed his smooth chin. "An alliance."

With Brutte's murderer? Impossible. "Your conditions?"

"You may stay in Stonevar."

How dare he offer what was already hers. "Continue."

"You'll supply us with food, cloth, and furs in return for gold." His marbled green eyes held no compassion.

She would never trade with this fiend. "Is that all?"

"You'll return the gold and jewels belonging to the Clan of Stonevar."

Thorne needed the valuables from Rustofona's treasure to buy supplies and to safeguard her followers from natural disasters that destroyed crops and animals. "I don't want your gold."

Thorne yanked off the serpent ring that Zarra had found among the Dragon's hoard and threw it at the Dwarf, aiming for his eye. He caught it. She yearned to pull the dagger from her sleeve, but must await the perfect moment.

"Your hand to seal our alliance."

Her dagger clanged to the floor. She couldn't have heard correctly. "You wish to wed me?"

He nodded, seeming as indifferent to her weapon as he was to his warriors' surprised, disapproving murmurs. Strumgued lifted an arm to quiet them.

Thorne would prefer death. But she must think. Her wrists throbbed, and dragonish fury made her head ache. Why did a Dwarf Lord want to marry her? This was no ordinary battlefield proposal where an alliance would benefit both sides. What would Strumgued gain? It made no sense. Thorne had nothing that the Dwarfs couldn't take. "You won't kill the whelp?"

"The beast must die," he said matter-of-factly.

"No!" Emera cried. "You can't harm Hellee."

The whimpering Dragon whelp stuck his nose under Thorne's arm, and she clung to him. "We can stay in Stonevar."

"Yes."

His grim visage was not how she pictured a groom. "What will you expect from me?"

"Only to share the eventide meal. Your answer?"

She collapsed beside Brutte and pressed his cold hand to her cheek.

Emera sobbed tearlessly and lowered her weapon. "I'm so sorry,

Thorne."

The Dwarf warriors' stony eyes shifted from her to Strumgued, then back. They wanted revenge. Killing Hellee would salve their pride. Under blond or red mustaches, their lips pressed tight.

Strumgued waited. A sour taste coated Thorne's tongue as she sheathed her dagger and strapped Brutte's knife to her thigh. She would go mad if she wed Brutte's killer.

CHAPTER FOUR

Brutte would know if she should marry Strumgued. She folded Brutte's arm over his chest, and instead of screaming, said calmly, "And if I refuse?"

"I'll recover my clan's wealth, evict your followers from Stonevar, and kill the foul wyrm's spawn." Strumgued hooked his thumbs inside his belt. "Your answer."

She stopped herself from blurting that if Hellee died, an adult Dragon would claim Hellee's territory and kill them all. This Dwarf Lord would never retreat. He might even slay Hellee to face a greater challenger for a more satisfying revenge.

The dragonish part of her urged attack, to die protecting her territory. Her Human part urged examining her choices. Without the Dragon treasure, she was penniless. The castle inhabitants were her family. How would they support themselves? The men were too old to resume soldiering. The families would end up beggars. The Dragon Guards had no other home. Women had no rights, couldn't own land. And she couldn't let Strumgued kill Hellee.

"You must let the Dragon whelp live," Thorne said.

Strumgued scratched his cheek. His warriors smiled, evidently confident he'd refuse. Their musky iron scent choked Thorne.

"Done," Strumgued said. "Control the loathsome beast, and neither I nor any Dwarf will harm him."

Thorne trembled like an animal. The trap had sprung. Behind her, Emera sniffled. The warriors pressed closer, murmuring displeasure.

"Silence," Strumgued ordered.

A youth with green eyes and a bulbous nose that resembled

Strumgued's spoke contemptuously. "Father, don't marry this . . . this Human."

"Waldemar." Strumgued's tone demanded quiet.

The young Dwarf scowled but said no more.

"Let us say the words to bind us," Strumgued told Thorne.

Thorne swallowed, but her throat was dry. He smiled. Evidently, her reluctance amused him. Brutte once told her, "Afraid or not, we must all face our fate."

She hadn't felt this alone since Da cast her out. "I'll speak the words."

Emera moaned. "No, Goddess. He slew Brutte."

Thorne took three deep breaths. "This must be done."

"I accept Thorne as my wife." Strumgued kissed the hilt of his blade and presented it to her.

She screamed silently; he couldn't expect her to pledge on the loathsome weapon that killed Brutte. She turned away.

"Say the vow."

"I accept Strumgued as my husband," she mumbled.

He lifted his sword higher. "Kiss the hilt."

She wanted to shove the blade down his throat, but instead pressed her mouth against it. The cold metal stung her lips. She pulled back, rubbing her mouth until it burned.

"You must swear allegiance to me as a warrior." Again, he presented his weapon.

Evidently, he distrusted marriage vows would ensure her loyalty. Thorne never knew taking one breath after another could be so difficult. She didn't kneel as was customary, and he didn't insist. When her fingers clasped the grip of his sword, Strumgued's callused hands imprisoned hers. Was joining him for the evening meal all he expected?

She bowed her head, not with respect but humiliation. "I pledge my allegiance to you."

He released her hand and sheathed his sword. "I expect you tomorrow for the eventide meal." Beside the fireplace, through a door that Thorne hadn't known existed, he exited, his Dwarf warriors following.

As she stumbled toward Brutte, Thorne's legs gave out, and she collapsed onto the floor. Hellee put his head on her lap.

Emera knelt beside her. "My fault."

Thorne put her arm around the Wanderling. "What happened?"

"I guarded the entrance, but they came through a secret doorway. I heard footsteps, and Brutte charged Strumgued." Emera's entire body shuddered. "I couldn't save him, so I ran to Hellee."

"You couldn't have stopped them. I knew there must be more than one exit."

"Magda's heart will break." Emera sobbed and stroked Hellee's bony head as he whimpered.

Death would be far easier than losing Brutte. Speaking one word after the other took all Thorne's strength. "He died a brave soldier. We'll prepare a fitting pyre." But that wouldn't comfort Magda.

Leaving Emera with Hellee, Thorne moved onto the Dragon ledge where she lit a signal fire to summon the Dragon Guards to protect the whelp. Inside the cavern, Emera chanted to soothe Hellee.

While Thorne waited for the others, she hugged the buckler Brutte had given her, trying not to think about telling Magda, trying not to fear that without Brutte to guide her, she'd blunder.

Past midnight, the other Dragon Guards arrived, and with Hellee defended, Thorne returned to Stonevar Castle. In the main hall, the children slept, and the adults watched from their pallets. Thorne couldn't summon even a weak reassuring smile. When Lott asked what happened, she waved him off.

Magda rose slowly from her rocker as if she'd aged fifty years since Thorne left her. "The blood on your tunic?" Her face paled. "Brutte?"

Behind Thorne, someone gasped. Others murmured.

Thorne couldn't speak. She ripped off her tunic and threw it down. She hugged Magda so they wouldn't see the other's faces and croaked out, "He joined your son."

Magda shuddered.

Thorne helped the older woman onto her pallet and stretched out beside her. "He said to tell you he's on his last campaign."

Tears washed Magda's cheeks as she stared into the hearth flames, while Thorne cradled Magda and stroked her hair. Neither slept, but they stayed like that until dawn.

After morning chores, the soldier-farmers built a funeral pyre near the river. Grief pinched Fehera's face as she sprinkled incense made with thyme, sage, and other oils to mask the scent of burning flesh. That evening, under a bad moon, Lott lit the pyre. Magda didn't rise from her pallet to attend.

Afterward, Thorne carried Brutte's shield and sword to the War Room. Someday, a warrior worthy of them would be born.

#

The next day, Brutte's funeral pyre still smoldered as Thorne watched Strumgued cross the temporary raft bridge. Her grandfather's book said that Dwarfs avoided water because they sank. Thorne willed the bridge to collapse so Strumgued would drown—and again the fates disappointed her.

The Dwarfs who'd camped across the river were setting stone pilings for a permanent bridge. On Stonevar's side, they'd raised a tent solely to feed her.

Thorne yelped when Raspberry-Frost yanked her hair. The Fairy flapped her wings hard to stay in place.

Thorne pressed on her scalp to reduce the pulling. "What's wrong?"

"Danger! Dwarfs!"

"I must eat with the Dwarf Lord."

The Fairy flew off, and Thorne had only taken a few more steps when Raspberry-Frost returned with a nightcrawler in her claws. The large worm twisted into a writhing mass.

"Eat, my Human."

"Thank you." Thorne held out her hand for the worm. "I'll save this for later. Now I must join Strumgued."

"Foolish Human."

"I have no choice."

Strumgued held the flap open and motioned her inside.

Raspberry-Frost's voice sounded higher than normal. "Run."

"He won't kill me." At least not tonight. Unless she offended him, which seemed likely. Thorne didn't carry Dracodurus, but she had Brutte's knife strapped to her thigh and a dagger inside her boot.

Raspberry-Frost flew off. Thorne left the worm outside before entering the tent.

Strumgued's square face was clean and his golden-red hair, the color of a ripe peach, neatly secured. "Sit before the wild boar cools, my wife."

My wife! She fisted her hands to prevent clawing out his eyes.

"After Brutte's funeral, my appetite is small." She made no effort to keep ire from her voice and sat board stiff, ignoring the savory aroma of the nuts and beans around the roast boar. She picked up a silver goblet of red wine. Drunkenness might make this tolerable, but drinking Dragon blood forestalled that.

Though she'd intended to speak as little as possible, she blurted, "How did you get into Redilik Cavern?" She needed the answer, even a worrisome one.

"I'll explain," he said evenly, "if you converse with me. Speak of your day."

His musky smell made her stomach roil. Did he roll in iron dust? "I hardly think what I do concerns you."

"You greatly interest me." He rubbed under his bulbous nose.

She straightened the skirt of her plain brown kirtle before telling him what he might observe himself. "The crops grow well. We've cultivated two more hectares." Then she blurted, "Brutte was no threat to you."

"He surprised me."

She gripped her fork so hard her nails dug into her palms. "You could've disarmed him."

He shrugged as he carved the boar. "That was his fate."

Heat climbed her neck. "Have you no heart?"

Strumgued smiled wryly. "Do not seek that which cannot be seen."

"How did you enter Redilik Cavern?" She hacked at the meat he set on her plate.

"A tunnel under the river. I'll show you, but first eat."

Thorne stabbed a chunk. The wild boar was well done. She preferred her meat bloody. "Why build a bridge if you can go under the river?"

"An enemy chooses the road he sees. How tastes the boar?" he asked with a full mouth.

She set down her fork. "A bit dry."

"Hrrr," Strumgued growled. "I'll speak to the cook."

Thorne flushed. "The food isn't deficient. My tongue lacks refinement." She took another bite, picturing herself chewing Strumgued's heart. She'd finally thought of an acceptable reason for him to void their marriage. Not that she cared about his pride, but he'd free her only with his honor intact. "I cannot bear children."

"I've nineteen and seek no more."

Nineteen Dwarf stepchildren. Unimaginable for someone who never wanted any. "You fail to understand. You may annul our marriage."

Confusion glazed his eyes. "I've no wish to annul it."

"But you must." Her voice squeaked, and she took a breath. "I'm not what I appear." This was her last desperate argument.

His round nostrils flared. "Tell me what manner of creature you be."

"A Dragon spirit dwells within me." That should drive him away.

"I knew they called you a Goddess of Dragons."

Unable to tolerate more, she left the tent. If that angered him, then so be it.

In the dark she paused, remembering he'd agreed to show her the tunnel. She retraced her steps and peered inside. Strumgued was eating with zest, not the least bit upset. His indifference set her blood boiling, and she returned to the castle, wanting to stomp on his head.

#

For a fortnight, Thorne spent her days with Magda. The older woman didn't mention Brutte, refused to eat, moved only between her pallet and a rocking chair. When she finally resumed supervising the castle, her mouth held a permanent scowl.

On the seventeenth day following Brutte's death, Magda stirred stew in a large pot hanging inside the hearth. "Dwarf families invade us. How can you allow it?"

Pride stopped Thorne from saying she lacked the power to make them leave. She'd postponed telling her foster mother the truth. "Strumgued is my . . ." the word stuck. "Husband."

Magda slammed the large wooden spoon on the table. "Husband!"

"On the battlefield. Part of a truce." Magda hated Dragons and wouldn't care that Strumgued threatened Hellee.

The older woman slammed down a bowl. "What poison does he pour into your ears?"

"None. He's most solicitous."

"Stab the stone he calls a heart." Magda's eyes narrowed. "Then pry it out and bring it to me."

"No," Thorne said, though she yearned for widowhood. At night she dreamed of wetting Dracodurus with Strumgued's blood and freeing Stonevar from this Dwarf pestilence.

Wisely, Strumgued had insisted she swear a warrior's loyalty.

CHAPTER FIVE

The ancient black Dragon, Gaspotine the Dark, was dead. But his spirit had escaped into the Dragon Continuum, where all time existed—past, present, future. He hadn't expected everlasting death to bestow peace. Neither had he expected to spend eternity in an endless struggle to remain sane. Ignoring the evidence, he thought he would conquer the Niede—a primordial urge like hunger or thirst but ninety-three times worse. The Niede served a useful function for the living, compelling them to return to the corporeal world before they perished. But it served no purpose for the dead, other than driving them mad by making their spirits yearn for nonexistent bodies.

Seeking to escape this torment, he traveled time's Silver River to watch himself in the past. The events immediately preceding his death fascinated him. A Fairy had led Thorne to Gaspotine's final battle. Afterward, Thorne guzzled his blood, then nibbled him like a wole-rat. Disgusting. When he'd first witnessed this, Gaspotine wanted to hide, but in the Continuum hiding got complicated. He couldn't go far. Time's Continuum imprisoned his spirit.

Reliving his memories made him yearn for physical sensation. A feral mating. An aerial Dragon battle to inflame his primordial savagery. The aftertaste of gristle stuck between his teeth. An itch. Most of all, for sleep to stop his endless thoughts.

Wanting only worsened the Niede, which made him roll his vaporous form into a ball. That was how Rustofona the Magnificent found him on the Silver River shore.

Rustofona clawed him. "Thorne intends to kill Hellestorm."

Gaspotine unrolled, cursing Rustofona's motherly instincts, still strong after death. "You chose the Human to raise him." Rustofona's endless prattling about her whelp exhausted his patience, which took less than a moment since Dragons had none.

Both Dragons were dead, so neither could aid her whelp, but Rustofona refused to accept this. Her fixation on Hellestorm would madden Gaspotine more quickly than the Niede. He departed before they bickered, though usually he enjoyed a good quarrel.

Gaspotine burst through faded-red clouds smelling like week-old lamb's blood. While he lived, the scent was fresh. Now the sky had dimmed, the purple mountains faded to gray. As the Niede's madness advanced, bits of him floated away, and his power to shape the Continuum diminished.

Only the Silver River still shimmered, having widened to accommodate the gold currents of the Humans who had drunk Dragon blood. At present the river was at rest. No Humans caused eddies, whirlpools, or undertows.

Below Gaspotine, Thorne's current beckoned. He despised Rustofona's obsessive scrutiny of Hellestorm yet suffered a similar compulsion to monitor Thorne. Downstream he viewed her yesterdays; upstream her tomorrows. Her future branched often, a sign of frequent changes of mind, which made viewing almost meaningless. Human behavior bewildered Gaspotine, an intolerable state for a Dragon, so he avoided Thorne's future.

Predictably, Rustofona waved at him. "Hurry!"

He would've ignored her, but she was his daughter and would continue pestering him until he joined her in Hellestorm's current.

"Look." Rustofona pointed at the waters.

Inside Hellestorm's lair, Thorne slid a dagger from her boot and approached the recently hatched whelp, who was the size of a calf. "I don't know why Rustofona thought I could mother him. I can't bear watching him suffer."

Without raising a ripple, Rustofona thrashed inside Hellestorm's stream. "She'll kill him."

Thorne shoved the pommel down her throat and vomited partially digested raw meat onto the rock floor. The whelp didn't even sniff.

Gaspotine rumbled laughter. "She's trying to feed him like a mother Dragon."

Rustofona snorted ice shards. "Thorne's a fool."

"A reasonable attempt."

A second Human called Zarra scratched under her narrow nose. Gaspotine liked Zarra's jutting teeth and long horsey face.

"He's persnickety and ugly." Zarra had short hair, the red-hot color of fire, which added to her appeal and made Gaspotine remember igniting his breath. Save for Thorne and the Wanderling, those that drank Rustofona's blood had red hair.

"Looks like a plucked bird with an oversized noggin," Zarra said.

Rustofona's vaporous form darkened. "That Human insults him."

Hellestorm's frailty shocked Gaspotine. Fragile bat-like wings folded against his gray body. Gaspotine doubted Hellestorm could unfurl his wings, lift his head, or stand. A mother Dragon would've let him die.

A fluttering near the whelp drew Gaspotine's gaze. Quist, the Fairy-Dragon, stalked dragon-mites along the whelp's skin, stopping on Hellestorm's snout, evidently checking whether the whelp breathed.

Thorne shoveled the vomit. "Someday he'll be handsome."

Hellestorm pawed weakly, missing Thorne and striking Zarra, who dropped her bundle.

"Aw. I've broken the quail eggs."

"Look." Thorne motioned at the whelp licking the raw eggs.

Zarra shook her head. "Even if Stonevar's hens each lay two eggs a day, it won't be enough. Though it might keep him alive till we find something else."

Sir-Sir the wole-rat crawled from inside Zarra's shirt onto her shoulder and stretched his strong jaws, displaying rows of pointed teeth. Thorne scratched under his pierced ear. He bit her and she yelped.

Gaspotine understood the wole-rat's behavior. Thorne's actions tormented him as well.

Rustofona asked, "Do you think Hellestorm will live?"

A useless question, since she could ride Hellestorm's current. A short distance up the Silver River, Hellestorm's future branched: one side to life, the other to death. The latter was wider, most probable. No wonder Rustofona obsessed over Hellestorm.

Gaspotine had seldom considered whelps while he lived. Yet Rustofona's fixation made him wonder how many he'd fathered.

CHAPTER SIX

Only Lily troubled Thorne more than Strumgued. Thorne carried a tray to the second floor and knocked outside the room Lily shared with the Giantess.

"Who is it?" Lily was seventeen, but the voice sounded childish.

Thorne wanted to say it was Rose, reveal that the Goddess of Stonevar was her sister, that she'd do anything to make Lily happy. Instead, Thorne made sure the necklace with the pouch Lily made for Rose was tucked inside her tunic. "It's Thorne. I bring food."

"I'll just throw it up." Lily was pregnant but not by her husband. Anders—a brash, blond sailor—had seduced her. "Go away."

Thorne waited until the door creaked open.

"Why are you still here?"

Thorne set the tray on the table beside an empty plate. Lily would eat the thick stew, then claim she'd thrown it up. Thorne wasn't fooled, pregnancy gave Lily a rapacious appetite. A trail of dried wine led to Grandfather's book. Thorne wiped the tome with her tunic. The bed linens mounded as if a family of wole-weasels nested there. Lily's few possessions scattered the room. Thorne picked up a skirt and hung it on a peg and brushed mud from Lily's boots. The leather had hardened, and Thorne resisted scolding her sister.

Lily folded her thin arms over her swollen belly. "Why did you bring me here?"

"Stonevar is your destiny."

"Stonevar is all you care about."

"Not true. I care deeply about you."

Lily's belly grew larger each day, but her gaunt face alarmed

Thorne.

Thorne rubbed her tunic below her throat, feeling the small leather pouch underneath. Lily had made it for Rose's fifteenth birthday. Her siblings seldom had money, but Lily had found a halfpenny and purchased red thread to embroider a bird in flight into the leather. Lily had loved Rose.

But no matter what Thorne did now, she couldn't recapture their closeness.

"Why do you care?" Lily asked. "What am I to you?"

Drinking Dragon blood had changed Thorne so much that Lily didn't recognize her. She'd grown a foot, reaching six-feet tall. Her brown hair turned white. Her brown eyes were now amber with elongated diamond centers—Dragon eyes. Rose had never been pretty, and neither was Thorne. Her jawline had become angular, and her high cheekbones more defined. Even her voice was deeper.

Thorne didn't enjoy lying or hiding behind her legend. But Lily hated Rose and might leave if Thorne confessed. "I heard your prayers. You wanted help leaving your husband."

Lily threw the empty plate across the room, shattering it against the stone wall. "You drove Anders away."

Had her sister forgotten that Anders would've returned Lily to her husband? Lily deluded herself, unable to accept that Anders didn't love her. Thorne nodded at the knitting on a chair. "Is that for the baby?"

Lily snatched it away. "I've heard that you don't like children. That you never wanted to marry. That you're unnatural."

Her words hit Thorne like a punch in the gut. How could her beloved sister be so cruel? Had Lily forgotten Daisy? Thorne was nine when Mother contracted childbed fever and couldn't nurse. Thorne fed newborn Daisy cow milk then goat milk, but the baby threw them up. Soon, her tiny arms and legs were thin as flower stems. After Daisy died, Da planted a yellow rose bush to mark her grave. Thorne vowed to neither marry nor have children. And she couldn't abide the smell of roses.

Now Thorne said, "A goddess explains herself to no one," and strode from the room.

In the hallway, Thorne leaned against the closed door, shaking, weakened by her sister's hatred. She jumped when Zarra said, "Lily shouldn't talk to you like that."

Moving away from the door, Thorne tripped over Sir-Sir, Zarra's wole-rat. Zarra caught her.

"My room," Zarra said, dragging Thorne down the passageway.

Thorne collapsed on Zarra's bed atop a patchwork quilt from Bekka. Zarra might've last occupied the austere room yesterday or last year. Having lived on the streets, she wasn't accustomed to possessions. She stored her armor, red Dragon leathers, and sword inside a nondescript trunk. Her bow was always on her back.

Zarra cracked the door so Sir-Sir could enter. "I won't tolerate Lily speaking disrespectfully to you."

"Promise me you won't upset her." Thorne took Zarra's hand, which Zarra allowed, though she didn't like others touching her. "I owe Lily a great debt."

Zarra smoothed the wole-lion skin rug, a gift from Thorne. "Seems to me Lily owes you the debt."

Thorne didn't trust anyone knowing the nature of her obligation to Lily. Thorne shivered, and Zarra wrapped the quilt around her.

After Thorne stopped trembling, she said, "I must consult Fehera."

Zarra accompanied Thorne to Fehera's herb-drying hut, a lean-to against a castle wall.

"I'll wait outside." Zarra stroked Sir-Sir's furry chestnut-colored tail.

Thorne knocked on Fehera's doorframe, knowing she'd have to tell Zarra something. Thorne wanted to tell her the truth, relieve some of the isolation she felt as Stonevar's Goddess.

The healer peered out the open door. "Come in but watch your head." She pointed a long, thick-knuckled finger at the ropes suspended from the ceiling beams. The lines supported drying oregano, chervil, and a red leaf from giant dragonwort. The latter stunk of rotting meat, but its scent soothed Thorne.

"I made dragonwort tea." Giant dragonwort was scarce. Inside one blood-red leaf, its deep purple spathe bloomed for a single day each year.

Thorne inhaled deeply, unable to resist the putrid odor. "When does it flower?"

"The hottest day of summer, when the smell carries farthest."

"How can you pick it without succumbing?" Fresh dragonwort sedated Dragons or Dragon Guards who approached too closely.

"I sent my trainee to harvest it and mark the spot. Sit." Fehera pushed aside thyme and rosemary heaped on a table. Drinking Rustofona's blood had changed Fehera's albino-white hair to pale red and added two inches to her height. As the oldest Dragon Guard, Fehera had grown the least and seemed to have the fewest dragonish compulsions.

Thorne swallowed the weak tea. "What troubles Lily?"

"She pines for Anders."

That part Thorne guessed. "I should never have made Lily drink Rustofona's blood." She'd believed Lily had Dragon-Fating and would want to become a Dragon Guard. She'd been wrong.

"She should've told you she was with child."

"I don't think she knew."

Fehera cocked her head. "Then how could you?"

"Too late, Raspberry-Frost told me the Dragon-Fating tingles I felt came from Lily's unborn child. Not Lily." If only she'd consulted the Fairy first. "I would never have asked Lily to drink if I'd known."

The healer sipped her tea, evidently considering this. "So this Dragon-Fating means the unborn will determine if a Dragon lives or dies?"

Thorne nodded. "What harm did Dragon blood do the child?"

"I see a healthy baby inside her womb."

Raising her hand, Thorne refused more tea, because it dulled her thoughts and made her sleepy. "The child steals her strength. Though Lily gets thinner, her belly grows huge." Thorne's voice cracked. "It will kill her."

"I cannot see her future, only the child's." The healer gathered dried rosemary to crush with a pestle.

Thorne wanted to save her sister and didn't care what the child's Dragon-Fating might portend. Many desperate women must've come to Fehera. "You know ways to make her lose it."

Fehera continued grinding. "She wants the baby."

"Only because she thinks Anders loves her. Will the baby come soon?"

"A month." The healer's gaze met Thorne's. "She'll bear no other."

Thorne rubbed her eyes. The fates seldom favored her. Maybe Lily could survive one birth, but she doubted both her sister and the child would live.

Outside, Thorne led Zarra from the bailey to a place where no one would overhear. Thorne stopped in the path between two newly planted fields with a clear view of anyone approaching. She looked into Zarra's dragonish eyes and saw that Zarra would never betray her.

"Swear never to tell anyone what I say."

"I swear." Zarra pressed two fingers to her lips.

"Lily is my sister."

"Why doesn't she recognize you?"

"Drinking Gaspotine's blood made me grow a foot and turned my hair white. Even my voice got deeper."

"That doesn't explain why she's so disagreeable."

"Lily wasn't always like this. Once she was kind. Never rude." Thorne needed Zarra to believe her.

Zarra rolled her eyes.

Thorne couldn't abide Zarra thinking ill of Lily. "Da pledged me to marry Farmer Rutmon."

"He broke my ribs when I tried to rescue Lily." Zarra massaged her chest. "How many wives has he buried?"

"Two. To avoid marrying him, I followed Raspberry-Frost to the lair of Gaspotine the Dark seeking gold to repay my bride price and save Lily from a similar fate."

"Your Da's a bugger."

"He needed a workhorse. Without one, my family would've starved. He believed he'd arranged a good match. When I returned with gold, Da accused me of stealing. When drinking Dragon blood made my hair fall out, he thought me diseased and cast me out. Then he gave Lily to Rutmon."

Zarra raised her hand but hesitated before patting Thorne's arm. "You didn't know what your Da would do."

"Marriage made Lily an angry woman."

"Maybe a baby will change her back."

Thorne hoped that was true, but doubted that would stop Lily hating her sister, Rose.

Somehow it seemed fitting that rain fell from dark clouds, though the sun was visible. A sunshower forecast a witch marrying. Lily considered Thorne more witch than goddess.

Thorne raised her face to the cooling drops. "No one must discover Lily is my sister. If Lord Bludwelt finds my father, he'll pay

Da a huge bride price."

"You're married to the Dwarf Lord."

"That won't deter Bludwelt." Nothing would diminish his dragonish determination to have her, and Thorne didn't plan on staying married to Strumgued.

CHAPTER SEVEN

Lord Bludwelt, the Head Constable of Seahaven, waited for the rabbit to hop away from the inn's urine-scented earth-closet and venture within range. The hare paused to nose a discarded turnip, and Bludwelt snapped his whip. The tip wrapped around the furred throat, and the rabbit fell on its side kicking. A second flick broke its neck. Bludwelt cut the rabbit's throat, checked to make sure he was alone, then licked the blade.

"Captain Hauk's here," Daxx yelled out the inn's rear door.

Bludwelt had waited months for those words. He coiled his whip and hurried inside, anticipating news of Thorne the Warrior Goddess. She'd captivated him the first time he saw her striding through Seahaven town square in black leather trousers, her white hair gleaming in the sun, her silvery scent inviting his approach.

Now as his eyes adjusted to the gloom, he handed Daxx the rabbit to skin. "Fetch two ales. Then wait outside. Ensure that no one disturbs us."

At a small table under a dirty window, Captain Hauk rose to his feet with the smooth, effortless grace of a breaching dolphin. A summer at Stonevar had dispelled his hungry look. His leather vest and linen shirt were new. His blond hair was clean and neatly secured at the nape of his neck. Daxx limped to the table on bowed legs, flashed a sour glance, and slammed a half-filled cup before Hauk.

After Daxx left, Hauk announced, "The Dragon's dead."

Bludwelt blanked his face, hiding his excitement. Fear that the Dragon would kill him had kept him from going after Thorne. So he'd arranged for Hauk to build Thorne a fishing boat at Stonevar and hired him to kill the Dragon.

"Your proof. The Dragon blood." Bludwelt had many uses for a strong poison.

Hauk lifted his harpoon from where it leaned against the wall. "The point pierced its eye."

Bludwelt examined the blade, wanting to impale Hauk. A few dried drops—worthless, even if it was Dragon blood, which he doubted. Until he smelled a familiar silver scent.

While Hauk resumed his seat, Bludwelt turned his back and licked the harpoon tip, tasting the same silver elixir that transformed him from Goadran, an impotent innkeeper's son, into Lord Bludwelt. Evidently, Dragon blood was far from poisonous. Three years ago, he'd stolen a waterskin from an inn guest, thinking it contained something important, but never suspecting Dragon blood until now.

Drinking it had made him grow a head taller than most men. His thin hair had fallen out and grown back into a thick white mane. His once scrawny arms now had muscles. People bowed when he passed, respecting him or fearing him—he didn't care which.

As Seahaven's tax collector, Bludwelt paid himself high fees and purchased property cheaply by paying back taxes. He wanted more. Someday he would rule the Isle of Elysia and have Thorne. She lived only a few hours' ride away, but while the Dragon breathed, an ocean might've separated them.

With the Dragon dead, he would leave for Stonevar, never to part from her again. Bludwelt retrieved a bag of gold and dropped it on the table before Hauk. He didn't begrudge the price.

Hauk lifted the bag and frowned. "Weighs light."

"I paid for your new mainmast. The Sea Runner's prepared to sail."

"What if I didn't return?"

"Then I'd own a ship." Bludwelt took a steadying breath, inhaling wood smoke, burnt pottage, stale ale, and rancid men's sweat; smells permanently imbedded in the walls. "Tell me about Stonevar."

"You've not asked about Lily." Hauk scratched his crooked nose, as if trying to hide his smile.

Bludwelt's shoulders tightened. He'd endured derision in his twenty-three years, but no one dared laugh at him now. "What of Farmer Rutmon's wife?" Rutmon had paid Bludwelt to recover Lily, believing Zarre the thief had kidnapped her.

"The Goddess insists Lily remain at Stonevar."

"Her husband will be disappointed. I'll inform him I located her." But Lord Bludwelt wouldn't refund the fee.

Beside him, rain cut rivulets down the dirty window. The storm would delay his departure for Stonevar. He twisted the ruby ring around his little finger, the wedding ring intended for Thorne. "What news of the Warrior Goddess?"

Hauk smirked. "Thorne was most agreeable."

Bludwelt's smile slipped a notch. "Few would describe her as agreeable. She has a sharpness about her." And he anticipated honing her edge.

"She's unlike any other. Handsome rather than beautiful. Thinks like a man. Maybe a goddess."

Bludwelt steepled his fingers. "Have you met many gods?"

Hauk chuckled. "Can't say I have."

"Perhaps she's a pretender."

Captain Hauk squinted to appraise Bludwelt. "Her hair is thick and white like yours. Her amber eyes have elongated diamond centers—like yours."

Though this pleased Bludwelt, he wanted to poke out Hauk's too-observant eyes. "The gods favored me."

"So it seems, Lord."

Bludwelt buttoned his coat. Without a hearth fire, the inn was danker than usual. He should've had Daxx build a fire. "Tell me of Stonevar."

"We built them a fine fishing boat." Hauk paused as if expecting praise. "The boat pleased Thorne, and my tales entranced her. I needed more time . . . I'd never considered a land marriage, though I've made my share of promises. But I asked Thorne to wed me."

Bludwelt wanted to castrate Hauk.

The Captain winked. "She told me if I wed her, you'd kill me."

"I'd heed her words."

Hauk laughed.

Lord Bludwelt ran his tongue over a pointed canine tooth and pictured shredding Hauk's throat. "Our business is done."

"Don't you want to learn about my slaying the Dragon and about the treasure?"

Fenks, Bludwelt cursed silently. The man tired him, but the treasure was interesting. "Go on."

"It was a hot day, unseasonably so for autumn. I approached your supposed ally." Hauk flashed a narrow-eyed, reproachful look. "The harlot betrayed me to Thorne."

"Whores are whores. Won't stay bought." Bludwelt had better ways to ensure loyalty.

"Fate smiled upon me. The Dragon scattered Stonevar's cattle and everyone scurried after the herd. While the beast devoured a heifer, I crept closer. The monster roared. Another man would've run, but I—"

"Spear your tongue on the point." The puttock was telling about the Dragon, not the treasure.

Without seeming the least perturbed, Hauk said, "I harpooned the Dragon's eye. But its death displeased the Goddess, when a sculpin could see I'd done her a service."

"Foolish to leave the treasure behind." Bludwelt fisted his hand to avoid crushing the captain's throat.

Hauk rubbed the misshapen black pearl on his coral necklace. "I'd only three men."

"Your Giantess is worth six."

"Willow-Bender remains at Stonevar. My crew would tolerate her no longer."

"So your sea-wife strained your crew."

Hauk eyes widened as if surprised that Bludwelt knew about his sea tryst, then Hauk shrugged.

Bludwelt nurtured an uncomfortable silence before saying, "Enough about the Dragon. Tell me about the treasure."

"I'll need help fetching it." Hauk's eyes glinted.

Lord Bludwelt snorted. He'd let Hauk acquire the treasure for him, but if the captain misled him, he'd remove Hauk's tedious tongue. "How many defend Stonevar?"

"Nine aged soldiers and some women imitating warriors."

"How many to fetch the treasure?" Bludwelt preferred predictable outcomes.

"A score."

He'd need time to recruit twenty who'd keep quiet. Waiting to claim Thorne tightened his chest, straining each breath like a blacksmith's bellows with a sticky valve. In autumn, when Dragons mated, his craving for Thorne became intolerable. But he needed that treasure. At his current rate of skimming tax revenue, it would take years to fill the Guildmasters' purses. Without their support, he'd never become Magister of Seahaven.

At the right time, Bludwelt would arrest the current Magister for devaluing property. The fool had a weakness for young virgins, and their fathers complained of lowered bride prices. When Bludwelt became Magister, he'd enjoy ordering his predecessor lashed.

Lightning lit the window and thunder rumbled, raising bumps on Bludwelt's skin. Storms cowed him and cold made him sluggish. Dragonish changes he didn't like.

Hauk surveyed the empty inn as if expecting to discover a lurker. "I got a plan."

"Enlighten me."

Captain Hauk leaned closer. "We'll easily overcome her nine soldiers."

"How well do you know these men?"

"Lived beside them and their families in Stonevar."

Apparently Hauk had no compunction about attacking those who'd befriended him. Bludwelt admired that. "Thorne will hardly watch us kill her soldiers."

"She may call down lightning bolts or some such, but I'll deal with her."

Bludwelt worried less about lightning than Hauk near Thorne. After retrieving the treasure, Bludwelt would kill him.

"I know where she goes alone," Hauk whispered, though no one else was near. "She climbs to a mountain brekka to commune with the Dragon."

Lord Bludwelt frowned. "There is no Dragon."

Hauk waved dismissively. "I'll make sure the Goddess isn't an obstacle."

If this puttock touched Thorne, he'd chop off Hauk's hands before burning him alive.

"I'll distract her," Hauk said, "while you lead an attack."

Bludwelt had no intention of fighting personally. "A captain doesn't fight with commoners. I'll command from a distance."

Hauk nodded. "We'll need supplies."

"I'll take care of that." He rose.

"You've forgotten our split."

"Ten percent," Bludwelt offered.

"Seventy-five."

Intending to give Hauk nothing, he could be generous. "Fifty."

"Done." Hauk grinned. "I'll need a place to swing my hammock while I enlist more crew."

Bludwelt grunted. "I suppose you expect me to house and feed you and your sailors." Hauk would look less pleased after tasting Daxx's cooking.

The Captain extended his hand, and Bludwelt squeezed until Hauk winced. While he served Lord Bludwelt's designs, he'd continue breathing.

CHAPTER EIGHT

A month after Strumgued's arrival, Thorne awoke gasping from her dream of a man with flowing white hair riding over Stonevar Plain. With Rustofona dead, Bludwelt would come. The dragonish part of her wanted him. The Human part despised him.

She stripped off her sweat-soaked shift. Shivering in the early morning air, she examined her reflection in the mirror. Her back was smooth, without dragonish deformity. Shoulders still Human-like. Seeing no wings, she breathed easier.

In the Great Hall, she greeted everyone, determined to make her people believe her alliance with Strumgued pleased her. Somehow, without endangering their lives, she must nullify her vows, retain Stonevar, and protect Hellee. Smiling until out of sight, she rode to Hellee, leaving behind the Dwarfs hammering stone into a bridge. Once it was completed, she'd never be free of them.

Inside the cavern, she found Hellee with his feet in the air. Thorne's heart slammed to a stop. Had the Dwarfs killed him?

The whelp's snore restarted Thorne's heart. She couldn't resist touching his warm snout. Hellee rolled over and wobbled upright, knocking her over. He straddled her and licked her face, all the while mewling apologies.

Spangle pushed him off and pulled Thorne to her feet. "He must weigh fourteen stone. When he doubles his weight again, his bumbling will kill someone."

Glitter, Spangle's identical twin, scratched the scar on her side. "He's only a baby." With a dancer's lithe body and grace, Glitter moved to Hellee.

The Dragon whelp stretched his neck toward her. He already

measured eight feet from nose to tail. Unless he cooperated, they couldn't move him, and he was only an infant. As Glitter rubbed Hellee's throat, the whelp rumbled a dragonish purr. "He'd never harm us intentionally."

While they talked, Quist the Fairy-Dragon flew on translucent wings, owlish eyes open wide, hunting dragon-mites on the whelp's hide. Suddenly Quist, the size of a man's fist, dove at Hellee's ear slit and speared a dragon-mite on his fangs. He stabbed a second pest on the hard tip of his long tongue, then flew to Thorne's shoulder where he devoured the pests with loud crunches. He nuzzled Thorne's neck before hunting more burrowing vermin.

Unaware and unconcerned, Hellee flopped on his side. Glitter scraped Hellee's leathery belly with a thorn brush, and his back foot thumped the wall.

"Spangle's right." Thorne rubbed her sore bottom. "We must train him not to accidentally injure us. Now, when he exhales into the hearth, his breath creates only a small fireball. As he grows so will the size of his explosions. Has anyone taught puppies to herd sheep?"

"Lott trained army dogs." Spangle brushed non-existent dirt off her brown tunic and trousers. After years of wearing seductive clothing for clients, the twins now preferred dour attire.

Glitter ran slim, callused fingers through her short red hair. "How do you know that?"

"He told me." Spangle's tone was guarded.

Apparently the twin knew more of Lott's history than Thorne realized.

A wrinkle creased Glitter's patrician forehead. "No one must think we're training Hellee like a working dog."

"Lott won't tell anyone." Spangle stared at the floor.

Thorne didn't know why Spangle avoided her gaze but intended to find out. "Hellee stinks of sulfur," Thorne said. "Spangle, will you help me bathe him, while Glitter cleans the cavern?"

Outside Thorne watched for the right moment to ask Spangle what troubled her, but Hellee's happy howls hindered conversation. Thorne poured pails of water over Hellee, and Spangle scoured his leathery skin with a birch broom.

The whelp licked Spangle's face.

"Stop!" The twin danced away. "You're scraping my nose."

When they finished, Hellee stretched out to dry himself, yawning and displaying sharp baby fangs. After a short doze, he jerked awake when a cool wind swept down the slope. Under roiling clouds, lightning blazed between Ventamar's twin peaks. Thunder sent Hellee dashing inside. Thorne and Spangle followed as far as the tunnel entrance.

Spangle shivered. "Lott asked me to marry him."

Thorne hadn't expected any Dragon Guard to marry—at least voluntarily. "Did you accept?" To hide her expression, she watched the rain.

"Put him off."

Thorne's breathing eased.

"I don't know what to do." Spangle pressed her temple against cool stone.

Thorne wanted to tell Spangle to refuse. "I'm a poor advisor. Bias taints my words. You must choose."

Spangle lowered her gaze. "When Glitter and I were girls, men did things I refuse to remember. I can please a man, but I've never shared myself with one."

"Withhold all you can," Thorne blurted.

"I never expected to meet a man I could trust."

So the overture tempted. Thorne relied on Lott to steward Stonevar. But should he be trusted with Spangle? Now a widower, he'd been a good husband. Nevertheless, his first wife was a draft horse, and Spangle a thoroughbred.

"I never thought I'd marry." Spangle's forehead wrinkled. "A wall inside me has crumbled. Did Dragon blood do this?"

Thorne forced her next words out. "It increased my desire to couple."

"Aah. That I understand. But why does Lott want to marry me?"

"Your grace cleaning barns; your lyrical voice calling cattle; your scent after butchering hogs. You please all the senses. How could Lott resist?"

Spangle groaned. "You jest, but beauty brings women only pain."

"I agree. Fathers demand a higher bride price for beauty; nevertheless, a woman must still obey her husband, bear his children, and work until her back fails without any say."

Spangle nodded. "What will happen to Glitter if I accept Lott's proposal?"

"What did your sister say?"

"I've not told her."

That surprised Thorne.

With a loud boom, a thunderbolt struck over Malwood. Inside the cavern, Hellee screeched and a torch exploded. Both Thorne and Spangle flinched. Training him to resist exhaling on torches or into the hearth proved impossible when anything frightened him.

"You scorched my hair!" Glitter scolded. "And it just got long enough to lay down." Drinking Dragon blood had turned the twins' hair deep red.

Hellee mewled.

Spangle stared down the tunnel. "I can't hurt Glitter."

"Brutte often said we must choose the most arduous route."

Spangle gazed up at Thorne. "You're wise."

Thorne didn't feel so. Foolish described her better. Her interference often caused disaster. "No need to rush a decision."

#

By evening the rain relented, but wind tore at Thorne's simple gown as she approached Strumgued's tent. Though the support poles rattled, she'd no doubt it would withstand a hurricane. Strumgued rose when she entered. Without pleasantries, they shared a meal of boiled fish. Strumgued, always a hearty eater, consumed little. Worried about Lily and Spangle, Thorne hadn't thought of new reasons for Strumgued to unyoke her. At least tonight he didn't insist she talk.

When she finished, he placed a foot-sized wooden chest on the table and opened it.

Thorne saw only white cloth. "What's this?"

His eyes sparkled with a child's excitement. "I planned this offering after apricots, but . . ."

An impatient Dwarf. Unusual. She doubted the box contained a divorce. "No gift will make me love you."

He grunted. "Human love is mist. What can I or any Dwarf know of it?" Strumgued set the contents before her and rubbed the back of his neck. "Unwrap it."

Curious, she opened the cloth. Inside was a miniature cutlass made from bone, similar to Dracodurus; a Dragon formed the grip, its tail the blade. Fine craftsmanship. She fingered the blade and felt a tingle. The bone must've come from a Dragon. "Who carved this?"

When Strumgued placed his hand on her arm, she stiffened rather than flinch.

"I shaped it from the wyrm's rib. I call this blade Fervid, for the wound it inflicts will burn like Dragon fire."

Thorne traced the shape before grasping it. "Priceless." Unexpectedly, her stomach swayed as if she soared amongst the clouds. This blade contained a trace of Dragon spirit. "Who gave you Rustofona's rib?"

"Willow-Bender."

Likely from bone still attached to the flesh they preserved. Thorne pressed her lips together. She couldn't refuse this present, but she'd never accept another.

She shook off his hand. "Don't think this will weaken me."

A crease cut the middle of Strumgued's brow. "You lack trust."

He yanked open his leather jerkin and shirt, exposing the thick, reddish-blond curls on his chest. "Upon my life, I swear never to betray or deceive you. I shall defend and honor you. Have no dread of me. If I cause you harm"—putting his hand over hers, he pressed Fervid's tip to his breast—"then plunge this blade deep into my faithless heart. I'll not resist."

Thorne pushed on the blade, hard enough to break the skin. Three drops of blood clung to his chest hair. Strumgued snorted and his eyes widened. This was her chance to be free of him.

Sighing, she set aside the knife. "Must you offer a Dwarfish oath that I know you'll never break? Our situation grows even more intolerable."

He rubbed the silk ends of her scarlet sash against his cheek. "It need not be."

She wrested the belt away. "I will never be the wife you hope for."

"Nonetheless, we are wed."

She pressed her cold fingertips against her temple. "I never wanted a husband."

"And I sought no wife after Lea-Lee."

"A precious knife and Dwarfish oath. You seek to ingratiate yourself."

Strumgued struck his breast with a fist, then offered an open palm.

49

Thorne eyed the exit longingly. "Will your solicitude continue until I'm worn smooth as a river stone?"

"Dwarfs can maintain a course for decades."

"So I either concede or suffer your attentions until my death bed."

He laughed. "My Lea-Lee declined to wed me for eleven years. Afterward, she was most joyful."

Thorne hid her smile behind her hand. "Let's sample the apricots, before your charm overwhelms me." She spooned fruit onto her plate.

"You mock me."

She concentrated on cutting the apricot. "Tomorrow we bring in the new calves."

His eyes narrowed. "You will return for the eventide meal."

"I may." Thorne tasted the apricot. Perfect, but she left half.

#

When Thorne returned to the castle, Magda met her at the door. "You care for the Dwarf Lord."

"Stroll with me outside." Thorne didn't want others knowing the truth about her unhappy alliance.

For the first time since Brutte's death, Magda left the bailey. The breeze carried the sweet scent of deadly oleander. As they sauntered beside the river stained red by the sunset, Magda held out a small flask.

"What's this?"

"Put it in his wine. Sprinkle it on his food."

Thorne glanced about but saw no one nearby; nonetheless, she whispered, "You want me to poison Strumgued?"

"You'll be free of him." Magda's eyes glistened wildly. The twilight emphasized the hollows of their sockets.

"Yes, but—"

"The others will leave once he's dead."

"They're carving a castle inside South Ventamar. The Dwarfs will stay."

Wind lifted strands of Magda's hair, setting them wiggling like tiny gray snakes. "You own Stonevar."

"I have title to the plain, not the mountain nor the adjoining land. Strumgued suffers us to live in the castle and plow the most fertile ground. With him dead, his eldest son will lead." She didn't mention that a new Dwarf Lord would kill Hellee, since this would please Magda. "He has eighteen sons. I can't poison them all, and if Strumgued dies, none will dine with their stepmother." She thought her observation amusing, but Magda shed tears.

Thorne hugged her. "I swore fealty to him. I cannot poison him." At least not until she could nullify their nuptials and her oath.

"You grow fond of him."

"I cannot let loathing rule my head. I bank my hatred deep inside, but it stills burns like blue fire." She took the poison from the older woman.

Magda shook her head. "Brutte will put everything right after he returns."

Thorne held her foster mother tighter. Was Magda going mad?

CHAPTER NINE

After the Humans discovered Hellestorm would eat raw eggs, his current in the Silver River widened.

Rustofona screeched. "The Giantess . . . the Giantess has . . ."

For someone with no need to breathe, Rustofona seemed short of breath. She pointed at the river where the whelp chewed the Giantess's hand.

Gaspotine moved closer. "Is he eating her?"

"Sucking her fingers."

"Disgusting." Gaspotine would've enjoyed watching Hellestorm bite off her arm. "Now what's he doing?"

"Licking fish offal from the Giantess's legs," Rustofona said.

Remembering the pleasing aroma of fish guts, Gaspotine sighed. "Hellestorm will live."

Rustofona's eyes leaked. Gaspotine cocked his head. Dragons couldn't cry. When a drop plopped into his eye, he looked up. Water pelted them from above, but it never rained here. Apparently, no Dragon before Rustofona had experienced such relief or joy or whatever it was. This realization disoriented Gaspotine, but the Continuum brightened.

The Dragon spirits edging the shore scanned the Continuum, looking for the source of this phenomenon. Gaspotine wound himself around Rustofona to block their view. Somehow he must stop her crying.

"Cease weeping."

"Am I?" She touched claws to face. "That's rain."

Gaspotine didn't see any point arguing since the rain was stopping. When scattered droplets created rainbows throughout the

Continuum, Gaspotine groaned. Rainbows were worse.

Dragon spirits huddled on shore, discussing possible causes of these aberrations. Gaspotine would never reveal the source, though telling might've brought him the renown he'd once prized.

In the physical world, Thorne hugged the Giantess. "Thank you."

"Need more fish." The Giantess's feet pounded the cavern's stone floor as she fled.

Thorne's nauseating gratitude made Gaspotine squirm. Dragons never thanked anyone, since they never helped anyone. He didn't want Rustofona knowing he'd protected her from Dragon scorn. Gaspotine might be dead but he still had pride.

After a day passed in the corporeal world, something compelled Rustofona to update Gaspotine about Hellestorm's progress. After nine days, Hellestorm had doubled his weight. After thirty-three, the Giantess couldn't catch enough fish to satisfy him so they mixed in wild animal guts. Gaspotine grudgingly admired Thorne's cleverness.

Now that Hellestorm thrived, Gaspotine thought Rustofona would stop worrying, but she said, "How can Humans raise a Dragon properly?"

Gaspotine needed somewhere to hide.

CHAPTER TEN

Two weeks after Magda insisted Thorne poison Strumgued, the older woman continued to deny Brutte's death, and her mind seemed to slip into the past. That night, thoughts of Magda kept Thorne awake. When she finally slept, a tortured wailing woke her. Were they under attack? Had Hauk returned? Or worse, Bludwelt?

Lily moaned. Thorne raced to her sister's room, which she shared with Willow-Bender. A single candle burned beside the bed, and the bitter scent of cold ashes saturated the stagnant air. Why had the Giantess left Lily alone?

Thorne opened the balcony doors before stroking her sister's damp forehead. "Is the pain great?"

Lily grimaced. "My womb's bursting like a milkweed pod."

Fehera rushed in, followed by Willow-Bender.

"Why didn't you wake me?" Thorne asked the Giantess.

"Lily needs Fehera."

Thorne flushed. "You're right. Thank you."

Lily's swollen stomach shifted as the healer examined her. Thorne remembered Hellee clawing through his shell and pictured a foot rupturing Lily's belly.

Lily gazed at the window. Was she remembering Anders? Determined to interrupt Lily's sentimental fantasies, Thorne wiped the perspiration coating her sister's brow, and her necklace swung forward.

Lily clasped it. "I made this pouch for my sister, Rose."

Thorne asked the others to leave, though she knew that Lily hated her. "Do you know me?"

"Dragon blood changed you, didn't it?"

54

Thorne nodded.

"You ran away." Her eyes seemed unfocused.

"No." Thorne took Lily's limp hand. "I went after Dragon gold to repay my bride price." Her journey to Gaspotine's cavern had nearly killed her, but she willingly risked her life to escape a lifetime married to a loutish, middle-aged farmer.

Lily gasped as another pain hit. Thorne wished she could take the pain on herself.

"When Rose left, Mother wouldn't stop crying. And Da beat me for the smallest mistake."

"I didn't know." But she should have.

Lily squirmed as if trying to get comfortable. "You left me."

"I came back with gold, but Da thought I stole it." She'd returned with enough to repay Rutmon and to save Lily from marrying some dolt.

"Da gave me to Rutmon in your place." Lily's condemning stare made Thorne cringe.

"I didn't know Da would do that. You weren't fifteen yet."

"Rutmon promised to wait, but every night he pawed me."

Bile churned in Thorne's stomach. "He shouldn't have done that."

The next contraction squeezed Lily into a fetal position. Afterward she spoke breathlessly as if she'd run miles. "During the day, I chased after his seven awful brats who fought with each other like wild dogs. I cooked and washed, milked cows and planted gardens. I never had a moment's rest."

"I sent Zarre to rescue you." Afterward Thorne discovered that Zarre was really Zarra.

"When I tried to leave with Zarre, Rutmon almost killed him. That night Rutmon took me to his bed." Lily gagged. "I'm going to be sick."

Thorne brought her a pail, and Lily vomited.

Glitter and Spangle finally rescued Lily almost two years later. No wonder her sister was angry. "But you weren't fifteen yet," Thorne said.

Lily gave her a disgusted look that said Thorne would never understand.

"At least you didn't get pregnant."

Lily choked. "I had two babies born too small."

Thorne couldn't breathe. Two babies dead. No wonder her sister was bitter. "I'm so sorry." Instead of sending Zarra to rescue Lily, she should have gone herself. "I brought you here to keep you safe."

"Rose deserted me. Thorne brought me here. Does one remedy the other?"

"Only you can say." But Thorne knew the answer.

Lily stared at her stomach. "Not so safe."

Thorne sank to the floor. Intending to return Lily to Rutmon, Captain Hauk had ordered his first mate, Anders, to seduce her. "Forgive me, Lily. I bungled everything."

"And you made me drink Dragon blood. And eat raw Dragon heart, brain, and tongue."

Thorne knew Lily hated the changes Dragon blood caused; losing her soft, blond hair and blue eyes. Most of all losing her vitality to five inches of dragonish growth while pregnant. And after drinking Dragon blood, Lily had become even more morose.

Lily threw off the blanket. Her stomach was twice normal size. "It did something to my baby."

"Maybe twins," Thorne suggested.

"Fehera says only one."

Lily arched her back as new pain struck. When it passed, she said, "I thought those who loved me cared about my happiness."

"What more can I do?"

"I want Anders."

Thorne groaned. So many had failed Lily—Rose, Da, Rutmon, Anders. "I should never have brought those sailors here."

"I would gladly endure the shame of a bastard child, if Anders—"

Thorne hadn't known Lily felt shame. ""Anders is nothing. Your life is everything. Here, no one will speak ill of you."

"They wouldn't dare because of you." Lily clutched the bedding and arched her back again. "Now I understand why childbirth frightened Rose."

When Thorne wiped Lily's face with a cool cloth, her sister smiled like Thorne remembered. She kissed Lily's brow. "I should've rescued you earlier, even if I had no safe place to take you."

Lily grabbed Thorne's hand. "I'm not brave like you or Rose."

"I'm not brave enough to have a child." If only Lily forgave her.

"It's coming!" Lily screamed.

Fehera hurried back and examined Lily a second time, then motioned Thorne into the hallway.

"What's wrong?" Thorne whispered.

Fehera frowned. "The pains are strong but Lily's womb remains closed."

"Her labor has only begun."

"It started some time ago, but she didn't wake Willow-Bender."

Lily was braver than she admitted. "Give her something for pain."

"That would delay the birth and endanger the child."

Thorne grasped Fehera's shoulders. "Save Lily."

"I'll do all I can."

Thorne hummed a calming Fairy tune for herself and Lily. Soothed, her sister quieted. Thorne sent Willow-Bender to tell Strumgued that she'd miss their eventide meal. When the Giantess returned, she held Lily's hand, which barely covered Willow-Bender's palm.

Lily moaned. "Water."

"Wipe her mouth with a moist cloth," Fehera said.

Darkness circled Lily's sunken eyes. Humming no longer soothed her. Thorne rubbed her sister's distended stomach with oil to ease the pain. At times Lily responded. At others, her eyes glazed, and she didn't reply. Throughout the day, the Dragon Guards and other women visited. In a lucid moment, Lily insisted on wearing a scarf to hide her despised tresses.

On the evening of the second day, a banging came from downstairs. To hasten the birth, the women opened and shut chests. The men shot flaming arrows into the sky. The noise seemed to reassure Lily, who'd been in labor forty-eight hours. Without drinking Dragon blood, she'd already be dead. How long would her strength last?

Fehera joined Thorne on the balcony where wispy gray clouds snaked across the night sky. "A bad moon."

Thorne gripped the railing. "How much longer?"

"The baby's large."

Lily shrieked hoarsely. Thorne resisted an urge to retreat to a corner and cover her ears. She'd go mad if Lily's pain continued much longer.

After Fehera examined Lily, the healer shook her head. "Don't tighten, Lily. Fear will close your womb."

"I can't help it."

Thorne had never felt more helpless.

The third day, the sun rose red, forecasting a storm. Lily couldn't lift her head and struggled for breath. She gagged but nothing came up. Even dim light made her cover her eyes.

Fehera told Thorne, "She must deliver now or die," and asked Willow-Bender to put Lily on the birthing chair.

Lily stiffened and screamed when the Giantess lifted her. Willow-Bender's eyes widened and she froze. Thorne's empty stomach cramped.

"Do as I ask," Fehera ordered.

When Willow-Bender set Lily on the horseshoe-shaped chair, she flopped forward, and the Giantess held her from behind.

Fehera knelt in front of Lily. "Wait for the pain before pushing."

"The pain never stops," Lily croaked.

"Thorne, put your hand on Lily's stomach. Tell her when the contraction starts." She told Lily, "When Thorne tells you, push hard."

"Now."

Grunting though gritted teeth, Lily pushed. Sweat coated her flushed face.

"The head's out."

Lily wept tearlessly.

Thorne exhaled, unaware she'd been holding her breath. "Don't give up, Lily. It's almost over." And her sister still lived. She couldn't believe it.

Unexpectedly, Lily screamed louder and longer than before. The sobbing afterward shredded Thorne's spirit.

"The head's going back in." Fehera moved back. "Put her on the bed. Hurry."

"What's wrong?" Thorne demanded.

"The turtle sign. The baby's shoulders are stuck. I must get it out quickly. Pull Lily's knees against her abdomen."

Willow-Bender raised one leg and Thorne the other. Lily's panting became a whisper. Fehera took out a knife.

"The water ceremony," Thorne said. Grandfather's book said this helped mothers and babies survive.

"No time."

Thorne insisted. Fehera cleansed her hands and the blade while offering a blessing. Then she nicked Lily's skin around the baby's head and slipped her fingers inside. Blood soaked the bed. The rusty smell sickened Thorne, and she held her breath, smothering a sob.

Too weak to squirm away, Lily whimpered for mercy.

Thorne wanted to yank Fehera off. "What are you doing?"

"Pressing on the baby's back to move the shoulders."

Imagining how that must hurt, Thorne clasped Lily's leg tighter. Unexpectedly, Lily quieted.

"How's Lily?" the healer asked.

"Unconscious." The word squeezed from Thorne's taut throat. She looked away, unable to watch. "Are the shoulders moving?"

"No. I have to turn the baby. Willow-Bender, when Thorne signals the next pain, push your fist on the side of Lily's belly, here, behind the bone."

"Now." Thorne's voice cracked a little.

"One shoulder's out." Fehera took audible breaths, "but to get the other, I must turn the baby again."

"Now."

Willow-Bender pushed. The child emerged, followed by the afterbirth and a gush of blood.

Lily opened her eyes while the healer tried to stop the bleeding. "The pain stopped." She smiled at Thorne. "I'm thirsty." Lily raised her arm, but it fell back on the bed.

Thorne held the cup for her sister to drink. Lily's cheek was cool, and her skin pale, almost moribund.

"Care for him, Rose." Lily closed her eyes.

There was so much she wanted to say. "Don't sleep yet."

Lily's lips were blue.

Thorne shook Lily's shoulder, but her sister's eyes remained closed. "I cannot wake Lily."

"Let her sleep while I check the baby." The healer stuck her finger inside the infant's mouth, clearing his throat.

Willow-Bender took Lily's hand. Red rimmed the Giantess's eyes. "An endless sleep."

"No." The floor shifted, dropping Thorne to her knees beside the bed.

Fehera's lower lip quivered as she pressed her fingertips against Lily's throat. "She bled too much. Her heart gave out."

59

Thorne took the vial of Dragon blood from around her neck and tried to force Lily to drink, but the blood dribbled from her sister's lips. More Dragon blood couldn't save Lily.

She blew into Lily's mouth until her chest expanded. Though Fehera shook her head, Thorne tried again and again, until Willow-Bender said, "Cease, Goddess." The Giantess had never called her that before.

Willow-Bender began a sorrowful drone. Thorne huddled in a corner. Fehera said something Thorne didn't understand. Her head ached as black dots, like a colony of careening bats, obscured her vision. Baby cries multiplied the spots.

Fehera held out the red-faced newborn, who must weigh a stone—a monster to deliver. As the healer swaddled him, Thorne saw the baby's shoulders and gagged. Willow-Bender's drone became a wail.

Thorne stumbled downstairs, away from the Giantess's mournful cries. She rushed through the Great Hall, unable to speak or meet anyone's gaze.

Outside, Bekka the hunchback sat on a stool, brushing a goat's undercoat, collecting wood in a basket, filling the air with a musky odor. Normally the rhythmic motions soothed Thorne, but now she wanted to smash the comb and strangle the bleating goat.

Bekka waited until Thorne gazed at her. "Lily?" Her gentle look made Thorne collapse at Bekka's feet.

Thorne rested her heavy head on Bekka's knees. "The child killed her."

Bekka dropped the rope, letting the goat dash away. "Oh, no." She stroked Thorne's hair. With her crooked back and small size, Bekka was among the least likely of women to become a Dragon Guard. "The baby?" Her dearest desire was to have a child, but her twisted spine prevented her birthing one.

Thorne trembled. "Malformed."

"Show me."

Inside, Peppa, thin and plain, nursed the newborn. During the winter, she'd delivered Stonevar's first healthy child, a girl. When Thorne and Bekka approached, the others parted.

"He looks healthy," Bekka said. "Show me."

Peppa opened the soft wool blanket. He was twice the size of most newborns and appeared well formed.

Bekka touched his hand. "He has his fingers and toes. Does he cry?"

"Yells like banshee." Magda stood at the table, slicing carrots into a pot.

The newborn's fingers curled around Bekka's. "Show me."

When Peppa turned the baby over, he wailed an objection at being taken from her nipple. On his shoulder blades, two hard knobs pushed against the skin. More than one person gasped.

Magda sniffed. "The Dragon marked him."

Thorne couldn't disagree.

"Who will care for him?" Bekka gazed at the crowd.

"I'll nurse him," Peppa said, "but my own children are all I can care for."

"Give him to me," Bekka whispered, as if saying the words too loudly might prevent her having what she believed impossible.

The others murmured approval.

Thorne put her hand on Bekka's twisted shoulder. "There could be other problems we cannot see. His needs may be great."

Bekka lifted him. "His greatest need is love."

"He'll be my brother." Emera the Wanderling had stayed uncharacteristically silent until now. "What shall we call him?"

Bekka rubbed her cheek against the top of his head. "His name is Aeron, for he will be strong." He stopped crying and looked at her with elliptical Dragon eyes.

"His eyes," Thorne mumbled. "His eyes."

CHAPTER ELEVEN

First Brutte, now Lily. The Dragon blood, which Thorne had insisted Lily drink, had made the newborn so large that birthing him killed her sister. Thorne could bear no more; she didn't want to see anyone and didn't want anyone seeing her. She followed the path across the valley from Hellee's cavern. Her legs wobbled as she ascended to her Contemplation Ledge. When her foot slipped on a mossy rock, she caught herself with one hand, skinned her palm, and welcomed the sting.

Each foot weighed as much as a boulder. Her skin stretched tight over her bones. She hadn't slept or bathed in three days. On the mountainside, her odor would offend no one. The rocks and branches blurred. When she shook her head to clear her vision, the treetops quivered. She hadn't felt this lost since Mother died.

After pulling herself onto the ledge, she collapsed under a stunted larch growing from a crack. She craved tears to banish the prickling behind her eyes, but Dragons couldn't cry. Neither could she. Thorne licked Fervid's blade, feeling a prickling of Rustofona's spirit.

She'd settled Stonevar to give Lily a safe place, but her actions had killed her sister. Too many following her had died. Lily's child would have a better chance in Bekka's care. A niggling voice urged her to act rather than wallowing in useless self-pity. Instead she sprawled across cold rock, yearning to embrace madness like Magda and deny events too painful to bear. Moments later, she fell unconscious.

Thorne awoke in darkness, smelling smoke mixed with evergreen, thyme, and burning flesh. A day must have passed, but she'd no memory. Pulling the cloak over her face blocked some of the odor. She should attend Lily's funeral; instead she vowed never to interfere again and escaped into sleep.

#

Hellee's whines woke Thorne. The morning sun made her squint. On the ledge across the valley, Spangle stroked under Hellee's chin, but failed to calm him.

Raspberry-Frost landed by Thorne and blocked her vision. Thorne blew on the Fairy, rippling the white tuft topping its head and fur covering its body. Raspberry-Frost folded its wings so they flowed from its shoulders like a white cape. "Hellee wants First Mother."

"Is that what he calls me?" She rolled over to disguise her shudders. She never wanted to be anyone's mother.

Raspberry-Frost nipped her ear with pointed teeth. That often preceded unpleasant news. "Fairy Queen swarms."

Thorne's chest burned. Da would say, "Your black bile's unbalanced." Mother would inspect the whites of her eyes, then offer nut charcoal or goatweed tea. Thorne rubbed above her stomach. "You won't go with the new hive."

"All Fae leave Stonevar." Raspberry-Frost's black-slitted yellow eyes had a feral aspect.

The burning worsened. "You can't." Raspberry-Frost had saved her life more than once. If her Fairy left, Thorne would lose not only her companion, but also her translator, guide, first friend. "I've lost Brutte and Lily. I can't lose you. Will you stay?"

"United Fae remains strong."

Thorne touched the port-wine stain marking the Fairy's face. "You have me." Her voice broke. "Please stay."

Raspberry-Frost ran a clawed finger in the folds of Thorne's ear. "Fairies need hives."

"Why is the hive leaving?" She knew as soon as she asked.

"Dwarfs will hunt Fae." The Fairy set its pointed chin.

"I'll make them go." How, she'd no idea. "Give me time."

"Dwarfs stay forevermore." Raspberry-Frost combed Thorne's hair with her claws.

Thorne's heart pounded as if she'd run miles. "Without you, I'll go as mad as Magda." She was halfway already. "I'll go with you."

The Fairy didn't titter laughter. "Whelp needs First Mother."

Where could she take a baby Dragon? She couldn't raise him alone. She lay back, forced flat by yet another obligation not of her choosing. "When will you leave?"

"After new hive thrives."

"Will you come back?"

Raspberry-Frost kissed Thorne's eyelid—her Fairy had never done that before—and winged to the hedgerow. Would she ever see Raspberry-Frost again? She gripped Fervid tighter. All because of Strumgued. More reason to hate him.

#

Late afternoon the same day, Thorne heard grumbles as her husband climbed to her Contemplation Ledge. She huddled under a small outcrop. How dare he?

She shouted over the edge, "Go away!" She wanted to scream, "Don't hurt the Fairies." Somehow she must get the upper hand so he wouldn't harm them.

Strumgued huffed as he stomped onto the ledge. "You avoid my table."

"I'm grieving."

He scanned the Dragon ledge across the valley, but Hellee was inside. Thorne hoped he'd stay there.

"Rain comes." He pointed north where dark clouds gathered. "Time to return."

"Why do you care if I get wet?" She immediately regretted her childish tone.

"You are my wife. It's my duty to care for you." He spoke matter-of-factly.

"We've an alliance. Nothing more."

"It is what you wish." He squatted beside her.

She wanted to crawl away from him but instead sat straighter. "I wish you hadn't killed Brutte."

"He died a warrior's death. Would he have it any other way?"

"I'm lost without him." She immediately regretted revealing this weakness.

"Rely on me." He held out a waterskin.

Thorne shook her head. Though thirsty, she would never drink where his lips had touched.

He held out an oilskin sack with a tempting aroma. "Fresh bread."

Her stomach rumbled. "You came all this way to eat with me?"

Strumgued lifted an eyebrow. "To my meals, you add spice."

His gaze gave her the sensation of centipedes crawling up her spine. "Why do you persist?"

"The quest satisfies as much as achieving the prize." He pointed toward her lap. "You value the blade."

Thorne flushed and sheathed Fervid.

"Your eyes storm." He grinned as if delighted. "I wrote you a verse."

"A verse?" The Dwarf had lost his mind.

"Humans call it a song." He pulled a hand harp from his pack. The delicate instrument looked ridiculous in Strumgued's thick fingers.

There was no refusing without covering her ears like a child.

Strumgued plucked the strings and sang in a baritone;

> "Thorne traveled Malwood Forest,
> and made a gallant stand,
> she conquered the constrictor,
> and freed a savage land.
>
> No mortal man could tame her;
> none but a Dwarf could claim her;
> Thorne the Dragon's guardian.
>
> A northman slew the Dragon,
> and was banished from her land.
> Thorne saved the Dragon hatchling,
> and trained her warrior band.
>
> No mortal man could tame her;
> none but a Dwarf could claim her;
> Thorne the Dragon's guardian.
>
> The mighty Dwarf Lord Strumgued
> led his warriors to her land,
> challenged her in battle,

then bargained for her hand.

No mortal man—"

Thorne's giggles turned into laughter. She laughed until she coughed and gasped for breath.

Strumgued frowned. "To amuse, it seems I need only sing."

Thorne resisted the urge to apologize; instead she opened the food sack and stuffed black bread into her mouth. She'd never tell him she enjoyed the song. "Can't you go back south?"

"I am the Dwarf Lord of the clan of Stonevar. Returning salvaged our honor. I'll not leave alive."

CHAPTER TWELVE

Gaspotine the Dark's spirit rushed to the present where the young Dragon, Solanie the Resolute, screamed and screamed. Entering Time's Continuum for the first time always evoked bone-vibrating cries.

Centuries ago when Gaspotine's mother joined his mind and took his spirit to the Continuum, the volcanic rock around them seemed to melt into swirling bands of red, gold, and purple. Simultaneously reliving all experiences overloaded his senses. Clamorous roars rammed his hearing slits. Slashes, claws, and bites scourged his skin.

Convention said younger Dragons had fewer memories, therefore the trauma was less. Gaspotine thought the degrees of torture irrelevant to the sufferer.

Erramon the Eldest chuckled, a deep gurgling sound. "She screams louder than Gaspotine."

Gaspotine's screams were legend. In his first two centuries, older Dragons had teased him unmercifully about his undragonish terror. But Gaspotine remembered his initial visit as the only time his mother had been kind.

In contrast, Solanie's mother, Lasmenda the Luminous, ignored the young she-Dragon's cries for help. The Dragons along the shore laughed. Scores had gathered, anticipating an entertaining event. Solanie was the youngest Dragon ever to enter the Continuum and reputed to be shy. Her mother called her Solanie the Sensitive. Nevertheless, Solanie had earned entry into Time's Continuum by killing a large predator.

Lasmenda yanked Solanie from the Silver River into the sky.

67

"Solanie, hear me. See what I see."

"Chaos." Solanie's voice squeaked.

More Dragon laughter. Gaspotine remembered the overwhelming odors, putrid and floral, burnt and fruity, that burned his snout until it threatened to explode. Flavors, sweet and bitter, salty and sour, swelled his long neck, triggering his instinctive fear of choking.

Vainglorian the Red scratched, slicing open his brumous belly, which formed anew. "This will be amusing."

Perhaps Lasmenda hadn't prepared her daughter, intending to provide a better show. Gaspotine suppressed an urge to reassure Solanie.

"Picture violet mountains." Lasmenda motioned with a wing.

"What?" Solanie flapped wildly throwing off the tips of her vaporous wings. "How?"

During Gaspotine's first visit, he'd folded his neck in an instinctive reaction to danger, climbed onto his mother's back, and fallen through her misty form. For once, Gaspotine's mother hadn't chided him.

Unlike his mother, Lasmenda's stern tone offered no comfort. "Golden snow adorns giant spruce." Evidently she'd explain only what Dragon Code demanded.

Solanie wrapped her wings around herself. "What is this horrid place?"

That she'd conquered her fear enough to ask a coherent question impressed Gaspotine.

"The Dragon Continuum." Lasmenda hovered mid-air. "Be grateful I brought you."

Clearly, Solanie wasn't. Nor did she trust her dam. Understandable, since she-Dragons raised their whelps with enough cruelty to insure toughness, fearlessness, and autonomy.

"In the Silver River memories flow into future dreams," Lasmenda said.

"I don't understand."

Gaspotine guessed it would take time for Solanie to appreciate the Continuum's glory.

The young Dragon peered over her shoulder. "We're made of fog. What are we?"

"Spirits."

"Where is our flesh?" Solanie's voice quavered.

"Inside my cavern," Lasmenda replied, impatiently. "Foolish whelp, you thought me sleeping when I visited the Continuum."

On Gaspotine's first visit, learning his mind had separated from his body made him shudder so hard misty bits of him flew off. In a sympathetic voice, which his mother never used before or after, she explained that fear stole his vapor. Her gentleness frightened him even more.

Lasmenda continued. "We owe Wanderers a debt. Never harm one."

"Debt?"

Erramon the Eldest stared at the river. The other Dragons looked away. Lasmenda hesitated. Gaspotine knew the debt embarrassed her. It did all Dragons.

"A Wanderer showed us the way to the Continuum," Lasmenda said.

"Will I meet a Wanderer here?" The young Dragon sounded more curious than repulsed.

"Our guide's spirit lingers. No other knows the way." Lasmenda paused as if gathering strength. "In the Continuum, we built our society. Before we learned the way here, Dragons were brutes. Only here, do we converse without fighting."

Solanie stared into the Silver River.

Gaspotine shook his head. Although this perceptive young Dragon had more intelligence than he first suspected, Solanie didn't seem to appreciate the momentous influence the Continuum had on Dragon-kind.

"Tell me how to return," Solanie insisted, as if she suspected her mother might forget.

Lasmenda pointed at the lustrous stream undulating below. "To return, view yourself in the river. Move your tiniest toe claw. When you feel the Niede, rejoin your body."

"Explain."

"Pain, peril, and appetite trigger the Niede." Lasmenda's rear claws trailed in the water.

As Solanie gained confidence, she lengthened her neck to look around. "What churns the water?"

"Igtimus." The name twisted Lasmenda's foggy, dual-tipped tongue.

"Which ones?"

"Giants, Dwarfs, Humans." Her mother named each one with contempt. "Anyone not Dragon."

With minimal wing movement, Solanie soared along the river. "I see only Dragon spirits."

"You cannot see them, but igtimus with the Power can make undertows, eddies, and whirlpools in your current."

"What is this Power?"

Lasmenda huffed, reluctant to answer, but Dragon Code compelled her to. "Dragon-Fating. An igtimus possessing this rare Power will determine if a Dragon lives or dies."

Solanie circled her mother, testing her gossamer wings, clearly too youthful to conceive of dying. "How will I recognize my current?"

"Your own stream shines brightest." Lasmenda flashed a fanged smile. "The Continuum brightens when a new Dragon enters and dims after . . ."

"One dies," Gaspotine finished silently. Living centuries, Dragons preferred to ignore both their own mortality and the spirits of the dead. When the Niede impelled the dead to return to their bodies and they could not, the bloodless went insane. So far only Gaspotine and Rustofona had escaped that. Lasmenda didn't explain this, leaving Solanie to discover for herself the dung-sized spirits of the deceased littering the shores of the past.

Gaspotine had no doubt Solanie would ascertain this and more. He'd watched many young Dragons enter the Continuum, but this small she-Dragon had recovered quickly. Perhaps she'd developed keen survival instincts under Lasmenda's barbarous care.

While he mused, Rustofona sneaked up behind him. "How will a Human, who knows nothing of Dragon code, instruct Hellestorm in the Continuum?"

"You'll be here to help him." Since no other bloodless Dragon spirit had remained sane for fifteen years, Gaspotine doubted Rustofona would provide much support.

"You will teach him also."

He jerked his head. Male Dragons didn't teach whelps. Nor did Gaspotine enjoy being reminded that his own sanity was at risk.

CHAPTER THIRTEEN

Intending to discover Strumgued's attitude toward Fairies, Thorne accepted a ride back to the castle on his short but sturdy horse. She tucked her feet so they wouldn't drag. He walked beside her, asking personal but trivial questions, which seemed cleverly designed to get her to reveal something important, but what, she'd no idea. She answered his questions; he answered hers. His attitude toward Fairies resembled Brutte's. He considered them tricksters, thieves, and spies, vermin to eradicate. His comments weren't directed toward any specific hive, but he was clever. She couldn't be certain.

With a bow, he parted from her at the castle.

Inside, Bekka the hunchback stopped rocking baby Aeron. "I thought I'd have to climb the mountain and bring you home." Climbing was difficult for Bekka, though she suffered less after drinking Dragon blood. She'd grown taller, standing an inch shorter than five feet now. Her soft brown curls turned into straight, coarse salmon-colored strands. But Dragon blood hadn't changed her disposition. She was still the kindest person Thorne knew, and Aeron would be safe with her. Every child Thorne loved died.

Thorne refused water to wash herself, but ate the stew so Strumgued's evening meal wouldn't tempt her.

That evening, Thorne heard voices when she approached the tent to join Strumgued for the eventide meal. Not having bathed, she stank. That suited her. She hadn't combed her hair, only tied it back, leaving the dried leaves and sticks caught in the tangles. She hoped Strumgued would send her away, offended by her disrespect.

The wind rattled the door flap, and Thorne secured it before entering.

71

Strumgued rose to his feet. "This is my daughter, Cayeseed." He raised a palm toward Thorne. "This is my wife." He frowned a bit at Thorne, but she doubted his daughter noticed. Like her father, Cayeseed had thick lips, a bulbous nose, and bushy eyebrows over small eyes, but unlike Strumgued, hers were blue not green.

The young Dwarf tugged the blond tuft growing under her blunt jaw as she inspected Thorne. "I'm pleased to meet my father's wife."

Thorne, dirty and unbathed, doubted that.

Strumgued carried a cloth and bowl of water to Thorne. "I hope you enjoy the meal. The cook stuffed doves with nuts, wheat, and apples."

Thorne washed and dried her face and hands. "I'm sure the food is excellent." Before she could object, her husband lifted her foot and yanked off a boot. "What are you—" Before she finished, he'd removed the other one.

He knelt to wash her feet. Thorne opened her mouth but nothing came out. Heat rushed up her neck. She'd not foreseen him demonstrating humility and devotion, especially before his daughter, and mumbled, "Thank you."

Strumgued nodded. Cayeseed's jaw tightened. Although Thorne wasn't hungry, she ate. The first bite had a sour taste. Rinsing her mouth with wine helped.

Cayeseed glanced sideways at Strumgued. "I'm relieved Father let his beard grow. His smooth chin embarrassed my brother."

Her father cleared his throat and continued eating. Thorne guessed Strumgued's beardlessness also embarrassed Cayeseed.

"Why did he cut it?" she asked, hoping to discomfort Strumgued.

"An ancient ceremony mourning Mother." Cayeseed speared a small onion.

Strumgued stopped eating, but stared at his meal.

She dared another question. "How did your mother die?"

"The black Dragon killed her while she protected me."

Thorne hadn't expected that. Gaspotine the Dark had killed Strumgued's wife. No wonder he hated Dragons.

"She speared him," Cayeseed said with pride.

Thorne coughed to disguise a gasp. That yew spear had poisoned Gaspotine's flesh, weakening him so Tallasha the Resplendent could kill him.

"Enough, Cayeseed," Strumgued said softly.

Cayeseed's answers had discomforted Strumgued beyond Thorne's hopes.

"Father, don't forget—"

He banged down his spoon, breaking the dish holding his cherry tart. Thorne jumped.

"I've a favor to ask," he told Thorne.

She wanted him in her debt but mustn't appear eager. "What do you require?"

Scratching his stubbled chin, shifting on his stool, Strumgued appeared decidedly distressed. Even in battle, Thorne had never seen this. "Cayeseed desires to see the Dragon."

Thorne couldn't have heard correctly. "Your daughter wants to meet Hellee?"

Cayeseed's eyes gleamed. "If you please."

"Dwarfs hate Dragons."

"She has a child's curiosity." Strumgued puffed out his cheeks and exhaled. "I trust you'll not let the beast harm her."

Clearly, he couldn't refuse his only daughter. "Hellee isn't a beast." Perhaps if Cayeseed became fond of Hellee, Strumgued's hatred might diminish. "She may accompany me now." He'd owe her a favor when she approached him about the Fairies.

Strumgued gulped down his wine. "Keep her safe."

Thorne motioned for his daughter to follow. Though Cayeseed seemed nice enough, a Dwarf wanting to meet a Dragon felt wrong. Cayeseed had seen Gaspotine swallow her mother and should hate Dragons as much as Strumgued. Thorne decided that she would never understand Dwarfs.

When Thorne and Cayeseed entered Redilik Cavern, Hellee lumbered to them in a duck-like walk, flapping his wings and squawking happily. He now weighed close to fourteen stone, the weight of a mastiff.

Nella, Emera's mother, rushed to Thorne. Nella claimed to be a simple goat herder's daughter, but she'd braved the wild to bring Emera to Stonevar, hoping her half-Human, half-Wanderer daughter would be welcome. Thorne doubted she'd ever meet anyone more courageous than Nella.

"We're blessed to see you've recovered, Goddess."

Thorne nodded, but would never be the same. She plucked a

cobweb from Nella's rust-colored locks. Like all Uplanders, Nella had pale skin and a round face with upturned eyes, which looked even more exotic with elongated diamond centers.

Hellee's head nudged Thorne's leg. She scratched behind his raised brow, which had begun to harden into a bony crown. His hide was the creamy color of freshly churned butter.

Emera the Wanderling joined them. Her willowy frame bore no resemblance to her mother's solidly built people. "Who's this?"

"Strumgued's daughter, Cayeseed. She wants to meet Hellee."

Emera smiled and pressed her palms together. "I'm pleased to make your acquaintance."

Cayeseed gazed at Emera strangely, as if she'd never met a Wanderer and never wanted to. Emera didn't seem to notice. Thorne, having little experience reading Dwarfs, decided she'd misread Cayeseed.

"Offer Hellee your hand," Thorne told the Dwarf.

Cayeseed reached toward him. When his tongue snaked out, she snatched her arm back. "His breath stinks."

"Let Hellee taste your skin so he recognizes you."

Instead Cayeseed sped into the center of Redilik Cavern where the floor shimmered like black water. "It's huge. The columns are magnificent." Magnificent echoed. The evening light angled through ceiling apertures, crisscrossing the stone columns surrounding her. She took a deep breath. "I adore the scent of granite. My ancestral home is as beautiful as Father said."

Eyes closed, she slowly turned with arms extended. Her blond braid swayed against her short, thick back. "I sense the spirits of my forefathers."

Thorne felt them also; they despised Hellee.

Cayeseed stopped. "What's that pile of refuse?"

"The remains of Rustofona's treasure."

"This isn't treasure." She picked up a helmet. "Rusty."

Hellee snatched it with his tongue and scurried into a corner, where he rolled it inside his mouth.

"He's afraid you'll take it."

"Why does he want this junk?"

"Dragons deem all metal and gems treasure and are born with a compulsion to return them to their source—inside mountains."

The Dwarf picked through the pile. "Nothing of value."

Unexpectedly, Zarra separated from the shadows. "Your father took most of it when he stole Thorne's ring."

Thorne jumped, although Zarra lurking shouldn't surprise her.

"What ring?" Cayeseed asked.

Thorne rubbed her finger. "A serpent of gold with a red eye. Strumgued reclaimed it with the Dwarf treasure." She didn't mention that she'd thrown it at him, hoping to blind him.

"My many-greats grandfather made it for his wife."

The ring's loss upset Zarra more than Thorne, who vowed never again to wear Dwarf-made jewelry. "How big is your family?"

"Only a few hundred. After we left Stonevar, our numbers dwindled, but now that we've recovered our homeland, others will marry into our clan."

Thorne suppressed a groan. To hide her reaction, she stared at the pails near the tunnel entrance. "Has Hellee eaten?"

"Not yet." Emera lifted the pail lids, revealing fish guts and animal intestines. Hellee devoured six meals a day plus a snack at midnight.

Cayeseed wrinkled her nose. "That stinks worse than he does."

Emera dumped the buckets into a tub. "He likes it."

Hellee buried his face in the unappetizing mess, then straightened his neck to swallow. Entrails dripped from his snout onto the floor.

Cayeseed looked away. "When will he fly?"

"It'll be some years before his wings are strong enough." Thorne shoveled the mess back into the tub.

Finished, Hellee licked his muzzle clean.

Cayeseed cringed. "When will he breathe fire?"

"He can't." Emera rubbed Hellee's shoulder. "But if you hold a torch close, he can ignite his breath."

Cayeseed smiled at Emera. "Show me."

Emera took a torch from the wall and held it three paces from Hellee. He burped, sending a blast of flame across the cavern, then pranced and squawked excitedly.

Thorne had enough. "Zarra, take Cayeseed home. I'll stay with Hellee."

"May I visit again?" Cayeseed curtsied.

"Perhaps," Thorne said absently, watching Nella cut a length from boiled wool.

Emera smiled. "I can bring her."

"If her father agrees." Thorne wasn't really listening because Nella was aligning pieces for a baby bunting.

After they left, Thorne sat cross-legged on a mat, and Hellee put his head on her lap. She missed Lily. Not the person who'd come to Stonevar, but the sweet sister she'd grown up with. Thorne pictured lopping off Anders's head for impregnating Lily.

She ran her tongue over the edge of her teeth, anticipating ripping out Captain Hauk's throat for killing Rustofona, which enabled the Dwarfs' return. Then Thorne pictured all the ways she'd like to watch Strumgued die: Dracodurus through his heart; a fireball exploding his chest; her warhorse trampling him. There was more, but Brutte once warned hating consumed strength better used doing something worthwhile.

Thorne would need all her cleverness to discover why Brutte's killer had married her.

CHAPTER FOURTEEN

Gaspotine's spirit floated beneath the Silver River surface, hiding from Rustofona and watching Solanie approach Erramon the Eldest. Solanie listened to Erramon and Vainglorian the Red discuss hunting, then left quickly, as if some danger triggered the Niede. Before he could investigate, Erramon snagged his interest.

"This year Tallasha the Resplendent wants an egg."

Vainglorian puffed himself up, evidently forgetting she'd rejected him last year. "I'll join Tallasha's first begattening."

Erramon fanned his front claws. "Count your toes afterward."

Vainglorian rumbled laughter. "I enjoy a fierce mating."

"So do we all." Erramon's fangs dripped fog.

"I regret there's no other bull to fight."

Gaspotine snorted, doubting that. This past century, Vainglorian hadn't visited the mainland even once for mating. The red Dragon was lazy. Tired of Dragon boasting, Gaspotine moved across the Silver River where she-Dragons spoke of whelps. Male Dragons never knew their offspring, since each season females mated with as many bulls as possible. Determining paternity seemed hopeless, and male Dragons labeled whatever they couldn't do undragonish. Reflexively, Gaspotine curled his back claw missing its smallest toe since birth. A similar lack marked Rustofona his daughter. Perhaps it would identify other progeny.

After countless matings, he must have numerous offspring. To satisfy his undragonish curiosity, he searched the currents of immature, flightless yellow Dragons looking for those without their tiniest toe. He found none. Surprisingly disappointing. Nor did he find missing toes among the orange Dragons who'd recently claimed lairs.

He examined these youngsters again, looking for his familiar bony crest or his wing spread or his snout shape. When that also disappointed, he compared scale patterns. Gaspotine had never questioned his virility before and didn't enjoy doing so now. Whether a female conceived had never concerned him, only that he copulate as often as possible during the short mating season.

Was his seed weak? He wouldn't believe that. The problem must lie with the she-Dragons. Pondering female fertility made his eyes roll in opposite directions.

Why did having whelps matter anyway? The Niede hit harder, demanding his spirit return to his dead body. He tucked his head between his back legs, fighting rolling into a ball.

One whelp was like another. The Niede punched him again and he rolled up tight. Something about having relatives seemed to lessen the Niede.

Rustofona's voice startled Gaspotine. "What troubles you, father?"

Her solicitude surprised and pleased him; though he replied gruffly, "Don't ask undragonish questions." With effort, he straightened. "What's your whelp doing?" Rolling some tree across the floor, no doubt, or chewing on a deer skull. Why these activities merited reporting, Gaspotine had no idea.

"Resting."

Why did Hellestorm matter so much to Rustofona? She must have raised other whelps. "Before Nar devoured your eggs, how many quickened?" Nar the Insidious was a giant serpent. After Thorne defeated him, Rustofona allowed Thorne to stay at Stonevar.

"Only two. Perhaps my eggs are too dense." Rustofona chewed her tail tip, a childish habit.

Even Gaspotine, known for his insensitivity, sensed he shouldn't ask about those. Instead he followed her current into the past, discovering that both eggs had hatched within moments of each other. The whelps weren't even dry before they began to fight. The strongest devoured the weaker. The victor had a broken wing, and Rustofona wouldn't care for him. Gaspotine didn't linger to watch the whelp's death nor Rustofona eating him.

Only Hellestorm still lived, which explained why her motherly devotion transcended even death. But why hadn't more eggs quickened?

"How many bulls mated you during the season?"

"Only Vainglorian. No other flew to Elysia."

Maybe numerous partners facilitated conception. Over the decades, Vainglorian's seed had only fertilized three eggs. Why? Because he fought no other Dragon before mating Rustofona? Did fighting increase male Dragon virility?

This didn't explain why Gaspotine couldn't find his whelps. He'd made yearly journeys to the mainland, lairing in a snug cave near Maehitabelle the Merciless. His mating battles with other suitors had been fierce. Most challengers retreated and lived. Those that didn't Gaspotine remembered fondly. He rumbled a purr while recalling the taste of his opponent's heart sliding down his throat.

If memory served, Maehitabelle mothered no whelps in three centuries. A thought came from nowhere—was Dragon age related to fertility?

He considered asking Maehitabelle the Merciless, now a black Dragon past a thousand years, if she'd raised any whelps in the past two hundred, but she'd probably rip off his wings. Unwilling to risk the shame, Gaspotine jumped into her current. After traveling some decades, he saw no eggs after she turned black and only a few after she turned maroon at around eight-hundred. None of those hatched.

Had he whelps only from his younger matings? During the short season, he'd no time to mate with young females. Though many invited him, he preferred the ferocity of Maehitabelle.

Before Gaspotine could investigate his distant past, Rustofona called him, probably to tell him minutia about Hellestorm. Gaspotine hadn't known fatherhood and grandfatherhood would be so burdensome.

He forgot about checking on Solanie.

CHAPTER FIFTEEN

"**W**here is this hive?" Strumgued set down his cup.

The wind shook the tent, as if warning Thorne that she shouldn't have said anything. She stared at her half-finished grouse. What she'd eaten seemed determined to upend her stomach.

"Malwood?" he guessed.

She stayed silent.

"I owe you a boon for letting Cayeseed meet the Dragon." He cocked his large head. "But I can't agree unless I know what I'm agreeing to."

He made sense, but could she trust him? If he destroyed the hive, the chrysalises inside would die. The Fairies would believe she'd betrayed them, and they'd be right. She'd no right to risk Fairy young.

But she couldn't let Raspberry-Frost go.

Now because of her, Strumgued knew the hive was close. He could order his warriors to follow the Fairies until they found it. She'd hate him all the more if he destroyed the hive, and too much hatred already muddled her thoughts.

"Inside the hawthorn hedge below Redilik Cavern," Thorne whispered, "near the opening."

He said something, but her heart thrummed her ears. "What?"

"We'll not destroy your hive or kill the Fairies who live there." He held up a stubby finger. "If they stay north of the river."

Thorne exhaled. It would be all right. First thing tomorrow, she'd tell Raspberry-Frost that the Fairies could stay.

\#

That evening on the wall-walk, Thorne gazed over the parapet, watching the earth exhale a soft breath of haze that blanketed the plain. She ignored the lights on the Dwarf side of the river and pretended they'd never come.

Dwarfish shouts and ribaldry intruded. At least twice a fortnight, they celebrated something or other. After three months, she was no closer to getting rid of them or divorcing Strumgued. She needed help, but who?

Soft footfalls, audible only to those who'd imbibed Dragon blood, sounded on the steps.

Zarra lowered the hood of her cloak. "Found you."

"Didn't know I was lost." Thorne forced a smile. "Even without a moon, a talented thief would detect me on the wall."

Zarra sniffed. "I smelled you. Can't say I enjoy every dragonish change. Thought I'd get white hair like you. Red belongs on Dwarfs and Giants. Makes people remember me."

"At least Bludwelt's constables won't recognize you." She immediately regretted saying his name. The man always lurked just below the surface of her consciousness.

"I have to tell you something, Goddess."

The word "goddess" put Thorne on guard. "Go on."

"Magda met a Dwarf."

Thorne's breath caught. "Who?"

"Emera introduced Cayeseed to Magda."

The Wanderling wanted everyone to be friends. "Magda rebuffed her?"

"She made them a sweet." Zarra sucked her teeth. "Fried them honey cakes."

Bumps rose on Thorne's arms. "Do we need a food taster?"

Zarra chortled. "Then something even more peculiar happened."

"Has Magda welcomed Strumgued too?"

Zarra shook her head. "Strumgued's son, Waldemar, joined Magda, Emera, and Cayeseed for a picnic."

If the sun had risen in the west, Thorne couldn't have been more surprised. If the Dwarfs didn't leave soon, something terrible would happen. "Promise to tell no one what I say."

"Course." Zarra moved closer.

"I must escape my marriage."

Zarra spit over the side.

81

Thorne continued. "I want the Dwarfs gone. I must discover their weaknesses."

"I'll see what I can dredge up." Zarra's amber eyes gleamed.

"Be careful." Lily's husband almost beat Zarra to death when she tried to rescue Lily. If Dwarfs caught Zarra, it would be worse.

CHAPTER SIXTEEN

Early afternoon the next day, Thorne rode to the hawthorn hedge and called for Raspberry-Frost. Fairies flew over without stopping, seeming uncommonly busy, and surprisingly uncurious. This didn't reassure her.

She led her warhorse, Wild-Eyes, to a shady spot and waited. At dusk, Raspberry-Frost, looking tired, landed on Thorne's shoulder and accepted the water Thorne offered.

"You don't have to leave. The Dwarf Lord has agreed not to bother your hive as long as all Fairies stay north of the river."

Raspberry-Frost tilted its head. "Fae likes honeysuckle."

"Eat the honeysuckle here."

"South sweeter." The Fairy nipped Thorne's earlobe for emphasis.

Thorne rubbed her ear as she opened her mouth, then closed it. "I'll bring you all the honeysuckle you want."

"Must be fresh."

Her fingers and toes went cold. "So you'll go south."

"Must."

"More than half of Elysia lies north of the river. That's not enough?"

"Fae must fly free." The Fairy gently flapped her wings, releasing the scent of autumn leaves.

It took Thorne a moment to accept that her plan had failed. She groaned. Would she never wake from this nightmare? Before winter the Fairies would be gone. She'd used her only bargaining marker with Strumgued for nothing.

#

The following morning, Thorne rode Wild-Eyes through the hawthorn hedge but saw no Fairies. She missed Raspberry-Frost already.

She climbed to the Dragon Ledge, gripping the tail of a brown rat killed in the granary. She was relieved not to encounter Zarra. Her wole-rat, Sir-Sir, would hate Thorne more if he saw her with his dead cousin.

On the ledge, Emera and Cayeseed huddled by the cavern entrance.

"Emera, take this rat to Hellee." She wanted time alone with Cayeseed.

The Wanderling grimaced. "He won't eat it. He'll gnaw on it and bat it around until it's disgusting."

Thorne motioned for Emera to go inside with the rat, and she did.

"Do you visit Hellee often?" Thorne asked Cayeseed.

"Whenever Emera guards him."

Though it was natural for Emera to befriend someone, why Cayeseed? "Does your father approve?"

"Of Emera, or the Dragon?"

"Both."

Cayeseed shrugged. "We quarreled, but he relented."

"I thought a river would wear away the mountain before he changed his mind."

Cayeseed smiled smugly. "With my brothers, he can be obstinate. Not so with me or my mother." She smoothed her blue dress, which appeared new.

"Was your mother happy in her marriage?" Inappropriate, but Thorne must investigate any potential weakness. If Cayeseed reported their conversation to Strumgued, he'd probably be flattered.

"Mother gave him nineteen children, eighteen sons. A sign of her deep regard for him. Dwarf mothers seldom have more than three."

"You wanted your father to regrow his beard."

Though Cayeseed smiled, her eyes had a haunted look. "Mother died protecting me, and Father's smooth chin never let me forget."

Enough talk of Cayeseed's mother and Strumgued's devotion. "Magda seems fond of you."

Cayeseed stroked the hair under her chin. "She's sweet."

Since Brutte's death, Thorne hadn't seen Magda's sweet side. Why would a woman who hated Dwarfs befriend one?

From the tunnel came the sounds of claws scraping rock. Hellee emerged and yawned, dropping the dead rat and displaying a gap where one eyetooth had fallen out. Adult teeth so soon, or did Dragons get more than two sets? Raspberry-Frost would know. Thorne needed her Fairy.

"Do Dwarfs like having Humans nearby?"

"Human and Dwarf have made alliances in the past," Cayeseed said glibly. "Farmers benefit us."

"Your father hates Dragons." Thorne put a protective arm around the whelp's neck. "Why don't you?"

"I like Hellee." She rubbed him between his nostrils, a particularly sensitive spot. "Father says hatred's a poison."

He would know, since he nurtured his as determinedly as Thorne. However, her suspicions of Cayeseed seemed unjustified. Thorne felt a kinship with Cayeseed: they'd both lost their mothers. She touched Cayeseed's shoulder. Dragon-Fating tingles raced up Thorne's arm. Would Cayeseed protect Hellee from Strumgued?

She must touch her husband to discover if he had Dragon-Fating. "I worry your father wants an excuse to harm Hellee."

"You are wise to worry."

CHAPTER SEVENTEEN

Gaspotine floated among the clouds, letting the Niede consume him. When surrender brought no relief, he lost hope of ever escaping the torment.

Rustofona joined him. "Father."

Gaspotine didn't immediately realize that she addressed him. Perhaps in a couple centuries, he'd respond. Had anyone overheard? He glanced around. The red clouds had combined into a single stratospheric continent. Odd. He dropped lower. At the river, forty-seven Dragons gathered, with more arriving.

A wayward wind rippled Gaspotine's foggy skin. "What's happening?"

"Something momentous," Rustofona answered.

Below them, a current bucked into a tidal wave, presaging an unexpected Dragon death. Two currents unwound, a sign of a Dragon whelp separating from her mother. This normally happened when a whelp turned fifty, but Solanie the Resolute was only thirteen.

A loud bang jarred Gaspotine. Mountaintops cracked and slid groundward. The squalling wind splintered spruce trees as if their branches were glass. The ground shook, shattering the grass and throwing sand skyward. Only breaching Code disrupted the Continuum so violently.

The spirit of Lasmenda the Luminous, Solanie's mother, roared as she jumped into the churning river. It spat her back. Her incandescence dimmed.

"Solanie . . . Solanie . . ." Whatever Lasmenda wanted to say wouldn't come out.

Gaspotine entered Solanie's current a short distance in the past.

While Lasmenda's spirit visited the Continuum, her daughter had killed her. Though starving, Solanie didn't eat her mother's flesh as Dragon custom demanded, further dishonoring Lasmenda.

The Code forbade killing a Dragon without a spirit, and Gaspotine had never known a whelp to slay its mother. Why had Solanie? Gaspotine swam further into the past.

Lasmenda told her daughter, "Hunt for yourself, since you're so clever."

Solanie's first outdoor kill was an old elk who'd tripped in a burrow and broken its leg. Solanie ripped out its throat.

Gaspotine remembered the scent of fresh blood and yearned for a taste.

Solanie cupped the still-warm heart with her tongue, but before she could swallow, her mother said, "You're too fat," and yanked the prey away.

Gaspotine shook his head. Solanie was starving. His mother had been fierce, but he'd feasted on the tenderest veal and venison.

Her mother devoured the elk, while Solanie licked blood off the ground.

"Stay out of the Continuum," Lasmenda told Solanie.

A mother Dragon banning her child was beyond Gaspotine's understanding.

"I earned the right," Solanie said.

Lasmenda clamped Solanie's throat between her jaws. Blood dripped from deep punctures, but Solanie didn't struggle. The youngster knew resistance would give Lasmenda an excuse to squeeze. Lasmenda released Solanie and finished the elk, leaving not even a bone for Solanie. "If you enter the Continuum, I will kill you." She rumbled laughter. "I think I will kill you anyway."

Evidently, Solanie believed her mother and at her first opportunity, ripped out Lasmenda's throat.

CHAPTER EIGHTEEN

Lord Bludwelt never imagined anything could stop him from pursuing Thorne. Then Fexx fell ill and finding a cure besieged Bludwelt. Seahaven's only healer, an old man who couldn't even relieve the aching in his own crippled joints, ignored Fexx's screams as he inserted a syringe and injected mercury into Fexx's penis. It hadn't helped. After that, Bludwelt refused to let the man touch Fexx.

Fexx and his brother, Daxx, were the only men Bludwelt trusted, and he was determined not to lose either. That witchy woman, Fehera, might have cured Fexx, but she'd gone to Stonevar. That unhuman place haunted him, reminding him of Thorne, who set his blood burning. But he could do nothing until Fexx recovered.

Bludwelt sent north for O'Haven's best healer. While they waited, Fexx's suffering pared Bludwelt's good humor down to the core. He sent again with promises of a larger purse; however, the Rose Moon waned before the healer traveled south. The small pompous man stank of distilled alcohol, which Bludwelt suspected he used for more than tinctures.

The healer examined Fexx in the sleeping room behind the inn bar. Considering how careless the two were about their persons, the sparsely furnished room—bed, chest, table, two chairs—was surprisingly neat, although it stank of smoke root and sick man's sweat.

The healer tugged his matted beard. "Visit a whorehouse this past year?"

Fexx nodded. "Madame Dulcia got new girls. The old ones had the burning."

The healer put his hand to Fexx's forehead. "Ache in your bollocks?"

"Terrible." Fexx's lower lip quivered.

"Pain passing water?"

Caressing himself under the blanket, Fexx nodded.

"Open your mouth." He opened a bottle and put three drops on Fexx's tongue.

Fexx gagged. "Water."

Bludwelt turned his head at the stink and handed Fexx a cup. "What did you give him?"

"Tincture of garlic and onion. Lowers fever." He took a shallow bowl and sizable knife from his travel pack.

Fexx heaved a resigned sigh and positioned his arm outside the blanket, palm up.

Bludwelt ground his teeth. "How will blood-letting cure him?"

"Purges bad humors. Clears out weak blood. Relieves water backing up."

As the healer shuffled forward, Fexx whimpered.

Lord Bludwelt moved between them. "His arm's on the bed."

The healer cleared his throat, clearly unaccustomed to interference. His tone was stern. "His sickness is quite severe. I need a breathing vein."

"How much?"

"Till he faints."

"He's skin and bones."

When Bludwelt didn't move, the healer said, "Step aside, sir, if you want him healed."

Bludwelt moved back. The healer tucked his beard inside his shirt and set the bowl beside Fexx's head. The sick man stiffened. The older man placed the knife against Fexx's throat.

Bludwelt grabbed the blade, slicing open his palm and scenting the air with silver.

The healer huffed. "Sir."

"Get out."

The man took a wide stance. "My fee."

Bludwelt threw a bag. The healer snagged it from the floor and stomped out.

If Fexx died, he'd burn down the whorehouse and order Madam Dulcia whipped until her back ran red.

Daxx, carrying a small bowl, limped into the room on bowed legs. Ribald noise from Hauk and his sailors followed him. Daxx kicked the door shut. "Better?"

"That quack tried to cut my neck." Fexx sniffled and pointed at Bludwelt. "Goadran stopped him."

Lord Bludwelt didn't correct him. He'd always be Goadran to these two.

Bludwelt took the bowl from Daxx and offered Fexx a spoonful of broth. "You must eat."

"Not hungry."

Loss of appetite alarmed Bludwelt more than blood letting. "You're always hungry." Fexx ate and ate, but never gained a dram. Bludwelt filled a spoon. When Fexx clamped his mouth shut, Bludwelt said. "For me, eat."

Fexx grunted but slurped the broth. Bludwelt rubbed his lucky coin inside the pouch around his neck. Was there a competent healer on the Isle of Elysia? He'd send south. Ample gold would hasten the response.

The sick man burped. "Soup tastes odd."

Inside the bowl, red pooled around the chicken fat at the bottom. Bludwelt's blood. He hadn't realized the knife had gone so deep.

Bludwelt spent the night at Fexx's bedside.

The next morning, Fexx sat up in bed. "I feel better. I'll have more soup now."

Bludwelt traced the scar on his palm. His blood had cured Fexx, not that fool's drops, but no one must know. "Appears the healer's tincture cured you."

Fexx chuckled, fondling himself under the covers.

Now Lord Bludwelt could retrieve Thorne.

CHAPTER NINETEEN

"**W**ife, I've a matter to discuss." Having finished the mutton, Strumgued wiped his fingers on the tablecloth. His dwarfish iron smell was stronger tonight. His gaze never wavered as he pushed back his stool, giving his stomach room.

After discovering Cayeseed's Dragon-Fating, Thorne remained alert for an opportunity to touch Strumgued and learn if he also had it. "Speak."

"Someone stole a ring from my sleeping chamber. One you returned to me from the Dragon's treasure."

"How does that concern me?" She knew nothing of his rooms except that they were across the river, inside the castle the Dwarfs were carving from South Ventamar. Or maybe he lived deep in the mountain. She didn't care.

"I suspect a Human entered my chamber."

Zarra. Refusing to meet his gaze, Thorne gulped wine. "Surely, your guards would stop them."

He coughed, clearly embarrassed. "The guard saw someone wearing Cayeseed's cloak."

To avoid looking at him, she smoothed her simple brown dress. "Perhaps Cayeseed took the ring."

"She denied it."

"Another Dwarf then." Thorne wanted to believe Zarra had kept her promise not to steal.

Strumgued's eyes hardened into marble. "Dwarfs never steal, but Humans are another matter."

Thorne shoved away her plate. "Have you proof a Human took the ring?"

"The guard recalled a hunched figure with small feet."

Thorne blanked her face. "What does this band look like?"

"A gold snake with a ruby eye."

"I remember." When Zarra found the ring in Rustofona's treasure, she insisted Thorne wear it to denote Nar the Incidious's defeat. "What's the penalty for stealing?"

Strumgued set his jaw. "Banishment."

Thorne's chest tightened. Losing Zarra would be like losing Lily again. "Perhaps you misplaced it."

"I never lose anything." His large chin jutted. "The one responsible must leave Stonevar or all Humans must go in a fortnight. Except for my wife."

"I'm sure no Human could breach your stronghold." She left the tent, shaking with hatred, which made it impossible for her to touch him without ripping out his throat, even to discover Dragon-Fating.

As she stomped from the tent, Thorne saw Zarra watching the Dwarfs place the final stone on the bridge. Thorne tapped Zarra's shoulder and motioned for her to follow. Once in her sleeping room, Thorne's words rushed out. "Did you take Strumgued's ring?"

Zarra crossed her arms and nodded.

Thorne leaned against the table. The temperature in the room dropped, though someone had lit a fire. "When I asked you to find his weakness, I didn't mean thievery." She held out her hand. "Give it to me."

"Can't steal what don't belong to him." Zarra dropped the ring in her palm.

"This bit of Rustofona's treasure came from the Dwarfs. Now how did you get past the guards?"

"Cayeseed left her cloak in Hellee's cavern. I wore it to follow a group inside. The first time—"

"You went more than once?"

"Six, seven times, till I knew the layout."

"And no one detected you?"

Zarra's eyes glistened. "Not difficult. Dwarfs don't expect trespassers."

"Do you know the penalty?"

"It's your ring. He made you marry him."

Until now, Thorne hadn't realized that Zarra's hatred went deep as her own. "If Strumgued finds out, I must banish you."

Zarra's lower lip trembled. After her friend left, Thorne held up the ring, which was delicate, feminine. Why did he keep it in his chamber?

She'd have to bargain with him to keep Zarra here, and she'd nothing he wanted except herself.

CHAPTER TWENTY

The day after learning Zarra had stolen Strumgued's ring, Thorne swung her staff, bashing driftwood beside the river, picturing Strumgued's skull. Nella, who'd made the staff, would've disapproved of Thorne's technique, but mindless hits strengthened Thorne's resolve.

If she couldn't expel the Dwarfs, then she needed the deed to Stonevar, not just Strumgued's pledge. More than that, she wanted North Ventamar, including Redilik Cavern, which contained Hellee's lair, and the tunnels leading into it.

A stick cracked behind her. She pivoted, pole ready.

Glitter bounded over a fallen tree. "Spangle accepted Lott." She lunged at Thorne with a shepherd's staff, aiming for her throat.

With a grunt and loud clack, Thorne knocked Glitter's staff aside.

Pole at the ready, Glitter circled, seemingly determined to win. A wet sheen slicked her face. "Spangle's changed."

"As have you." Thorne rotated her pole, striking Glitter's hand. The twin yelped and backed away. "Now you wear trousers." The twins had grown until they stood only three inches shorter than Thorne's six feet. Inside they'd changed in ways Thorne hadn't expected—Spangle's engagement for one. She sensed Spangle wouldn't marry Lott if she hadn't drunk Dragon blood, though marrying seemed undragonish. Dragon blood had effects she didn't yet understand.

While these thoughts distracted Thorne, Glitter shrieked and struck upward. Thorne stumbled backward, more surprised by the screech than the blow. One foot hit cold water. She hopped out.

Both feet in water lost the match.

"She's familiar with the evil inside men." Glitter feinted left.

Not fooled, Thorne moved right. "Lott's as good a man as I've met." Alive, she added silently, remembering Brutte.

The twin twirled her staff, letting it slip upward at the top of its arc, then slamming it down at Thorne's head. Thorne blocked a moment late, catching the twin's staff on her pole tip. Her fingers lost feeling, forcing her retreat.

Glitter's eyes glazed. "I asked her why. Says she cannot explain what she doesn't understand."

"Does she want children?" Women seemed willing to risk their lives to birth them.

"Not something we discussed, since it can't happen. The Guildlord saw to that." Glitter and Spangle had been four years old when their father sold them to a man they called grandfather.

With a yell, Thorne rushed Glitter, stabbing between her eyes. With an upward thrust, the twin batted her staff away and thumped her back. Thorne whirled. If she weren't careful, the twin would maim her.

"Before Lott, Spangle and I shared the good and especially the bad." Glitter balanced her staff with both hands.

Thorne gripped hers tight, trying to guess Glitter's next strike. "If you feel a lack, I can always find bad to share."

Glitter's laughter verged on manic, as she struck with the swiftness of a snake, dropping Thorne to one knee.

"Spangle and I lived the same life. Each knowing what the other did. But I know nothing about what happens between them." The twin waited for Thorne to rise before pretending a poke to the gut.

Thorne knocked Glitter's pole sideways. "I wouldn't want to know. Better be careful with your staff or—"

"Why Lott? Many men are handsomer." Glitter struck a head-cracking blow.

Thorne's clumsy deflection slammed her staff into her own mouth. She wiped blood from her lip. "Yes, vile. Works hard. Always polite. Keeps himself clean. Terrible man."

"Don't tease. I suppose he's less odious than most, but he's got dark parts. I just don't know what they are."

When Glitter jabbed half-heartedly, Thorne leaned sideways. Sisters shouldn't lay claim to each other. "Choosing for a sister can have a dire outcome." If she'd left Lily with Rutmon, her sister would still be alive.

Glitter hung her head.

Thorne leaned on her staff. "Would you have Spangle choose for you?"

"We always chose together." Without raising her eyes, Glitter hit low.

Thorne tumbled into the chilly water. Sitting on the river bottom, she groaned. She had a split lip, bruises on her legs, contusions on her buttocks, and dented dignity.

"I suppose I must consider her happiness before my own. Like Mother taught." Glitter seemed to reach a decision, then appeared surprised about Thorne in the river. "I claim victory." She pulled Thorne to her feet.

Across the river, Dwarfs clapped and cheered. Thorne bowed deeply and motioned for Glitter to do the same.

"Has Spangle consulted Bekka?" Thorne asked. The diminutive hunchback had a talent for sensing destiny. Didn't assure happiness, though.

"Bekka said Spangle's future and Lott's entwine."

"Then I can only wish them joy." Thorne left, biting her tongue.

#

"I've spoiled it." Glitter stared at the white cloth, holding a ox-hair brush dripping with lavender paint.

"The brush is too wet," Spangle said.

"I wanted it perfect for your wedding banquet tomorrow." As Glitter painted lilacs on the tablecloth, she tried to slip into the character of an excited girl helping her sister. She had years of practice suppressing her real emotions, but today hiding the devastation she felt over losing Spangle was almost impossible. Her hand holding the paintbrush shook and her sight blurred.

Seeming unaware of Glitter's struggle, Spangle resumed stitching gold gauze from one of their dancing costumes into a wedding dress.

Glitter scanned their sleeping room, which would soon be hers alone. Tapestries with cavorting, naked gods and goddesses insulated these second-floor castle walls. In Lott's cottage, the winter wind squeezed between the logs. Glitter kicked off her slipper and rubbed her toes against the soft sheepskin rug. In Lott's cottage, scratchy reed mats covered the floor. A cushioned chair cradled her bottom. In Lott's cottage, you sat on hard wood stools and crude benches. Here she smelled lilac perfume. In Lott's cottage, she smelled musk and waste from the animal barns. In Lott's cottage, her sister would live like a peasant.

Spangle set aside her sewing. "Do you remember running away from grandfather?"

Glitter nodded. He wasn't really their grandfather; their father had sold them to him. Twenty years before, grandfather had been the Guildlord, the most powerful man on the Isle of Elysia. He took them to his home in a town called Seahaven. That night, their nursemaid brought them to his bedchamber. The four-year-old twins cried and begged for their mother. Their tears brought only punishment from the nursemaid.

"Mother will find us," Glitter told Spangle.

The twins waited for months, but Mother never came. Early one morning, they fled through an unlocked gate. Holding hands, the twins dashed over the deserted earthen street. The nursemaid followed. Her long stride overtook the twins' short steps. When she grabbed Spangle, the girl released Glitter's hand. Momentum moved Glitter forward, and she could've escaped.

"You wretched girl." The nursemaid slapped Spangle.

Her sister screamed. Glitter dashed back and kicked the nursemaid. After that, each escape attempt brought harsher punishments, but none left visible scars.

Now Glitter asked, "Why remember this?"

"You didn't leave me."

"Of course not." Glitter dabbed at the extra paint with a rag. "I'd never leave you."

Spangle turned away and picked up an ornate box from the bedside table. "I'll be close by." Her voice was weak.

Glitter stared out the window. At night, when the nightmares came, who would sing her back to sleep?

"You'll visit me," Spangle said gently, "and I'll visit you."

"I know." But she'd be alone when the faceless shadow-man came. He poked her and poked her. She kicked and fought. He laughed and shoved her inside his slobbery mouth. She screamed. Spangle always shook Glitter awake before he swallowed her. Who would wake her now? Glitter breathed slowly to calm herself. The dreams had almost stopped after she drank Dragon blood, but now she feared they would return.

Spangle took earrings from the box. Bells jingled on the wires. The twins had worn them to dance for customers. After all they'd lived through, Glitter couldn't fathom why Spangle wanted to marry.

Glitter knocked over the paint getting to her feet, but hardly noticed. "It's not too late to call off the wedding."

Spangle paled. "I need to marry Lott."

Glitter shambled to the balcony where she leaned over the stone banister. Thin clouds slithered across the moon. This kind of bad moon preceded a storm.

For the first time, Glitter regretted coming to Stonevar. Better to remain a whore than lose her sister.

CHAPTER TWENTY-ONE

What have I done, Spangle asked herself, looking at the plain ring weighing her finger after exchanging vows with Lott. She knew nothing about loving a man or being loved.

When Lott kissed her, everyone cheered. In the shadow of the barn, Spangle saw the pink, covered wagon that the twins had lived in before Stonevar. They'd lined the inside walls with silk and furnished it with elegant, spindly-legged chairs and tables painted white with gold trim. Tasseled pillows mounded on their beds. Most of their customers had never seen the like. The twins assumed the roles of vulnerable girls from a patrician family. They danced on tiptoes and sang sweetly. When the men were light-headed with wine, the twins disclosed their daring side and threw knives at targets. Many paid double.

Spangle pushed away memories of men pawing her and recalled happy times with Glitter. Bargaining for an ornate jewelry box in a dusty shop. Bartering for exotic perfumes with a canny sea captain. Buying fruit in the market, gorging themselves, and laughing as juice stained their gowns.

The vision was so real that Spangle stood up, intending to join Glitter inside the wagon, but instead heard her sister congratulate Lott.

Glitter said, "I'm going to relieve Nella." Nella guarded Hellee.

Spangle clutched her sister's hand. "Please stay."

Glitter shook her head. As she rearranged the layers of sheer gold gauze weighing Spangle's shoulders, she whispered, "I'll always come back."

Her sister's smile fooled the others, but Spangle saw deep lines at the corners. Once Glitter left the great hall, all desire to be Lott's wife vanished.

The groom led to her to the head of the long table, where the aroma of roasted veal tormented her stomach. Consume a bite and she'd spray the feast with it.

Lott's younger brother, Edz, offered a toast, making all manner of comments about marriage and the night ahead. Though everyone laughed, Spangle couldn't grasp the humor. Nevertheless, she returned Edz's toothy grin. Edz resembled his brother. Both were short and stocky, but Lott was clean-shaven. Edz's beard covered the battle scar running from his jaw down his neck. When Edz finished, he hugged Spangle, which signaled everyone to congratulate her. She reminded herself to smile.

Lott, his lips feverish, kissed her often. After the meal, they moved outside to dance around the bonfire. Edz refilled Lott's cup so often that Spangle lost count. She wanted to reject Lott's ale-soured kisses, but couldn't with the others watching. When Lott finally let her sit, she tugged at her gauzy gown, which clung to her clammy skin.

The Goddess approached, brows knit with concern. She wore a blue linen dress and red ribbons woven in her long white hair, garb for holidays. "I wish you joy." Thorne squeezed her hand, gave her an encouraging look, then climbed the stairs to the bailey wall.

After that, Spangle danced until her legs wobbled. Stonevar's first wedding ended too soon for her, although the celebration lasted into the next morning. In predawn, Lott took her hand and led her to the cottage he'd built for his first wife.

Spangle stood in the center of the room, shivering as Lott added logs to the hearth. When he came toward her, she retreated until her spine pressed against stone. Rush mats rustling under foot, Lott coaxed her into a chair near the fire.

He knelt beside her. "What wedding gift may I give you?"

She shook her head, unable to think. The door was only steps away. She wanted to flee to Glitter in Redilik Cavern. With his crippled leg, Lott couldn't catch her without saddling a horse. Then she'd hide in the long grasses until he passed.

While she plotted escape, he removed her shoes and rubbed her tired feet between his callused hands. The one-room cottage was all browns and grays, no speck of pink or yellow or bright color anywhere. Grim. Foreign. Except for a patchwork blanket, a gift from Bekka, covering the lumpy bed dominating the room. Her breath stuck in her throat, but she couldn't look away.

What if she felt nothing when he touched her?

With other men, she'd turned off her mind to protect her spirit. Afterward, she refused to remember. With her husband, her mind should stay. But what if her mind slipped into that place where she couldn't feel?

And she had secrets.

If she told him about the gold she and Glitter had saved, would he claim it? The urge to run overwhelmed her, but before she could rise, Lott kissed the foot he'd been rubbing and hugged her lower legs. Under her fingers, his gray-streaked brown hair was damp. His long silence was atypical. He was nervous. He couldn't know that she wasn't prepared for a wedding night and feared she'd disappoint him.

She ran her fingertips over the back of Lott's neck. His skin was smooth and soft there, protected from sun and wind by his long hair. He trembled, and as his arms tightened about her legs, he gazed up at her with tenderness. Maybe love.

He pushed up her skirt and kissed one knee and then the other. "Nothing that happened before Stonevar concerns me."

She believed him. She traced the lines on his weathered face and felt kindness. Though the odds were small, she decided to gamble on Lott.

CHAPTER TWENTY-TWO

The Council of Elders' roll call pulled Gaspotine to the present. He arrived in time for the last member.

"I am Vainglorian the Red, fifth councilor."

The five council members faced each other in a circle. More than a hundred living Dragons gathered around them. Where was Solanie?

Erramon the Eldest lifted his nose, avoiding looking at Lasmenda who'd rolled into a ball. "All councilors are present. The council begins. A grievous crime has been perpetrated against Lasmenda the Luminous." He explained the circumstances.

The crowd gasped, though everyone must've known.

"Quiet," Vainglorian ordered. Puffing out his chest, the Enforcer of Order gazed out the corners of his eyes, as if confirming Tallasha the Resplendent was watching. She was.

Rendeius the Terrible covered his mouth with talons longer than his legs, mocking Vainglorian. A gaggle of yellow Dragons laughed.

"Enough dragonfoolery!" Erramon motioned for their mothers to remove them. A glance from their dams sent the gigglers scurrying to the rear. The she-Dragons didn't want to miss this. Neither did their whelps.

"May I speak?" Maehitabelle the Merciless, second councilor, floated at Erramon's right, as always seeking to address the council first.

Gaspotine blissfully recalled the many times he'd almost drowned while they mated.

"With your permission," Maehitabelle said.

Erramon ignored her, evidently wanting to resolve the matter of

Lasmenda's death quickly. "Solanie has broken Dragon Code. She tore out her mother's throat while Lasmenda's spirit visited the Continuum."

The spectators roared and bared their claws, demanding justice for a Dragon killed at her most vulnerable.

"Solanie is absent. Will anyone speak for her?"

The crowd quieted. No one expected anyone would.

Gaspotine coughed. "I will."

The gathering uttered a collective gasp.

Erramon searched the crowd. "Will someone living speak for her?"

Gaspotine resisted withdrawing. "Lasmenda intended to kill her."

Lasmenda's spirit clawed Gaspotine. Reflexively, he retreated.

"Solanie is weak." Lasmenda snarled. "A Dragon must be strong."

Erramon raised a claw. "The facts are undisputed."

Maehitabelle tapped her front claws together. "Shun her. The Second petitions the First to oversee a vote."

The rest of the council concurred. All together, the crowd raised their wings and began to whirl, faster and faster, cyclones of teeth and talons.

When the crowd reached a whirling blur, Erramon opened his wings. "We will vote to shun Solanie the Resolute."

The Dragons stopped swirling and resumed their vaporous shapes. Though Dragon disorder commonly slowed these rare meetings, this one advanced quickly.

Gaspotine couldn't restrain himself. "Visit Solanie's current. She was starving and afraid for her life."

Vainglorian guffawed. "Undragonish."

Too late, Gaspotine realized his mistake. Better dead than afraid.

Skallegrim the Pugnacious raked vaporous claws over his fangs. "The Third Counselor votes to shun." He was supposed to vote after Maehitabelle, but enjoyed jumping ahead, claiming it spurred her to greater conjugal savagery.

After all council members voted, Erramon the Eldest announced, "All Dragons will shun Solanie the Resolute."

The Eldest dispatched a Dragon to devour the corpse. Unless Solanie hid, she'd be eaten also.

CHAPTER TWENTY-THREE

The stolen serpent ring, which Thorne kept inside a pouch hanging around her neck, seemed to weigh a hundredweight as she slogged to the Dwarf side of the river. She would rather have slept in after the wedding. Instead, wanting Strumgued in a good mood, she'd accepted his invitation to watch him train a horse. She intended to return the ring and ask him to forgive Zarra. But at what price?

Strumgued's whip rent the air. At the end of a long halter rope, the mare reversed direction, its hooves softly clopping packed earth. Thorne forced a smile, propped one foot on the lowest corral rail and her elbows on the top.

A breeze lifted loose strands of Strumgued's golden-red hair. His body language showed concentration and patience as he worked the horse. Night-Arrow—so called because of her shiny black coat and white triangle on her forehead—was small, swift, and spirited. After half an hour, Strumgued held out an apple, and the horse trotted to him. When he stroked her neck, the mare tolerated his familiarity.

"My wild beauty," Strumgued crooned in her ear. "A few more days and you'll carry my saddle."

"Why take so long to train her?" Thorne asked. His method took weeks longer than necessary.

Night-Arrow snorted and galloped to the opposite end of the corral where she pranced, head held high.

Strumgued smiled and rubbed his short beard. "Because, my inestimable wife, she'll serve me better if she serves willingly. I'll preserve her spirit. Then we'll be stronger together than separately."

As though on cue, Night-Arrow whinnied.

Strumgued, smelling of horse sweat, stepped onto the fence. His smiling face was a hand's length away. "She learns what I want, and I discover what pleases her." He pulled another apple from his pocket and offered it to Thorne.

She accepted it, wanting to preserve his good humor.

"Tonight, wear a gown with a scarlet girdle."

Thorne raised an eyebrow, but she'd wear a dress, hoping he'd feel an obligation, albeit a small one.

That twilight, the wind snarled Thorne's loose hair and crept up her bare legs. Her gown tangled her legs, making her stumble. She hoped this wasn't an omen.

Inside the tent, fresh rush mats covered the floor. On a red tablecloth, three candles circled a bottle of grape wine. A carving knife and fork with giant deer antlers for handles lay beside Thorne's favorite meal; mutton with mint sauce; sage and onion dressing made with oat bread, and fresh pears. Her rumbling stomach hoped the meat was rare.

Strumgued pushed back the full sleeves of his rust-colored shirt. He'd cleaned his leather jerkin and oiled his hair.

Why all the bother since they'd be eating alone?

Strumgued smiled. "Would you slice the mutton?"

In a flash of insight, she recognized what he was really asking. She picked up the carving set and hurled them at him. The knife missed but the fork struck his jerkin. If the curving handle hadn't unbalanced her throw, the knife might've hit him.

Frowning, he plucked the fork from his chest. She was pleased to see bloodied tines.

"Have your wits forsaken you?" he asked.

"I've only recently recovered them."

"If you didn't wish to carve the mutton, you'd only to speak. I'll slice it." Pressing his palms on the table, Strumgued leaned forward. "I'll spoon feed you, if that pleases."

"You cannot please me." She trembled with fury. "You cannot saddle me."

"You talk nonsense."

"You've been trying to break me, as you do Night-Arrow."

Strumgued's eye twitched. "I never break horses. I gentle them."

"You seek Night-Arrow's devotion. So the horse will follow you like a dog. Carry you in battle, die for you."

"The animal is destined to obey my commands."

"But I will not."

"Dear wife, I have no illusions about what you'll allow. I am

105

your husband. You have my respect and regard. If I ask you to cut the mutton, it does not seem too arduous a task."

She unfurled her skirt. "The dress, the tablecloth, my favorite meal."

Strumgued gestured at the table. "This pleasant repast provokes you?"

"You try to beguile me."

Strumgued cocked his head.

"You love me," Thorne said.

He laughed. "Human love is mist. What do I or any Dwarf know of it?"

The door seemed leagues away. Thorne collapsed on a stool. Someday she'd skewer his liver and roast it inside Stonevar's hearth. Through her dress yoke, she felt the ring. Begging him to pardon Zarra was impossible now; her tongue would shout only curses.

Strumgued cut the mutton into small morsels and offered her a one on the tip of his fork. She looked at it for a long time before opening her mouth.

CHAPTER TWENTY-FOUR

Spangle counted the days of her marriage by her blunders. Their second night, her flowery perfume made Lott sneeze. On the third, he insisted she wash her kohl-ringed eyes. The next, he turned away from her practiced seduction. Her feigned wantonness had satisfied countless others. Why not Lott? On the fifth night, her provocative talk made him cringe. Although she was no virgin, she was one in her marriage bed.

"Be yourself," Lott told her.

But she'd no idea how. The next night, she gave up, lying unresponsive on the narrow bed, letting her mind retreat into a familiar corner. When Lott still refused to consummate their marriage, she pulled the covers over her head, wondering how normal wives behaved.

For the next week, Lott was affectionate but no lovemaking. By the eighth morning, misery gouged lines from the corners of his mouth down to his chin. Spangle never wanted to hurt him.

That night as they lay in bed, hips and shoulders touching in the sinking middle, Spangle threw back the covers and said, "I don't know you want."

"Keep your eyes open."

She couldn't retreat unless she closed her eyes.

Lott stroked the inside of her arm. She stiffened, pushing away memories of other men's hands.

"My coarse fingers scrape your soft skin."

"Your fingers are fine." She examined the ceiling beams.

"You are safe with me."

She wanted to believe him, but no man had ever cared about her feelings.

He kissed her shoulder. "You must want to become one flesh."

"I offer myself to you, is that not sufficient?"

"Does my presence alone satisfy you?"

Did he expect lust from her? Impossible. Lott had shown infinite patience with his first wife, a childless shrew. She loved Lott for his sufferance, not for animal cravings.

He lifted her hand like it was made of glass and rubbed it against his cheek.

"Mmm." She liked his warmth, his scent of earthy sweat.

When he touched her stomach, she flinched, and he stopped. But when he grasped her hips, something inside began to burn. She tried to suppress it, but the heat spread through her center like wild fire. Did her dragonish side cause this?

She pictured Vainglorian the Red's claws gripping Rustofona's haunches as they mated in the sky. "Dig your fingers into my hips," Spangle said.

Lott grunted softly with surprise. Her hands moved down his strong arms, along his sides, pausing at the scar where the spear pierced his thigh. Lott was a warrior. He would fight anyone trying to mate her. This fueled the fire inside her until it burned white hot. She scarcely noticed when her Human side warned against surrendering to dragonish desire.

"Now," she murmured.

The bed creaked as they joined. But her memories were too strong. Her eyes closed. The fire died.

"Look at me," Lott said.

She did. He supported his weight, which made his gentle rocking movements soothing rather than threatening. He didn't make noises, which might have repulsed her. He didn't kiss her, which might have smothered her.

Spangle pressed her palms against Lott's chest, feeling his heartbeat and stilling her mind. Instinctively, her body matched his rhythm. Her muscles tightened. He rocked faster. Waves built inside her. Her Human side tried to resist, but it was too late. The waves crashed against her spine. Afterward she lay limp, bewildered by her response.

Lott moaned and collapsed beside her. As they clung to each other, water streamed down Lott's cheeks and wet her face.

"What's wrong?" she asked. Lott hadn't teared even when his first wife died, though he'd stayed drunk for two days.

He wiped his eyes then laughed until he couldn't catch his breath. When he could speak, he said, "You surprised me."

#

As the days passed, Lott's gentle lovemaking made her impatient. "Would you bite the back of my neck?" When he nibbled cautiously, she said, "Harder."

Her marriage was going better than she'd dared hope, until the trip to Seahaven.

"Stop!" Spangle told Lott at the edge of town as they traveled home.

A haggard woman nursing an infant pointed to a girl of about three. "Ten gold."

The child's tangled hair hadn't seen a comb or a wash in weeks. Behind her mother, two ragged boys fought with sticks. A gaunt man who might be the girl's father napped on a poorly mended chair, while flies buzzed his open mouth.

The wind changed, carrying the stink from an earth closet. Spangle held her breath as she jumped from the wagon and opened the purse holding Stonevar's profits. The woman pushed the girl toward Spangle. She couldn't leave the child to be sold to flesh peddlers.

"Do not buy that child!" Lott shouted from the wagon seat.

Glitter moved between them.

Memories of grandfather's slobbery kisses emboldened Spangle, and she emptied the purse into the woman's hand. Lott had been proud that they'd traded everything and for the first time, would return with gold for Thorne.

The woman counted on her dirty fingers. "That's only seven gold and five pennies."

"It's all I have."

"Not enough." The woman held out her hand.

Spangle didn't take the money back. She'd gold at Stonevar, but if she left and came back, the child would be gone. She couldn't live with herself if that happened. "I'll add a bag of salt and a bottle of wine."

The gaunt man jumped to his feet and snatched the gold.

"That'll do."

The woman looked as if she wanted to say something, but the man shot her a warning glance.

"Take the girl, Glitter."

As her sister carried the crying child to the wagon, Spangle pushed away memories of being separated from her own mother. She couldn't spare the child that pain, but could offer a future free from daily assaults.

When the man followed Glitter to retrieve the salt and wine, Lott said, "Put those back."

The man paid no attention and disappeared into the hut.

Spangle slowly faced her husband. She'd never seen him scowl, and she hugged herself. Buying the girl was madness. She and Glitter knew nothing of raising children, and Lott was angry.

In the back, Scatt whistled as he made room for the child. At thirty-six, he was the youngest soldier-farmer, a small man with a gray-streaked black mustache who'd been an army scout. He also loved gossip, which made him invaluable for collecting information in Seahaven. But he'd tell everyone at Stonevar that she and Lott had quarreled. Spangle cringed at embarrassing her husband.

"How much did you give her?" Lott growled under his breath, clearly not wanting the others to hear.

"All of it."

"Outrageous." Lott shook his head. "If we buy this one, her hag of mother will have another and another."

"If I didn't, she'd be sold to some whore-master." At least, impoverished families kept boys until they were old enough to work.

"Will you buy every poor child?"

"If need be." He had wanted a child with his first wife, why not with her?

"You'd disobey your husband?"

Spangle spoke with great weariness. "If need be." Even when she and Glitter were children, good people scorned them. Now when they rescued a child from the same fate, Lott disapproved. She'd never understand people. "The child cannot care for herself."

Lott grimaced. "What will the Goddess say when she finds you've spent her gold?"

"I'll repay her."

Lott cocked his head; his eyes narrowed. "How?"

She'd never told him about the small chest of gold hidden in the twins' pink wagon and now couldn't use it to repay Thorne without him finding out. Unable to tolerate her husband's disapproval, Spangle jumped off and motioned Scatt to the front. "I'll ride in the back."

Glitter gave the sobbing girl a honey drop. The child stopped weeping and nestled into the crook of Glitter's elbow. "Her eyes are blue. I think her hair will be yellow once we wash it. What's her name?"

"I forgot to ask."

With her pink scarf, Glitter wiped the child's tears, smearing the dirt. "Let's call her Una."

Lott called gruffly, "Ready?" Without waiting for an answer, he flicked his whip, and the horses trotted toward Malwood.

"Could she stay with me tonight?" Glitter asked.

Spangle glanced at Lott, but his tucked chin signaled a bad temper. "That would be best."

He didn't say anything until they reached Malwood where the twisted trees seemed locked in a silent battle for earth and light. They grew enormous because Dragons used the forest for their toilet. Every year the men had to clear overgrowth from the road. Overhead the wind-jerked leaves made sounds like panting tongues.

Before entering the tunnel of green tree branches, Lott asked Spangle to take the reins. Spangle urged the horses to pull. Lott and Scatt pushed the wagon over roots and out of holes in the road.

After they traversed the forest, Lott joined her on the seat. On their way to Seahaven, he'd held Spangle's hand, often pressing it to his lips. Returning, he offered no such attentions. If his love for her was so small that a child could divide them, its loss was insignificant. Still, a heaviness in her arms and chest made breathing difficult. She would've been relieved to end this miserable journey, but what if spending the profits angered Thorne? Spangle loved Thorne nearly as much as Glitter and hated disappointing either.

At dusk they arrived at Stonevar. Thorne, white hair gleaming, wearing black tunic and trousers, moved toward them with the grace of a wole-lion, taller than everyone save the Giantess, carrying the weight of Stonevar's survival. Anticipating Thorne's disapproval made Spangle want to crawl under the wagon.

However, Thorne was less concerned about spending the gold

than using it to buy a person. "But I trust your judgment." She put an arm around Spangle.

Thorne's touch lifted some of the weight from Spangle's shoulders.

Zarra stepped from the shadows. "When no one would buy, you gave away our wares, and now you purchase another empty stomach. You two are quite talented traders."

Glitter laughed. "You would've done the same."

"And thrown in the wagon and horses, too," Zarra said.

Una scratched her arms. Thorne pushed up the child's sleeve. Red spots covered the thin arm all the way up to her shoulder. "Have Fehera treat these after a bath."

Well past dark, after settling Una with Glitter, Spangle entered Lott's cottage. He leaned against the hearth, puffing his pipe, his gaze cold. The previous week, he plastered the walls with a mixture of sand, lime, and horsehair. She'd hung scarlet and gold curtains fashioned from a costume.

Below the window, their bed dipped in the middle, forcing them to sleep close. She hadn't minded before. Now she opened a wooden chest at the foot and gathered her clothes and piled them inside a basket to take with her. Glitter and Una would welcome her.

Lott flushed. "What are you doing?"

"I cannot be a proper wife." She'd always known that.

"A proper wife stays and fights it out. She doesn't pack up and leave."

Her head throbbed. "I do what I must." She was sick to death of 'musts.'

He rested his elbow on the wooden mantle. "I must approve of everything you do or you'll leave me?"

"You don't want me."

He inhaled his pipe then exhaled a cloud of smoke. "So I want you only if you obey me."

"That's the way of men." Caring for a man invited disaster. An enormous resentment ruptured like a festering boil. In a smooth motion, she slid her hand through the slit in her skirt, unsheathed her knife from her thigh, and threw it. The point thwacked the mantle and stuck only a finger width below his arm. She could've killed him, but at the last moment, affection altered her aim.

Lott didn't flinch. "Ha. Olga threw supper to get me over a sulk.

Should've remembered your knife." He yanked it out. "I'll hold this till we're done conversing."

"I'm done." Spangle picked up her belongings and hurried to the door. Better leave before she killed him. Since drinking Dragon blood, her temper burned hot.

Lott ripped the basket from her hands and threw it against the wall. An explosion of pastel dresses fluttered over the floor. "Do you think I'd let you go?"

"I don't know." She also didn't know if she wanted to stay or leave, but she wanted one of them desperately. "So you were sulking by the fire?"

"Pouting some, too." The corners of his mouth turned up.

She collapsed on the bed. "I couldn't leave that child."

Sitting beside her, he traced her jaw with a resin-stained finger. "Seems I love you all the more for it."

Her mid-section twinged in an unfamiliar way. Lott's musky scent had once repelled her, but now smelled familiar like her bed fur. "You wanted children. Why not Una?"

He pulled her close until his lips brushed her ear. "I'm reluctant to share you."

The following day, Lott carved Una a wooden doll.

CHAPTER TWENTY-FIVE

In a chilly downpour, Thorne's nightly march to join Strumgued for the evening meal seemed longer than usual. This wasn't the night to talk of Zarra, but she'd only one more until she must banish the thief or the Dwarf Lord would evict them all. How could she cast out her friend? Stonevar was Zarra's home, her first since her mother's death had forced her, at seven, onto the streets and into thievery to survive.

Every time Thorne planned to beg Strumgued to pardon her dear friend, something interfered. Even touching him to determine if he had Dragon-Fating had proved impossible. Yet both must be done.

Ahead, rain blurred the light in the triangular window of the newly constructed stone cottage, a permanent building to replace the tent. Clearly Strumgued was preparing for a long siege. Tonight Waldemar would join them—first Cayeseed, now his son.

Beyond the river, lightning flashed in the pattern of an uprooted tree. Thorne's heart hammered her breastbone. Panting, she dashed to the cottage, awash in a dragonish fear of lightning.

Inside, she could breathe, but at the next thunderclap, she crouched in a corner, hugging herself. When her trembling eased, she looked around, relieved to be alone, though fresh bread sat on the table and something bubbled in a kettle within the hearth. Strumgued would arrive soon. She must regain her bearing, act the dutiful wife, get him in a benevolent mood. She lifted the kettle, but in her haste, seared a finger. She slammed the pot on the table, slopping stew over the sides.

From the torrent outside, Strumgued said, "My stomach's as empty as a sluggard's purse. Hurry along."

Hastily, Thorne wiped the pot.

"I can't hurry. I have a blister," Cayeseed said. "My new boots pinch my toes."

"Your toes are as big as apples," her brother teased.

"Cease your bickering." Strumgued nodded at Thorne as the group entered. "My apologies for our late arrival. Assembling my family is more troublesome than mustering an army."

Thorne forced a welcoming smile as they hung up their wet capes.

"My fault. I wanted to wear my new boots." Cayeseed held up her skirt to show boots embossed with a leaf pattern.

Thorne felt the soft leather. "Fine workmanship. They'll soon mold to your toes." She glanced at Strumgued who smiled. Good.

Waldemar snorted. Cayeseed punched him. In mock pain, he rubbed his thick arm. His hair was redder than Strumgued's, and his beard brushed his chest.

"Enough." Strumgued pointed to a seat. "Sit before you shame me further."

Waldemar braced hands on hips. "On stools?"

Strumgued grunted. "I'll carve four fine chairs."

Chairs encouraged one to linger. "These seats serve." Thorne ladled stew onto thick slices of bread while Strumgued poured the wine.

His son ate nothing, only sipped from his cup. Strumgued made no comment about Waldemar's lack of appetite, although Thorne found it odd. From what she'd observed, Dwarfs enjoyed eating.

Cayeseed fidgeted and picked at her food, also evidencing little appetite.

Strumgued frowned. "Why do you flop about like a fish on shore?"

Waldemar answered, "Torvald wrestles me tonight."

Cayeseed glared at her brother.

Strumgued nodded at Cayeseed. "A fine young Dwarf."

His daughter flushed red as madder root.

"I've never seen a wrestling match." Thorne raised a fork full of bread dripping gravy coated with lamb, peas, and onions.

Her husband smiled. "Then you shall be my guest."

Waldemar's eyes grew larger and rounder than Thorne thought possible. "Father, I don't think an outsider—"

"My wife's no outsider." Strumgued's booming voice echoed among the rafters. "Your disrespect shames me."

Thorne sipped wine, trying to conceal her eagerness to enter the Dwarf stronghold and discover their weaknesses. Brutte had been a spy and called it a worthy profession. "I've no desire to intrude."

"My wife cannot intrude." Strumgued smiled, but his eyes were hard as blue diamonds.

"Your pardon." Waldemar hung his head. "I bid my father's wife attend the contest and will forfeit if she refuses."

Cayeseed's lower lip quivered.

"It's time you visited the new safehold," Strumgued told Thorne. "The main level nears completion."

So soon. "Have you named it?" Thorne asked.

"Not yet. Perhaps you'd do the honor."

That surprised Thorne. "I don't know what name would please you, Lord." Her dissembling gave her a sour taste, and she gulped more wine.

"One will occur to you."

Waldemar frowned, and Thorne doubted he'd like any name she picked.

"Are we finished?" Cayeseed asked.

Eyes glowing with mischief, Waldemar scratched the side of his round nose. "Have you placed a wager on Torvald?"

Cayeseed flushed crimson again.

Waldemar fluffed his thick whiskers. "Do you like Torvald's hairless chin?"

"He has a beard." Cayeseed pursed her mouth. "It's pale, almost white."

"So you've gotten close to his buck teeth." Waldemar grinned.

Cayeseed punched his arm. "I'll hold our seats." With a nod toward Thorne and Strumgued, she gathered her skirts and left.

Waldemar, holding his breath, looked near bursting. Strumgued's eyes twinkled, but he waited a few moments before chuckling. Waldemar exhaled loud guffawing laughter.

Thorne brushed crumbs off her lap. "You two are cruel."

Strumgued glanced at the doorway. "She didn't hear us laugh."

Thorne shook her head. "Whether she did or not, she knows."

"A brother must ensure his sister finds a worthy mate." Waldemar lifted his chin. "She needn't have hurried off. No one will sit on father's bench. At least she's acting the fool over Torvald, not that Dragon." His face twisted in disgust.

Thorne's mouth went dry, and she downed the last of her wine. Waldemar hated Dragons as much as Strumgued. If Waldemar disobeyed his father and killed the whelp, would Strumgued be secretly pleased?

Strumgued offered Thorne his arm. "Let us proceed to the wrestling match."

Thorne took his arm and felt—nothing, only coarse cloth. No Dragon-Fating. Strumgued wouldn't harm Hellee. He would honor his word, though he wanted Hellestorm dead. She was almost disappointed that she could trust him, preferring more reasons to despise him.

Strumgued escorted her to a small covered wagon. Halfway across the new stone bridge, lightning flashed, thunder rumbled, and Thorne clasped Strumgued's arm. His smile made her want to rip his arm off. Instead, she relaxed her grip. Through the rain, a tetrad of three-sided windows carved into South Ventamar glowed like the eyes of four monsters. The wagon stopped before a triangular wooden door, five paces tall, similar to Stonevar's. A guard opened one side.

Wall torches lit this Great Hall, which was thrice the size of Stonevar's, easily holding four hundred Dwarfs. Seeing them all made Thorne's knees wobble. She pretended to stumble, then stiffened her spine.

Strumgued escorted her through the crowd. No point trying to blend, since she stood two heads taller than any Dwarf. When Strumgued nodded at those sitting on split log benches, Thorne did also. Conversations became whispers as they passed. Some hid behind large mugs of ale. Many didn't disguise shock and disapproval, though Thorne doubted anyone would publicly slight the Dwarf Lord's wife.

Cayeseed sat in the front row, chatting with those sitting behind. Thorne joined her. Newcomers acknowledged Strumgued before selecting their seats under the domed ceiling five times a man's height. The Dwarfs laughed often, their round eyes shining above bulbous noses. If she'd met them under other circumstances, she might have enjoyed their company.

An aproned female gave Thorne a mug of ale. The redhead

filling Strumgued's cup flipped her curls. She fingered Strumgued's bristled chin as if admiring the new growth and leaned close, saying something Thorne couldn't hear.

The Dwarf Lord laughed and slapped his thigh. "Thank you, Valhilda." He watched her stroll away with her orange and blue skirt swirling about her legs.

Strumgued must like thick ankles. For no reason she could think of, Valhilda's conspicuous flirting gave Thorne the urge to yank those red curls. She'd never considered that she-Dwarfs might consider Strumgued attractive. Evidently, the Dwarf community didn't expect her marriage to endure. Why else would that thick-ankled trollop flirt so openly? Unless . . . a Dwarf could take more than one wife. What if he already had another spouse somewhere, and she was second? Thorne stiffened. She wouldn't tolerate that indignity.

She gazed at the rock floor and high ceiling, counted eighteen pillars, looking anywhere but at Strumgued. In a corner a dozen smooth-chinned youths whispered. They were dressed like the adults: boys in maroon or brown shirts and leather jerkins; girls in colorful blouses and full skirts.

Near the hearth, which was large enough to roast a giant deer, a gray-haired Dwarf with a round belly inflated his cheeks and blew a ram's horn. The crowd quieted. A Dwarf in battle regalia—copper helmet and breastplate—pulled aside the heavy tapestry by the fireplace.

First through the doorway was an elderly Dwarf whose white robe and white whiskers both brushed the floor. With each step, he banged his six-foot staff. Waldemar and Torvald followed, their unshod feet slapping the floor. Thick hair covered the competitors' bare chests, arms, and legs. Torvald seemed plenty hairy to Thorne.

The spectators shouted and stomped in a reverberating rhythm.

The elderly Dwarf stopped in the center of the white circle and quieted the crowd by banging a staff topped by a conch-shaped gnarl. The contestants bowed before taking their positions at opposite sides of a larger yellow circle.

Each contender knotted his beard, Torvald having just enough to do so. When he glanced toward Cayeseed, she flushed. For her sake, Thorne hoped Torvald won.

"Who's the Dwarf holding the staff?" Thorne asked Cayeseed.

"The Ombud. He declares the winner."

"Is he very old?"

"As old as the trees. He's forgotten the year of his birth, and only he knows his birth name."

What knowledge might this elder have? "Would he speak to me?"

Before Cayeseed could answer, the Ombud thumped his staff, startling Thorne. The Ombud's voice crackled with authority. "He who forces the other outside the ring wins the match." He bowed at Strumgued, who nodded in return. Thorne nodded also. Too much respect was better than too little.

The cymbals clanged, signaling the first round. Waldemar and Torvald planted their feet a shoulder-width apart and clasped their left hands on the other's right shoulder.

The two swayed like young trees in a storm. Veins popped on their thick arms. Perspiration curled the hairs on their backs. They shuffled inside the ring, huffing and grunting, their feet gripping the floor so tightly that their plum-sized toes turned purple.

"Force him back!" "Haul him out!" More voices joined the first two, creating a cacophony.

It was unclear whom they encouraged. Thorne's heart beat faster. If Waldemar lost, that would upset Strumgued.

A foot gained by either wrestler caused cheering, though each advance was soon lost. Torvald stood two knuckles taller, but Waldemar was heavier. Behind Thorne, someone commented that one would make a decisive move soon.

"Push! Push!" the audience called.

Unable to resist, Thorne joined them.

Torvald leaned into the crook of Waldemar's elbow, forcing him back. Countering, Waldemar grabbed Torvald's arm and used his opponent's momentum to lift him.

The crowd stood and cheered.

Waldemar, scarlet-faced, dropped Torvald outside the circle. Strumgued raised his fist and cheered.

Cayeseed stared at the floor, lower lip quivering. Thorne squeezed Cayeseed's hand. With her dragonish hearing, Thorne heard someone mumble that Strumgued intended to betroth Cayeseed to Torvald. Someone else remarked that after the Dragon ate Strumgued's first wife, five-year-old Cayeseed had vowed to avenge her mother's death. For years, Cayeseed practiced slaying the Dragon with a wooden sword. Normal childish play under the circumstances, Thorne thought. But Cayeseed would never have revenge since Gaspotine the Dark was dead.

Everyone quieted when the Ombud struck his staff on the floor three times. Thorne turned her attention to the circle where the contestants, both breathing raggedly, now waited.

The Ombud's voice boomed. "The first round goes to Waldemar." When he held out the staff, Waldemar grasped it.

The crowd cheered again. The two contestants retreated to their stools. The contest would've been more exciting with clawing and biting that drew blood, but it satisfied Thorne nonetheless.

During the break, Valhilda with the red curls and thick ankles topped Thorne's cup. Thorne glared at her. Valhilda, seemingly oblivious, refilled Strumgued's tankard while he grinned.

Thorne wouldn't tolerate Strumgued taking another wife, even if it were Dwarf custom. Yet why did it matter?

"A fine match," Strumgued said.

"A bit reserved." Thorne would never admit that she enjoyed watching. "More bloodshed would've added interest."

Strumgued's woolly eyebrows raised. Before he could respond, the Ombud banged his staff. The wrestlers took their positions.

"He who first pins the shoulders of his opponent wins," the Ombud announced.

Cymbals signaled the second round. Thick arms open, the two competitors circled in a slight crouch. Waldemar grabbed Torvald's arm, leg-hooked him, and dropped. They tangled on the floor in a mass of flailing limbs.

The crowd stomped. "Pin him! Pin him!"

Torvald, nose bloodied, scrambled on top. He pressed his knee into Waldemar's back and hooked his arms through Waldemar's. Strumgued groaned. Cayeseed clasped her hands so tightly that her fingers turned red.

Waldemar's wide shoulders prevented Torvald from linking hands. With Torvald clinging to his back, Waldemar struggled to his feet.

The clapping crowd stood. Thorne jumped up, yelling encouragement.

Torvald struck a leg between his opponent's. Waldemar fell. Torvald scissored Waldemar's leg and rolled, forcing him onto his back then pinned Waldemar's shoulders to the floor.

The crowd roared. Apparently, an exciting match mattered more than who won. As Torvald blotted his bloody nose, he winked at Cayeseed, who giggled and waved shyly.

Strumgued frowned. Thorne enjoyed her husband's disappointment.

Shaking his head and huffing, Waldemar rose slowly, rubbing his leg. When he growled at Torvald, the crowd clapped. Thorne smiled, enjoying the drama, until she remembered wanting the Dwarfs gone.

The Ombud swept into the center of the chamber, long robes trailing behind. Three times, he struck his staff on stone, each time pausing to let the sound ring. Everyone quieted. "The second round goes to Torvald."

The winner grasped the Ombud's staff. Again, the crowd cheered. The wrestlers retreated to their stools. Bruises blossomed on their arms, legs, and trunks.

"Lady Strumgued," the red-haired, thick-ankled trollop said, "more ale?"

Thorne's face went slack. She couldn't feel her lips. The Dwarf called her . . . she struggled for breath—Lady Strumgued. Thorne held out her cup.

"Honored to serve you, Lady Strumgued."

"Ah. Ah. Yes," Thorne mumbled. She glanced at Strumgued, who was watching the wrestlers. He must've heard what Valhilda called her; however, for once, he wasn't grinning at her discomfiture. For the remainder of the break, she inspected the two-headed axes mounted on a wall rack.

When the Ombud's staff banged, the wrestlers took their positions.

"The victor will lift both opponent's feet from the floor," the Ombud said.

Cymbals clashed for the final round.

Torvald charged, grabbing Waldemar's arm and leg, making him fall sideways. Torvald landed on Waldemar's stomach with a loud "ooofff" then scrambled to his feet.

Waldemar grabbed Torvald from behind.

The crowd called, "Lift him! Lift him!"

With a long groan, Waldemar leaned backwards to hoist his squirming opponent. Torvald hooked an ankle around Waldemar's calf, and Strumgued's son fell, elbow hitting stone with a loud pop. Cayeseed gasped.

His opponent stepped back, letting Waldemar rise. As he rubbed his injured left elbow, the crowd mumbled approval for Torvald. When Waldemar nodded, the wrestlers resumed their hunched circling. Sweat soaked their bushy eyebrows and chin hair.

Torvald grabbed the wrist of Waldemar's injured arm, jammed a hip into his belly, and threw Waldemar over. On the floor, pain dug trenches into the corners of Waldemar's mouth, but he made no sound. Many in the crowd whistled. Cayeseed beamed at Torvald. Strumgued groaned. Thorne's pulse quickened.

The Ombud strode into the ring and struck his staff three times. "This was a mighty contest. Both wrestlers earned our admiration. The match round goes to Torvald."

Cayeseed jumped to her feet, clapping and grinning. Torvald grasped the Ombud's staff. The crowd cheered.

Thorne reminded herself that she didn't like Dwarfs and sometimes hated them. She shouldn't have enjoyed this.

The wrestlers bowed at Strumgued. He nodded at Torvald, then Waldemar who cupped his injured left elbow. Strumgued took Thorne's arm.

"No need for you to leave the celebration," Thorne said. "I'll find my way back."

Strumgued grunted. "I'll escort you through the mountain."

When she hesitated, one side of his mouth twisted upward. If she refused—shaming him in front of hundreds—he'd never pardon Zarra.

CHAPTER TWENTY-SIX

Why did Strumgued insist on taking her home this way? A little rain wouldn't bother her. Better than relying on him to guide her through dwarfish mountain mazes. As Thorne followed him behind the tapestry where the wrestlers had first emerged, into an anteroom with three doorways, she banished every pleasant memory of that evening.

Strumgued took a torch from the wall, passed through the left door and descended into a room half-filled with debris from hollowing a massive fireplace. Thorne stayed close, avoiding the roughly hewn walls where they angled in, checking her balance on uneven floors. After running her hand over the rust-colored walls, she licked her fingers, savoring the iron taste. She sniffed, expecting the sweet scent of carbide, but inhaled wole-rat and Zarra. They'd passed this way. In the dimness, Thorne didn't see Zarra, Sir-Sir, or Strumgued.

Surveying the scattered rubble, she saw torchlight in the new fireplace. Strumgued's voice echoed inside the chimney. "Enter the hearth and step left."

Odd, but she did as asked. The fireplace was two paces deep with a place for a grate a foot below floor level. Strumgued stood on a side ledge. Hands against the wall, she sidled next to him. He shone the torch on handholds carved into the rock.

If Stonevar's hearths were similar, it presaged nothing good. "Where does it go?"

"You'll know soon enough." He climbed the wall. "Hand me the torch."

She passed it over, then followed. The ladder led to a newly excavated tunnel where rock dust powdered the floor. Thorne ducked to avoid an overhang. If she crouched and shuffled she could move without slipping or hitting her head. Something scurried down a passageway on her right, and she smelled wole-rat again. Sir-Sir? If Strumgued caught Zarra, he'd banish her immediately. Thorne couldn't bear losing her after Raspberry-Frost.

Strumgued poked the torch down a tunnel. "Leads to the mines. Stay close unless you've skill at wayfinding."

"Don't Dwarfs get tired of working in the dark?"

His echoing laughter made rock dust rain. "We draw strength from stone. Our castles are mountain monuments to our future, evidence of our clan loyalty."

She refused to admire this. "You cannot eat rocks."

"We trade, but keep the finest gems and purest gold."

She remembered the serpent ring. "I knew Dwarfs made superior weapons, but hadn't realized they fashioned adornments."

"Not surprising. We never sell what we value, and we value our time most of all." He wiggled his thick fingers. "Crafting the perfect necklace for a wife might take decades."

She didn't want anything like that. Distracted, she collided with a cobweb. Peeling it from her face, she noticed shimmering strands hanging from the ceiling and walls. "Why do the spider webs sparkle?"

"Diamond dust. We've entered an old tunnel." His eyes glistened as if hoping she appreciated it.

Bringing her to see the webs was some kind of lure. Unintentionally, she frowned. Strumgued shrugged. If diamond webs didn't impress her, he'd apparently spend a lifetime discovering what would.

His resolve made her more determined to resist. But she must get on his good side. "This is lovely." Saving Zarra was more important than avoiding his traps. His grin made her want to break those square teeth, but she forced a weak smile.

At the next junction, he stopped and touched the wall.

"What do you feel?" Thorne asked.

"Our location." He lowered the torch to show slashes in the rock. To the untrained eye or finger they could be random chisel marks. "The first denotes the tunnel slope. The bar crossing the second line indicates the direction. The third, our level in the mountain. The fourth, our position on the level."

Almost giddy, she hurried to the next branch to touch the small indentations. "This marking shows a rise, but we're descending."

"Only temporarily." Evidently unaware of what he'd revealed, he smiled, pleased by her excitement.

Now she wouldn't lose her way. But what secret doors led into Stonevar? At her first opportunity, she'd examine the castle.

After ten more minutes, a breeze fluttered the torch flame. The scent of water intensified, and the air grew heavier. Moss slicked the walls.

Strumgued offered a hand. "Step careful. The floor's wet."

Refusing would only amuse him. She didn't mind his touch, still too excited about the markings. The sounds of water rushing crescendoed, until they emerged behind the waterfall splitting Ventamar Mountain. The half moon quivered in the cascade.

Under the spray, she shivered as she followed him along a ledge a pace wide. In the center, she stopped to watch the stars shimmer through the water. "I'd like to come during the day."

He smiled. "I'll show you the secret. Now hurry along before a chill settles into your lungs."

"Have no worry for me." Dragon blood made her immune. On the other side of the falls, she followed her husband into a tunnel with smooth walls, smiling at her plan. "I've a name for the new castle."

Strumgued pointed the torch toward a pathway branching right and down. "Speak, wife."

The word "wife" conjured thick-ankled Valhilda. "Have you other living wives?"

"Does sharing me concern you?"

Thorne pictured his delighted smirk, but wanted information more than the pleasure of a nasty retort. "Races have different customs." Being his second wife was more than an insult; it would invalidate her marriage.

"Steep here." He took her elbow. "Watch your step."

She snatched her arm away when the floor leveled. "Well?"

"No Dwarf wife would permit it." He looked at her. In the torchlight, his large teeth magnified his grin. "Were you concerned?"

She hoped the gloom concealed her flush. "Only curious."

"I am also curious. What name have you chosen?"

"Dyadzan."

"Well spoken. Two mountains it shall be."

Since he meant nothing to her, Thorne couldn't understand why his compliment pleased her; she'd named the castle only so he'd pardon Zarra. Maybe Magda was right, she'd let her hatred cool. She must never forget that he killed Brutte, and that she occupied her home on Strumgued's sufferance. She must choose the right moment to unleash her dragonish fury. Until then, she must learn all she could, especially about the Dwarf tunnels.

As they advanced, more passageways burrowed downward, evidence of heavier mining in North Ventamar than across the river.

Strumgued extended his arm. "Halt or fall." Ahead the tunnel dropped sharply. He handed her the torch and climbed down. "Pass the firebrand," he said from three paces below.

Above her, stars twinkled at the top of a chimney. She wasn't certain where she was, but had a premonition. On her belly, she slid over the ledge, and he guided her foot into a toehold. She stepped from the chimney into Stonevar's lower level—inside the War Room.

She wanted to scream and claw his face, but said calmly, "So these markings beside the fireplace indicate a tunnel."

"Indeed, my wife." Looking around, he frowned at the sacks and barrels of stores.

The word 'wife' made her teeth ache. "Does a tunnel like this lead into Hellee's cave?"

"Yes."

If Strumgued chose to kill the whelp she could do nothing.

She'd seen similar marks beside her fireplace. "In Stonevar's sleeping rooms?"

"Dwarfs don't care to be trapped."

Yet Strumgued constantly plotted to trap her.

Thorne hugged herself. "Nothing will keep you out of Stonevar if you choose to enter."

Strumgued lifted the torch so it illuminated his face. "Nothing."

CHAPTER TWENTY-SEVEN

When all the Dragons in the Continuum avoided Solanie, she approached Rustofona. The Magnificent looked up from Hellestorm's current and explained the shunning.

Gaspotine paddled closer, below the river surface.

Solanie's spirit appeared as gaunt as her flesh, making her large eyes more prominent as they widened. "Will I be shunned forever?"

"Through winter. They expect you'll be dead by spring." Rustofona stuck her head back in Hellestorm's stream.

Solanie sucked her tail tip. A mother Dragon would reproach her for this whelpish behavior, but Gaspotine sensed her loneliness. When he neared fifty, his mother's tolerance for company became shorter than snow on a sun-baked rock. By the time he left her lair, he preferred solitude to her nipping jaws. He desired only to hunt, sleep, savagely mate, and ride the Silver River. Ideal Dragon goals. He'd obeyed Dragon Code—until he devoured the Dwarf mother with the Power. That lapse led to his death.

Why did Lasmenda judge Solanie deficient? The young Dragon was sufficiently savage and fearless.

Solanie stopped mouthing her tail. "I don't know how to hunt. Will you teach me?"

When Rustofona didn't answer, Gaspotine burst from the river. "You must have patience."

"Gaspotine the Dark." Solanie appeared impressed. "What is patience?"

"Quietly waiting. It develops slowly in Dragons. One reason whelps stay with their mothers fifty years." From his observations, the newest generation of whelps learned more slowly than the one before.

"An empty belly destroys patience." Solanie quivered. "I must go. The Niede compels my return."

"Follow a wole-wolf pack and take their kill," Gaspotine said. "Or locate their prey's remains. You may find scavengers to devour."

"Why help me?"

"No reason." At least none he understood. "Why seek council from the dead?"

"The Fairy Queen suggested Rustofona."

"How would a mainland Fairy Queen know about her?"

"Not she. The one in the Continuum."

"A Fairy in the Continuum! Where?" Gaspotine shouted.

The other Dragons mumbled approval, evidently thinking he chastised Solanie.

She ignored them. "The Queen hovers down river."

Gaspotine squinted. A speck moved. He huffed and swung his head. Why had he never seen it before? When he approached, the Queen moved away.

"Stay still!" he ordered.

The Fairy Queen dove into the river. This invasion was intolerable.

CHAPTER TWENTY-EIGHT

Time had run out. Thorne must beg Strumgued to pardon Zarra for the stolen ring today. She pulled the blanket over her head, as if staying in bed would hold back the sun.

Mid-morning, she forced herself to rise and dress, although a nightmare of Strumgued invading her chamber still weakened her. She shoved wood into her fireplace. If he entered that way, he'd burn his feet. After a hasty meal in the Great Hall, she entered the bailey where Nella fed the chickens.

"What are those?" Thorne pointed to the leafy vines with tiny red buds climbing the stones below her balcony.

"Fire vines."

Thorne's knees buckled, and she leaned against the wall. Autumn had come too quickly.

Nella hurried to her. "What troubles you?"

"In Gran—in Lily's book it says:

> When fire vines bud, it stirs a skylord's blood.
> When fire vines bloom, it makes a skylord loom."

"What does it mean?" Chickens pecked at Nella's toes, asking for grain.

Though Thorne had read Grandfather's words many times, she hadn't understood them until now. "Fire vine flowers mark the Dragon mating season." She glanced around, almost expecting Captain Hauk to appear. This time last year, her body had betrayed her, and she'd sought Hauk in his bedchamber.

Mother often said, "Nothing's so wretched that it can't get

worse." The flowers wouldn't open for a day or two, and when they did, she'd stay in her chamber and send word to Strumgued that she was ill. Today she had other plans. She must gather the words that would convince Strumgued to pardon Zarra. Thorne left Nella in the bailey and rode to her Contemplation Ledge.

On the mountain outcrop, she sat cross-legged, stroking the bone cutlass made from Rustofona's rib. Brutte would counsel the hard decision, but losing Zarra would be like losing her sight. She must bargain and access to her bedchamber would be Strumgued's price.

Thorne longed for Raspberry-Frost or Quist. She hadn't seen her Fairy for some days; presumedly the new hive occupied it. Before Hellee hatched, Quist attended her constantly. Now he spent his time grooming the whelp.

Across the valley, Hellee, now large as a cow, lumbered outside the cavern, squawking and flapping leathery cream-colored wings. Bekka the Hunchback followed, carrying Lily's baby.

When Quist's claws pinched her shoulder, Thorne sighed, feeling encouraged beyond what the Fairy-Dragon could possibly offer. He nuzzled her neck, giving her a brief moment of peace.

Behind her, a male voice said, "Still climbing the brekka."

Thorne drew her sword as she jumped to her feet. The bone cutlass fell from her lap, clattering against stone. Screeching, Quist flew to a scraggy pine above.

Captain Hauk laughed, hands braced on hips, shirtsleeves billowing. "No need for alarm. It's I, the Dragon slayer." His levity didn't amuse Thorne. He motioned at the Dragon Ledge. "So the winged wyrm left a whelp." A few wisps of white-blond hair had escaped the lace tied behind his neck and fluttered about skin made golden by sun and sea wind. A leather jerkin hugged his strong chest.

"I'll kill you before I let you harm him." Thorne placed her sword tip beneath his chin.

"Would you cut me after the bond we've shared?"

She didn't want to be reminded. Especially since the fire vine would bloom soon. Killing him seemed the wisest course, so she wouldn't run to his bed again. "Why have you returned?"

"To beg forgiveness." He held up his hands. "There's no need for discord between us. I did you a service when I harpooned the Dragon."

"You killed our protector." The Dwarfs would never have returned while Rustofona lived. Thorne yearned to see Hauk's blood stain the ledge crimson.

Even with her blade pressed to his throat, he seemed relaxed. "Behind you, Goddess."

On the Dragon Ledge across the valley, a dozen sailors surrounded Hellee and Bekka. Still holding Lily's baby, Bekka drew her sword and pointed it at Anders, the child's well-favored, blond father.

Hellee squawked and scrambled toward the cavern, but Anders blocked the way and struck the whelp's nose with the flat of his sword. Hellee squealed and retreated behind Bekka.

"Tell your sailors to withdraw," Thorne said, "or I'll slice your throat." His fear smell encouraged her.

"If I die, they'll kill the Dragon and the child. But they'll let Bekka live to remember her failure, as you will live with yours."

Her sword arm shook with fury. Dracodurus pricked his neck and blood trickled around his Adam's apple. Baby Aeron's death would devastate Bekka. Add to that breaking her oath to protect Hellee.

A monstrous evil had hatched this plan. She'd never thought Hauk capable of this. Dragonish fury burned inside her. She must kill him. "Anders would slay his own child. You'd destroy Bekka though you know her gentle spirit."

"Only if you resist me." Cruel lines cut into the corners of Hauk's mouth. "Surrender your sword."

She wanted to sheath Dracodurus in his bowels, but couldn't let either infant die. "What do you want?" Probably Rustofona's treasure.

"Come with me."

"Where?"

"Lower your weapon."

She pushed back her dragonish rage, so she could think. She'd only herself to blame. The Dwarfs gave her a false sense of security, and she'd relaxed her vigilance. "Order your men from the Dragon Ledge, and I'll surrender my sword."

Hauk waved an arm. The sailors backed off, and Bekka and Hellee hurried inside the cavern. The wind changed, carrying the stench of sweat mixed with whale oil.

Thorne held out Dracodurus. When Hauk took it, its loss reverberated, second only to Brutte's death.

"A wise decision, Goddess." He motioned for her to descend.

Someday, she vowed, Dracodurus would skewer him. For now, she must remove Hauk and his sailors from Stonevar.

#

For the remainder of the day, Thorne and her captors traveled north. She spent the ride picturing the dagger from her boot piercing Hauk's eye. After she allowed Stonevar time to prepare, she'd escape.

As the waxing Predator's Moon rose in a cold starry sky, they rode into a camp, passed a dozen fires, and halted before the largest tent. Hauk disappeared inside.

Although she was thirsty and her buttocks ached, she held her head high. Townsmen she didn't recognize emerged from smaller tents to gape. In the firelight, she detected fear in their eyes. If she really were a goddess, she'd curse them all.

Hauk reappeared. "Follow me."

CHAPTER TWENTY-NINE

Before Lord Bludwelt saw Thorne, her metallic scent rolled over him like a fervid breeze. He shivered, though his veins burned as if venom flowed there.

He had planned to take Stonevar and marry Thorne, but without an army to engage the Dwarfs, he'd changed his scheme. They'd waited five days for Thorne to visit her Contemplation Ledge. Hauk would've rushed in immediately, but Bludwelt demanded patience. When a Dragon whelp lumbered onto the ledge across the valley, Bludwelt devised a delightful plan to threaten Bekka and the baby.

Now when Thorne stumbled into the tent, Hauk grabbed her arm to steady her.

Bludwelt jumped up from the table. "Don't touch her."

Captain Hauk backed away. "Didn't want her to fall."

Gaze locked on Thorne, Bludwelt waved Hauk out. "Leave us."

Hauk waited until Thorne nodded, then stomped out. For now, Bludwelt would ignore Hauk's insolence. Hauk thought they would ransom Thorne, but Bludwelt would never release her. He moved closer, breathing harder, resisting an urge to kneel and embrace her thighs.

She backed away, tripped on his oversized pallet, and caught herself on the table. "I should've recognized your handiwork."

For a long moment, they looked at each other, breathless, marveling. When she shivered, he swung his cape about her shoulders. Her nearness melted the hoarfrost icing his heart, made him tremble. Though he intended to never separate from her again, he must accustom himself to her, savor what was to come.

Gazing at the door, she fingered the blue gauze covering the tent walls. "This abduction won't gain what you hope."

He knew different and motioned to a stool. "You must hunger. Join me."

"Wine." She made no move to sit or remove his cape.

As he poured wine into a silver goblet, she rubbed her cheek against his cloak. His heart missed three beats, and he yearned to press his skin against hers. She wanted him but must be won. He blocked her view with his body, then sprinkled dragonwort into her glass.

She drank quickly. The wine made her skin glow. When he refilled her goblet, she tore the whip from his belt and backed toward the entrance.

He approached.

"Stay back."

The fire in her eyes enthralled him, enticing him closer.

Thorne flicked the lash, but so clumsily he easily grabbed it. Bludwelt yanked her to him and wrapped her in his arms. He cupped the back of her long neck and licked the scar on her chin. Her head fell back, exposing her throat. He nipped hard enough to bruise. Her breathing changed to short gasps.

Unexpectedly, she slumped to the floor. Bludwelt groaned at the sudden, unendurable deprivation and knelt beside her. His reflection in her elongated pupils imprisoned him.

She licked her lips. As he leaned to touch his tongue to hers, metal cut the air between them.

Hauk pressed his blade to Bludwelt's throat. "Leave now as we agreed."

Lord Bludwelt had agreed Thorne would occupy this tent alone, but hadn't anticipated how difficult leaving her would be. Pretending to accept Hauk's leadership was even more galling. He backed away, mumbling, "I'll kill you for this." Shoulders hunched, he charged from the tent. At the right moment, he'd enjoy ending Hauk's delusions of command.

CHAPTER THIRTY

Thorne couldn't catch her breath, as if separating from Bludwelt had ripped open her chest and removed something vital. She pulled his cape tight around her, hating her dragonish need for him, but bereft without him nonetheless.

Hauk offered his hand. "Are you hurt?"

"No," she whispered. "A moment." She took several deep breaths before extending her arms.

He pulled her upright. "I'll protect you."

"Leave before he returns."

Instead, he kissed her knuckles.

Thorne yanked back her hand. "Get out." His attention left her cold.

Seeming puzzled, he massaged the broken nose that marred his northern handsomeness. "I'll guard your door."

Again she laughed. No one could protect her from Bludwelt, not even herself. Hauk frowned and stomped outside. She collapsed on a stool. With Bludwelt gone, she regained herself. He must never touch her again. The next time, she might not resist. She groaned, recalling her half-hearted opposition. Maybe she did owe Hauk something.

At least Bludwelt's Dragon-Fating had vanished, meaning for now, he'd no plans to kill Hellee or any other Dragon. Without Dragon-Fating amplifying his allure, he'd be easier to resist. She downed a second glass of wine. Hereafter, she'd be prepared.

A small voice told her not to deceive herself; she'd never think clearly with him near, especially while fire vines bloomed. The voice also warned that if Bludwelt mated her even once, she'd never escape him.

135

When the camp quieted, she'd flee. Wrapped in Bludwelt's cape, Thorne tried to stay awake, but couldn't. Surprisingly, she slept deeply.

In the morning, Bludwelt woke her, urging her to dress quickly. She cursed herself for failing to escape. After breaking camp, they rode until they reached the edge of Tallasha the Resplendent's territory. If the Dragon found them trespassing, she'd kill them. Rather than going around, Bludwelt risked everyone to remove Thorne from Stonevar.

In the northwest, a black spot on the mountainside marked the entrance to Tallasha's lair, once Gaspotine the Dark's Cavern of Diamonds. There, three years prior, Raspberry-Frost made Thorne drink Dragon blood, starting a life-changing journey. Thorne shivered. If only her Fairy and dearest friend were with her. Raspberry-Frost would warn Thorne about Tallasha's movements, and she could escape.

Now waiting for Tallasha to appear, Thorne's kidnappers, more than a score, surrounded her. Bludwelt wouldn't risk her bolting. In early afternoon, the orange Dragon finally took to the sky, heading away from them. Lord Bludwelt raised his arm and kneed his horse into a gallop. Thorne raced after him, though riding into Tallasha's territory invited death. As they traversed the plain, the sky remained clear of anything larger than a buzzard.

On reaching the mountains, they dismounted. The eldest townsman pulled his wide-brimmed hat low and led them through a rocky ravine. Bludwelt often looked over his shoulder, making certain Thorne followed. Mid-afternoon found them still navigating the cramped passage. No air moved inside the sun-baked crevice. The horses' heads were bowed, their breathing rough, their progress slow. They needed water and rest, but they'd get none until they left Tallasha's domain.

With a high-pitched screech, Tallasha the Resplendent swooped from the clouds.

Bludwelt vaulted onto his horse and yelled, "To the other side!" He slapped his ebony stallion's haunches and galloped past Hauk, setting rocks sliding and horses shying.

Thorne soothed her mount. Bludwelt was a fool and a coward, and she despised him. The Dragon wouldn't fly into the narrow ravine. Tallasha would wait for them to emerge, then kill them.

A guard behind Thorne screamed. She was wrong. Tallasha was small and nimble, apparently practiced at plucking prey from this crevice. The Dragon straddled the chasm and speared the man with her back claws. As Tallasha devoured the rider, his horse dashed toward Thorne. She scrambled up the rocks out of the way. The remaining guards dashed past, leaving her to face Tallasha.

The Dragon wrapped her forked tongue around Thorne, who sensed the ferocity of ten wole-lions surging through Tallasha. Thorne didn't struggle. Instead she pressed her cheek against the raspy tongue. The scent suggested Tallasha neared estrus. The desire to mate made Thorne light-headed.

"Thorne!" Bludwelt shouted, approaching on foot.

"Go back." He had no Dragon-Fating. Tallasha would kill him. Too late, Thorne remembered she wanted him dead. Or did she?

Tallasha dropped Thorne and roared. Bludwelt yanked her upright. His Dragon-Fating had returned, a hundred and seven times stronger, giving him a shimmering dragonish aura that mesmerized her. As the Dragon flew off, Thorne intuited that Bludwelt's strong Dragon-Fating confused and frightened Tallasha. The Dragon had no way of knowing if Bludwelt's Dragon-Fating predicted he would save or take Dragon lives. Thorne suspected the later.

"I thought the Dragon killed you," Bludwelt said, pulling her away.

Had believing Tallasha killed Thorne made him so angry, so vengeful, so empowered that he could kill every Dragon? As she tried to grasp the implications, Bludwelt embraced her. He'd overcome his fear to return for her. She sensed Bludwelt would never fail her nor would his devotion falter. He might betray others but never her. This she knew.

His mouth pressed against hers. She'd little experience with kissing, both times finding it smothering. This kiss traveled the length of her spine, leaving a hot pool at the base. If he threw her on the ground and took her now, she'd welcome it.

"Let her go!" Hauk clasped Bludwelt's shoulder with one hand and his sword with the other. "We must leave before the Dragon returns."

Bludwelt shook him off, all the while watching Thorne. She wanted to kill Hauk for intruding, and knew Bludwelt felt the same. Deferring to Hauk or anyone wasn't like Bludwelt, and she doubted it would last. As they continued through the ravine, Bludwelt's Dragon-Fating vanished; he no longer intended to kill every Dragon. Even without Dragon-Fating, his allure lingered. As he led her though the canyon, everything was brighter, the air sweeter, the sky bluer.

They emerged into a small plain where her guards huddled, clearly terrified. Two more had joined the group: Fexx, gaunter than she remembered, and Daxx, whose dark hair was greasier. Thorne had broken the third brother's neck.

When Daxx whispered something, Lord Bludwelt's answering smile gave her shivers. His spell had lessened enough for Thorne to pull away, but his hand had an iron grip.

"Get the horses!" Bludwelt shouted and the men scurried after their mounts.

They rode a short distance before wading into a stream to water the animals. Thorne checked the sky. Tallasha's absence suggested they'd left her territory. They resumed with Hauk in the lead, and Bludwelt riding beside her, his jaw clenched as if grappling with an unpleasant task. Neither spoke. Though his proximity tormented her, separation was worse.

All day she observed her guards. This one fell asleep in the saddle; that one loved to talk; another stared into the distance. They seemed less vigilant today. Their complacency suited her. She must leave before she lost the will.

At dusk, clouds blocked all but three determined shafts of light cutting the gray haze. Thorne swung her leg over the horse's neck, slid to the ground, and rubbed her tired bottom. She bent backward, stretching her tight muscles, ignoring the drizzle. She welcomed the cooler air as long as a thunderstorm held off.

Three guards followed Thorne as she strolled around the camp, silently berating herself for falling asleep the previous night. That would not happen again. The damp wood smoke stung her eyes and nose, but she'd endure that and worse before entering Bludwelt's tent. If necessary, she'd walk all night.

Then she saw Anders laughing by the fire. Thorne wanted to tear out the throat of the lowborn uzzard—three levels of bastard. Ignorance didn't excuse threatening to kill his own son.

Murderous thoughts distracted her until Hauk snagged her arm and said, "Careful now. There's a—"

"Release her." Bludwelt took her other arm, trapping Thorne in a tug-of-war.

Hauk grinned and let go. "Stopped Thorne from stepping in horse shit."

After giving Hauk a nasty look, Bludwelt escorted Thorne inside his tent. She didn't protest. He'd exchanged riding clothes for a royal blue robe embroidered with two gold dragons, tails at the hem, snouts nosing the shoulder seam.

"Do you require anything, Goddess?"

His fingers seemed to melt into her flesh, and she liked the feeling. "You're a hospitable jailer." She rested her head against his shoulder.

As his breath warmed her ear, he whispered, "You have feelings for Hauk?"

"Perhaps." Dividing her captors might facilitate her escape. And she did feel something—a desire to cut out his heart and grind it to gristle.

Eyes narrowing, Bludwelt clenched his jaw. "Stay inside."

"I need water to wash my clothes and something to wear."

He untied the belt of his robe, letting it fall from his wide shoulders. Curls shimmered on his muscular chest. She grabbed her wrist to keep from touching those white coils.

Bludwelt handed her the robe, and she resisted burying her face in the cloth. He dressed and swept on a black cape that brushed his boot tops. The lines around his mouth softened. "I'll send water, and there's food in my packs. I may not join you this night."

Good. If he stayed away, she might escape. After he left, she undressed and slipped on the silky robe still warm from his skin. The back of her legs shivered like a mare in heat. Thorne downed the wine he'd opened for her and refilled her glass.

After washing her clothes, she chewed jerky from the pack, willing the guards to sleep. She washed down the dried meat with more wine. She must flee before Bludwelt overcame her weak resistance.

Her behavior would seem inexplicable to those who hadn't drunk Dragon blood. She couldn't predict Strumgued's reaction. Would he believe Bekka? How would he interpret her leaving with Hauk when no Dwarf would ever kidnap another? Might her absence anger him enough to cast out the Humans?

After refilling her wine glass, she watched smoke rise from the fire and escape through the opening overhead. A Fairy-Dragon flew down the hole, making her jump. Chirping happily, it landed on her shoulder.

"Quist!"

CHAPTER THIRTY-ONE

After Thorne fell asleep, Quist flew out the tent's smoke hole, holding his breath to avoid inhaling fumes. Nevertheless, he perched on the roof, coughing and sneezing.

Quist liked Thorne, but then he liked everyone, including Hellestorm's many Human mothers. Mostly though, the large races confused him. They fought over shadows, and came and went for reasons having nothing to do with eating or mating. Mostly he ignored them, and would've ignored Thorne's absence, but the Dragon whelp mewled for her, and Hellestorm's Little Mother moaned, which made baby Aeron cry. Quist couldn't bear all that sadness, so he'd decided to tell Thorne to return, then everyone would be happy again.

However, when he'd stuck his tongue in Thorne's ear and said, "Home," she stayed in that smoky tent, making him turn from black to red. What would convince her? She wasn't gathering food; they'd plenty at Stonevar. She'd had plenty of time to mate with the males here, so why stay?

Now as he cleaned his hide, he decided Thorne didn't understand him, and someone else must tell her. To find his way back, he marked the stars' positions by opening the scales protecting his third eye, which detected even the tiniest change in light or shadows. Then he started toward Stonevar.

At sunrise, he met the Dwarf Lord and his party waiting by the forest marking Tallasha's territory. Strumgued batted at Quist. Since Dragons were rarely kind to their Fairy-Dragons, dwarfish behavior didn't offend Quist, who stuck his tongue in Strumgued's ear and said, "Thorne."

When the Dwarf tried to crush Quist, the Fairy-Dragon decided he'd have to go all the way back to Stonevar to tell someone smarter. But then Raspberry-Frost arrived with Hellestorm's many mothers.

After Quist told the Fairy about Thorne, Raspberry-Frost bit Strumgued's ear, which delighted Quist.

The Fairy spoke to the Dwarf. Quist understood less than half, but grasped the part about the Dwarf following the Fairy-Dragon. Quist was the only Fairy-Dragon here. That must mean him.

"Lead the way, beastie," Strumgued said, pointing in the wrong direction.

Quist wasn't sure what a beastie was, but he was certain the Dwarf wasn't praising him. At the first opportunity, he'd put a sour-tasting bug in the Dwarf Lord's beer.

While they traveled, Quist sat on the Dwarf Lord's shoulder. If Strumgued turned the wrong way, Quist nipped his ear. The Fairy-Dragon didn't like the taste—Dwarf blood tasted like rusty iron—but Strumgued would heed nothing else.

Even after Quist led them safely through Tallasha's territory, the Dwarf still called him a beastie. Did Strumgued also call Thorne names? Was that why she didn't like him?

CHAPTER THIRTY-TWO

Lord Bludwelt ordered ten men to surround Thorne's tent. No one should leave or enter. He wanted Thorne secured while he dealt with Hauk. But first he moved to the trees where the horses were tethered, and pressed his cheek to Thorne's saddle. Her nearness made separation unendurable. He'd known she was meant for him since he'd seen her in Seahaven's town square. Only he could win a woman that strong, and only she was worthy to be his wife.

Boisterous laughter interrupted his thoughts. Hauk brayed loudest. Picturing the whip around his neck quickened Bludwelt's pulse. Hauk's overly familiar attitude toward Thorne suggested the captain had taken improper liberties. Hauk would pay for that, along with not knowing the Dwarfs returned to Stonevar.

Fexx tugged his arm. "Is your head paining, Goadran?"

Lord Bludwelt moved away from Thorne's saddle, glancing to see if anyone had heard Fexx call him by his birth name, but no one was nearby. "Kind of you to inquire." He rubbed his forehead. "It aches a bit." Although it didn't; after drinking Dragon blood, he never sickened.

With thin fingers, Fexx scratched his straw-like hair. "Ma recommends feverfew."

The brothers' mother had returned to Seahaven after more than a decade of silence. Her two living sons provided her with all coin she needed, so she'd retired from whoring. Fortunate for her; toothless, she attracted few customers. Regardless, Fexx and Daxx were pleased. Bludwelt not as much, since she caused the brothers to neglect their duties, and he abhorred inconvenience.

Now barrel-chested Daxx, carrying an armful of firewood,

scuttled toward Bludwelt on bowed legs. With his dark hair and complexion Daxx looked nothing like the fair and lanky Fexx. Clearly, the brothers had different fathers.

"Unsaddle this horse," Bludwelt ordered.

"Right away, your grace." Fexx gave an exaggerated bow for the others' benefit.

Bludwelt smiled a half-smile as he strode to Hauk's tent where the captain and five sailors joked around a fire. "Hauk," Bludwelt called from the shadows, "walk with me."

Hauk, flashing a familiar insolent grin, brushed debris from his bottom. "Need help handling the Goddess?"

His sailors laughed. Bludwelt wanted to whip them; instead, he strode toward a stand of pines. Hauk caught up. When Anders followed with a torch, Bludwelt didn't object.

"Speak respectfully to me before the men." Bludwelt kept his tone friendly.

"No disrespect intended. No one knows better than I how difficult Thorne can be. I spent a summer with her."

Bludwelt took three deep breaths. "Your irreverence toward her strains my good nature." He cleared his throat. "We should split up. Take your men. Create a false trail leading to the sea. I'll take the Goddess north, and we'll meet at O'Harbor."

Hauk cocked his head. "Better if I stay. Anders and my crew can prepare the ship."

Bludwelt had foreseen this. "Very well." He motioned for Hauk to follow.

When they reached the forest, an animal scurried away through fallen pine needles. Bludwelt sniffed. Wole-weasel.

Hauk rubbed his eye. "I'll give orders in the morning."

"Tonight."

"I'm done in. A seafarer, not cavalry." Hauk rubbed his thighs.

Bludwelt put a hand on Anders's shoulder. "Tell the crew to avoid waking their captain when they leave at dawn."

Hauk shook his head. "I'll tell my crew."

"Stay," Bludwelt said. "We've a detail to discuss."

"I'll relay the message, Captain." Anders passed Hauk the torch.

Hauk nodded, and Anders left.

"After we have Thorne safely aboard your ship, I'll send our demands to Stonevar."

"Good." Captain Hauk's gaze followed Anders. "I'll check on the Goddess."

"No need."

A smirk twisted Hauk's mouth. "You object?"

"Tonight, my men guard Thorne." Under his cape, Bludwelt slipped a dagger from its sheath. "This'll take only a moment." The fool was so predictable. He deserved to die.

CHAPTER THIRTY-THREE

How could she fall asleep again? Thorne groaned. She'd probably still be unconscious if the racket from breaking camp hadn't woken her. She jumped to her feet and knocked over her cup from last night, disturbing three flies. Her slumber couldn't be from the wine; brew didn't affect her. The spill had the appealing scent of rotting flesh. Dragonwort.

Bludwelt had drugged the wine. With the camp odors, his dragonish scent, and him muddling her, she hadn't detected it. To contain her dragonish fury, she held her breath, squeezed her mouth shut, and fisted her hands. She'd been foolish to think she would easily escape him. Worse, if he knew about dragonwort, then he knew she'd drunk Dragon blood. What else did he know?

She needed Raspberry-Frost's help. Even Quist had deserted her. She'd no time for self-pity; she must make an escape plan. But all she could think about was cutting out her captors' hearts and stomping on them. Being barely Human, they probably wouldn't notice until next spring when they changed shirts.

Until she thought of a scheme, she must act naturally. She called for water, and a dirty hand passed her a jar. She stripped and washed.

"After you eat, we'll resume our journey," Lord Bludwelt said from the doorway.

Not bothering to cover herself, she faced him. "How long have you . . ." It didn't matter.

His eyes raked her. She threw the contents of the water jar at him. Dragon blood had stolen her modesty, but violating her privacy was a good excuse for throwing something. Watching water dribble down his clothes delighted her.

He lifted a hand. Thorne stepped closer, daring him to strike her. If he did, she'd claw out his eyes.

"Do not vex me." He brushed drops from his face and crumpled shirt. "I've had no sleep." His voice was tight. The irritation narrowing his eyes flared into malevolent fire, his temper more strained than a sleepless night warranted. "When your horse is saddled, be ready." He set a bowl and bread on the table then left.

By the time Thorne found her horse, Hauk and his sailors were gone; yet no one remarked or seemed uneasy. What if they'd returned to Stonevar? If Hauk's crew harmed anyone, she'd never forgive herself. She must escape, but the morning offered no opportunity. With Lord Bludwelt in the lead, they followed a path through grassland toward the northern coast, stopping often to rest the horses despite a late start.

After the midday meal, Lord Bludwelt flicked rocks off a log with his whip. The shadows under his eyes were dark as muddy water. "Bring me wine," he told no one in particular.

A boy of about twelve approached carrying a silver goblet. Eyes on the cup and tongue protruding, he pushed dirty blond hair off his forehead as he stepped over a tree root.

Bludwelt rewound his whip. "Now!"

The scurrying boy bumbled into Lord Bludwelt's side, splashing wine down his trouser leg.

"Oaf." Bludwelt pointed to an ironwood tree. "Fexx, tie this clod to that branch."

"He didn't mean it." Fexx squeezed the boy's shoulder. "He's only a lad."

Lord Bludwelt snorted disgust over Fexx making a pet of him. "Daxx, you tie him."

Bandy-legged Daxx secured the boy's bony wrists to the tree while Fexx sniffed. Thorne couldn't believe Bludwelt would flog a boy for so small an offence.

Bludwelt snapped the lash with a loud crack. The tip flicked the boy's back. The strike could've hurt no more than a bee sting, but he yelped and squirmed.

Thorne's stomach cramped as she remembered arriving in Seahaven three years before, hoping to find work to repay her bride price. Instead she witnessed a girl flogged for disobeying her father after he caught her kissing Anders. No boy would be whipped publicly for so small an offense. Thorne still heard the girl's screams in her nightmares.

Thorne cringed when a second crack ripped the boy's shirt.

He wailed and tugged at his bonds, as blood wet his shoulder. "Your lordship, forgive my clumsiness!"

Fexx wiped his nose and mumbled. Lord Bludwelt's grin dug cruel lines into the corners of his mouth. Rose couldn't stop that girl's whipping, but Thorne could stop this.

She risked clasping Lord Bludwelt's forearm. No Dragon-Fating tingles. For now, he'd no intention of harming a Dragon. He'd changed his mind. "Do me a service. Spare this lad. I distracted him."

Lord Bludwelt spoke through gritted teeth. "You're too forgiving, Goddess. Leaders must show strength."

On tiptoes, she brushed her lips against his ear. "Daxx and Fexx worship you. Would you have the same from this lad? Show him mercy, and he'll never forsake you. Fear or loyalty—you choose."

Bludwelt relaxed. "Daxx, release him."

The sniffling boy ran to Lord Bludwelt and kissed his knees. "Thank you, your lordship. Thank you."

Lord Bludwelt's smile made Thorne shiver. Fexx nodded thanks at Thorne. She returned the nod, but knew he was no friend.

Witnessing more of Bludwelt's cruelty changed nothing. Thorne couldn't hate him more or resist licking her lips, tasting him in the breeze as they rode.

She saw no occasion to escape while passing through woodland, but how hard was she looking? She could resist Bludwelt no more than Fairies resisted the raspberries used to trap them.

At twilight they made camp. Thorne hurried inside the tent. After her guards slept, she'd cut a hole, kill a guard if necessary, and escape. Her plan depended on Bludwelt staying away. Would he?

She dug inside Bludwelt's pack for something to eat, but instead of barley cakes, found Hauk's shell necklace. She squeezed it so tight her knuckles blanched. Bludwelt had stolen her revenge. At least Thorne's sword wouldn't bring Willow-Bender more pain; the Giantess had once almost died taking a sword cut Thorne intended for Hauk. Why Willow-Bender loved the self-serving Hauk, Thorne never understood. His charms were as false as his tales.

Thorne stroked the necklace's misshapen black pearl. Why leave it where she'd find it? Had Bludwelt thought she'd be grateful, or was it a warning? Whichever, if she didn't go tonight, she never would. She stuffed the necklace inside her tunic pocket and listened.

The chatter and shuffling suggested only two guarded the rear. She slipped the knife from her boot and slowly cut a knee-high slit between them. Then she willed the guards to sleep.

Before hearing snores, she smelled Bludwelt. Bumps rose on her skin. She arranged the blue tent lining over the cut, sheathed her dagger, and scrambled to the stool, where she posed goddess-like, haughty and bored. At least so she hoped.

Bludwelt pushed aside the tent flap and stepped inside, his head grazing the ceiling, his silvery musk scenting the air. Thorne held her breath to keep her thoughts clear a little longer. She must convince him to leave. But how?

Desperate for air, she breathed him in, undercutting her determination to focus. "Where are Captain Hauk and his sailors?"

He unbuckled his scabbard and passed it to the guard outside. "Readying the ship."

Good. At least they hadn't returned to Stonevar. However, for herself, nothing could be worse than Bludwelt's plan to take her from Elysia—on a ship he'd always be close. Light-headed, she clutched the stool seat. Would Strumgued look for her? Dwarfs didn't have ships and hated ocean travel. Once at sea, no one would find her, and she'd have no way to flee. Knowing all this, she couldn't look away from Bludwelt.

"Wood," he called to someone outside. He took the logs provided and lit a fire.

"Does Hauk trust you enough to leave me alone with you?" His telling the truth shouldn't matter so much.

Bludwelt removed his leather vest and damp shirt. Sweat dotted his chest as he stretched backward. This show was for her. Still she grew hotter than the small fire warranted.

He extended his arm out the tent opening. "Water." He tipped the jar provided over his head, letting water stream down his chest onto the hairs curling over his trousers.

Thorne dropped her gaze to banish thoughts of sucking droplets from those white coils. "Why send Hauk away?"

His eyes narrowed. "I found his attendance on you distasteful."

She sensed this was true.

With his shirt, he dried his face and chest, then handed it out the tent flap with orders to wash it. "Do you pine for him?"

"I long for no man." Her skin was hot, and she hugged a knee to stop herself from moving closer. The fire vines must be in full bloom.

His mouth turned up a little as he retrieved a bottle of wine, two cups, and a pipe from his pack. "Then I'm fortunate to be more than a man."

She stiffened. He couldn't know everything. He'd no one like Raspberry-Frost to explain how drinking Dragon blood changed a person. Still he was clever. Though she tried to sound imperious, her voice quavered. "Imprisoning me will have dire consequences."

When he handed her wine, his little finger brushed hers. She flinched, expecting to see a burn. Nothing. Mustn't touch the raspberries, Thorne reminded herself, remembering how Raspberry-Frost couldn't resist the berries baiting a Fairy trap.

He packed and lit his pipe, then slowly exhaled gray smoke. The scent of smokeroot kindled memories of Brutte, lowering her guard further.

Bludwelt's eyes softened. "We'll make a magnificent pair."

Her mouth was dry, but the wine smelled of dragonwort, so she only pretended to sip. "Are you suggesting marriage?"

"I am."

Evidently the irony of imprisoning her while trying to win her eluded him. "I cannot bear children."

"Disappointing, but I never cared overmuch for them."

Thorne's resolve thinned even more. She stood, but her voice was weak. "Leave, so I may retire."

He set his pipe on the table. "Not this night."

With the confidence of a wole-lion, Bludwelt offered his hand. She tottered back. His shadow darkened the tent walls around her. He gripped her wrist and nipped the inside, sending fire flashing up her arm. His low character repelled her, yet she couldn't pull away. He breathed harder. She stopped.

"Some say I desire only power and gold, but that's not true. I want Stonevar's Goddess." The elongated pupils of his amber eyes widened.

He held her wrists behind her back and pushed her shirt away exposing her shoulder. She didn't resist. When he bit, an involuntary rumble erupted from her throat. For a long moment, nothing existed but the overwhelming sensation of rising higher. Her dragonish strength surged, convincing her that she could lift the world. Now she understood how Rustofona gained stamina enough to keep herself and Vainglorian airborne while the two Dragons mated.

When Bludwelt released her, Thorne swayed and touched her chest, feeling skin. Her shirt was gone, her trousers low on her hips. She turned away, yanking them up, reminding herself that he'd threatened to kill Aeron and Hellee. She reached for the dagger sheathed inside her boot.

He clasped her waist from behind. When she leaned against him, the voice insisting she stab him faded. She'd kill him after they mated.

"Bludwelt," she whispered.

His tongue traced her neck. With Gaspotine's blood binding them, their joining seemed destined, the reason she'd seen no opportunity to leave him. He mouthed her shoulder. She shivered. If she let him take her, he'd think he owned her. Unable to escape and unwilling to surrender, she'd no choice.

Thorne joined Bludwelt's mind and took their spirits into chaos.

CHAPTER THIRTY-FOUR

Thorne had vowed never to return to the Dragon Continuum, convinced her spirit would fail to rejoin her body a second time. Knowing what to expect did little to ease this visit. The first time she'd felt as if something had ripped apart her ribs to yank out her spirit.

Now Bludwelt flailed in the Silver River, jerking and screaming as he clutched at Thorne's misty form. Their spirits floundered inside a hurricane of swirling reds, blues, yellows, and colors she couldn't name. High and low pitched squeals battered her ears. The odor of fungi, spoiled meat, and rotting seaweed burned her nostrils. Worse, the stink of roses—Da planted them over graves—seemed to predict her death. The first time Thorne thought she'd lost all reason, but Rustofona the Magnificent, who'd brought Thorne, taught her to shape the jumbled sights, sounds, and smells into the familiar.

Now Bludwelt bellowed, "What's happening?"

"Memories overwhelm you." Thorne pulled him from the river, where the wide band of water undulated up, down, and sometimes sideways. "Picture this. We kneel on blue grass by the shore of time's Silver River. Crickets sing and wole-wolves harmonize."

"I hear them." He sounded calmer.

"Violet mountains rise before you. Golden snow crowns azure spruce." The mountain peaks and trees were more vivid this time. Could Bludwelt be the reason?

"I see them."

His voice was strong. He didn't beg to return as she had. His trust surprised her.

"Where are we?" he asked.

152

"The Dragon Continuum, where all times exist. Past, present, and future."

"Did you bring us here?"

"Yes." Thorne was amazed it worked.

"We have wings." He rubbed his against her, with the velvety touch of a thistle bloom.

When Bludwelt's vaporous wings enfolded her, she couldn't tell where her misty form ended and his began.

"What are we?"

"Spirits."

Thorne moved her wings, and they rose into the heavens where sapphire stars sparkled in a yellow sky. Her wingspan was bigger than last time, four times her height, as if she'd grown more dragonish. She'd worry about that later.

They swooped as one toward the glistening Silver River. She sensed a dragonish bond growing between them. Too late, she realized that escaping to the Continuum was another kind of snare.

"Are those Dragons along the shore?" He sounded more curious than concerned.

"Yes. The elder Dragons spirits are white and larger here than in the flesh."

They banked into a grassy mountain valley where they caught an updraft. She didn't want this to end. Maybe in the Continuum, it didn't have to.

"Can they hurt us?" he asked.

"I don't see how."

"Why do they come here?" Bludwelt asked as they ascended into ruby clouds smelling like deer blood.

Thorne licked her lips. "This is the only place they can gather peacefully."

"Why do they travel the river?"

"To see their pasts and futures." The river was quiet, suggesting nothing endangered Dragon-kind, and Thorne didn't want their Human presence to agitate it. When Erramon the Eldest considered Thorne a threat, he sent Vainglorian the Red to kill everyone at Stonevar. Before she or Bludwelt did something that threatened Dragon destiny, they must leave. But once again, she didn't know how to return. And if they did, would their passion fade or burn brighter? She suspected the latter.

"How can I see the future?" Bludwelt asked.

She felt compelled to explain. "Ride your gold stream."

"How do I find it?"

"Your own glows brightest. Jump in and you'll land in your current."

Below them, a half-dozen Dragons traveled the past. Two swam into the future. Those on the bank discussed raising whelps. All agreed that Dragons must be tough and fierce.

Thorne and Bludwelt entered the river where their gold streams entwined.

Bludwelt opened and closed his wings while peering into the river. "I see us inside the tent."

"Our present." She and Bludwelt lay on the floor, her back to him, his arms tight around her, so close they could've been mating. Maybe they were. She couldn't remember.

A ball of mist, the size of a cow, came toward them from the past and unrolled into Rustofona the Magnificent, a ninth her living size. "Raspberry-Frost's Human returns."

"I never thought I'd greet Rustofona the Magnificent again."

Behind Thorne, Bludwelt said, "That Dragon's dead. Hauk killed her."

"I am one of the bloodless." The Dragon swung head and tail, then seemed to lose the battle with an invisible enemy, stuck her head between her legs, and rolled back into a ball.

"Why did she do that?" Bludwelt asked.

Rustofona answered, "It eases the torment of the Niede, which demands I return to my body."

"You have none." Thorne immediately regretted saying this.

The Dragon shuddered. Thorne wanted to help Rustofona. But how?

Rustofona unrolled partway. Her smoky tongue flicked the scar on Thorne's chin. "My whelp eats fish guts."

"The Dragon Guards work hard to mother and protect him." She was proud of that.

"You destroy him."

"What do you mean?"

"He eats entrails. How will his teeth become sharp without tearing flesh and bone? How will he grow strong without red blood?"

The Dragon raked the grass with her claws, ripping off her talon tips. "He plays like a kitten. A Dragon must attack and kill."

When Bludwelt swept his wings protectively about Thorne, she was grateful. "Hellee's only a—"

"You gentle Hellestorm like a dog. Never let him feel fear." Rustofona's foggy fangs lengthened.

Thorne spread her wings to appear larger. "He's a baby."

"Desist, daughter." Gaspotine came from the future. His large spirit was similar to his living size of fifteen workhorses.

"You're Hellestorm's grandfather?"

Rustofona swung her head. "Erramon the Eldest says Hellestorm will never be a proper Dragon."

"You chose a Human to raise him," Gaspotine told Rustofona. "Now endure what Hellestorm the Great will become."

"Who's this?" Bludwelt asked Thorne.

"Gaspotine the Dark."

"How does he know the whelp will be great?" Bludwelt's curiosity put Thorne on guard.

Rustofona answered, "Gaspotine is the supreme current rider."

"Meaning?" Bludwelt seemed to have lost all fear.

"Gaspotine can ride other Dragons' currents and see their tomorrows," Rustofona said proudly.

"Can I view someone else's future?" Bludwelt closed his wings as if that would hide his thoughts.

"I don't know." Thorne hoped he couldn't. No good would come from it.

Bludwelt moved against the current into his future. Ahead his gold stream churned and branched. What did it mean? Nothing good.

Gaspotine pointed a claw at the swirling water. "Humans change their small minds often." He wrapped his smoky tongue around Thorne's head.

She didn't resist, though she sensed his attraction and abhorrence for Humans with Dragon-Fating. "I won't disturb the river." She couldn't say the same for Bludwelt.

"Then why bring the Dragon-killer here?"

Did he know Bludwelt hired Hauk to kill Rustofona, or was it worse? "If Bludwelt intended harm, he'd have Dragon-Fating." Defending Bludwelt felt right. Being with him felt wonderful. This couldn't be good. She must escape before the link between them became unbreakable.

"He hasn't the Power at present, Blood-drinker." Gaspotine clawed Thorne's wings, shredding them. "But the Dragon-killer's future is uncertain. Keep him from Hellestorm. Choose the future where your streams twine. That will provide safety for Hellestorm."

"You said to keep him from Hellee." Thorne pieced her tattered wings together.

"Heed my words, Blood-drinker, and Hellestorm will be great."

From the waters at Thorne's feet, Strumgued shouted, "Release my wife!"

CHAPTER THIRTY-FIVE

The Dwarf Lord had come for her. How unexpected. She'd always had to rescue herself.

Strumgued pressed his fingers to Thorne's neck, as if determining whether she lived. His touch tugged her consciousness. Her little finger twitched. Thorne opened one eye, then the other, took a deep breath. Strumgued's musky iron scent, seasoned with horse sweat, cleared her mind.

Her husband stood with sword drawn. Lines cut into the corners of his mouth. Dust coated his helmet and armor, as if he'd ridden without rest. Outside Bludwelt's tent, metal clanged against metal. Warriors yelled battle cries. The rusty smell of Human blood blighted the air.

Lord Bludwelt groaned, lying on his side, still holding her. "What in hellfire happened?"

Strumgued stomped closer. "Release my wife."

"Your wife?" Bludwelt repeated. He adjusted his trousers and rose, pulling Thorne with him.

One look at her husband's narrowed eyes and bared teeth, and she crumpled, forcing Bludwelt to let go. Cold hardened Thorne's nipples. She refastened her trousers and felt around for her shirt but couldn't find it.

Fury flashed in Bludwelt's eyes. Clearly, he wanted Strumgued dead. But Thorne knew the Dwarf Lord would prove difficult to kill.

"Who is this beastly creature?" Bludwelt asked, seeming reluctant to believe Thorne had wed Strumgued.

She scooted away on her buttocks, croaking, "My husband." She hadn't told Bludwelt about her coerced wedding. Admitting it shamed her.

Strumgued glared at his opponent. "You've assaulted my wife."

It surprised Thorne that Bludwelt wasn't already dead. Maybe finding them unconscious startled her husband out of an impulsive strike.

"Thorne neglected to mention that she'd wed." Bludwelt reached toward his pack.

"Stand fast." Strumgued's tone was calm, though his sword pointed at Bludwelt's heart.

Bludwelt gestured at his naked chest. "May I retrieve a shirt?"

Strumgued nodded. Thorne suspected that honor stopped him from skewering the unarmed man.

Under Strumgued's glower, she held up the knife from her boot. "I intended to kill him."

Bludwelt's laugh broadcast his disbelief.

The Dwarf gestured toward Lord Bludwelt's crotch. "Not before he pierced you with his dagger."

Strumgued didn't believe her, either. Saying she'd hoped her sanity would return after mating wouldn't calm her husband. So she pressed a palm to her heart. "Pray continue with my rescue."

Strumgued's mouth tightened. Evidently, he wasn't amused.

Bludwelt held up his hands. "Will you slay one unwitting of his offense?"

Would Bludwelt talk his way out of this?

Deep lines split Strumgued's forehead. "The Goddess did not willingly accompany you."

Lord Bludwelt offered a lazy smile, though his amber eyes smoldered. "I'm not the sailor who took her. In truth, I killed the scoundrel."

Thorne nodded, then wondered why she'd helped Bludwelt.

Strumgued appeared unconvinced. "You detained her."

"She came willingly," Bludwelt said.

"To remove him from Stonevar," she explained.

Eyes hard as granite, Strumgued said evenly, "You've dishonored my wife. But her abductor's killer has earned a warrior's death." He shouted for a sword, and someone passed him one through the tent door.

Thorne took this opportunity to locate her shirt under the table and listen for sounds outside—the battle continued. War cries, screams, swords clanging against metal.

Strumgued gave the weapon to Bludwelt, who immediately struck at the Dwarf's head. Though Strumgued blocked with the flat of his sword, his snort indicated a strike stronger than anticipated.

Unexpected heat rushed up Thorne's neck at the dragonish thrill of two males fighting. Perhaps the fates would finally favor her, and they'd kill each other.

"To the death!" Strumgued cried as he lunged, following through with his body to add force. Thorne envied his technique. She should've asked him to train her. Too late now. She'd live happily with that regret.

Bludwelt parried with a loud grunt, face twisting with strain. Strumgued could easily best a Human fighter, but not this dragonish man. Thorne's blood surged.

Lord Bludwelt aimed his sword between the Dwarf's eyes. "When did you creep from the bowels of your mountain into the light?"

Strumgued grunted. "Years before you crawled from the whore that birthed you."

Roaring, Bludwelt swung a circular cut. Strumgued ducked and counter-cut to his opponent's knee.

The tall man jumped back. The Dwarf's short height disadvantaged him little inside the confining tent. Though less elegant than Strumgued's, Bludwelt's attacks were powerful and his blade fluid. "You're a niggling troll, with a nose like goat bollocks."

"Have care when you wipe your beak that you don't cut your hand." The Dwarf Lord smiled and slashed.

Thorne's heart battered her ribs. She hoped they battled for hours before killing each other.

Lord Bludwelt deflected, arcing his blade into a high cut, slicing open the tent roof as he attempted to split Strumgued's skull. The Dwarf let Bludwelt's sword slide off his own and moved into a counterstroke—a cleaving blow toward his opponent's arm.

Bludwelt dodged and returned an off-balance jab. "Binding a goddess to a Dwarf is a perversion."

"We shall see who proves worthy."

Bludwelt's silvery musk intensified, making her breathe as heavily as the combatants.

Strumgued feinted. Bludwelt jerked sideways, then thrust hard, dashing Strumgued's sword aside, forcing the Dwarf back and preventing a counter-hit.

If she distracted Strumgued, Bludwelt would kill him. Afterward, she'd stab Bludwelt even if she must mate with him first. Then she'd be free from them both.

While Thorne plotted, Bludwelt hurled his sword at Strumgued and yelled, "Now."

The Dwarf jumped aside.

Bludwelt's shoulder struck the back of the tent. Someone whipped up the cut bottom, and he rolled under. Voices outside urged Bludwelt to hurry. Saddles creaked. Hooves pounded grassland.

Strumgued, eyes wide with astonishment, stood braced for battle. "He's run off." Clearly, he'd never witnessed such dishonor.

"Bludwelt's a coward." But surely he considered his expeditious escape essential.

"A false jewel in a rich setting," Strumgued observed before rushing outside.

Surely Strumgued would divorce her now.

CHAPTER THIRTY-SIX

Cramps struck her mid-section, dropping Thorne to her knees. Her burning insides clenched, disabling her for some minutes, which she spent loathing herself for still wanting Bludwelt.

The fighting outside had stopped. Thorne stumbled to the door, dagger ready. The tent flap flew open, and Thorne raised her knife, planning to slit the intruder's throat.

A blackened face peered inside.

She checked again before lowering her arm. "What's on your face?"

Zarra's crooked teeth gleamed in the firelight. "Soot."

Thorne followed Zarra outside. In the eerily quiet night, dark clouds scuttled across the moon. The odor of Human blood was stronger. Torchlight illuminated a small band striding over the hill, and Thorne inhaled the sweet scent of the Dragon Guards. She embraced each one. Bekka came last, wearing an uncharacteristic frown.

"Not your fault." Thorne hugged her longest, soothing her tearless sobs and apologies. After Bekka calmed, Thorne asked with trepidation, "Who protects Hellee?"

"Emera," Nella answered.

Thorne inhaled sharply. The last time Emera guarded Hellee, Strumgued killed Brutte. They must return before something terrible happened.

The Giantess seemed to sense something amiss. "You well?" She held out Dracodurus.

"Well enough." Thorne took her sword, vowing never to surrender it again. She welcomed Quist to her shoulder, not minding his pinching claws. "Where are Bludwelt's men?"

"Here and there." Willow-Bender held up a torch, illuminating the bodies.

"Any of you hurt?" After everyone reassured her, Thorne pressed the shell necklace into the Giantess's hand.

Lip quivering, the Giantess stared at it. "The endless sleep?"

Thorne nodded, grateful she hadn't had to slay Hauk. "By Lord Bludwelt's hand."

Willow-Bender slumped.

Thorne clasped the Giantess's arms. "You couldn't save him this time." Willow-Bender had almost died protecting him from Thorne's sword. To save her life, Thorne had offered her Dragon blood. The Giantess drank. What choice had she?

Now Willow-Bender bent over, shaking. Thorne helped her to a log and motioned the others away. Her shaking became shudders, as if she battled to hold her grief inside.

Grandfather wrote that while Dwarfs expressed their feelings, their Giant cousins repressed theirs. Shaking preceded violent Giant behavior. If restrained, they chewed the ropes until their teeth broke. Some jumped off mountaintops or stormed towns, forcing the townspeople to flee. Some overturned wagons and tossed animals. Only death ended their rampages.

Years of suppressed emotions—her clan's rejection; Hauk mating Thorne; grieving for Lily—clearly tormented Willow-Bender. But whatever happened, Thorne didn't think she could kill the Giantess.

Thorne hugged Willow-Bender and hummed. The other Dragon Guards also embraced the Giantess until her shudders subsided. A rampage seemed deflected for the present.

Afterward the twins sat on either side of Willow-Bender. Thorne would thank Lott when she saw him. Few husbands would be so tolerant of their wives leaving to rescue Thorne.

"Do nightmares still trouble you?" Spangle asked Glitter.

"They've almost disappeared." Glitter didn't say she slept in Willow-Bender's room now.

Thorne jumped up, pointing Dracodurus in the direction where dry grasses crackled. "Who's there?"

From the darkness, Torvald, the young Dwarf who'd won Cayeseed's affection, stepped forward.

Thorne lowered her sword. "Thank you for aiding me."

He bowed. "It is my duty to serve you."

Thorne nodded, surprised but pleased. "We'll tarry until Lord Strumgued returns."

As more Dwarf warriors emerged from the darkness, she thanked them. Each replied, "No need, Lady Strumgued. It is my duty."

The title made her cringe. Still, Thorne couldn't quite believe that fifty Dwarfs had come. She hadn't thought Strumgued valued her this much. She looked for Waldemar, who hated Dragons as much as his father. Evidently Strumgued's son had stayed behind. Chills struck Thorne. With Strumgued gone and Emera guarding Hellee, Waldemar might invent a reason to kill the whelp. She must return quickly.

While they waited for Strumgued, Torvald said, "An unsatisfying battle. Kidnappers are unworthy of a warrior's death."

They quieted as Strumgued approached muttering, "Vile coward. Cur, blackguard," and less polite names.

Thorne sped to him, and he reined in his horse.

"Have you slain him?" She was uncertain what she hoped to hear.

"He runs like a craven wole-weasel vanishing into a hole. Darkness hides his trail."

"He's clever." A gift of Dragon blood, which besides making him dragonish, intensified traits he already possessed. She bowed her head but watched Strumgued. "I've stained your honor. Divorce me."

In the torchlight, Strumgued's green eyes glowed. "I disbelieved you were a goddess until tonight. Your spell stopped his foul intent."

His reasoning, so close to the truth, surprised her. She supposed taking Bludwelt into the Dragon Continuum would appear like a spell. She stifled a groan. Escaping into the Continuum had stolen Strumgued's reason to divorce her. If only she'd waited.

But Thorne still needed his good will so he'd pardon Zarra. "No living man has bedded me." She looked away, despising the necessity of her words. "I would've killed Bludwelt."

From the saddle, Strumgued patted his horse's neck. His tone was gentle. "I doubt the coward will return."

She met his gaze. "He'll return for me until his last heartbeat."

"Then I shall rest easier, anticipating another opportunity to slay him." He motioned for her to follow and they rejoined the others. "Bring the prisoner forward."

Two Dwarfs hauled the bound boy, the one who'd spilled Bludwelt's wine, before Strumgued. The boy fell to his knees, blood matting his hair. The Dwarf Lord clutched the grip of his sheathed sword. Did he intend to kill the boy? She wouldn't tolerate it.

Strumgued removed his helmet and wiped his brow with a forearm. "Tell all you meet of the alliance between Goddess and Dwarf. Tell them Stonevar's Dragon lives and will spew a fiery death on invaders."

His mercy pleased Thorne, along with his reference to Stonevar's Dragon. Was he finally accepting Hellee?

"Remove his bonds." After the boy sped off, Strumgued bellowed, "We ride!"

At his signal, the group galloped after the torchbearers, following a river winding south. Thorne pressed her cheek against Wild-Eyes. The warhorse was a smoother ride than the bony nag Lord Bludwelt provided. Strumgued rode beside her. Light from the torches illuminated his cheeks, still flushed with lingering anger.

Hooves shushed through the long grasses and splashed through streams. A night breeze stroked Thorne's face. Strumgued didn't question her about Bludwelt. Did he think Lord Bludwelt an ordinary man? Did he think her resemblance to Bludwelt coincidence? Thorne couldn't guess.

Strumgued's saddle creaked as he shifted. "Your Dragon Guards fought well."

"I'm honored to call them my friends." Strumgued seemed calmer so she risked a question. "How did you find me?"

He grunted. "An enigmatic journey. First I followed a false trail."

Of course Bludwelt would've made one. Now she realized that for the last few days, she hadn't been thinking clearly, hadn't seriously considered the Dragon Guards or her husband rescuing her.

He pointed to Quist perched on Thorne's shoulder. "That beastie pestered me. Kept sticking his tongue in my ear." Strumgued made a fist. "I tried to crush him, but he eluded my grasp. Then that wretched Fairy of yours bit me. Afterward a devilish thing happened. I understood its uttering."

Thorne didn't tell him that Raspberry-Frost had given him a bit of Fairy glamour. He wouldn't welcome the gift.

"The Fairy insisted I follow that beastie on your shoulder."

Quist chewed her hair affectionately. When they stopped, she'd overturn rocks until she found the Fairy-Dragon a juicy grub. But where was Raspberry-Frost? Thorne felt deserted.

"What words did Raspberry-Frost speak?"

"Heed the Fairy-Dragon. Though simple and carefree, he followed my Human, who has need of thee. The beastie perched on my shoulder as I rode. If I didn't go where he wanted, he nipped my ear. Seemed to enjoy my blood."

Thorne smiled. "Thank you for aiding me."

His disgusted grunt made his horse jerk its head. "A husband's duty."

His duty. "Did you rescue me so you wouldn't be dishonored? Did you expect me to take my own life before disgracing you?" Wild-Eyes shook her head until Thorne loosed her grip on the reins.

"I don't presume to judge a goddess."

"If you do, expect disappointment." Was he jealous, or did his tone suggest something else?

His eyes gleamed. "Marrying a goddess entails traveling an undetermined road with an uncertain destination."

"Remember that." Too late she bit her tongue, remembering Zarra.

From inside his jerkin, he removed the knife carved from Rustofona's rib. Thorne slipped Fervid into her belt, drawing strength from it.

"Thank you." Her fingers squeezed the ring in the pouch around her neck. Tomorrow. She didn't trust her temper tonight, nor want to admit how much separating from Bludwelt unsettled her.

They rode until midnight, then camped. At dawn, as they saddled their horses, before her husband could irritate her, she held out the ring. "This is yours."

He smiled knowingly as he continued cinching his saddle. "So the thief was Human."

"I ask for leniency." Begging twisted her gut, but this was for Zarra.

Strumgued didn't take the ring, but tapped his heart with a fist. "All must bow to justice."

She'd rather sheath Dracodurus in his chest than plead. "Can you say you found the ring in your chamber? Perhaps under a table."

"You ask me to play the fool." He raised his eyebrows. "I'd never misplace something so precious."

"The ring isn't valuable. The ruby is small."

"My many-greats grandfather fashioned the ring for his wife at the birth of their first child. After the Dragon chased us from Stonevar, I never expected to see it."

Thorne leaned against Wild-Eyes. "Please, accept my regrets. It won't happen again."

"The culprit must be punished."

She tried to keep her voice confident. "Is there no alternative, my Lord?"

His eyes widened, clearly pleased about the 'my Lord.' She didn't like herself for manipulating him. She'd rather lop off his head.

Strumgued stroked his palm-length beard. "One way—"

"I'll do it."

"Put the ring on the fourth finger of your left hand."

She slipped it on, pleased to prevent Zarra's banishment so easily. He probably hadn't told anyone the ring was missing.

"I'll say I found the ring on my wife's hand. That she wears it in accordance with Human marriage customs." For the first time, he looked at the ring.

His trap closed around her. Thorne opened her mouth, but no words came.

Behind him, the rising sun gave him the golden aura of a fire god. "The ring must never leave your finger."

She wanted to throw the ring into a sinkhole and Strumgued after it for gaining another advantage. He was clever. Grandfather's book described Dwarfs as superb warriors, excellent metallurgists and miners, but uncurious about other races. Either the book was wrong or Strumgued was exceptional.

A half-league later, a growl rumbled in the back of her throat. How had he learned about Human marriage customs? And what other webs did he spin to trap her?

CHAPTER THIRTY-SEVEN

Quist, screeching alarm, flew to Thorne's shoulder.

"What's wrong?" Thorne had ridden hard for two days. Ahead, outlined by twilight, Ventamar's peaks loomed above Stonevar.

Quist vibrated his tongue in her ear. "Hellestorm."

Thorne's heart hammered. She yelled for the other Dragon Guards to follow and urged her warhorse into a gallop. Strumgued shouted something Thorne couldn't hear. She bent low for speed, ignoring the horse's dark mane whipping her face.

Below the Dragon Ledge, she dismounted and dashed up the stairs, stumbling near the top when she heard the whelp yowl. The smell of Dragon blood made Thorne draw her sword.

Was Hellee dead? In the moment she took to push back her crippling fear, Zarra caught up with her. Thorne nodded toward the tunnel, grateful for help. Together they scurried down the passageway. In the gloom-shrouded main cavern, the sure-footed thief slipped on meat pies littering the floor. Sir-Sir the wole-rat squealed. Thorne caught Zarra, and they sidled around the corner to peer into the hatching alcove.

Hind end pressed against the wall, the whelp swung his bloodied snout, teeth bared, throat rumbling. Emera was on her knees, her thin face longer than usual. Cayeseed lay on the floor, the front of her green dress soaked with blood.

Thorne hurried to the Dwarf and touched her throat. No pulse. A heaviness weighed Thorne's chest. Cayeseed had become a daughter of sorts, and Strumgued doted on his only daughter. Her death would devastate him. "What happened?"

Emera heaved a dry sob. "Hellee clawed Cayeseed. I tried giving her Dragon blood, but she didn't swallow."

"How long after the injury?"

"I don't know." Her palm-sized ears, flushed scarlet, poked through straight white hair. "I left to get Magda's meat pies. I hurried, but—"

"Get Strumgued," Thorne ordered. Too late, she realized that her husband would kill Hellee for this and ran after, but Strumgued was already climbing the mountain. "Quickly," Thorne told Zarra. "Fetch the Dragon Guards."

Thorne covered Cayeseed with Emera's cloak. In the corner, Hellee raised his head and roared. When she approached, the whelp's wild thrashing forced Thorne back from his whipping tail. She pressed against the cavern wall, closed her eyes, and hummed, picturing him gliding through blue sky among peaceful white clouds.

After a few moments, Hellee calmed and bumped Thorne's chest with his triangular head. Fresh rivulets of silver-scented blood ran down his snout. She wiped it with her tunic, revealing a gash in one nostril. She could've prevented this if she'd escaped Bludwelt a day earlier. Or banned Dwarfs from Redilik Cavern. At the very least, she should've insisted that two Dragon Guards always defend Hellee.

Thorne hugged his neck, murmuring, "Who did this?"

Her head snapped up when Strumgued bellowed from the entrance, "Where's Cayeseed?"

One arm protectively about Hellee, Thorne nodded at the floor. Strumgued yanked off the cloak and moaned. The sound cut deep into Thorne; she'd never seen him so unguarded.

Torvald, Cayeseed's beloved wrestler, sprinted to her body. Tears wet his cheeks. Strumgued's son, Waldemar, followed wearing a miner's filthy shirt, his face colorless, his mouth a thin line.

Strumgued drew the war axe from his back and advanced toward the whelp, filling the hatching alcove with his looming shadow. "Step aside."

Thorne moved between him and Hellee. "I vowed to protect him with my life."

In the main cavern, the Dragon Guards raised their weapons. They wouldn't survive a fight with three Dwarf warriors. Hellee butted Thorne's back. She ignored him, keeping her eyes on the Dwarfs. She must stop this, but how?

"My Lord." Thorne pretended calm. "My Lord, I'm sorry for

your loss. I loved Cayeseed, too, but we don't know what happened."

In the dim light, Strumgued's face appeared dull as clay. "This one," he pointed toward Emera, "told me the evil monster clawed my daughter."

Moisture slicked Thorne's palms. Even if she'd asked Emera to say nothing, she couldn't hide Cayeseed's death. "Hellestorm's no more evil than you or I. We each have our own nature."

His face turned scarlet. "You talk like a fool."

He'd never spoken disrespectfully to her before. Her hands curled into claws, but she forced her fingers straight. Torvald sniffled. Thorne was grateful that Waldemar stayed uncharacteristically quiet.

"I understand your sorrow," she said. "But killing Hellee won't wake her. Let me discover what happened."

Madness glazed Strumgued's eyes. "Move aside!" His voice thundered inside the cavern as he raised his axe. "Blood must flow."

Thorne knew his need to kill Hellestorm went deeper than Cayeseed's death. Deeper even than the shame of losing their homeland. Gaspotine the Dark had killed Strumgued's beloved first wife. For twenty years, he hungered for revenge.

Thorne's voice quavered. "I implore you to wait."

"You provoke me." He stepped toward her, double-bladed war axe readied. "Move aside."

"You don't want to do an injustice."

"Killing a Dragon is never unjust." A drop of liquid balanced at the corner of his eye.

Sweat? It couldn't be a tear. Seeing Strumgued cry would weaken her when she needed all her strength. Behind her, Nella ordered the Dragon Guards to attack on her command. Thorne couldn't let them. The Dwarfs would kill anyone who threatened Strumgued.

Thorne's hope rested with Strumgued's attachment to custom and duty. "You've given me no wedding gift." She held out an imploring hand. "Give me until you light her pyre to find the truth."

For a long moment she waited. He looked fierce as an enraged wole-lion. Their marriage was in name only, with no love bond to sway him. Strumgued would refuse.

"I will spare you the sight of his beheading. Leave Redilik Cavern."

Emera sobbed.

"You have every right to want revenge." Desperation squeezed

Thorne's voice. "Give me a day."

"No." He sped around her, faster than she thought possible.

Hellee skittered, but he was already pressed against the wall. Strumgued swung his axe. Thorne pulled the buckler from her belt and lunged, taking the full force of the axe on the small shield. She screamed. Pain made spots swim before her eyes. The buckler dropped from her numb fingers.

The Dragon Guards rushed to her.

"Back," Thorne said through clenched teeth. "Do nothing."

Strumgued edged away, breathing as if he'd run miles.

When Fehera touched Thorne, she moaned. "You've dislocated your elbow," the healer said.

Before Thorne could reply, Fehera gave it a quick tug. Thorne screamed again. Behind her, Hellee pranced and whimpered. Thorne took the buckler in her other hand, preparing to block another blow.

Growling, Strumgued pounded the axe handle on the floor. The sound rang inside the cavern. "I won't hit you again. You have one day."

"Swear."

The battle raging in Strumgued twisted his mouth. One wrong word from Waldemar or Torvald would reignite his killing rage.

For Hellee. "Escort me to my chamber." Her voice was stronger than she expected.

Shock seemed to mitigate his fury, as he realized what her invitation implied.

Through gritted teeth, Strumgued told Waldemar and Torvald, "Take Cayeseed away. I'll not have her lie near this vileness."

They carried the body to an open door beside the hearth.

Thorne gestured for the Dragon Guards to move between Hellee and Strumgued, and told Zarra, "Learn the truth."

Zarra nodded. "I'll not fail you."

"Come," Strumgued told Thorne and followed Waldemar.

Thorne staggered down the passageway, cradling her elbow. With only hours to discover the reason for Cayeseed's death, she'd no time for pain.

Strumgued would expect a night in her bed. Perhaps she should've suggested his, a lesser violation. Still in the end, did it really matter? Keeping him with her was the only way to protect Hellee. But once he'd bedded her, he'd think he owned her. Sweat trickled down the hollow of her spine, although the tunnel's dampness made her shiver.

He took a torch from the wall, lighting the way ahead. Thorne hummed to soothe him and herself. Maybe it was her imagination, but after a few moments, his tightly hunched shoulders appeared to relax, while hers tightened with each step. Only her determination to save Hellestorm kept her shuffling through the dark tunnels twisting through Ventamar Mountain.

Strumgued turned right as Waldemar and Torvald continued on, leaving Thorne alone with her husband. After hundreds of steps, Strumgued stopped and faced the wall. He inserted a finger into a crack near the markings and pushed. The rock door pivoted almost soundlessly, not loud enough to awaken a sleeper. He motioned for her to precede him through the low doorway. She ducked and moved inside her chamber. Entering from the side made everything appear strange. Especially the bed, which seemed twice its normal size.

She bit her lip. She should've known Strumgued would make it a priority to learn where she slept. Nevertheless, his easy invasion of her chamber, where she'd once felt safe, made his trespass more egregious.

Strumgued slid the torch into a notch by the hearth and knelt to build a fire. He'd not spoken since leaving Hellee's cavern.

When Thorne swayed, he pointed to the bed. "Sit."

She did, trying not to jar her arm. He helped her remove her tunic. As he moved her elbow, she turned her head to avoid his musky scent.

"Give me your shift."

When she hesitated, he ripped the hem and rent it upward. She'd lived in close quarters with both sexes for most of her life, but his closeness made her squirm.

"Stay still." He tore a strip from the garment, wrapped her elbow, and tied it to her naked chest.

Thorne shivered. He wet the cloth and cleaned the dust from her face. After removing her boots and woolen socks, he washed her feet. His ministrations made everything worse. If only he'd stop touching her, give her a few moments alone to compose herself.

"Where's your gown?"

"Gown?"

"Your sleeping dress."

"You ripped it off me."

"Do you have another?"

She pointed to a chest. He retrieved a fresh shift and pulled it over her head.

He opened the balcony doors and moved outside, giving her privacy to remove her trousers. Cool air fingered her legs. Grandfather's book said Dwarfs disliked heights. Perhaps her husband would get dizzy and fall. To her disappointment, he stood solidly, outlined by the thunder moon, fists braced on his hips, imposing as a Giant.

She itched from travel dust and sweat, most severely on her head. She untied the lace holding back her hair, but couldn't pull the brush through her thick tangles.

When she cursed, Strumgued approached. "Give it to me." As he combed her hair, she closed her eyes, resenting the gentle strokes even though they soothed.

After he finished untangling her hair, he removed his boots and shirt, but with the thatch of glistening curls covering his chest, he hardly seemed bare-chested. He intended to stay. She wanted to run.

Her buttocks ached after days of riding, and Thorne longed to stretch out. However Strumgued sat on her bed, staring not at her, but into the fire, face drooping as if anger had deflated him, leaving only grief. Though they both were exhausted, she doubted either would sleep this night. She couldn't offer him the comfort a wife might give without opening up, and that she would never do.

His jade-green eyes were bottomless craters in skeletal sockets. His large, square hands rested on his knees, statue-like, as if enduring the unendurable had stolen his strength.

Her chest tightened with sympathy. That plus fatigue, grief, and pain were all too much. And this was her dreaded wedding night, too. Clenching her teeth, she crossed to the fire to warm her cold hand. Mating with Strumgued didn't frighten her. Nor did she worry he'd impregnate her. But the act of submitting appalled Thorne.

He patted her bed furs. The serpent ring weighed her wedding finger. Strumgued had no Dragon essence to inflame her; only her Human self would lie with her husband.

CHAPTER THIRTY-EIGHT

Thorne took one step toward her bed, offering herself for Hellestorm's life. Strumgued rose to his feet. A cool breeze swept in from the balcony, plastering Thorne's damp shift to her skin.

She took a second step on legs heavy like slogging through water. Surrender seemed impossible. She wiped a sweaty palm on her shift, unsure how she could take those last three steps, four if she shortened her stride.

She'd braved Gaspotine the Dark's lair and faced Rustofona the Magnificent—she must do this for Hellee. A soft moan leaked from her lips. She pressed her knuckles to her mouth to smother further sounds. She was behaving like a child but couldn't help it. Consoling herself with thoughts that he might possess her person, but those thick fingers would never capture her spirit, didn't work. Instead, she tasted blood where she'd bitten her knuckle.

Her bargain must be kept. Two long strides and Thorne slid under the furs, pulling them to her neck, feeling like a rabbit hiding in a fox's den.

The fire backlit Strumgued's stocky form, illuminating the hair on his arms and head so they appeared wisps of flame. Shadows concealed his face, but not his musk.

She retreated to the middle of the bed, where the sheets felt cool.

When Strumgued sat on the furs rather than crawling under, she willed herself not to wiggle away, to meet his gaze. She wanted to tell him again how much she regretted Cayeseed's death, how much she sympathized, but her mouth was too dry.

His green eyes hardened. "Your hand."

She lay her uninjured arm atop the fur. He raised her hand to his mouth but didn't kiss the back as she expected, rather he sniffed her palm. His tongue flicked the inside of her wrist. She flinched and curled her long fingers. He slipped a finger under hers, forcing them open. For what seemed hours, he ran fingertips over her hand, bent and unbent her fingers and wrist as a sculptor might scrutinize his model.

By the time he reached her elbow, she wanted to beg him to get it over with. But he stopped there, reclined on the furs, and pulled his cape over himself. He imprisoned her hand until he slept, evidently finding comfort. All night he mumbled and thrashed in troubled slumber.

Thorne lay awake, worrying about the whelp, and what her husband would do on the morrow.

#

Spangle had killed a man. As she stabled her horse and moved toward Lott's cottage, she remembered severing his neck when he bent to pick up his sword. Before drinking Dragon blood, she wouldn't have had the strength.

He died without making a sound, still groggy from sleep, a campfire illuminating his surprised face. She should at least know his name, but had no way to learn it. Returning to Stonevar after rescuing Thorne, Spangle wondered if the hollow feeling inside her chest would ever go away.

Lott would understand. When she opened his cottage door, three candles burned beside a mound of wax nubs on the table. He'd kept a vigil for her.

He raised his head from the table. Deep lines cut into the corners of his eyes as if he hadn't slept. She heard anger in his voice though he whispered to avoid waking Una. "You left without telling me."

"I told Magda," Spangle said softly as she removed her outer clothing.

"You should have told me."

"I couldn't find you." She didn't look outside the cottage.

"I was in the cow barn."

"No time." To justify why she must go.

"Did you think I would try to stop you?"

"I thought you'd want to go in my place."

He opened his mouth then closed it, clearly surprised that she'd guessed. She wet a cloth in the washbowl. The damp fabric felt cool against her neck. "I'm a Dragon Guard. I vowed to protect Thorne and Hellestorm the Great." Lott honored his vows but would he respect hers?

"I'm your husband. It's my duty to protect you."

Her obligations and Lott's had never conflicted before. "I have duties also."

His face reddened, as if a battle raged within him.

She used a bootjack to remove her boots, which she'd worn for days. When she pulled off her socks, the air hitting her toes was bliss. She couldn't remember feeling more tired.

She looked at Lott and said, "I don't need protection." At least not in the way he meant.

Lott inhaled in short sniffs. He drank ale from a cup then stood up. "Hereafter, you can protect me." In his knee-length nightshirt, he appeared vulnerable. "You shouldn't have left me undefended."

Spangle tried not to smile. A titter skittered across her tongue, then a giggle, then a laugh exploded. Una squirmed under a blanket. Spangle covered her mouth.

Lott stopped smiling when she told him about Cayeseed.

He took her hand. "Do you think Strumgued will kill Hellee?"

In less than a day, the Dwarfs had changed from allies to adversaries. As they rode to rescue Thorne, Spangle had bonded with Strumgued and his warriors. How could she fight them? She wanted Lott's advice, but not enough to reveal her uncertainty.

"Thorne will stop Strumgued," she said confidently. Thorne had to. "I wanted to tell you what happened and have a kiss before I guard Hellee." She'd started to enjoy his lips pressing against hers.

After softly kissing her in the way she liked, Lott held her and whispered, "Don't let the Dwarfs kill you."

#

In gray dawn, Strumgued rose from Thorne's bed with a hard-edged glint in his eye.

Thorne kept her voice soft. "Promise me that you'll not harm the Dragon this day."

Strumgued grunted what she hoped was agreement as he pulled

175

on his shirt. Dark circles emphasized the drooping pockets under his eyes. His full lips formed a tight slit. She didn't trust him and decided to question Emera in Hellee's cavern.

"I'll join you for the eventide meal." She clutched the bed furs one-handed, wishing she wore her Dragon leathers rather than a thin shift.

He nodded and left using the exit beside the fireplace. She hated him more for violating her sanctuary than her bed.

The door flew open and Magda rushed inside to hug Thorne. Her foster mother must've been waiting outside until she heard movement. Thorne groaned, favoring her sore elbow as she sat up.

The older woman's eyes widened. "You're injured."

"My elbow. It's better today. I can move my arm." She didn't bother explaining since Hellee's death would please Magda. Nor did she did tell Magda about the kidnapping.

Magda picked up a leather jerkin from the floor and sniffed. "Strumgued. You promised me you'd never open your bed to him!"

Thorne struggled to put on clean trousers one-handed. "Do you think I surrendered easily? He rescued me."

Magda tossed the jerkin toward the flames but came up short. "So you've mated?"

Saying nothing happened meant enduring this scene on subsequent mornings. Strumgued would surely exercise his husbandly rights tonight. "I could think of no other way."

"You broke your oath."

Thorne took a deep breath. "Hellee killed Cayeseed."

Eyes wide, Magda croaked, "Not sweet Cayeseed."

"Strumgued wanted to kill Hellee. Still does. I had to stop him." Not that Magda would care.

The floor seemed to mesmerize Magda. "Waldemar should've killed that monster."

"What does Waldemar have to do with this?" Although Cayeseed's sweetness may have broken through Magda's hatred of Dwarfs, Waldemar was a different kettle of turnips altogether.

Magda wouldn't meet Thorne's gaze. Her voice trembled. "How copes Emera?"

"Distraught. Everyone tries to protect her, but twice that's ended in death." Thorne picked up her dirty shirt, which smelled of Bludwelt and Strumgued and threw it into the hearth flames. She

176

kicked Strumgued's jerkin and missed. Just as well. Leather burning in the fireplace would stink up her room. "Was Waldemar in Hellee's cavern with Cayeseed?"

"Told you that monster was dangerous." Magda pounded the table. "You should've destroyed the egg before it hatched."

"Did Waldemar visit Hellee?"

Magda turned away. "Waldemar hates dragons."

Thorne, ignoring the pinching in her elbow, grasped Magda's shoulders and spun her around. "Was Waldemar in Hellee's cavern?"

The middle-aged woman tried to squirm away. "Taking meat pies to Emera and Cayeseed seemed harmless."

Thorne released her. "Waldemar carried pies into Hellee's cavern."

Magda moaned. "Emera's too young to guard that Dragon alone. I worried about the lasses when Cayeseed didn't come."

"Cayeseed? You should've worried about Waldemar."

"A Dragon killed her mother. I couldn't help worrying."

Thorne tried to keep fury from her voice. "What did you do?"

Magda crossed her arms above her protruding abdomen. "I sent the pies with Waldemar and asked him to make sure Emera and Cayeseed were all right."

Heat climbed Thorne's neck, remembering Zarra slipping on those pies. "Why did you befriend Strumgued's children?"

Tears wet Magda's cheeks. "To please you."

"The outcome displeases me."

Magda flushed. "That vicious beast must die."

"Someday Hellee will become our protector. He's not vicious. Something must've frightened him." Thorne pulled on her boots. "Waldemar wouldn't go near a Dragon unless he intended to kill it. And you sent him with meat pies."

The older woman shook her finger. "You've changed, Lass."

"More than you know." She'd comfort Magda later.

Magda's lip trembled. "Brutte will come home soon."

Her delusions seemed worse. Thorne hugged her foster mother. "We must do our best without him."

#

Thorne rode Wild-Eyes to the Dragon Ledge under a rising red sun—a bad omen. Traveling the tunnels might be shorter, but the mountain passageways stank of Dwarfs. She approached the hawthorn hedge, seeing only a single Fairy, a lookout for the old hive, perched on a thorn. No Raspberry-Frost.

Her mood didn't improve as she climbed to the Dragon Ledge where Zarra met her. "Emera has much to tell you."

"Fetch her." To avoid upsetting Hellee with her black mood, she waited outside.

Shoulders slumping, Emera joined Thorne. "I rode back to the castle to get Magda's meat pies, but Magda had already given them to Waldemar."

Thorne rubbed the tight muscles in the back of her neck. Were Wanderers bad luck as Fehera said? Could Emera appear harmless, yet cause disaster?

"You left Cayeseed alone with Hellee."

Emera nodded, rubbing her dry eyes with thin fingers; Dragon blood had stolen her tears.

Thorne resisted yelling. "Why not send Cayeseed for the pies?" First Brutte, then Cayeseed. Until now, she hadn't realized she blamed the Wanderling for Brutte's death.

"Cayeseed said she had a surprise." Emera sniffed. "She wasn't a Dragon Guard, so I should never have left Hellee."

"That's right." To stop herself from slapping Emera, Thorne stared across the plain, watching the morning mist dissolve over Malwood until she'd calmed enough to speak. "Did you see Waldemar with the pies?"

"No. He must have come through the mountain." Emera rubbed her thin upper arms. "When I returned, Cayeseed was dead and Hellee wounded." The Wanderling supported her forehead in her palms, clearly miserable.

Thorne didn't comfort her. If Emera hadn't left Cayeseed alone with Hellee, she'd be alive.

Hellee loped toward them like an ungainly puppy, wearing what Thorne considered a Dragon smile. She inspected his snout, which Fehera had stitched. Someone's sword sliced his nose. An attack or a defense? And where was the weapon?

While Thorne examined Hellee, Zarra comforted Emera and narrowed her eyes at Thorne. Zarra was right; Thorne shouldn't blame the Wanderling. Zarra motioned for Thorne to speak, then disguised this as scratching her head.

"Pardon my short temper," Thorne told Emera. "Strumgued gave me one day."

"If Strumgued kills Hellee, it'll be my fault," Emera said.

"No. My shortcomings did this." Ignoring the warning flutter beneath her breast, Thorne sent word for Strumgued to have his son join them for the eventide meal. She must rely on a Dragon-hating Dwarf (was there another kind?) to save Hellee. What Waldemar told his father would either condemn the whelp or spare him.

CHAPTER THIRTY-NINE

Solanie appeared no better fed the next time she entered the Continuum. Above her, Gaspotine had thinned himself until he blended with the blood-red clouds.

Rustofona, as usual, had her nose in Hellestorm's current. Since the whelp slept eighty percent of the time, her scrutiny seemed pointless, but lessened her Niede. Gaspotine also felt stronger; apparently, an undragonish concern for others loosened the Niede's grip.

Solanie traveled the river, listening to Dragon gossip before jumping into Hellestorm's current. "Your whelp lives."

"Yes," Rustofona said distractedly.

"He's plump."

"They overfeed him."

"He's twice the size I was at his age." Solanie bared her teeth. "Are those Humans?"

"Yes. Always at least one stays with him, though he needs solitude."

"Why?"

Rustofona shrugged her wings. "It's the Dragon way."

Solanie's snout drooped. "I hate it. When Lasmenda was in her cave, she slept or visited the Continuum."

"Obviously she didn't teach you Code."

"What's that?"

"The first law is 'She-Dragons must teach their whelps Dragon Code.'"

Gaspotine surmised Lasmenda hadn't expected Solanie to live long enough for others to discover this deficiency.

"Will you teach me?"

"Never been done. She-Dragons only teach their own whelps." Rustofona buried her snout in the current. "Hellestorm occupies me."

In Hellestorm's cavern, Thorne rolled a log toward the whelp.

"What are they doing?" Solanie asked.

"Playing."

"Explain."

"Something igtimus and animals do."

"Hellestorm appears to like it. Is he happy?"

Gaspotine dropped from the clouds. "Dragons don't need happiness."

"What then?"

Her question seemed sincere. "To kill. Eat. Sleep. Protect our territory. Visit the Continuum and ride our currents in the Silver River, looking for changes but seldom finding any. If we do, we're ..." For the first time, he realized that change terrified Dragons. "We compose riddles. She-Dragons rear their young. Oh yes. In autumn we mate. That's all."

"What's our purpose?"

Gaspotine lengthened his neck to see her better. "You're a strange whelp."

"My mother said I was inquisitive. Why is that bad?"

"Dragons are skylords. None are greater. There's nothing to be curious about."

"Why are Dragons so ... I don't know the word. They don't care about anything."

He waved her off, not knowing the answer.

Solanie looked into the river. "Why do they touch Hellestorm?"

"Scratching where he itches." Rustofona growled. "Suffering makes Dragons strong."

"Animals comfort their young."

Rustofona bared her fangs. "I understand why Lasmenda threatened to kill you."

The more Gaspotine observed Solanie, the more she puzzled him.

CHAPTER FORTY

Strumgued had removed Cayeseed's chair from the Eventide House—what he called the stone building where they shared supper each night.

Thorne tried to keep her voice normal, although time was short. "Will Waldemar join us?"

"In a moment." Strumgued's sunken eyes had a haunted stare. "First, I would have you understand my thoughts." He leaned forward across the table. "The Dragon must die tonight." His voice was low and calm. "Then Cayeseed's spirit will find peace in the Citadel of the Slain."

Thorne matched his tone. "If something other than Hellee caused Cayeseed's death, will you let him live?"

A furrow cut between Strumgued's eyes. "I cannot promise that which defies sense." He struck the table with a fist. "Foul claws raked my daughter's flesh."

Thorne's heart battered her ribs like a caged wole-munk. "But if there are special circumstances?"

"There's no doubt."

"Since it's impossible anything else caused Cayeseed's death, will you promise?"

His thick brows joined in irritation. "I cannot pledge the impossible."

"I understand, but will you give me your word?"

He exhaled a disgusted grunt. "I will."

Thorne had only a moment's relief before Waldemar joined them, his mouth squeezed tight, refusing to look at either Thorne or his father.

Strumgued asked Thorne, "What do you require?"

"Waldemar will speak the truth?"

Waldemar half-rose from his chair, but Strumgued motioned for him to sit and gave Thorne a tolerant smile. "A Dwarf will die before falsehood takes his honor."

Thorne wasn't so certain. "Waldemar, did you carry meat pies to Cayeseed and Emera?"

The young Dwarf gaped at Strumgued. "By what authority does this Human question me?"

Strumgued regarded his son through narrowed eyes. "Answering my wife would please me."

Thorne tried to speak without emotion. "Did you enter Redilik Cavern?"

Waldemar scowled. "I did."

Strumgued lifted an eyebrow.

Thorne was convinced that Waldemar had attacked Hellee. And when Cayeseed moved between them, Hellee killed her accidentally. "Had you visited Hellee before?"

"Never."

"Why yesterday?"

The young Dwarf huffed as if he'd run leagues. Strumgued waited, mouth tight, gaze locked on his son.

Sweat trickled from between Thorne's shoulder blades down to her buttocks. "Will Waldemar answer?"

Strumgued leaned back in his chair. "He will."

Thorne kept accusation from her tone. "Did you cut the whelp's snout?"

The young Dwarf folded his arms.

Strumgued cocked his head. "Did you play a role in your sister's death?"

"I never wanted Cayeseed hurt." Waldemar shifted as if preparing to bolt.

Thorne failed to keep the anger from her voice. "Did you attack the Dragon whelp?"

"Answer my wife."

Waldemar's eyes met her gaze. "I did not attack the beast."

Strumgued smiled, evidently believing Waldemar.

Risking everything, Thorne demanded hoarsely, "Tell us what happened."

Strumgued nodded.

With the side of his thick finger, Waldemar rubbed his full lips. "I've a weakness for Magda's dove pies." His ear tips flushed. "She promised me one but gave me three, asking that I carry the others to Cayeseed and Emera before they cooled. In the cavern, I called to Cayeseed from the doorway. She smiled and motioned. 'Come, Waldemar. The Dragon naps.'

"When I approached, she pointed at the sleeping beast and said, 'Kill it.' "

Waldemar assumed a shocked expression. "I told her Father forbids it."

Strumgued smiled. Thorne suspected Waldemar exaggerated.

"Cayeseed slid my sword from its sheath. Grabbing for it made me drop the pies. I told her to give it back, but she swung the sword and laughed. Her eyes gleamed eerily, and she held it out, taunting me to 'Avenge Mother's death.'

"I told her this whelp didn't harm our mother.

" 'The black Dragon killed her,' she said and raised the sword. 'And Thorne took Father.' "

Strumgued coughed and inspected his hands. Thorne hadn't realized that Cayeseed hated her.

"I tried to calm her. Said that after she wed Torvald, she'd gibber no more childish nonsense. But she said, 'I'm no child,' and slashed the air with my sword.

"I grabbed for her arm, but she jumped back. I looked around for something to subdue her: a length of rope, a cloak, a branch to trip her, but saw nothing.

"I told her, 'So this is why you conceal your sword skill from Thorne; why you pretend meekness and befriend Magda. You contrive to disobey Father.'

"She smiled and said, 'Father didn't forbid me to kill the monster.' The venomous glint in her eyes alarmed me more than the sword she brandished."

Strumgued slammed his fist against the table. "Cayeseed would never disobey me."

"Let him continue," Thorne said.

When Waldemar gave his father a wary gaze, Strumgued motioned for him to proceed.

"I suspected Cayeseed had lost her wits and pretended I'd help her. She scraped the sword tip across the stone floor, waking the Dragon. The beast lumbered toward her, tail wagging like a dog.

"When she lifted the sword, I batted her arm upward. My sword cleaved the creature's nostril. He yowled and clawed Cayeseed's chest. She fell to the floor, screaming. I'll never forget the sound. But the silence afterward was worse. I chased the beast away and used my shirt to staunch her wounds until she coughed blood. The Dragon's claw must've punctured her lung. After a few gurgling gasps, she stopped breathing.

"When I heard footsteps from outside, I snatched up my bloody shirt and hurried into the tunnel. I knew Father would avenge her."

Strumgued shook his head. "You say Cayeseed plotted to kill the wyrm."

Thorne found it hard to believe gentle Cayeseed wanted Hellee dead. "Do Dwarf females use weapons?"

"Some," Strumgued said.

"Your daughter was skilled?"

"She was a member of the Bellacassisa. A female guard."

Thorne cocked her head at Waldemar. "Thank you for the truth." Speaking it couldn't have been easy.

The young Dwarf nodded and left. Misery cut dark shadows under Strumgued's eyes, as he bowed and followed his son. Unsure of her husband's intent, hoping he'd recognize Cayeseed had manipulated Magda and Waldemar, Thorne decided to spend the night with Hellee.

After Hellestorm the Great survived the night, Thorne knew Strumgued believed Waldemar.

#

The next day at full dark, Thorne and the other Dragon Guards marched across the bridge. At the riverside funeral pyre, Emera stood bravely, although grief twisted her face. In Malwood, wole-wolves howled, as if heralding the hundreds of torch-bearing Dwarfs spilling from the mountain.

So many. The impossibility of defeating this horde squeezed Thorne's chest.

They covered Cayeseed's body with a shimmering gold cloth that captured the moon's glow. Using a torch, Strumgued ignited the pyre, chanting in a language Thorne didn't understand. Gray smoke carried the smell of burning flesh as the Dwarfs sang;

> "One of us has gone,
> never more to see the dawn,
> scores more will follow ere long.
> Though earth's bond we sever,
> life's gift forgotten never,
> we will cherish her forever.
> Her mortal life was short,
> but death we cannot thwart,
> find lasting peace in heaven's port."

The Dwarfs' love song to the dead raised bumps on Thorne's skin. After the ceremony, she sent all the Dragon Guards to protect Hellee while she went to her sleeping room.

#

Strumgued came late to Thorne's chamber. Thorne pitied him, yet refused to lower her guard. He collapsed beside her, head on one arm, staring at her, eyes asking. She turned away, determined to give nothing freely. Strumgued must take what he desired.

He touched her neck. Dwarf women scarcely had one, so hers must seem freakishly long. Callused fingertips, scratchy as cattails, traced the muscles of her throat. When his finger lingered in the hollow, she stiffened, thinking he might nuzzle or lick her neck, but instead he enclosed it with one hand. She tried not to squirm.

With her throat pulsing under his palm, he slept atop her bed furs. He was gone when she awoke, but his metallic scent lingered.

When she met him for the evening meal, they didn't discuss the previous night. He picked at the baked quail. When she spoke of the ram's aggressive behavior now that the ewes were in heat, his gaze never left hers. His finger grazed her hand when she spoke of moving cattle. Seemingly by accident, he drank from her wine glass, placing his lips where hers had touched. He apologized, but it was no mistake. He seemed unguarded in a way she'd never seen. Another time she might have used this to her advantage. Not today.

That night, as she lay looking at the ceiling's pointed arch, he traced the contours of her cheeks with his coarse fingertips, making circular motions as if polishing stone. Her cheekbones were high and

186

sharp, not the apples of Dwarf females. When he stroked her narrow nose, heat rushed to her face. He must prefer round noses, so why study hers so intently?

She rolled over. He rubbed her shoulders, pushing aside the bed fur to massage the hollow between. She didn't resist his familiarities. When he stopped, she looked over her shoulder. He was asleep above the covers. Postponing the inevitable offered little relief. With him near, sleep eluded her.

The next night, Thorne felt certain Strumgued would mate her, but he stayed away. The delay drove her mad.

In the morning she blinked awake to his hulking shape watching her with dull eyes.

"I'll not hold you to the bargain between us. Cayeseed . . ." He left, unable to speak of his daughter's undwarfish betrayal.

For all she cared, he could lie above the covers for the rest of his life. However, she'd given her word, allowing Strumgued access to her body, knowing, perhaps not consciously, that he'd never force her.

But she'd not fulfilled her implicit promise that they'd consummate their marriage. Now he dared negate her obligation. She pounded the mattress with her fist. She must give herself to him.

Fire char him. This was too much, too cursed much.

CHAPTER FORTY-ONE

The following day, the wind carried Dragon musk. From her balcony, Thorne watched Vainglorian the Red swoop beneath the clouds, flying north to mate with Tallasha the Resplendent.

On her way to meet Strumgued for the eventide meal, Thorne saw the fire vine was in full bloom. The creeping plant climbed the mountainside, almost reaching her balcony. Bees clustered on the crimson, belled flowers, gorging themselves, legs covered with yellow pollen.

The roots were too deep to pull, the stem too thick to break, so Thorne picked all the wretched blooms she could reach, as if destroying them would stop her hipbones from swelling and tame her thoughts of Bludwelt. Then she rushed to meet her husband.

From the doorway, she told Strumgued, "We made a bargain. I will honor it." She didn't mention how dragonish obligation compelled her.

Strumgued's eyes widened, then narrowed. "You invite me under your—"

"Yes." She couldn't bear to hear the words.

He stopped cutting the venison roast. "Your favor is freely given?"

Heart tolling inside her ears, she nodded.

After setting down the carving knife, he stared at her with steady green eyes. "You are ready to become my true wife?"

"I'll do it. Cease questioning me." She crushed the red blossom inside her tunic pocket, releasing the floral scent, which gave her queer sensations in her belly.

Later that night, Strumgued, carrying a sack, entered Thorne's sleeping room through the secret door while Thorne performed her toilet. Although nude, she neither tarried nor hurried. Finished, she slipped into bed and pulled the furs over her chest.

Only then did Strumgued remove his boots and jerkin, and loosened his shirt from his trousers. He threw aside the covers and grasped her ankle. She retracted her ticklish foot, but he pulled it into his lap. She wouldn't tolerate him sniffing, licking, or sucking her toes.

He removed a jar from the sack and opened it, scenting the air with aloe. He massaged the cream into her foot. She was unaccustomed to anyone touching her feet, but when he pressed his fingertips into her arch, she groaned with unexpected bliss and uncurled her toes.

His thumb circled the ball of her foot. She moaned. He curled her toes, straightened them, and tugged gently on each one. If she'd been a cat, she'd purr. He patted her hip, signaling her to roll onto her stomach. He kneaded cream into her calves, squeezing and stroking up her legs, like a sculptor with clay. Under his tireless fingers, her mind floated. Not long ago, he'd brushed a horse until it accepted him, even welcomed his touch. He was treating her the same, but this felt so good she didn't care.

He traced her spine upward, lingering on her neck before removing his hand, then replaced the fur. "We must speak."

The time had come. The hearth cast grasping shadows across her bed, as she tucked the fur around herself and sat up.

"To a Dwarf maiden, I'd have no need."

She didn't disclose that she was no maiden. He didn't need to know. "I hope I've wit enough to understand."

"You're clever for a Human." He scratched his whiskers. "Before we're truly wed, we must settle a concern between us. Your hand."

She placed hers on his callused one. His palm was half again the size of hers, but their fingers were of similar length. Thorne resisted snatching it back.

"To each other," he said, "we will speak only the truth. Your secrets you may keep as I'll keep mine, but the words we share must be without deceit." He placed his right hand over hers.

She raised an eyebrow. "You think me a liar?"

"Humans value deceit. My words to you will be true."

This pledge touched her as no declaration of love could do. "I swear, Lord Strumgued, that my words to you will also be true."

He clamped his fingers around her wrist. Instinctively, Thorne pulled back, but Strumgued held her tight. From his belt, he took a dagger with a curved blade and wicked tip. Instinct warned that he might cut her wrist, but he'd had many opportunities to kill her. She held her breath and made herself relax.

With the tip, he nicked the fleshy part of her hand, then his. At the sting, she stiffened. He pressed his wound to hers, letting their blood mingle. Her palm burned. Strumgued jerked as if her blood seared him. He quickly recovered and said in a growling voice;

"Marriage vows and blood unite us.
Lies and deceit will never divide us."

She doubted this was a customary Dwarf wedding night vow, but she repeated it.

He removed his shirt before sitting beside her. In the firelight, his eyes flashed like bloodstones as he motioned for her to lie on her stomach. She did. His hand rasped over her buttocks, as if polishing her flesh. Thorne was no soft stone, like amethyst or garnet; she was hard as a ruby. He touched her like a carver searching marble for the tiniest flaw. By the time he slid under the bed furs, he knew her flesh better than she.

The breeze from the balcony carried the sweet scent of the fire vine flowers, reminding her that while the red bells bloomed, dragonish desires would stir her. When Strumgued's patience exceeded her own, she climbed atop him.

Eyes closed, she touched his arms and chest, feeling muscles as hard as mountain rock. His metallic scent overpowered even the fire vine. She pictured their joining as two sliding past each other, never melding. But a fire burned within her, hot enough to melt iron and stone, a primordial need ready to erupt from her center.

Tremors rocked her. She leaned forward but couldn't stifle her shaking. Only when Strumgued stopped shuddering did she open her eyes.

Afterward, he slept with her wounded palm clasped over his heart.

Their days remained unchanged, but at night, Stonevar mantled their secrets.

#

Three months later in early winter, Thorne couldn't deny she'd become Strumgued's true wife. She strolled beside Ventamar Falls, feeling something flutter inside her abdomen.

Thorne had always known where she'd meet death. She accepted that whatever grew within her would kill her. After bedding Hauk, she asked Fehera to look inside her womb.

The healer told her, "You shall bear no man's child."

Evidently, she couldn't birth a Human baby, but the spawn of a Dwarf would grow under her breast.

The remainder of the day, Thorne sheltered under willow branches dusted with snow, breathing cold crisp air, hidden from the castle, developing her plan for Stonevar.

The next morning, the place where Strumgued slept was empty. When she sat up, her stomach roiled. Even after a night's rest, she lifted her head with effort. The thing inside, what she called an igle— a leech—drained her. No amount of sleep refreshed. She fell back and woke the second time with sunlight pooling on her bed, having slept half a day.

Nearby, Magda rocked, stitching a tunic for Brutte. Each day, the older woman slipped more deeply into the delusion that her husband would return. "Are you ill, Lass?"

"A storm assaults my stomach." She refrained from mentioning her tender breasts and swollen ankles. Clearly, Strumgued's seed disagreed with her.

Magda pressed her palm against Thorne's forehead. "You're warm. Stay in today and help me sew."

Thorne laughed. "I've no talent with a needle. I'll feel better moving around." And she did.

That day they prepared Hellee's cavern for more snow. Thorne tried to hide her weariness as she and Willow-Bender carried in stacks of sweet rushes for bedding, and the soldier-farmers used a pulley to haul firewood up the mountainside. While they worked, Hellee nosed a hollow log across the floor, then scrambled after it like a giant kitten.

Mid-afternoon, Emera trotted into the cavern. Hellee dashed toward her, tripped over the log and fell end over end. Quist hovered, chittering anxiously.

Willow-Bender laughed. "Odd Dragon behavior."

Thorne enjoyed seeing Willow-Bender mirthful and couldn't stop laughing herself.

"How are Dragons supposed to act?" Emera asked.

Thorne stopped laughing. Hellee shook his head. Thorne doubted his tumble hurt him, but she inspected his cream-colored hide anyway, looking for bruises and finding none on his tough skin. A mother Dragon would ignore minor injuries, but she couldn't. Rustofona was right; he didn't behave like a proper Dragon. In the short time left, what could Thorne do?

"We must train Hellee to be a proper Dragon." Even if Thorne knew how, right now she hadn't the strength. She collapsed on a stool and removed her boots. Only twenty-one years old, she'd never had swollen feet or experienced a constant dull pain in her back. She'd expected her condition to kill but not enfeeble her. Every woman she knew, including Mother, continued working until delivery.

While Thorne tried to ignore her weakness, Hellee nudged Emera. The Wanderling kissed his snout. "You're a perfect Dragon. But I'm neither Wanderling nor Human."

"You are what you are," Willow-Bender said solemnly.

Thorne had an unexpected revelation. "Being unlike other Dragons could be a good thing." She wanted to believe Hellestorm the Great would still fulfill his destiny if they raised him with kindness rather than harshness.

Hoping she was right, Thorne returned to the castle. The nauseating odor of rutabagas in the Great Hall sent her upstairs, where she crawled into bed and slept. She didn't join Strumgued for supper. Sometime during the night, he joined her.

He touched her hot cheek. "What ails you?"

She shook her head and turned from him, refusing to tell him about the igle growing inside her.

CHAPTER FORTY-TWO

When not watching Thorne or Hellestorm, Gaspotine observed Solanie's less than successful hunts. What was special about her? A talent for self-preservation. Uncommon intelligence. She'd need more to survive.

After failing to catch an old buck, Solanie appeared in the Continuum, spinning like a whirlwind. "No matter how fast I strike, deer evade me," she told Gaspotine.

"They smell you." He considered himself an expert hunter.

"Teach me."

Her request flattered him until he remembered that only mother Dragons taught whelps to hunt. He checked to make sure no one was listening. "Fly against the wind." He moved his wings as if resisting the wind. While alive, he could create gusts in the Continuum.

"I get more speed with the wind."

"Stealth catches prey, not speed." Apparently Lasmenda had neglected to teach Solanie stalking techniques. Another indication Lasmenda planned to kill her.

"I'll try." Her eyes grew larger.

Gaspotine's desire to reassure her was undragonish. "Did you hunt with Lasmenda?"

"Never. She wouldn't let me watch, either."

"Maybe she wasn't skilled." Every Dragon scavenged when necessary.

Solanie's stomach deflated. "She killed enough to feed herself, but not me."

"A first whelp often suffers," Rustofona said, joining them while Hellestorm napped. "Some mothers ignore their first altogether."

193

"Lasmenda preferred my male nest-mate."

"Only one whelp can survive." Rustofona's voice trailed away. "Sometimes neither does."

"Lasmenda fed him. After I hatched, he attacked me. But the large meal slowed him, and I broke his neck." She snapped her jaws.

Gaspotine had heard enough about hatching. "Come. I'll show you how I hunt."

Solanie followed Gaspotine into his past where he tracked and killed a giant deer.

"Is there a name for a male who acts like a mother?"

"Father," Gaspotine answered automatically. Did Solanie consider him her father? "Go hunt." The Niede had receded while he spoke with Solanie, but now it returned like a headbutt in the gut.

CHAPTER FORTY-THREE

Fisting and unfisting his hands, Strumgued approached Fehera, who was cleaning her herb patch, preparing for next spring's planting. Afternoon clouds chilled as the healer tucked her chin-length, pale red locks into a scarf. For a middle-aged, angular woman, Fehera moved gracefully. Strumgued liked watching her red, blue, and yellow striped skirt swirl around her ankles, although the design was undwarfish.

Of late, too many of his thoughts were undwarfish, especially his obsessive desire for Thorne. Warming her bed had done nothing to cool his ardor.

Fehera stretched her back. "Lord, how may I serve you?"

Strumgued shifted his weight, not knowing how to speak about Thorne. His wife's behavior mystified him, and of late, she'd been stranger than usual. Still he had an uncommon compulsion to understand her and hoped Fehera would enlighten him.

Fehera rinsed dirt from her hands in a water bucket, dried them on her apron, then motioned for him to enter her herb-drying hut. "May I offer you tea?"

Strings of drying nutmeg and light-scented lovage hung from the rafters and over the fireplace. Anise was heaped on a small table. The other herbs he didn't recognize. Absently, he rubbed his thick eyebrows.

Fehera pointed to two chairs with curved runners underneath. "Please sit." She hung a pot of water from a hook over the fire.

He'd never sat on an unsteady chair like this. When it jerked, he grasped the arms. Apparently mastering this seat took skill.

Fehera rocked smoothly. "Many drink tea with me and speak

195

their thoughts."

His tongue tangled when he tried to speak Thorne's name, so he puffed out his cheeks and nodded.

After the water boiled, she took a mortar and pestle from the mantle, ground a pungent yellow root, and spooned it into two cups. "You are the first Dwarf Lord to visit me."

Strumgued forced a smile. He'd mastered the chair, and they rocked companionably sipping tea, warming hands around their cups.

He stared into his drink. "I'm loath to speak my concern."

"Hmm," Fehera said encouragingly.

"My wife behaves most strangely."

"She conceals her condition from you."

Condition! Did some female disease rot her bowels? The cup leapt from his fingers, spilling hot tea in his lap. He sprang to his feet, brushing his legs. "What ails her?"

"She refuses to accept what grows within her."

A tumor from too much black bile? That would explain her discontent.

Fehera refilled his cup. "What was your first wife's name?"

"Lea-Lee. Her beard was soft as lapin." He rocked with quick jerks.

Fehera touched his arm to slow his pace before giving him fresh tea. "I've heard Dwarf females bear few children, but she gave you nineteen."

"Her gift to me." Fighting a wole-lion pack alone frightened him less than losing another wife. He must know what ailed Thorne. But needing a moment to recover his evenness, he blew into his replenished cup. "Thorne has a Dwarf spirit."

Fehera looked thoughtful. "Thorne is many things."

He gulped tea. "Human or bastard child of a god, her lineage matters nothing to me. What ailment has stricken my wife?"

"Thorne carries your child."

Strumgued laughed loud, deep howls of relief. "I hadn't thought our mating would bear fruit."

"Are you pleased?"

"Pleased for the joy this will bring Thorne."

Fehera frowned.

"Why scowl? Is something amiss?"

"She's healthy."

An almost unthinkable thought hit him. "She doesn't want my child."

"I cannot say, since she refuses to speak of it." Fehera's eyes said she suspected more.

"She told me she couldn't bear children. I sense she spoke the truth."

"I have the gift of seeing inside a woman's womb. When I looked into Thorne's, I saw no man's seed would root there and told her so. Even now I cannot sense your child."

"Why does my wife reject the truth?"

Fehera sipped before answering. "She's no simple woman desiring marriage and family. To her, husband and child symbolize enslavement and drudgery. Death frightens her less than surrender."

"Unnatural." He shook his head but couldn't shake off the wound of Thorne rejecting his child.

"Don't expect her to behave like other females. Do you love Thorne?"

He grunted derisively. "Human love is a seed in the wind, landing by chance, with shallow roots easily ripped from the earth."

Fehera smiled. "I humbly offer this advice. Tread lightly."

He extended a leg and wiggled his foot. "Unfortunately, my feet are large."

Fehera laughed, as did Strumgued. They rocked and drank tea until his rumbling stomach reminded him of supper. He didn't want to be late and give Thorne an excuse to leave, but he had one more question.

"How might I please my wife?" An undwarfish question, since Dwarf wives weren't reticent about voicing their needs.

"She wants the Fairies to stay."

Strumgued thanked Fehera and left muttering, "Fairies. Aaach." Why his wife wanted the vile creatures nearby, he'd never understand. They were pilferers, liars, and spies, unable to stay on Stonevar's side of the river. But Humans formed incomprehensible bonds—that thief and her wole-rat for one.

Human behavior impacted not only him but also his son. Three months past, Waldemar had caught a wole-weasel kit. An annoying, energetic, strong-jawed beast larger than common weasels, but devoted to Waldemar who spent hours training the animal. Strumgued disapproved but said nothing.

Now he passed through Stonevar's bailey unmolested but as he hurried through the orchards, a farmer waved. Distracted by thoughts of his wife, Strumgued couldn't remember how a Human Lord acknowledged a thrall and ignored the man. He arrived at the Eventide House before the cook brought the meal or Thorne arrived. Strumgued puffed out his cheeks and blew, deciding to wait at the river.

On the arched bridge, he watched the water rush from the mountain. For the first time, he wanted to flee Thorne. He'd never believed in magic, but she must have bewitched him; there was no other explanation. From the moment he tasted her blood—a dwarfish battle custom—he'd known he must have her. He slapped the stone railing. Since Thorne wanted neither him nor his child, pride should make him release her from their marriage.

Still the thought of losing Thorne made his chest ache as if he'd broken a rib. He remembered a Dwarf proverb: You will decide a lover's value by your desire for them.

If it took decades, he would win her loyalty and devotion. For Thorne, he'd find where the Fairies were building their new hive. Demolishing it would force the Fairies to spend the winter in their old hive near Stonevar. The new hive would be in Dragon territory, either near the orange Dragon in the northwest or the red monster in the south. Wherever, the new hive would be difficult to destroy.

CHAPTER FORTY-FOUR

Lord Bludwelt, Head Constable and tax collector for Seahaven, pounded the whitewashed door so hard it rattled. "Farmer Dale, come out." After escaping the Dwarf Lord, Head Constable Bludwelt's minimal good humor hibernated. If that loathsome Dwarf hadn't interfered, he and Thorne would be together.

"That you, Bludwelt?" Farmer Dale mumbled from inside.

Bludwelt surveyed the property that might soon be his. The stone walk was swept, the yard neat. Curtains fluttered at the windows of the spacious four-room house. The breeze carried only a faint stink of pig manure.

"Official Seahaven business," Bludwelt announced. If the farmer couldn't pay his taxes, Bludwelt would make him sign a paper saying the Magister had seduced his oldest daughter. If he refused, Bludwelt would take his farm. A win either way.

Farmer Dale lifted the bar. In the open doorway, he appeared more hunched than Lord Bludwelt remembered.

"Your taxes are past due." Bludwelt rested a hand on his coiled whip as he eyed the middle-aged man.

The farmer slid his thumbs into his belt and cocked his head toward a pile of charred rubble. "Fire took my cattle and barn. Last year my swine sickened. I'll pay after next year's harvest."

"Unacceptable."

The farmer flushed red as madder root. "Now Goadran—"

Bludwelt's lackey, Fexx, stomped forward in his knock-kneed gait. After adjusting his constable hat, he poked the farmer's chest. "Lord Bludwelt, dolt. Goadran bought that title."

"Enough, Fexx. Back." Bludwelt didn't like being reminded that he'd been an innkeeper's ineffectual son. "Pay your taxes or I'll claim your farm."

The pig farmer lost all color. "Now be reasonable. I've never been late before—"

"The law's the law." Bludwelt smoothed his long white hair. "Perhaps you own some other property to satisfy the tax."

"I need my stock to survive winter."

"I suggest you sign this." He motioned to Fexx, who handed Bludwelt a rolled document.

"What is it?" After Bludwelt explained, the farmer hunched. "You ask me to attest that the Magister shamed my daughter. If I sign, he'll send his constables for me."

Bludwelt waved a dismissive hand. "My constables will do as I say. Refuse to sign, and I'll take your farm."

"You're a reasonable man—"

"Not at all."

Fexx chuckled as he scratched his chicken neck.

"Your indentured girl." Bludwelt motioned at the house, where the girl peeked out the window. "Gene the pig thief's lass."

The farmer's color faded. "She's been with us three years. She's like a daughter to me."

"She's not worth much. Sign this, and I'll mark your taxes paid."

"I—"

"Keep arguing and I'll remember whose sword killed my predecessor." The Magister had pushed the previous Constable onto the farmer's sword.

Hand over his heart, the pig farmer collapsed on an upended bucket. "Girl!"

The twelve-year-old sped from the cottage to offer the farmer tea. Willow bark by the smell. Bludwelt motioned for Fexx to take her. She slapped and kicked.

The farmer looked away.

Bludwelt smiled. One more farm to seize today. Soon, he'd rule the Isle of Elysia.

#

Thorne stopped unloading cloth from Stonevar's wagon when Glitter said, "I heard some interesting gossip."

Magda moved close. "Tell."

Glitter dug through her shopping bag and gave a new pack of needles to Magda, who tucked them in her tunic pocket, mouthing thank you.

"Tobitt the talebearer says that last year some farmers lost their pigs to disease and can't pay their taxes. Constable Bludwelt wastes no time confiscating their property. There's a farm between here and Seahaven."

Thorne had once hoped disaster would force a farmer to sell her land. How could she have been so heartless?

"Which farm?" Magda asked.

"Kale's."

Da's farm. Losing his farm would break Da's spirit, and Thorne couldn't let her family become beggars. She must pay Da's taxes. But how without Bludwelt or Da knowing? Brutte would've known.

The following day, she consulted Lott, who suggested an inheritance. Who would Da inherit from? His family lived on the mainland, and Thorne had never met them. Then she remembered an older brother who'd never married. He'd do.

She'd ask Lott to sort through her coins, make sure all were common, and put them in a plain purse. Neither Thorne nor any Dragon Guard would touch them. Lott would entrust the purse to Tobitt and swear him to secrecy. The talebearer would enjoy foxing Bludwelt. Da wouldn't question the windfall.

#

When Head Constable Bludwelt found Kale planting winter crops instead of preparing to leave, he should've been forewarned.

Fexx slouched in his saddle. "I'm hungry."

Scrawny Fexx was always famished, and Bludwelt reminded him to remain alert.

"I doubt Kale will provide a repast," Fexx grumbled.

Accustomed to Fexx's constant griping, Bludwelt smiled tolerantly. "Hello, Kale!"

Before lumbering to Bludwelt, Kale told his three sons to keep working. The youngest was little more than a toddler. "What brings you to my property, Constable?" Kale offered a slack-jawed smile.

Why was the stocky man so calm? "To collect taxes."

Kale rubbed his sweaty brow with his thick forearm, leaving behind a dirty smear. "Taxes are serious business."

Bludwelt shifted in his saddle. This wasn't proceeding as expected. Confident he'd seize the property, Bludwelt had given Kale seven more days. Demonstrations of generosity would help Bludwelt become Magister. "I've no time to dawdle. Do you have the money?"

"In the house. Would you like a cup of cider?"

"No." Bludwelt didn't want the taxes, either. He wanted this farm.

"I'd like a drink," Fexx said.

Bludwelt raised his arm, signaling silence.

Fexx mumbled under his breath. Kale returned with a small sack and no cider.

Bludwelt judged the weight of the sack. "Delighted you acquired the tax money." He assumed a practiced smile. "Seems like a miracle."

"An inheritance from my brother."

"Fortuitous." Bludwelt barely resisted whipping the grin off Kale's doughy face.

"Never expected he'd amount to much, but people surprise you."

"Don't much care for surprises."

Kale laughed. "Seems my luck has changed."

Bludwelt didn't believe in luck. Or miracles.

As he let his horse amble back to Seahaven, he planned to investigate this windfall. Receiving funds just in time defied common sense.

The payment might hold a clue. He loosened the tie closing the sack-like purse. The coins were worn. He held one to his nose and sniffed. A faint scent of lye soap. Odd. He checked each one. The largest had a gouge. If he didn't know better, he'd say an animal clawed it, but the groove was too deep.

Fexx interrupted. "Can we get a meal at the next farm?"

"In Seahaven." He tossed Fexx a coin.

Fexx grumbled but seemed resigned. Bludwelt tongued a copper coin to help him think. He sniffed the bag; also freshly washed. As he poured the coins back, he noticed the purse seams were sewn in a familiar crisscross pattern. Magda—the fat, old, interfering cow. Before his father died, Magda cleaned and cooked at the Honey Lodge, and repaired their clothing. Now she lived at Stonevar. Why would she send coins to Kale?

While thinking, he worked the copper coin with his tongue until it zinged against a canine tooth.

Kale's daughter, Lily, ran to Stonevar. Why?

"Fexx." The man gathered gossip like bees collected pollen. "Why did Lily leave Rutmon?"

"She weren't fifteen when Rutmon married her."

"Why so young?"

"Kale promised his eldest daughter, but she took off, then came back sick. When Rutmon refused her, Kale didn't want to return her bride price and gave his younger girl to Rutmon."

Bludwelt was only dimly aware of passing cultivated fields, orchards, and farm buildings. "What illness did the older girl have?"

"Dunno. Wedding guests said her hair fell out. Kale sent her to the Holy Women so she wouldn't sicken his sons."

Everything made sense. "Any other symptoms?"

"Kept insisting she weren't sick."

Bludwelt's horse shook its head, asking Bludwelt to loosen the reins. He did. "Did she join the Holy Women?"

"Can't say." Fexx pulled bread from his saddlebag.

"How long ago?"

Fexx answered with a full mouth. "Three years or so."

"Someone should confirm she's with the Holy Women. I'll send word. What was her name?"

"Rose."

CHAPTER FORTY-FIVE

Infuriated Fairies swarmed above the hawthorn hedge. The Fairy hive was inside the thicket, by the path Thorne had cut to reach Hellee's cavern.

"Wole-weasel razed new hive," Raspberry-Frost told Thorne, from its perch on a thorny branch.

Thorne had missed Raspberry-Frost terribly and tried not to look pleased. But why had a wole-weasel attacked them? The hawthorn hedges where Fairies built their hives discouraged most predators. "What about the foul smell?"

"Rammish undone." Fairies coated their hives with a malodorous substance they called rammish. Raspberry-Frost rubbed her narrow nose. "Jelly plugged wole-weasel nose."

Strange. Then Thorne had a suspicion. "Did you see Dwarfs nearby?"

"Son of Dwarf Lord tracks Fae."

Waldemar's wole-weasel? The Dwarfs wanted the Fairies gone, so why force their return to Stonevar? "Does that mean you'll stay?"

"Through wintertide."

"I'm glad." Thorne choked on a dry sob. At least during her last months, she'd have Raspberry-Frost nearby. She composed herself and looked around. The Fairy clutch seemed smaller.

"How many killed?"

"Many." Raspberry-Frost nipped her ear then licked the drop of blood.

Thorne was accustomed to nips and hardly noticed. "The chrysalises?"

"Perished."

"Oh no." Unconsciously, Thorne hugged her stomach.

#

Often Thorne was sleeping when Strumgued entered her chamber, but that night, she waited up. "Where's Waldemar?"

"In the north." Strumgued closed the stone door.

"What business has he in Tallasha the Resplendent's territory?"

Strumgued unbuckled his belt and said slyly, "A mission for me."

"Raspberry-Frost tells me the new hive is destroyed."

"Good." Smiling, he removed his jerkin.

"Many Fairies died defending it."

"No matter." He waved a dismissive hand. "You wanted them here. Now they'll stay."

Perhaps she misunderstood. "You sent Waldemar to destroy the new hive for me."

"I did."

Nausea knotted her gut. "Their chrysalises perished."

"Fewer pests."

"Their babies are dead!" She waited for him to say something but he said nothing.

He stripped off his remaining clothing and crawled under the furs beside her. She burrowed into the covers—if only her husband slept in a nightshirt.

"Do not turn from me," Strumgued said.

She rolled to face him, her nails digging into her palms to prevent clawing his eyes.

He rubbed under her chin as if expecting a hairy tuft. "Now that Fairy of yours will stay."

The knot in her gut tightened. "If Raspberry-Frost had been in the new hive, it would be dead."

Strumgued shrugged. "One's like another."

She closed her eyes and gripped her wrist to avert punching his short neck. Telling herself that he intended to please didn't quell her revulsion, but an unexpected realization made her vomit into the chamber pot. To charm her, what other horrors might he commit? Must she pretend contentment, even pleasure, during her last days to halt his ceaseless courting?

CHAPTER FORTY-SIX

Cold woke Thorne on Long Night's Moon. In the fireplace a single ember glowed, and she was alone under the bed furs. Strumgued might arrive later or not all. What kept him at Dyadzan Castle? She didn't know and neither asked nor cared. But he would've put wood on the fire.

She dashed to the hearth, her breath frosty, her woolen socks little protection against cold stone. After she piled wood on the grate, the air soon carried the comforting scent of pine.

For the past two days, the clouds dumped snow, and a boreas wind had whipped up deep drifts. Now a wole-wolf howled and another answered. The bailey gate, three times a man's height, kept the pack out and the stock protected. Good to be inside safe and soon warm.

On her way back to bed, something scratched the thick window glass.

She sped over and grabbed the latch. Hoarfrost singed her fingers. With her nightshirt covering her hand, she tried again. The window frame held fast. She pounded, but it was frozen tight.

"Dying," the wind seemed to whisper.

She lit a brand, moved it along the window seam, and pulled. With a loud pop, the window opened, and frigid air oozed in. Shivering, Thorne leaned out. On the sill, a Fairy cocooned its body with delicate wings that made a fragile shield against winter. Carefully, Thorne scooped Raspberry-Frost into her palms.

Thorne carried the Fairy to the hearth and set it atop her furs. After checking for more Fairies, she closed the window. What dire events forced Raspberry-Frost out in this frigid night?

"I'm relieved you live, my Fairy."

"We perish," Raspberry-Frost whispered in a quavery voice.

"The Fairy colony is dying?"

"Hurry, my Human."

Thorne dressed in her warmest fur boots; her winter-white wole-wolf cloak; and rabbit-fur mittens. The basket she used for firewood would transport the Fairies. The fur covering her pillow would shelter them. Using fireplace tongs, she conveyed four river-smoothed stones, the size of her fist, from the hearth to the basket. She lifted Raspberry-Frost onto her shoulder and sped downstairs.

Inside the Great Hall's hearth, flames cast undulating shadows. The odor of onions and beetroots from last night's meal mingled with the scent of wood burning. Along the walls, sleepers snored on their pallets.

The floor rushes crackled as she tiptoed past Magda's pallet to squeeze Edz's shoulder. "I need your help."

He reached for his trousers. "At your service."

"Close the bailey gate after me and open it when I return."

His brow creased. "Where you off to?"

"To retrieve the Fairies."

Scatt jumped up. "You'll need my help."

Someone lit a candle. More than one asked, "What's going on?"

From behind, Magda grabbed Thorne's arm. "Are we under attack?"

"The Fairies are dying. I must help them."

"Good riddance. Troublemakers. Soul stealers."

"Don't speak so."

Magda folded her arms. "Don't risk your life for creatures who bring ill fortune."

"Raspberry-Frost saved me more than once."

"How'll you get through the snow?" Edz pulled on his boots.

She hadn't thought about that.

Scatt had dressed. "I'll harness Young Dobb to cleave a path."

Clad for outside, Zarra lit a torch. Thorne smiled, unsurprised that her friend followed, bow across her back.

"Haste," Raspberry-Frost said.

The group met Scatt at the gate where he'd tied a bell to the workhorse's bridle. "Stay close. Too cold to look for stragglers."

Sharp-edged stars punctured thin clouds as Young Dobb

snorted white plumes of feathery mist. His bell tinkled as he cut a path through three-foot drifts.

Under Thorne's fur hood, Raspberry-Frost huddled by her neck. Needle-sharp cold stabbed any exposed skin; her numb toes resisted bending. Despite the bitter night, they traveled half a league without complaint, through low clouds of ice crystals sparkling in the moonlight.

At the hawthorn hedge, Raspberry-Frost took the lead. The others followed the bobbing iridescent point along the brambles until the Fairy disappeared inside.

Where Thorne had slashed a path, the snow's weight flattened the thicket, destroying the windbreak protecting the Fairy's home. The wind had ripped the barrel-sized hive in two, exposing them to cold and blowing snow. Silver chrysalises and adults with glistening wings clung to the shimmering mother-of-pearl interior.

Thorne's blood crystallized. She'd caused this.

Raspberry-Frost hummed. Able-bodied Fairies crawled into the fur-lined basket that Edz presented. Thorne offered an open palm to Fairies less able.

Scatt squeezed his nose. "Stinks worse than skunk."

"Bad odors don't trouble Fairies." Thorne had learned that in Gaspotine's sewage pit.

"Let me help." Zarra extended her arm.

Thorne shook her head. "Don't touch them, Let them crawl onto your palm."

Raspberry-Frost flew a large-headed chrysalis to the basket, and the adults inside cocooned it with their wings. When the survivors were tucked away, Thorne covered them with fur. They left five small bodies behind: a gray Fairy that had helped carry Gaspotine's eye, and four chrysalises. Thorne must ensure the rest survived.

As they retraced their steps, Raspberry-Frost hummed a dirge inside Thorne's hood.

Behind Thorne, Zarra whispered, "Hurry."

Thorne looked over her shoulder, seeing only darkness. "What do you see?"

"Wole-wolves flank us."

They were still five hundred paces from the castle.

Thorne rushed to Edz. "Pass Scatt the Fairies and take the torch. Tell him to get home and bar the gate."

Edz did and slapped Young Dobb's haunch. The workhorse jerked into a trot that set its bell ringing.

A whoosh; a thwack; a wole-wolf yipped. Zarra had hit one with an arrow. Around them, a dozen pairs of red eyes gleamed. Their white winter fur blended with the snow. After the storm, they'd be ravenous.

Thorne drew her sword. Another whoosh, thwack, and a wole-wolf yelped. Zarra's arrow had hit a second target.

As the three backed toward the castle, Edz swung the torch back and forth. Red eyes followed them, closer now, lower, as if the beasts crouched.

Thorne glanced over her shoulder. Scatt and the horse were gone. The bailey gate was open a crack. Bekka held up a torch, but four hundred paces separated them.

A wole-wolf growled. A gust ruffled Thorne's fur hood.

Raspberry-Frost tugged Thorne's ear. "Wing-wind."

"Pass me the torch," Thorne told Edz. "Run."

Edz and Zarra sprinted toward the castle.

Thorne threw the torch high toward the center of the wole-wolf pack. With a loud whoosh, the sky exploded into flames. As fire and sparks rained, Thorne covered her face with an arm.

Blazing wole-wolves howled and yelped, filling the air with the stink of burning fur. Some ran in tight circles, while others dashed for Malwood.

Evidently, Vainglorian the Red had been tracking the wole-wolf pack. He roared an exhale and a burning wole-wolf exploded. Bits of flesh pelted Thorne.

The bailey gate rattled open. With Scatt in the lead, eight soldier-farmers rushed toward them, brandishing swords and shouting. When they reached Edz and Zarra, they stopped to gape.

Vainglorian swooped over a smoldering wole-wolf and exhaled. Its fur caught fire but it kept running. The Dragon circled the plain, herding the pack, exhaling and exploding wole-wolf after wole-wolf until black flesh pocked the snow and the air reeked of charred meat.

The Dragon landed near a growling wole-wolf. Crunching bone, Vainglorian devoured it.

Thorne rushed to the others. "Return to the castle." She sensed the wole-wolves had only stimulated Vainglorian's appetite.

They dashed home, snorting white mist. Ahead, two second-floor lights gave the mountain flickering eyes as Bekka waved them into the bailey. "Hurry!" She held the torch while Thorne and Edz closed the gate.

Thorne motioned. "Get the torches inside, Bekka. Everyone go with her."

Overhead, Vainglorian flew low, blocking the moon as Thorne dashed inside and shut the door. "Put out the fires." Though she took deep breaths, her heart pounded. She hoped that smoke from the dying fires wouldn't incite Vainglorian to exhale down the chimneys.

Thorne stared at the hearth for what seemed hours, while Scatt distracted the others by describing events. When she was certain the Dragon had gone, she asked Edz to relight the hearth fire. Thorne checked on the Fairies.

Bekka set a shallow bowl of water beside the basket. "What do Fairies eat?"

"Berries. Bugs. Maggots."

Magda shook her head, mouth twisting as if she tasted bitter cherries. Raspberry-Frost hovered over the basket, humming. The Fairies crawled or flew to the dried berries and water, gripping the bowl lip with bird-like feet. The castle residents moved closer to watch.

"May I touch one?" Emera reached out.

Thorne grabbed her arm. "You might injure it. Offer an open hand."

The Fairies ignored Emera, who bit her lower lip. The smallest Fairy moved feebly, too weak to climb out.

"Try this." Bekka dropped some honied bread into Emera's palm.

The weak Fairy crawled onto Emera's slim hand and ate. Hair-thin veins spread through its silver wings, circled its yellow eyes, traversed its narrow nose and thin lips. The fine white fur covering its body was damp from snow. Its needle-sharp claws must've pricked Emera's palm, but she held steady.

Without looking away from the Fairy, Emera asked Thorne, "What's its name?"

"I don't know. Name it and it may accept you."

"Silver-Frost." Emera blew gently, ruffling its fur.

The Fairy nipped the fleshy part of Emera's palm.

Emera frowned but didn't flinch. "It doesn't like me."

"It's taken a bit of you and given you a bit of Fae. Fairy glamour will no longer deceive you."

The Wanderling's eyes glistened. "So it likes me."

"I believe so."

When the Fairies finished eating, the strongest perched on Nar's beam and chattered.

Magda harrumphed. "How can I sleep with those noisy insects overhead?"

"They're beautiful and gentle." Evidently, Emera had already forgotten Silver-Frost's nip.

Magda shuddered. "I can't abide them peering at me."

Zarra crossed her arms. "Will they stay?"

"Until the weather warms," Thorne said. "For now, they need a cool place to become dormant again."

"The turret," Emera suggested. Above Thorne's sleeping chamber was a small circular room, entered through the ceiling.

"They'll cause no end of mischief," Magda said.

She had valid concerns. At the bottom of the broken Fairy hive, Thorne had found Magda's needles, believed lost over the years. Fairies had no concept of ownership or thievery, nor did lying to Humans or deceiving them violate Fairy code.

Strumgued would welcome the Fairies even less than Magda. They brought Stonevar at best a challenge and at worst a disaster.

CHAPTER FORTY-SEVEN

A northern winter was cold, windy, and long. Solanie's breath froze into droplets, which clinked on the cavern floor. Gaspotine could count her ribs. A half-grown Dragon needed sustenance and warmth to withstand falling temperatures.

Gaspotine switched to Hellestorm's current where a hearth fire glowed in the cavern. The Humans fed Hellestorm, cleaned him, played with him. Solanie had only herself. Even her mother's Fairy-Dragon had fled, evidently convinced Solanie would perish.

When Gaspotine resumed watching Solanie, she'd woken from her winter torpor and tunneled through the snow blocking the cave entrance. Snow whitened the sky, preventing her from hunting. On sunny days, finding game was challenging; on snowy days impossible. Giant deer hid in forests eating twigs and bark, evergreen and moss, sheltering under spruce, fir, and hemlock.

With the snow blocking the entrance gone, icy wind whistled through the cave. Solanie escaped to the Continuum and bumped Gaspotine. "Were you watching?"

"I was."

"I cannot last much longer."

He didn't want her to perish, but didn't know why. He'd always thought only of himself. "After the storm breaks, go to a lake. Fish gather in open water when the sun shines brightest."

"Have you been there?"

He'd ridden every Dragon current. "In spirit. Do not let ice trap you."

Two days later, Solanie left her cave. Closing her nictitating membrane against the sun reflecting off the snow, she flew to a flat expanse where ice chunks floated in a modest opening. As she dove, the ice-cover broke around her with loud cracks. The opening was small, easily missed underwater. Gaspotine should've told her to enlarge the hole first.

In the frigid lake, the slow-moving fish made easy targets. Gaspotine thought she should come up for air, but Solanie dove deeper. After eating her fill, she swam upward and bashed into frozen lake. Over and over, she tried to surface through unyielding ice. Her panicky thrashing could kill her.

A short distance away, the opening was darker than the snow-covered ice. Gaspotine yelled directions, but she couldn't hear. She went limp. Dead? In the Continuum, Gaspotine clawed at the ice.

"Hole?" Solanie said breathlessly, poking her head above the Silver River surface. Her aura had dimmed.

Gaspotine pointed, certain it was too late. "The dark spot."

In the lake, her flesh drifted upward. Floating or moving deliberately?

When Solanie's head broke the lake's surface, she coughed up water so forcefully that Gaspotine thought her neck would explode and protectively retracted his own.

She struggled onto the ice, back legs kicking seal-like, body trembling. The ice beneath her collapsed.

"Move!" Gaspotine shouted. "Get off the ice!" He should never have suggested this.

Solanie fell through, then resurfaced, gasping. She snaked onto the ice again, moving away from the opening. When she tried to stand, her front foot punched a hole.

Instinctively, Gaspotine reached out, but no matter how far his front legs stretched, he never reached her. "Crawl, Solanie, crawl!"

As if hearing him, she dug in her toe claws and pushed herself toward shore. The ice cracked around her. Firm ground was too far.

He couldn't tolerate this.

Solanie opened her wings, letting the wind push her. When she reached shore, Gaspotine's chest stopped hurting like he'd collided with a mountaintop. If this was friendship, he wouldn't wish it on anyone.

#

After surviving the lake, Solanie took a winter nap before visiting the Continuum. She lingered by the pink rock before telling Gaspotine, "The Fairy Queen says Hellestorm and I must form a pair bond."

Gaspotine hadn't thought anything could shock him. "Preposterous. Dragons mate freely."

"She says that's Hellestorm's destiny."

"Ridiculous. Impossible. Undragonish." Gaspotine would've continued ranting, but dark fog poured from his hearing slits. "Your words foul my ears."

"I must join Hellestorm on Elysia."

"You're too young for so long a flight."

"The Fairy Queen says you can teach me to fly sea air currents."

"Dragon droppings. Lizard piss. Wole-wolf vomit." He repeated every foul curse he knew. "Dragon-kind will never forgive this." Black sparks burned inside his mouth—a memory from inhaling when he should've exhaled.

"You'll be remembered well."

"For what?" He spit but nothing happened. Sometimes he hated the Continuum.

"Being Hellestorm's Grandfather."

His spirit turned the deep scarlet of Dragon blood. "Curl your tongue. Where did you hear it?"

"Dragon-kind must accept Hellestorm and me."

"It cannot be done." That should end it.

"The Fairy Queen says you can help me."

"May dragon-mites devour that evil sprite. I'm dead. Is that not enough? Must you bring more infamy?"

Other Dragon spirits stared, then lifted their noses and looked away, seeing Solanie and Gaspotine—spirits of no consequence.

Rustofona approached. "Are you discussing Hellestorm?"

"I must help him, but Gaspotine refuses to assist me."

"Father," Rustofona said. "Hellestorm needs Solanie. The Humans—"

"Father. Son. Grandson. I cannot abide this. I'll not become some igtimus who knows all his relations." The Niede doubled Gaspotine over. "A Dragon breeding pair. Love birds. Disgusting." The Niede rolled him tight. "Both of you, get away!"

He would suffer the Niede rather than lose everything that made him a Dragon.

CHAPTER FORTY-EIGHT

Strumgued woke Thorne. "Did you cross the plain after dark?"

She nodded.

His jade-green eyes glowed in the dark. "You might have frozen to death or worse."

Apparently he hadn't discovered the wole-wolf pack. She hoped Vainglorian had eaten the evidence.

"Promise me you won't leave the castle after dark."

"I foresee no need."

Strumgued scowled and pointed at Raspberry-Frost perching on the bedpost. "What's that doing here?"

"The snow destroyed their hive. They'll be staying above us." She pointed to the trapdoor in the ceiling. She'd made a makeshift hive by winding a blanket around a tripod.

"Will it roost above our heads all wintertide?"

"Yes." Thorne didn't hide her smile.

Her smile vanished, when the leech inside her kicked. Strumgued rubbed her stomach and the igle calmed.

Evidently Strumgued misunderstood her vexation and said, "You think me vile for destroying the Fairy hive?"

She looked at the hearth. Over and over again, the flames speared upward, seeming determined to escape. But they wouldn't and neither would she. When he smoothed her hair, she resisted jerking away.

"Do you know why Fairies build their hives in the thickets around Dragon holds?" he asked.

"For protection." Fairies were small and vulnerable, relying on deceit and mimicry to survive. That didn't make them wicked.

"They spy for the evil wyrms. A Dragon could never have driven a Dwarf Clan from their keep without Fairy spies." His voice had a sharp edge.

He must be mistaken. "You believe Fairies help Dragons kill Dwarfs?"

"I do, and they did. Fairies are not the innocents you think."

She'd never thought them innocent. But she hadn't believed Fairies capable of nanicide—slaying whole Dwarf clans. Though she resisted believing Strumgued, she knew Raspberry-Frost had advised Rustofona the Magnificent. "Is a Dragon attacking so different than destroying a hive?"

Strumgued snorted and removed his hand. The igle resumed kicking.

#

Though Thorne had banned men from the castle's second floor, everyone quickly learned Strumgued spent nights in her sleeping room. Thorne couldn't decide which was worse; going back on her word or admitting Strumgued came to her bed. For once she was relieved to be a goddess who needn't explain her behavior.

On a frigid morning late in winter, Thorne lay in bed after Strumgued left. "What traits do Dragons have?"

Raspberry-Frost raked its claws through Thorne's hair fanning it across the pillow. "Vain, vicious, prideful, territorial, selfish, churlish."

Less than encouraging. "Any good ones?"

Raspberry-Frost wrapped one of Thorne's white hairs around her arm. "None."

Thorne laughed, though the sound hinted at hysteria. "Dragons are strong and fearless."

"Skylords flee lightning and hurricanes," Raspberry-Frost said.

"Understandable." She rubbed the scar on her chin. "Hellee must be different."

Raspberry-Frost tittered. "My Human cannot change Dragon nature."

"I don't want to change his nature. Well, maybe I do—to temper it. Make him think before he acts. Train his mind so logic, not instinct, rules him."

"Foolish Human."

#

Later that morning, when Thorne entered the Great Hall, the stares and whispers made ignoring her growing girth impossible. Her condition was the Dragon in the castle that everyone pretended not to notice. Flushing, she tugged at her tunic, which stretched tight over her belly, then pulled her shawl around it.

She'd stayed upstairs until the sun was full up and the men left to tend stock. A few laughing wives lingered over bread soaked in bacon fat. The greasy odor made Thorne's stomach lurch. Even so, she longed to join them in a few moments of forgetfulness.

Instead she sat at the other end of the long trestle table, knowing she'd find no comfort or comradery. Two were expecting, and all welcomed pregnancy. Thorne's unhappiness would shock them. They accepted a mother dying in childbirth as normal, at the same time denying it would happen. They didn't talk about babies dying, though each had lost at least one infant. Some kind of motherhood enchantment seemed to fool them.

Thorne ran her fingers over the wooden tabletop scarred like the one in Da's cottage. Da had called her unnatural, but to Thorne, dying giving birth was unnatural. Dragon blood hadn't changed her in that regard. She tried not to think about Lily's long, painful labor and demise, but the igle kicking reminded her that she had only a short time.

She mustn't delay implementing her plans for Stonevar. Thorne motioned Bekka to join her. As if sensing something, Bekka patted Thorne's cold hand, but even Bekka's Dragon-Fating didn't reassure.

Thorne nodded toward the hearth where Magda napped in her rocker. "Confusion prevents Magda from managing the castle."

"Don't worry. I'll care for her and the castle when your time arrives. You've been so good to us all, and we want to lighten your burden."

At this point nothing could. Unable to find any place for her trembling hands, Thorne tangled her fingers in her shawl fringe. "I've only a short time."

Bekka squeezed Thorne's hand. "During your lying-in you can still order us about."

Thorne stared at the hearth's glowing embers. Of late, the castle was too warm, though no one else complained. Perspiration wet her shirt, and she let her woolen shawl fall from her shoulders, holding it around her thickening waist. The igle stole her strength when she'd much to do.

Evidently observing Thorne's distress, Raspberry-Frost swooped from Rustofona's skull, which was mounted above the hearth, onto Thorne's shoulder where the Fairy flapped its wings, cooling her face.

"Are you afraid?" Bekka's eyebrows arched incredulously.

Thorne forced a smile. "Have no worry for me. Only Stonevar's future matters."

Bekka wrapped her small hands around Thorne's. "I sense your path is the right one."

"I never chose the common path, but this"—Thorne lifted the shawl to expose her belly—"forces it upon me."

Bekka's positive tone cracked. "Fehera will see you through the birth."

Not even a healer as skilled as Fehera could save her. Thorne smiled weakly.

"How else can I calm your mind?"

"I'm quite calm," Thorne lied.

Bekka's voice shook. "Dragon blood will give you strength."

In a cradle beside Magda, Lily's baby fussed, but this time Bekka ignored him. Leaving Aeron in the cradle, Thorne checked his back. His disfigurement was growing.

"It didn't save Lily," Thorne blurted before she could stop herself.

"Anders's betrayal stole her will to live."

Before Thorne could say Dragon blood had deformed Lily's child and might hurt hers, Willow-Bender stomped in from the cold, leaving the door open. "Baby crying." She hurried to snatch up Aeron, as always unable to tolerate his hoarse sobs. In her ample arms, he stopped wailing and smiled. "What ails you?" the Giantess asked Bekka.

Thorne had never heard Willow-Bender sound irritated, but Bekka didn't seem to notice. The small woman slumped. Her large eyes dimmed, as if realizing that Thorne fulfilling her destiny might mean disaster.

CHAPTER FORTY-NINE

The Seahaven Guildhead marched into the Honey Lodge, took Bludwelt aside and said, "The Magister touched my thirteen-year-old."

After losing Thorne to that deplorable Dwarf, Bludwelt needed good news. He'd brooded these last weeks without even one foreclosure to cheer him.

"I want the Magister arrested." Only the Guildlord had more influence than this man.

The Magister had finally seduced the wrong girl. Bludwelt bowed his head, hiding a smile. This was what he hoped for. "Not that easy."

Bludwelt motioned to the indentured girl, who pushed back her limp blond hair. With her eyes lowered, the thin girl set two ale cups on the table. The inn was half full, a busy night. The girl had improved the inn's cooking and banished the inn's dirt, encouraging former patrons to return.

After she moved away, the plump Guildhead took a purse from his belt and dropped it on the small table. "Will this suffice?"

Bludwelt enjoyed being paid for what he intended to do anyway. "It will do." For luck, he clutched the black pouch around his neck containing the coin covered with Thorne's blood. She'd sent both to him before going to Stonevar. "Pass the word to the Guildmasters so they stand with us."

The Guildhead's nod squeezed his double chin. The Guildmasters had previously bypassed the Honey Lodge's meager offerings. After tonight, that would change.

With Guild support and Farmer Dale's signed complaint,

Bludwelt convinced the Magister to resign and leave Seahaven. The Magister sold his businesses to Bludwelt and with his family, embarked on Captain Anders's ship to O'Haven.

With popular backing and well-bribed Guildmasters, Bludwelt became Magister.

Before the first winter snow, the new Magister learned Rose never reached the Holy Women. Rose and Thorne were one. He spent the winter weaving a plan to marry Thorne. This time, she'd come to him.

#

At the first spring market, Lord Bludwelt spied on Glitter from behind the barrel maker's shop. He waited to approach until she was alone by Stonevar's wagon. She was taller than he remembered, with darker red hair. Though she had balanced features, graceful arms, and long legs, she had little appeal until he smelled her silvery scent. Then he stumbled but caught himself on his Magister's staff.

He inhaled deeply. Her dragonish musk was less compelling than Thorne's. However this unexpected development offered a unique challenge and promised more pleasure than he'd anticipated. He prided himself on his ability to change plans.

After a gaggle of gossiping shoppers passed, Bludwelt cleared his throat.

Glitter turned, quickly masking her surprise. Her gaze moved from his face to the staff.

"Welcome," he said as if meeting her for the first time. "I am Lord Bludwelt, Magister of Seahaven."

Glitter crossed her arms. "We've met."

He bowed, sweeping off his broad-brimmed hat and shaking his head so his long white hair glinted in the sun. "This is a new day."

"New for some." She inspected his tall frame. "We at Stonevar remain the same."

"I doubt that." He enjoyed her cautious regard. Before he drank Dragon blood, everyone treated him like an insignificant boy. Afterward, he grew taller and appeared older than twenty-three. Sometimes his very thoughts didn't seem to be his own.

Glitter seemed to choose her words carefully. "You're too important a man to linger with a middle-aged woman."

He laughed. She must be still in her twenties. "I enjoy passing

220

time with elderly women who serve the Goddess. They've had uncommon experiences."

She laughed until the wind shifted, carrying his scent to her.

"Good selling." Bludwelt put on his wide-brimmed hat and moved away, thumping his staff on the packed earth. He'd expected her cool reception, although she'd warmed up toward the end. He doubted she'd tell Spangle or Thorne. If she did, Bludwelt had only offered his respects.

Throughout the spring, Bludwelt chatted with Glitter whenever Stonevar's wagon came to Seahaven. After two months, her eyes brightened when he greeted her. He brought her excellent wine and sweetmeats made with honey and chestnuts. Since Glitter's silvery scent attracted him, his interest was real, though no one compared with Thorne.

His original plan called for manipulating Glitter with his wealth and power—a whore would respond to that—but since she'd drunk Dragon blood, he relied more on his dragonish appeal.

He prepared a room in his house. Purple and gold tapestries on the walls. Softest down pillows and mattress. Silver pitcher and washbowl beside a bottle of lilac water. Women might prefer roses but he couldn't abide their odor. Last he draped a blue velvet dress with flowing sleeves over a chest of new clothes.

Bludwelt stepped back to admire the stage set for Thorne's return.

CHAPTER FIFTY

A knock rattling the door sent Una running to Spangle. She lifted the child onto her lap as Una clutched the yoke of Spangle's sea-green dress.

"There, there, little one." Spangle patted the child's back. "It's only Glitter."

Una's kiss made Spangle's heart jump in a way no other could. She brushed blond hair from Una's winter-chapped cheeks, wondering if all mothers felt like this.

When the hut door creaked open, Thorne rather than Glitter entered. Thorne commonly dressed in black trousers, but now wore heavy wool stockings and a loose brown skirt borrowed from Magda. In front, the hem stopped just below her knees. The Goddess was big with child, though three months remained before she'd deliver. Even Spangle, who'd never borne a child, knew birthing such a large baby would be difficult.

Pregnancy had thinned Thorne's face, as if the unborn drained her vitality. Her eyes had a hunted, hopeless look, as though the world denied her sanctuary. Most alarming was her resemblance to Lily, which Spangle had never noticed.

"Sit, Goddess." Spangle set Una on a stool and retrieved a jar from a shelf. The child held out her hands, eager for a glob of clay. Spangle rolled up the pink sleeves of Una's soft, wool gown, exposing the child's thin arms, which Spangle wanted to kiss.

Thorne hung her cloak on a peg near the door. "What are you making, Una?"

"Bowl." Una concentrated on working the lump.

Spangle would be forever grateful that Thorne hadn't objected to buying Una. "What brings you out on this rainy day?"

Never one for pointless pleasantries, Thorne said, "We must be less dependent on Seahaven and produce more trade items. We need guilds."

If only Thorne asked Spangle to cut off her hand instead. "The guilds won't tolerate those they can't command."

Thorne shifted on the stool, as if trying to get comfortable. "I want you to engage guild journeymen suitable for Stonevar."

That meant dealing with the Guildlord. As the ground crumbled beneath her, Spangle struggled to think. "We don't need the guilds."

"We need skills. Masonry, millers, shoemakers, and more."

Spangle sensed a desperation in Thorne, which made refusing more difficult. The twin rubbed her forehead. "I cannot find so many."

"You needn't hire them all at once. But they must agree to train women."

Spangle didn't want to disappoint Thorne, but this was impossible. "The Guilds don't employ women."

Thorne set her chin the way Spangle knew meant that she wouldn't be dissuaded.

"They must also accept female Guildmasters."

Spangle felt dizzy. Anyone unfamiliar with Thorne would think she'd lost her wits, but the impossible never deterred her. "We'll learn the trades ourselves."

"Only guild craftsmen know trade secrets. Even if we had the skills, discovering them on our own would take too long."

Behind Thorne, Glitter flung open the door. "Wet out there." She hung up her cloak and hugged Una. "You two look grave."

"Thorne wants to form guilds."

"Good. We'll sell more." Glitter inspected Una's clay bowl, which resembled a plate.

Spangle pressed both hands against her temples. "Thorne wants women to become Guildmasters."

"Wondrous." When Glitter clapped, so did Una.

"Impossible." Spangle wanted to scream.

"What about widows who know their husbands' craft?" Glitter asked.

"Excellent," Thorne said. "Daughters might also know a father's trade."

To avoid Thorne's gaze, Spangle picked up a half-sewn nightgown for Una and began to stitch on a lace collar. "The guilds will kill anyone who teaches their secrets."

"Not once you charm the Guildlord." Glitter batted her eyelashes.

Spangle never expected Glitter to suggest this. "He's a horrible man."

Thorne pressed on her belly as if trying to reposition the child. "You've the skill to deal with him and run our guilds."

"You flatter me, Goddess." Spangle fortified herself to refuse.

"I'd approach him myself if I could." Thorne frowned. "Do you need Lott's consent?"

Glitter sniffed derisively.

"That's not why," Spangle said, though doubted her husband would approve.

"For the others, become the Guildhead of Stonevar."

"I would die for you, Thorne, but don't ask this."

Glitter raised a hand. "I'll do it."

Not Glitter! Spangle stabbed her finger with the needle and bled on the gown. "All right. I'll try." She stuck her bleeding finger in her mouth. Her sister must never meet the Guildlord.

"Thank you." Thorne turned to Glitter. "I'd like to appoint you Stonevar's Merchant Guildmaster."

"Whatever you ask." Glitter puffed out her chest. "I never thought I'd be so respectable." She swung Una into her arms and danced around the room. "Don't you think I'm important, Una?"

Giggling, Una nodded vigorously, loosening the red ribbon confining her blond hair.

Glitter set Una down. "Bow to the Guildhead of Stonevar." Glitter and Una curtsied before Spangle.

Spangle's laugh had a hysterical edge. "Please take Una outside to play. I want to speak to Thorne."

Glitter gave Spangle a puzzled look but complied.

With a lace handkerchief, Spangle blotted sweat on her forehead. She'd no desire to relive her past, yet she owed Thorne an explanation. "The Guildlord will levy a high price."

Thorne's eyes widened. "I'd never ask you to sell yourself."

Spangle cackled, a mirthless, grating sound. "If only it was that easy. I would sleep with a thousand diseased men before forgiving my father."

"Your father?"

Spangle tossed a handful of Fehera's herbs into the hearth, but their juniper scent failed to banish memories of her father's stench. The sparks scattered like flies brushed from rotting meat.

Rather than answering Thorne, Spangle picked up Una's wooden doll from the table, rattling the arms and legs. "Glitter and I had many dolls, fine porcelain ones. The old man we called Grandfather, the man our father sold us to, enjoyed watching us play with them." Spangle spoke without emotion as she inspected the sweet face that Glitter had painted on the smooth wood. "He sold us when we were twelve to a man called the Master. My mother had taught us to speak properly, so he presented us as well-brought-up innocents left to our own devices. Our vulnerability appealed to men."

Thorne squeezed her hand. "I'm so sorry."

Spangle felt nothing. She'd walled off those feelings long ago. "Years later, after we bought our freedom, we needed a license to practice our trade. I took the Guildlord a generous bribe. Most Guild leaders are rich and fat, but he was gaunt with a shock of gray hair that seemed to weigh down his skeletal head. The stink of sickness clung to him." She sipped barley beer to relieve her dry mouth. "His green eyes were familiar, and I recognized our father. To prevent his recognizing me, I hid my face inside my hood."

"What do you want?" he had asked, sitting behind a vast table on a dais. With bony fingers, he picked up a ripe apple from a silver bowl. He polished it with a purple scarf, studying it with lustful eyes.

What did she want? To hide her pain. To have him beg for her forgiveness. To watch an army violate him. She breathed slowly to calm herself.

He seemed to have forgotten her. Rather than show impatience, she inspected the elegant furnishings. Beyond the table, frankincense's smoky haze lingered over a blue velvet divan framed by tapestries. She stood on a fine wool carpet embroidered with silver chariots racing over a green field.

After a proper interval, she said in a business-like voice, "I wish to purchase a license to ply our trade throughout the Isle of Elysia."

The Guildlord didn't look up. "What trade do you practice?"

He baited her. There was only one that women were licensed for. "I am a whore," she said evenly, careful to keep her face hidden.

"I'll deal with your master." He dismissed her with a wave of his cadaverous hand.

"We have none."

He inspected her then, up and down, with rheumy eyes underlined with sagging skin. "We?"

"My sister and I."

He scowled at her. "Fifty percent."

Outrageous. Twenty was customary. She'd give the Innkeeper ten plus the cost of their room, another fifteen to local law enforcement. This she'd learned from the Master.

"I see how you became rich." She removed a leather purse from the belt cinching her plain brown dress and set it on the table. "Percentages vary. I offer a fixed amount."

With one eye he peered into the bag, then balanced it on his palm. His veined nostrils flared, reminding Spangle of a cat sniffing a half-dead mouse. He smiled. She preferred his scowl.

"Let me see the whore who earns this much gold."

Deliberately, she lowered the hood of her cape. "Men pay generously for identical twins."

Shaded by bristling caterpillar eyebrows, his squinty eyes widened. The apple tumbled from his bony fingers, thumping down the two dais steps, rolling over the marble floor and carpet.

Evidently, nothing had shocked him in a long time. Without looking away, he dug in the pocket of his brocade robe and pulled out a palm-sized oval painting. As he glanced at it then back at her, his pallid face turned gray.

He knew her now. "Are you ill?" she asked politely, rubbing her nose to hide a satisfied smile.

"My stomach." He clutched his mid-section.

She'd heard his ailment started after Mother died. She retrieved the apple and set it on the dais. "Should I send word to your wife?"

He groaned. "Gone."

Market gossips said his next two wives left him because of impotence. He wasn't old, so this was attributed to a curse—an incantation chanted over a closed lock, then key and lock thrown down separate wells. The Guildlord offered a large reward; however, the cursed lock and key weren't found, though a surprisingly large number had been recovered.

Spangle lowered her eyes. "My condolences."

He dismissed her sympathy with a flick of his hand.

"Perhaps a rest on your divan would help," she suggested.

"No use." He rubbed his eyes.

Lack of sleep explained the deep lines in his face, common for a man of seventy, not fifty. He pointed at a chair near the table.

After sitting, she folded her hands on her lap. Under normal circumstances, she'd never question someone with the power to withhold her license, but this was hardly normal, and she would never see him again. She slipped her hand through a slit in her skirt and unsheathed the knife strapped to her thigh. "Do you want to know what happened to us?"

His plaintive eyes had a self-pitying look. "Your life couldn't have been so bad. He was a rich man."

Had he given his daughters even a cursory thought before today? She doubted it. "An old man's wet kisses stinking of stale wine and rotten teeth," she said with disdain. "Gnarled, thin-skinned hands as dry as dead leaves pawing us. He claimed our father sold us. As if that justified what he did."

The Guildlord shrank into his brocade robe, mouth open, spittle on his lower lip.

"Why would Father sell us, my sister asked. Were we bad?"

His eyes sank into the gloomy well of their bony sockets.

"The old man told us he'd named Father his heir."

The Guildlord closed his eyes, rubbing his forehead as though it pained mightily. She hoped it did.

His knuckles reddened as they curled around the painting. "He said he wouldn't hurt them."

She laughed scornfully, as she pressed her palm against the knife blade. The physical pain helped. "When we were twelve and too old for him, he sold us to a whore master for a fortune. I know, because we repaid him. We were valuable, not only because we were identical, but because scars prevented us from conceiving."

He moaned and buried his face in his withered hands. "Did my wife send you to torment me? Her spirit won't let me rest. She comes in my sleep, crying for her daughters. She beats my breast until my heart pounds, and I can't breathe."

Spangle smiled. He deserved more.

He rubbed his swollen eyes. "I'm awake, yet I see her before me."

"I am not your wife!"

Squinting, he leaned toward her. "Her eyes were blue and yours are green."

"Like my father's," she said in a venomous voice. "You poisoned Mother." More gossip.

His furry gray eyebrows met. "She poisoned herself."

That surprised Spangle. "Why?"

"To kill my son inside her belly."

Mother had been pregnant when Father sold her daughters. A suspicion came alive deep inside Spangle, in the place where hope is born. "She must have hated you."

"She poisoned me as well!" His voice drooled with self-pity.

Some of the cords strangling Spangle's spirit unraveled. She'd never lost faith that Mother loved them.

He fell back against a wooden armchair too hard for his brittle bones. "I've suffered."

"Not nearly enough." She stroked the cold blade. What punishment fit his crimes? "Do you expect pity from me?"

The Guildlord appeared to shrink, seeming weaker, more fragile. "Not pity, forgiveness. If you forgive me then my wife's spirit will rest."

His selfishness roiled Spangle's stomach. "My mother died because of your greed."

He nudged the purse with his fingertips. "Take it and your license." He scribbled his name then pushed the paper toward her.

Spangle snatched both, then flipped her knife, catching it by the tip, ready to throw. "Before forgiving you, I'll remedy my mother's failure."

Rheumy eyes watering, he dropped the painting, which hit the carpet with a soft thud. He leaned forward on the table, covering his head with his arms.

She retrieved the small portrait, then strode from the tomb-like Guildhall, vowing never to see Father again. She'd die before letting him hurt Glitter again.

Now Spangle told Thorne, "I didn't kill him, because he might find peace in death. Nor will I forgive him and grant him serenity in life." With a poker, she prodded a log, splitting the wood, which spewed sparks. "I never told Glitter that he's our father or that our mother killed herself. Knowing would only hurt her."

Thorne leaned forward to push an errant lock of hair behind Spangle's ear. "Do you think your father regrets what he did?"

Spangle bit her lower lip so hard she tasted blood. "He may regret my mother's death and may even have cared for her as one cares for a prized horse. Her feelings concerned him not at all. Still, I sleep better knowing my father cannot."

"Though I haven't tried it myself, Bekka says forgiving salves a person's bitterness."

"If I forgive him, he might let Stonevar have Guilds. Forgiving would be easier if he'd been poor like Una's father."

Before Thorne could comment, Glitter returned with Una, and soon after Lott entered the cottage, smelling of cattle, horses, and dried grasses. Una ran to him. Spangle wanted to also. Instead, she concentrated on sewing.

"I'm all muck, little one. I cannot lift you."

Una sobbed as though he'd broken her heart.

"She fears you no longer care for her and thinks you'll sell her if she doesn't please you." Spangle's heart thump-thumped, thump-thumped. When age stole her beauty, would Lott discard her?

Lott wiped his dirty hands on his trousers. "Very well, but your nice clothes will get soiled."

Una put her arms around his neck and kissed his dirty cheek. A few days after her arrival, she fell asleep in Lott's lap. He'd let her remain until he retired. Now she did that every night.

"Don't worry." Lott squeezed her. "I'll keep you till I find you a husband."

Una sobbed until a river of tears flooded her cheeks.

Frowning, Lott shook his head. "Never met a group of females so averse to marriage. Unnatural."

Glitter chuckled. Spangle moved beside him but stopped herself from touching his arm. Her feelings made her vulnerable, and she hated that any man could make her so.

"Shush, child." He wiped Una's tears away with his thumb. "You may live with me until your teeth fall out. Now, what new exploits are you women plotting?" He looked from Thorne to Spangle.

When Spangle didn't answer, Glitter picked up the blood-spotted nightgown and gave her sister a puzzled glance. Spangle held up her poked finger.

"Thorne asked Spangle to form Guilds," Glitter told Lott, daring him to object.

Spangle wanted to gag her sister and slap Lott for roaring with laughter. He seemed determined to think his wife fragile rather than accept that she'd survived what had killed many and turned even more to strong drink. When he paused for breath, he must have realized that he'd offended her and passed Una to Glitter so he could take Spangle's hand.

He bowed his head toward Thorne. "After following the Goddess, I've seen strange marvels."

Spangle tore her hand from his. He would never understand her.

Evidently Thorne detected Spangle's mood and told Lott, "Since Brutte passed, you've managed the fields without proper recognition. I now appoint you Master Farmer and Head Plowman. Select a parcel of land."

Grinning, Lott hugged Spangle. "I'm a landowner."

Spangle hid her face in his shoulder. Thorne had always intended to deed the soldier-farmers property, but did she do it now to prevent Lott from being jealous?

He released Spangle to snag Una from Glitter. "This little one brings good fortune."

Una hugged Lott tight around the neck. Instead of reassuring Spangle, Una's love for Lott pinched her throat. The child would be heartbroken if Lott cast them out. How Spangle would ever learn to trust her husband, she didn't know. Expecting the worst was easier.

Una tugged Lott's hair. He tickled her, making the child wiggle and laugh. Watching them, Spangle's heart felt as if it would burst through her chest. For those she cared about, she must face Father again.

CHAPTER FIFTY-ONE

Solanie wrapped her spirit around Gaspotine. "Thank you for helping me survive winter."

Gaspotine moved away, unaccustomed in life or death to touching another Dragon for any reason besides killing or mating. Death had stolen his ability to do both. But he had an undragonish urge to protect Solanie. He was no better than a bird caring for its nestlings. Revolting.

"I'll go south before the next cold season." Solanie set her long jaw in that determined way Gaspotine recognized.

"Good." He couldn't tolerate another winter worrying. "Where?"

"Elysia. The Fairy Queen's suggestion. She's quite insistent."

Somehow he would destroy this Fairy Queen. "Where does she hive?

"Elysia."

Too many odd things happened there. When had it started? With Thorne moving to Stonevar?

Gaspotine bellowed. "Rustofona!"

His daughter swam to him.

"What gave you the idea Humans could raise Hellestorm?"

"What do you mean?"

"Did a Fairy suggest it?"

"I had no choice."

"I understand. Hellestorm the Great must survive." Gaspotine wasn't accustomed to remaining calm when he wanted to tear off limbs. He twisted his tail so hard it disconnected. "Who was nearby?"

Rustofona narrowed her eyes. "My Fairy-Dragon Quist."

Gaspotine hadn't expected this. Fairy-Dragons weren't bright. Gaspotine's own Fairy-Dragon never looked further ahead than his next dragon-mite. Would one devise something so farseeing? This stank of the Fairy Queen.

"Did Quist advise taking Thorne to the Continuum?"

"I don't consult Fairy-Dragons."

He didn't believe her. A harpoon sticking in her eye might have clouded her memory. "A Human in the Continuum is undragonish."

"Necessary for Hellestorm."

Gaspotine's gut told him the Fairy Queen had proposed this via Quist, but Rustofona either didn't remember or wouldn't admit it. While he questioned her, Solanie stayed nearby, pretending not to listen. Now he turned to the young Dragon. "My old eyes don't see so well." A lie. "Can you show me the Fairy Queen, Solanie?"

She led Gaspotine to a small pink rock that he'd passed many times. Now alerted, he smelled his own scent even from a distance. Clearly, the Queen had eaten his flesh.

The Queen, appearing as a hazelnut, rolled into the river. Size here bore no relation to size in the physical world; nevertheless, her tininess helped her go unnoticed.

For the first time, Gaspotine realized Dragon spirits wouldn't notice what they didn't expect. He'd no intention of enlightening others about the Queen. They detested him enough for polluting the Continuum with igtimus like Thorne and Bludwelt. Even saving Dragon-kind hadn't overcome this, only reduced their criticism to mumbles.

Somehow he must kill this Fairy Queen. But first he must do the impossible and convince her to talk to him. More than impossible, he needed her to speak the truth.

CHAPTER FIFTY-TWO

Like ropes drenched in blood, Spangle's hair hung in rain-soaked braids. She'd delayed visiting her father until it was nearly time to leave Seahaven. She crawled under the oilcloth covering the back of the wagon, circled her eyes with kohl, and slipped gold bracelets on each arm.

Glitter peered under the oilcloth. "Where are you going?"

"To see the Guildlord."

"Shall I come?" Glitter asked eagerly.

Spangle hopped off the wagon, sneezing from the damp or from anticipating the Guild Hall's stench. "Ask about that child tied to the money lender's stall."

Glitter nodded, then hugged Spangle as if sensing her sister needed strength.

"I'll return soon." Clutching her cape, Spangle scurried across the square.

When she identified herself to the guard as the Guildlord's daughter, the thug looked her up and down, but didn't step aside.

"You don't want to insult me, you great oaf." She pictured blood spurting from his thick neck. Since drinking Dragon blood, stupidity loosed her savage side.

Scowling as if he'd sooner punch her, he opened the door and made to lead her inside.

She brushed past him. "I know the way."

Grunting, he adjusted the oversized helmet on his undersized head.

Atop the dais, Father penciled in a ledger on his expansive table. "Yes, yes. What is it?" His voice cracked. His face was more crimped

233

than she remembered. A heavy brocade robe clothed him in the sweltering room. She doubted he'd survive another winter.

When she didn't speak, he looked up. "What do you want?"

"Have you forgotten your daughter, Sopia?" Declaring her given name after two decades made Spangle feel more exposed than disrobing.

"You lie. Get out."

Spangle stepped forward, holding up the small painting of her mother. "I kept this from my last visit."

"A thief as well as a whore."

"I'm flattered you remember."

He set down his quill. "What is the purpose of this distasteful surprise?"

"I . . . I . . ." He no longer seemed to want her forgiveness; the one thing she'd counted on.

He squinted as if trying to bring her into focus. "Speak up, trollop."

The cassia incense filling the air with a cinnamony haze failed to ease her breathing. She stowed the painting in her purse and stroked the knife grip through the slit in her skirt. "I am a handmaiden of the Goddess. Appoint me Guildhead of Stonevar."

He cackled until tears flowed down the deep crevices of his face. "You."

First Lott, now Father laughing at her. Her resolve strengthened. "I am your eldest daughter and heir."

His face darkened as he shook a bony fist. "You dare blackmail me? ME!"

She doubted anyone had dared question him for years. Having nothing to lose gave her power. "If the Guildlord dies without a son, his eldest daughter inherits. That's the law."

"I've not acknowledged you."

"On the day we were born, you wrote our names in the town registry."

His smile chilled Spangle. "A woman cannot become Guildlord."

"My husband can." The image of Lott's shocked reaction almost brought a smile.

Father templed his fingers. "It's not wise to be so clever."

She bowed. "My sire is known for his shrewdness. I'll surrender my claim for your signature." From beneath her cloak, she retrieved a parchment.

He unrolled it, then flicked it with yellowed, inch-long fingernails. "I sign and you go?"

"Yes."

"How do I know you'll not present yourself after my death?"

She pulled another parchment from under her cloak. "This renounces my inheritance." Thorne had prepared both documents.

He slumped on his ornately carved chair. "Why should I? You cannot prove you're my daughter. With your hideous red hair and great height, you don't resemble your diminutive mother. No one will believe you."

"The illegality would interest the man who bought my inheritance."

"You repulsive tart!" Father's skeletal face turned red as fire vine berries. "How dare you meddle in men's affairs?"

"It's my affair as well." Gossip said Seahaven's Guildhead paid her father more gold than a man could carry. "The Guildhead will be displeased to learn you've a legitimate heir. He'll demand his payment back with interest."

Wrinkles circled the Guildlord's pursed mouth as he slouched in his chair. "I've enough misery. The new Magister demands more taxes. My bribes are insufficient." His bony neck stretched. "I'm an old man. Leave so I can rest."

His feigned yawns didn't fool her. "After you sign."

"Remove yourself or I'll call the guard."

"Sign and I leave."

He picked up his quill and scribbled his name. Contemptuously, he flicked the second parchment toward her. His eyes widened when she signed her name like Thorne taught her.

He drank from his wine cup and licked his thin lips. "You've swindled an old man."

She blew on his signature to dry the ink, then said sarcastically, "Thank you, Father."

The Guildlord sniggered. "Maybe you are my daughter."

Although she wanted to run from this depressing place and its skeletal ruler, she strode out deliberately, neglecting to remind him that he had two daughters. Glitter could still claim her inheritance.

Outside, the rain had washed the air clean. Horse hooves

clopped cobblestones in Seahaven's most prosperous area. Glitter chatted with the guard. Spangle snagged her sister's forearm and pulled her away. The guard frowned.

"Why are you here?" Spangle whispered.

"Did he make you Guildhead?"

When Spangle nodded, Glitter hugged her. Spangle unwound her sister's arms and hurried her past the other Guild Halls into the market.

As they passed the cobbler's shop, Spangle said, "I'm worn out. Next visit, I'll try to recruit guild journeymen. What did you learn about the child tied to the moneylender's shop?"

"She's collateral. I'll check on her when we return." Amid scents of beeswax and animal fat, Glitter planted her feet before the candlemaker's shop and refused to move. "While I was waiting, I remembered overhearing Father and Mother arguing."

"They fought a lot. Don't think about it."

"Mother was crying. She said the price was too high. Father said he wanted to be Guildlord." Glitter searched Spangle's face. "Is he?"

Spangle hesitated before nodding. Glitter ran back the way they'd come. Spangle rushed after her and caught Glitter's cape, forcing her to stop.

"I want to see him."

"Trust me. You don't."

Glitter must have seen something in her sister's eyes and let Spangle lead her away.

When they reached Stonevar's wagon, Spangle said, "Don't be cross."

Dragon-eyed pupils emphasized Glitter's glower. "I barely want to talk to you."

"I had to protect you."

"So you lied."

"By omission." Spangle took out Mother's picture, gave it to Glitter, and told everything. "Forgive me."

Glitter took the picture. "You can pack up. I'm going for a walk."

CHAPTER FIFTY-THREE

"**Y**ou must come," Zarra told Thorne.

Hellee whimpered, wanting Thorne to stay.

When Thorne hesitated, Zarra took her arm. Odd, since the thief normally avoided touching anyone. Thorne hugged Hellee and reassured him that Fehera would stay. The healer offered him a deer thighbone to distract him.

Thorne followed Zarra though the secret door beside the cavern fireplace. "What's happened?"

"Spangle will explain." Zarra rushed through the tunnels, the fastest route to Stonevar. Only she had mastered the Dwarfs' stone burrows.

Thorne pestered Zarra for information, but she wouldn't answer.

They emerged inside Glitter's chamber where Spangle lay sobbing on the bed. Willow-Bender stood in a corner, breathing through her mouth, clearly overwhelmed by Spangle's suffering. Bekka stopped patting Spangle's back and let Thorne take her place on the lavender coverlet.

"Tell me," Thorne said.

Spangle tried to sit up, but fell back. Willow-Bender sat beside her, letting Spangle lean against her. The bed creaked but didn't collapse. The Giantess looked out of place in this room draped with pastel gauze and spindly-legged white furniture.

"Glitter's betrothed to Lord Bludwelt." Spangle's breathing sounded labored. "She stayed in Seahaven. Scatt said Bludwelt had been courting her for months. She never told me."

Thorne gathered Spangle in her arms. She should've warned the twins about Bludwelt's dragonish appeal.

"Glitter would never agree to wed a man like that or any man for that matter." Spangle clung to Thorne. "She never keeps secrets from me."

Thorne had never seen Spangle like this. For the first time, Thorne realized that the whorish trappings—wall tapestries of cavorting forest gods, violet-scented silk curtains, sheepskin rugs under impractical furniture—prevented others from seeing two vulnerable women.

"Bludwelt has charms even I can't resist." Ignoring the fluttering inside her chest, Thorne told them how Bludwelt had stolen the waterskin with Gaspotine the Dark's blood.

Spangle pulled away. "You mean you knew this could happen?"

Thorne couldn't meet Spangle's gaze. "I hadn't thought about him affecting you and Glitter, but I should have." How could she explain? "I'm sorry. I was ashamed. You have experience with . . ." She didn't know the words.

Shouts from the Great Hall joined Spangle's sobs. Thorne sent Zarra to investigate.

Zarra rushed into the room. "Lott's on his way."

Spangle hid her face in Thorne's shoulder. "I don't want to see him."

"Ask Lott to wait."

Zarra nodded. The shouting moved outside then stopped.

"This happened because I married Lott."

Bekka joined them on the bed. "You love him."

"I've loved Glitter longer." Spangle gasped thrice as if she couldn't breathe. "The Guildlord distracted me. I should've seen what was happening and protected Glitter."

Willow-Bender clicked her tongue. "The heart sparks fires that reforge lives."

No one knew that better than Willow-Bender. Her love for Captain Hauk had almost killed the Giantess.

Thorne stood. "Don your Dragon leathers. We ride to Seahaven."

Spangle sat up. "You can't. You're pregnant."

Thorne ignored that.

#

The Goddess of Stonevar rode into Seahaven on her bay warhorse, wearing the black hide of Gaspotine the Dark. Four Dragon Guards followed, riding two abreast, eyes straight ahead; Willow-Bender and Spangle, Fehera and Nella, all in red Dragon leathers. The townspeople watched silently. The eight-foot Giantess attracted the most interest; evidently most had never seen one. That diverted attention from Fehera, who Bludwelt had threatened to arrest if she returned to Seahaven.

They reached the Magister's house, where Bludwelt imprisoned Glitter, without incident. Outside, nothing had changed since Thorne's last visit four years before; poplars still circled the one-story house with its wide front porch.

Seeming to sense Thorne's mood, Wild-Eyes shook her head. Thorne loosened the reins. While they waited for Bludwelt, Seahaven's uniformed constables formed a half-circle around the Dragon Guards. Unlike the town folk, the constables seemed unsurprised at the Goddess's return.

When his constables were in position, Lord Bludwelt, who had evidently been watching, stepped onto the porch. "Goddess, welcome to Seahaven." His white hair flowed forward as he bowed.

Fehera had given them peppermint oil to smear under their noses. Even so, Thorne felt a primeval attraction to Bludwelt, though less compelling than before her pregnancy.

Thorne glanced at the constables. "A most ardent welcome, Magister."

"I'm pleased that you're honored. It's been some years since you graced our streets."

"Only one since you visited Stonevar."

He grinned, showing pointed canine teeth. "A most eventful sojourn."

Unrepentant about her kidnapping then. "Transformative, I would say."

He smoothed his long white hair. "I've changed. My betrothal made me a different man altogether."

On a visit with a less serious purpose, Thorne might have enjoyed their banter. "Your betrothal induced my journey."

"Not to call on me?" Bludwelt feigned disappointment, but his amber Dragon eyes glistened.

"A visit with you is always memorable. Today I seek my

handmaiden, your intended who is still in my service."

He scratched his heavy jaw. "That presents a quandary."

"No quandary. She'll return with me."

The crowd beyond the constables murmured.

Bludwelt smiled and waved at the gathering. "Her betrothal rescinds her commitment to you."

"I don't see how. She swore allegiance to me first."

"Her father pledged her to me."

Behind Thorne, Spangle gasped. Without looking behind, Thorne raised her hand, signaling silence. The Dragon Guards, especially Spangle, were supposed to avoid displaying any reaction. The throng seemed to enjoy Spangle's upset. They murmured dislike for her red hair, a dark shade common only to Dwarfs. They disapproved of women in trousers. They considered her height unnatural.

Thorne smoothed emotion from her face. "Why would her father do that? She's nearing thirty, past marrying age."

"For a substantial bride price." Bludwelt licked his lips.

The constables guffawed. All were clean shaven and wore tidy, blue uniforms.

"How dare he sell her a second time!" Spangle shouted.

"Quiet," Thorne whispered. Spangle knew the answer. The Guildlord dared because both he and Bludwelt had wealth and power. Spangle had been wrong; her father hadn't forgotten about Glitter's inheritance. Thorne knew Spangle was thinking that the Guildlord wouldn't have given his daughters a thought if she hadn't threatened his legacy.

The crowd mumbled questions.

"May I speak with Glitter?" Thorne asked.

"She's quite busy, preparing for our nuptials."

Thorne wished he'd look away. "What price to free her from your captivating charms?"

"No captive. She came willingly."

"Like a hare willingly leaps between a wole-wolf's jaws."

The throng sniggered. Lord Bludwelt laughed. Thorne had an unwelcome vision of swimming with him naked in the lake where Rustofona and Vainglorian had mated. Bludwelt caught a silver fish and bit into its raw flesh. She licked the blood trickling down his chin.

As if sensing her thoughts, Bludwelt swept an arm toward chairs on the porch. "Join me, so we may speak privately."

Thorne thought it safer to look down at him from atop Wild-Eyes, but if the town couldn't hear them, perhaps he would bargain. "May I bring my handmaiden, Spangle?" She didn't trust Spangle to stay quiet or herself so close to Bludwelt.

"Certainly." His long aquiline nose flared as he inhaled deeply. "Two are sweeter."

The crowd tittered.

On the porch, his silvery scent made her shiver. "What will free Glitter from her betrothal?"

"You mean Gwyna."

Beside Thorne, Spangle clasped the knife strapped to her thigh. "How dare you speak my sister's true name."

Thorne gave her a warning glance. "Your price?"

"A superior bride." As he twisted the ruby ring on his little finger, he gave Thorne a meaningful look.

"I'm sure many are available."

"The Magister grants divorces."

Thorne hadn't anticipated this. She'd no intention of divorcing Strumgued to marry Bludwelt. "Let me speak to Glitter."

"She's resting after a glass of wine."

Thorne twitched. "Did you spice it?"

"You enjoy my special wine."

Dragonwort. He'd sedated Glitter.

"My friend, Daxx, has skill with plants."

Thorne rubbed her nose. "And a tolerance for smells." Dragons and Fairy-Dragons found its decaying animal scent irresistible. So did Thorne and anyone who drank Dragon blood.

Bludwelt laughed. "I've missed you."

"Yet you settle for another."

He lifted an eyebrow. "You taunt me. I've no intention of settling."

The small hairs on the back of Thorne's neck rose. "My handmaiden will never wed you."

"The penalty for a woman breaking her betrothal is public whipping."

Spangle covered her mouth, smothering a cry.

Thorne jumped to her feet. "You wouldn't dare."

"Head Constable," Bludwelt said, "fetch my fiancée!"

Fexx stomped past, wearing a gold badge on a spotless uniform. His scraggly blond hair was clean and neatly tied back. Thorne barely recognized him.

Spangle clutched the porch column. "Don't harm her."

"I will uphold the law," Bludwelt said.

The crowd muttered agreement. A few men drew their weapons, as if hoping for a fight. Apparently, Bludwelt was a popular Magister. Thorne wanted to warn them that they succored a snake, but would they believe her?

With Fexx grasping her arm, Glitter shuffled onto the porch.

"Are you hurt?" Spangle asked.

Eyes glazed, Glitter shook her head. Her thin face was ashen.

"Will you honor your betrothal and wed me?" Bludwelt asked.

"No," Glitter whispered.

"Tie her," Bludwelt told Fexx.

The crowd shouted encouragement. As Fexx secured Glitter to the porch post, she tugged weakly at her restraints. Fexx cut the laces closing the back of Glitter's blue velvet gown, exposing her pale skin. Bludwelt loosened the whip from his belt and snapped it. When Thorne saw Spangle palm her knife, she grabbed her arm.

"I won't let you whip her," Thorne told Bludwelt.

"Neither will I." Spangle tried to pull away, but Thorne held tight.

Bludwelt nodded toward the constables who outnumbered the Dragon Guards five to one. The constables unsheathed their weapons. Willow-Bender growled through closed lips. Nella and Fehera looked serene, but Thorne knew they were ready.

"Do you want blood wetting your doorstep?" Thorne asked Bludwelt.

The throng muttered. They'd enjoy that. One shouted, "He bought her."

Another, "You can't take a man's property."

"She's my handmaiden. Her father had no right to sell her a second time."

That brought confused rumblings from the observers.

Bludwelt coiled his whip. "Your marriage means nothing, Thorne. Stay and I will free Glitter."

"You are not my destiny."

Bludwelt's slow smile sent chills up Thorne's spine. Before she could react, his whip nicked Glitter's shoulder. She moaned.

An arrow thumped the pole above Glitter.

Face hooded, Zarra stood on the roof of the Magister's stable, bow readied. "Free her now."

"Now!" Scatt echoed from a tree, bow drawn.

"Now!" Emera shouted, balancing on a temple dome, arrow aimed at Bludwelt's heart.

"Now!" Edz perched on a house roof, bowstring taut as he sighted on Bludwelt.

All wore hoods masking their faces.

"They'll kill you first, Magister," Thorne said. "Then, anyone raising a sword."

Spangle escaped Thorne's grip and threw her knife, cutting the rope tying Glitter. Before she fell, Bludwelt caught her. She squirmed lethargically. A few in the gathering laughed. A standoff.

"Release her," Thorne demanded.

Bludwelt licked the blood from Glitter's shoulder. "We are betrothed. I'll do as I wish."

Even if Glitter refused, her father's consent was enough.

Thorne wanted to slide Dracodurus across Bludwelt's neck and watch his blood gush. "Nullify your betrothal."

"I'll marry her, unless . . ." He raised Glitter's red hair and sniffed her neck. "She smells like a rose."

Thorne couldn't breathe. He knew her real name.

"Some like lilies. I prefer roses."

He knew Lily was her sister. She wanted to cut out his tongue, but her arm wouldn't move.

"A rose can be very expensive." He smiled knowingly.

Da had betrothed her to Bludwelt for a large bride price. Bludwelt would free Glitter only if Thorne agreed to his terms.

Thorne nodded. "Release Glitter."

"I release Glitter from our betrothal." Bludwelt shoved her away. Spangle caught her sister.

As Bludwelt started to say the words that would divorce her from Strumgued, Thorne shouted, "I must be won in battle!"

Pointing her sword at his neck, Thorne leapt off the porch, rushing him. He deflected her blow with the whip butt. For a moment they were arm to arm. This close, the peppermint did nothing to block his dragonish scent. Perhaps because of her pregnancy, desire to kill was stronger than desire to press against him.

He fell back, drawing his weapon and unhooking the buckler, a small shield, from his belt. She readied her dragon-hide buckler and struck at Bludwelt's head. He ducked and countercut to her leg. His blade didn't penetrate Dragon leather but bruised her knee. When she hopped back, favoring her leg, he smiled. The observers cheered.

She lunged. He parried. Thorne's technique was weak. His smile showed he knew it. Pregnancy had slowed her.

He swung at her neck. Deflecting the blow with her buckler made her shoulder ache. She chopped at his side. He sidestepped, and her blade sliced air, leaving her off balance.

She wouldn't win this fight.

"I alone am like you." Bludwelt swung his sword toward her ribs.

Ignoring the pang in her elbow, she blocked with an upper cut. "There's no resemblance." She slashed at his face.

He easily deflected by swinging his weapon in a half-circle, countering with a second blow to her bruised thigh. "Only I am worthy of you."

She grunted and stumbled backward. "Only a fool judges his own worth."

Willow-Bender groaned. The others gripped their swords.

Thorne jabbed at his eye. He batted her blade aside, then thrust at her belly. Instinctively she retreated, catching his point with her buckler.

Thorne tried a figure eight, but he flicked her blade away. He circled, looking for an opening. In a few moves he'd win, pronounce her divorced, and make her marry him. Her only chance was letting him think she wanted him to win.

She winked at him and struck a light blow at his head. He ducked and his weapon hit hard. Her elbow collapsed, slamming her buckler against her chest. Fire smoldered in his eyes. Apparently, Bludwelt didn't trust her.

She stabbed at his heart, a small target. He knocked her sword away to nick the side of her neck. Blood streamed.

"Thorne!" Spangle called.

"Stay back." She felt no pain now but soon would.

"Surrender," he said.

Though she wanted to say "never," Thorne whispered, "In time." Her breath came in short gasps. Though every instinct resisted, she must let him disarm her.

Bludwelt licked her blood from his blade, making the fire in his eyes burn brighter. "We are meant to share the same harness."

"A sweet proposal. But you must vanquish me first." She swung her blade low.

He batted Dracodurus from her hand. Bludwelt lowered his sword, his smile claiming victory.

She moved close. "I carry the Dwarf Lord's child."

His jaw fell open.

Thorne hit him hard in the side of the head with her buckler. He dropped. Brutte once told her to "Strike a hard blow that knocks your opponent to his knees. Then lop off his head." By the time she retrieved her sword, Fexx separated her from Bludwelt.

"She killed the Magister!" Fexx shouted, tears streaming down his bony cheeks. "Arrest them!"

The constables looked at Fexx who was sniffling beside Bludwelt, at Stonevar's bowmen, then at each other.

"A fair fight." Thorne mounted Wild-Eyes. "Let us pass."

The constables raised their swords.

"Our dispute ended honorably." Inside her, the igle thrashed. "Move aside."

When the constables hesitated, Thorne urged Wild-Eyes forward. The warhorse burst through their line. The constables fell back. After Thorne and the Dragon Guards passed, Stonevar's bowmen vanished from the rooftops.

With Seahaven behind Thorne, the road ahead dimmed until it shrank into a narrow tunnel. When it went black, she tumbled from Wild-Eyes.

Even after Fehera bandaged her neck, Thorne couldn't ride. Willow-Bender, atop her shire horse, cradled Thorne all the way to Malwood. By then night had fallen, and they made camp. Thorne lay on the ground, head propped on a rolled up blanket, trying not to move. After Edz and Scatt fell asleep, the Dragon Guards sat around a campfire. Zarra hacked a leg from a half-cooked partridge as it roasted.

Glitter rubbed her forehead. "Bludwelt beguiled me, though I didn't believe any man could. I wanted no husband, yet I couldn't resist him."

Spangle took her sister's hand. "This went on for months. Why didn't you tell me?"

"I was ashamed that a schurk attracted me."

"A schurk?" Afraid she'd pass out again, Thorne resisted moving her head, even to lessen the stink of decay and fungus wafting from Malwood.

"A rogue. A blackguard," Glitter said. "A northern sailor taught me the word."

"I should've warned you that the Dragon in him calls the Dragon in us. We must never return to Seahaven."

"Maybe you killed him," Spangle said.

"He lives. I saw his chest rise." Each defeat only increased his determination to have her. "If he sees anyone from Stonevar, he'll arrest them."

#

"What happened to your neck?" Strumgued asked, but before Thorne could answer, he demanded, "What's this I hear about you riding to Seahaven?"

Thorne pulled the bedding under her chin. Of late, his admonishments occurred when she was in bed. Her marriage was becoming even more disagreeable. "Do you have me watched?"

He harrumphed. "Since you neglect to tell me your plans, it seems I must."

Mentioning Bludwelt wouldn't improve his temper. "I hadn't planned to visit Seahaven."

Firelight flickered across his jutting chin. "I cannot let you endanger my unborn child."

"I'd leave it behind, but my condition compels me to take it."

"Give me your word that you won't go to Seahaven again before you deliver."

"I won't return to Seahaven."

"Very well. What about your neck?" When he touched the bandage, she knocked his hand away.

"A small wound, which will heal quickly." It would've killed anyone who hadn't drunk Dragon blood.

The back of his trembling fingers touched her cheek. "I feel no fever."

She let his hand stay, hating apologies even more than explanations. "I had no intent to worry you."

"I doubt you thought of me at all."

She couldn't deny it.

"Strive to extend me the smallest courtesy by notifying me of your whereabouts." He stomped out.

Thorne should've felt relieved but for the first time, she would've welcomed his presence.

CHAPTER FIFTY-FOUR

Thorne awoke screaming. She reached for Strumgued but his side of the bed was empty.

She'd dreamed Da planted rose bush after rose bush until hundreds bloomed, each marking a grave. Her sister Daisy's was in the center, between Mother's and Lily's.

Holding her breath, Thorne felt her stomach. Still there. No rose bush for her child. As if to reassure her, it kicked. She felt what might be a foot. A separate being, yet part of her.

In the morning, she'd tell herself this was all a dream, that she'd been only half awake and deny wanting to hold her child or press it to her breast. She'd deny wondering what it would look like or who it would become.

For a brief moment, in the middle of night, she forgot that when she was nine, her newborn sister, Daisy, had died in her arms. She forgot her vow to neither marry nor have children.

Instead she pictured nursing her child under a summer sun and smelling its hair. She pictured a world where babies didn't starve, where no one buried living newborns with dead mothers, where children survived childhood.

Maybe if she hadn't read about the dangers of childbirth in Grandfather's book, she would've healed after Daisy's death. Perhaps she would've married Rutmon and been content.

Strumgued would be a good father. He'd do everything in his power to protect his child, but sickness not swords slew most children.

Bekka had suggested Thorne sew a baby gown. Thorne replied that she was poor at needlework. True but she'd sew no gown that might be a shroud.

She fell back asleep, thinking laying eggs would be less troublesome. The next day, Thorne denied waking or remembering her dreams.

#

That afternoon, Thorne had confidence that the Giantess would do as asked. She found Willow-Bender herding sheep into the bailey.

The ram butted Willow-Bender as she enticed the flock into the pen with a bucket of grain.

"Hey!" Thorne shouted to distract the ram as she waddled closer. Minding the gate was the one chore she could still do.

Willow-Bender dumped the grain in a trough and scratched the animal's head. "No harm."

When all the sheep were inside, Thorne latched the gate. "Stonevar needs her own merchant ship to trade with the mainland."

Willow-Bender wiped sweat from her forehead with her arm. "Ships are a muckle of work."

"We need a captain."

The Giantess nodded, replying with measured words. "One who understands the sea and your purpose."

"I know only one."

Willow-Bender plodded into the sheep barn, an abrupt departure that surprised Thorne. Had the Giantess misunderstood? Thorne followed.

The barn stunk of wool and sheep droppings. As the Giantess shoveled waste into a bucket, Thorne opened a shutter. The smoky air smelled of scorched weeds from burning a field.

As Thorne turned around, Emera came through the door, carrying a stool. "Mother sent me to help."

"Your mother doesn't trust me." Everyone treated her like she was brittle, although women commonly worked until delivery. "Willow-Bender, aren't you curious about who will captain Stonevar's ship?"

Willow-Bender shrugged and continued shoveling.

Emera's eyes looked dreamy. "Could we find my father?"

"First we need a trustworthy captain familiar with the mainland."

"Willow-Bender knows the mainland," the Wanderling said excitedly. "Don't you?"

"Aye."

Thorne smiled. "Willow-Bender, I want you to captain Stonevar's ship."

The Giantess grabbed her full pail in one hand and Emera's half-empty one in the other, and stomped from the barn to dump them into a wagon.

Emera danced around Thorne. "We'll find my father." She skipped around the barn until Willow-Bender flung the buckets on the floor.

The Wanderling seemed unable to stand still. "Will you captain the ship?"

Willow-Bender, head twitching, shoveled both buckets full then lugged them outside.

Emera's lip trembled. "Will she?"

"I don't know." Thorne rubbed the top of her stomach where her skin stretched tight. "Perhaps she needs to think about it."

"For how long?"

"However long it takes." Thorne didn't want to agitate the Giantess further. "Please, don't bother her."

"I've waited my whole life to meet my father. I can't wait any longer." She sped toward the door.

"Where are you going?" Thorne asked, afraid that Emera might annoy the Giantess.

"To tell mother that I'm going to find my father."

Thorne shook her head. Find a Wanderer. Impossible. Grandfather wrote that only Wanderers knew the location of their homeland. Outsiders attempting to find it invited a Wanderer's curse.

Willow-Bender shoved past Emera and hurled the foul buckets, missing Thorne's head by a hand's breadth. With a bang, one wooden bucket shattered into slats. Outside, bleating sheep rushed the closed gate.

The Wanderling jumped back. "What's wrong?"

Thorne shook her head. "I've angered her. But how?"

Willow-Bender leaned against the wide doorway, shoulders hunched forward. The trembling that started in her head spread downward. "Hate shoveling shit."

"Then don't." After Hauk's death, embracing Willow-Bender had calmed her. "Fetch the Dragon Guards," Thorne told Emera. "Close the door after you."

The Giantess growled like an angry bear. "Air."

"Stay." Thorne grabbed her arm to prevent the Giantess from doing damage.

Willow-Bender yanked back her arm, kicked the door open, and stomped outside. Smoke blackened the sky. The baaing sheep milled by the gate, further agitated by the fire. The Giantess waded into the flock, scattering them.

"Stupid beasts. They shhhit and shhhit." Willow-Bender grabbed a ewe by the legs and flung it against the fence with a loud crack. It hit the ground, kicked once, and was still. When the ram charged her, she grabbed him by his curled horns and shook him. "Mutton."

"Willow-Bender, please stop," Thorne pleaded.

The Giantess cast down the ram. It baaed and tried to rise but one leg was injured.

"Horse." Willow-Bender strode toward the corral.

Not the horses! Thorne grabbed the Giantess's arm, but Willow-Bender threw her off.

"Stop, Willow-Bender!" Thorne shouted. What took Emera so long? Hours seemed to have passed. Then the emergency bell clanged, summoning those in the fields home.

"Hate horses."

The Giantess's smile chilled Thorne. Willow-Bender never liked riding, but Thorne hadn't known she hated horses.

Willow-Bender swung a leg over the log fence. "You." She pointed at Wild-Eyes.

The warhorse pawed the ground. Thorne lumbered over the fence then dashed between the Giantess and the mare.

Gasping, Thorne held up her palms. "I'm sorry I offended you. Don't let a Rampage control you." She'd read about Giant Rampages in Grandfather's book. He advised avoiding rampaging Giants. Or killing them.

Willow-Bender's shudders worsened. "I'm an ill-beseeming Giant." She shoved Thorne aside.

Thorne landed on her bottom. Pain ripped through her tailbone. Feeling like an upended turtle with her pregnant belly, Thorne clasped the fence rails to pull herself upright.

The Giantess's eyes flashed maliciously. Fueled by dragonish fury, she'd be even more dangerous. The horses trotted to the other side of the corral. Thorne suspected killing a horse would inspire greater atrocities.

Lott entered the bailey carrying the torch used to ignite the field. "What's going on?"

"Fire!" Willow-Bender burst through the gate, snatched the torch, and strode toward the cow barn.

A crowd had gathered, but not a single Dragon Guard. Were they all with Hellee?

"Stay back!" Thorne rushed after the Giantess, remembering Dragons found fire irresistible and relished explosions. "Dear friend, please calm yourself."

The rage in Willow-Bender's eyes flared brighter.

"Hear me!" Thorne moved between the Giantess and the cows. "Calm yourself."

Willow-Bender held the brand to the barn roof then clomped toward the castle. Lott and the others carried buckets of water and wet down the smoldering roof. Bekka carried Lily's baby to the front of the crowd. Thorne motioned her back.

"The well's dry!" Lott shouted.

Refilling would take an hour.

Emera dashed to Thorne. "The others are coming."

She'd been gone only moments, which seemed like hours. "Fetch my bow," Thorne told the Wanderling and shouted for everyone to move back.

"Hate willow." The Giantess threw the torch on the willow branches piled beside the castle and watched the flames before striding toward the horses.

Agitated by the fire, the animals trotted back and forth inside the pen. Thorne lurched after Willow-Bender, holding her stomach with one hand and her bow with the other. The Giantess yanked open the gate and snagged Emera's yearling.

"No!" Emera launched onto Willow-Bender's back.

The Giantess released the filly to yank Emera off and held her up as if she were vermin.

Nella shrieked from the bailey entrance. The crowd gasped.

Thorne drew back her arrow. "Put Emera down!"

As the horses thundered from the pen, the Giantess dropped Emera and caught Wild-Eyes's halter. The warhorse dragged the Giantess until she lost her footing, then she let go and stumbled into Bekka.

Bekka fell on her twisted back, emitting a high-pitched cry as the wailing baby tumbled from her arms. The Giantess swung her head as if seeking the source, then picked up the screaming child by his foot. Blood streaked his gown where his tiny wings had ripped the cloth.

The crowd murmured surprise. "A chimera," someone said.

Thorne pulled back her bowstring, aiming at Willow-Bender's heart. "Don't throw the baby!"

The onlookers held their breaths.

Only Bekka moved, scrambling to her feet and limping to Willow-Bender. "Please, give me Aeron." When Bekka reached upward, the Giantess shook her head, seeming confused.

Thorne blinked away the perspiration leaking into her eyes. She couldn't risk delay. "Give Bekka the child!"

Willow-Bender dangled the baby above Bekka's head, making him wail louder. Bekka clutched the Giantess's waist. Nella hugged Willow-Bender from behind. Emera ducked under the Giantess's arm to hold her side. Willow-Bender shook them off. They threw themselves at her midsection.

"Please." Thorne's hands shook as she aimed. Her first shot had to kill; she couldn't risk a wounded Giantess. One last chance. "Please. Give Bekka the baby."

Thorne's fingers couldn't feel the string. Though she'd rather die herself, she let go. Too late, she saw the fierce light dim in her friend's eyes and moved her bow hand.

The Giantess yowled, dropping the child. Bekka caught him. Willow-Bender clutched the arrow protruding from her shoulder.

For the first time, Thorne was happy she wasn't a skilled archer. Hands shaking, she lowered her bow. "Take Willow-Bender upstairs."

Fehera rushed to the Giantess and told the crowd, "A fever possesses her."

Thorne was grateful to the healer and relieved that Willow-Bender's flushed face supported Fehera's claim. Thorne didn't want everyone fearing the Giantess. Though unresisting, Willow-Bender stumbled often on the stairs. It took both Thorne and Fehera to steady her. Inside Willow-Bender's sleeping room, Fehera treated her wound. Afterward the Giantess refused to remain seated, instead yanking open the narrow window to suck in air.

Thorne motioned for Fehera to leave, telling her to lock them in. The room still had Lily's sweet apple scent. Thorne's imagination? When they were children, they put apple blossoms in their hair and pretended to be grand ladies.

After Thorne led Willow-Bender to the bed, which occupied half the room, she sat beside her. Willow-Bender hugged Lily's embroidered pillow. Lily's small bed was gone. In a corner stood three tall drums of different diameters. Hauk's flag—a sea serpent crushing a ship—covered one wall.

The Giantess groaned and buried her face in Lily's pillow. Her coarse copper hair poked in every direction. As she rocked side to side, Thorne put an arm around her wide shoulders, refusing to be shaken off. Could a Rampage re-ignite?

Willow-Bender clutched Hauk's shell necklace at her throat. "Bad luck."

"Hauk didn't believe that. He said you were born to race a sea wind. Made you his sea wife." Thorne's skin prickled. Should she have mentioned Hauk?

The Giantess moaned. "My bad luck killed him."

"Lord Bludwelt killed Hauk." Grandfather's book said nothing about Giants after a Rampage passed. Perhaps none survived.

Willow-Bender's cheeks turned the color of a late autumn apple. She held up her hand, asking for silence. "If not for me, Hauk would live."

"Why say that?"

"Bad luck damaged his ship. Bad luck anchored him here."

"The Sea Runner was damaged in battle. One person doesn't lose a fight."

"No proper Giant."

After drinking Dragon blood, Willow-Bender had grown until she stood eight feet tall. No longer short by Giant standards. But clearly, she still felt inadequate.

"No proper sailor. No proper wife."

Thorne massaged Willow-Bender's slumped spine until the Giantess breathed easier. "Everyone fails sometimes."

Willow-Bender stiffened. "Failure unacceptable."

If Giants thought they should never fail, no wonder they went brainsick. "I don't expect perfection. Your best is good enough."

"No proper Captain." The Giantess's eyes glazed.

What would soothe Willow-Bender? Up till now, Thorne's instincts hadn't been good.

"A Dragon trusts herself." As far as Thorne knew, Dragons never questioned themselves.

Willow-Bender grunted.

"A Dragon never yields to fear." Not quite true.

Willow-Bender's shoulders jerked. This must have aggravated her wound, but she gave no sign. Her mental state seemed more painful.

"A Dragon Guard never goes back on her word. You promised to protect Hellee and Aeron." Thorne paused to let Willow-Bender digest her words.

The Giantess covered Thorne's belly with hands the size of pail bottoms. "With my life, I pledge to protect your infanta from harm."

Thorne hadn't expected that. If the igle died, she didn't want Willow-Bender going on another Rampage. "Thank you."

Now Willow-Bender looked up with clear eyes. "Once I wanted to see alltihap—the whole world."

"That's what I want, too." But Thorne would die in childbirth. She'd never sail with Captain Willow-Bender.

CHAPTER FIFTY-FIVE

Gaspotine recited;

> "What cannot pass through hills,
> but hills cannot keep out?
> What soughs and whistles,
> but cannot shout?
> What lifts trees and beasts,
> but cannot lift itself about?"

Vainglorian the Red nodded, clearly appreciating the intricacy of Gaspotine's riddle.

Erramon the Eldest scraped a vaporous talon against a fang. "I shall attempt to solve your riddle."

Gaspotine smiled as he moved away, almost feeling alive again. Frustration had forced him to cease searching for hazelnuts that might be the Fairy Queen in disguise. Devising a riddle had improved his humor. He'd let Solanie and the Fairy Queen distract him from finding his offspring long enough.

He jumped into the Silver River, planning to seek his whelps at an age before they entered the Continuum. He watched she-Dragon after she-Dragon kill her whelp in the year before the young Dragon might enter the Continuum for the first time.

Although the whelps were dissimilar in temperament, all demonstrated undragonish traits. One was cheery. Another fearful. Or too quiet. Too calm. Too small. Undragonish in some manner.

They shared in common the viciousness of the predator their mothers selected to test them. Even a small wound was cause enough for the mother to kill it.

Catulicide—Dragon-kind's secret. How many superior whelps had died? Was this why so few of his own survived?

Gaspotine rode the currents of a dozen survivors. They learned slowly. They were cruel. Narcissistic. Lazy. Uncurious. Fleshly urges and animalistic instinct controlled their actions. Perfect Dragon grubs. He didn't know whether to be relieved or ashamed that he'd passed this secret test.

Unwilling to investigate further, he let his current carry him to the time of his death. Without flesh's instincts, Gaspotine saw things differently, as if he'd raised the nictitating membrane shielding his brain.

She-Dragons killing their whelp didn't shock him; he'd do the same. However, discovering that this behavior would cause long-term deterioration of Dragon-kind required reflection, like a difficult riddle. Made him see how simple his riddles were.

CHAPTER FIFTY-SIX

Since Thorne's kidnapping, Zarra had stayed close. But after Willow-Bender's Rampage, Zarra seldom let Thorne out of her sight. Thorne didn't mind, especially today when she wanted a private dialogue. As she walked through the blooming orchard, everything smelled fresher. These last few days food tasted better; water, sweeter.

Standing on a small rise in the morning sun, Thorne removed her cloak and folded it over a branch. Below them, the river, high from melting snow, swept over the sandy banks. She brushed a honeybee from her shoulder.

"Sit beside me." Only a few weeks until the igle killed her. "Will you be Stonevar's Head Constable?"

Zarra guffawed. "I'm a thief." She pointed at the serpent ring on Thorne's finger.

"I trust you."

The thief sniffed. "I don't trust myself." She threw a stone at the river. It slapped the water nine times then sank. Before drinking Dragon blood, she couldn't throw so well. "Why me?"

"You understand people." Her friend needed this.

Zarra fired pebbles faster. "What if the others object?"

Thorne couldn't read Zarra's face. Did Zarra stay in the shadows because she feared judgment? "The soldier-farmers?"

"And their wives." Zarra stared at the water.

"In Stonevar we work together to survive."

Zarra met Thorne's gaze. "What you see in me others cannot. For the greater good, I cannot accept."

For the first time, Thorne understood that something divided Stonevar.

Thorne spent the next two days observing the castle folk without noticing anything different. They worked with minimal conflict. She didn't quiz them, lest she seem intrusive and foolish. On the third day she asked Emera to join her upstairs, intending to continue implementing her plans.

"If I cannot act as Stonevar's Goddess, I need you to stand in my stead."

They sat at a small table in Thorne's sleeping room, which smelled of the wole-munk oil that she worked into her leather boots.

Emera's hand-sized ears poked through her hair. "Me, a Goddess?"

"Your hair is white like mine. Your upturned eyes and slim build give you an ethereal mien."

The Wanderling touched Thorne's sleeve. "Don't leave us."

This was proving more difficult than Thorne expected. "I was kidnapped not so long ago."

Emera's honey-brown skin paled. "That won't happen again. We won't let it."

"If something does, will you take my place?"

Emera stared at Thorne's stomach, evidently thinking Thorne's pregnancy affected her mind. "If that will ease your worries."

"It will." The tightness in Thorne's chest lessened. Or maybe the igle—the leech—inside her had moved off her lungs, letting her breathe easier. It was seldom still, rolling and kicking, day and night.

Moments later Nella joined Thorne and Emera, and asked playfully, "What schemes do you two spin?"

The Wanderling hugged her mother. "Thorne asked me to be the Goddess if she cannot."

Although Emera seemed to consider this a game, Thorne knew how important the Wanderling's role would be.

White-faced, Nella said, "Emera, go help Bekka."

The Wanderling did as asked.

"You honor Emera." Nella pressed her palms together. "Remember she's the daughter of a goat herder."

"She's fifteen, a marrying age. I was only two years older when I drank Dragon blood."

"Such responsibilities burden a mother's heart."

"I should've spoken to you first." Clearly Nella still worried that Thorne would alienate Emera from her mother.

Nella lowered her almond-shaped eyes. "In your wisdom, I'm sure you considered how others will receive this?"

"What others?"

"One as observant as yourself has noticed the division."

Thorne shook her head.

"In my humble opinion, the men begrudge we red-haired women counseling you. Though Lott pacifies them."

"Will they resent Emera?"

"Why should they agree to follow a girl?"

Brutte would be disappointed. A good leader would've foreseen. "Would you stand behind Emera. Become Stonevar's Magister?" Emera might resemble Stonevar's goddess but Nella's steady head would make the decisions.

Nella jerked as if slapped. "I'm unworthy."

Afraid, but why? "Have you seen something playing your flute?"

Nella bowed her head. "I play no longer."

Bumps rose on Thorne's skin. "What have you seen?"

"A giant snake squeezing Emera."

Thorne pressed her lips tight, smothering a gasp.

Nella continued, "Metal pierces its nose."

Tiny hairs on the back of Thorne's neck rose. "Nar the Insidious."

"Who?"

"The giant constrictor who devoured Rustofona the Magnificent's eggs. After I banished Nar, Rustofona let me live at Stonevar. Where is Nar in the dream?"

"In the Great Hall."

After Thorne died, the snake would reclaim Stonevar. "I must find Nar and transfer his allegiance to Emera."

"No." Nella grabbed Thorne's arm. "Your lying in is too close."

Heat climbed Thorne's neck. No one spoke of the igle inside her—at least within her hearing.

Nella's voice was shrill. "Your husband won't allow it."

Thorne wasn't fooled; Nella was really saying that she wouldn't permit it.

"Strumgued has nothing to say about this." Unless he heard of her plan. He was still grumpy about her journey to Seahaven. She'd find Nar as soon as the spring rains stopped, before her strength failed. Until then, she'd another challenge for Emera. This time, she'd discuss it with Nella first.

Thorne took Nella's hand. "I must show Emera the Continuum."

Nella blanched. "The place of fog and phantoms."

"Someone other than myself must have the knowledge."

"Losing a daughter cannot be borne."

"When Emera knows how, I believe her father will come to Stonevar. She can show him the way." Thorne didn't mention how difficult returning was.

Nella's eyes glowed with the hope of seeing her lover again. Thorne stared at the door, regretting the necessity of manipulating her friend.

#

"Our spirits will return from the Continuum by nightfall," Thorne told Nella.

Nella moved between Thorne and Emera. "If they don't?"

"Fetch Zarra. She'll get us back even if it means killing us."

No one laughed.

"Hunger and thirst will bring us back. So will danger." And Strumgued somehow helped Thorne, seeming to anchor her in the physical world.

"I want to go." Emera hugged her mother. "Don't worry."

Hands clasped, Thorne and Emera lay side by side in Thorne's bed. Thorne's mind touched Emera's and took them into the Continuum. Going ripped apart Thorne's ribs and yanked her spirit out. The igle twisted and kicked.

Emera screamed, though Thorne had warned her. Every sound, color, and odor she'd ever experienced battered her senses.

Thorne pulled Emera from the river into the yellow sky. "Emera, hear me. See violet mountains covered with golden snow and blue leaved trees."

"I see them."

"We float through red clouds smelling like fawn's blood." Thorne stuck out her tongue, tasting them as she passed.

"We have wings. How is that possible?" The Wanderling glided, adjusting more quickly than Thorne had during her first visit.

"Because we drank Dragon blood." Rustofona and Gaspotine could see Thorne so she knew those Dragon spirits would also see

Emera. Thorne suspected all Dragons could see a Wanderer, but she didn't anticipate what happened next.

A golden aura encompassed Emera, which Thorne doubted portended anything good. She'd show Emera what she needed to know. Then they'd leave.

Emera swooped into a smooth glide. "Thank you for bringing me. I love it here."

Though Thorne couldn't say the same, she slipped into the Silver River and motioned for Emera to follow. "Listen carefully. The Silver River flows into the past. To see the future, swim against the current. Those who drank Dragon blood have gold streams, which branch when we change our minds."

Emera pointed to what appeared to a knot. "Our gold currents intertwine with Hellee's silver stream."

She observed more than Thorne could ever hope to. "We have Dragon-Fating for him."

"Upstream our gold currents and Dragon streams roil."

Thorne swam to it. "Vainglorian. Hellee. And a Dragon I don't recognize. The churning prevents me from seeing what will happen." She followed her current into the future. After a short distance her stream thinned to a thread—as if only one improbable choice offered life.

No stream separated from hers. The igle had no current—no future. Inside her, its large transparent head and cord-thin arms and legs flopped about. She cupped it. Even here, it felt warm. She could pull it from her womb. On her return, she'd deliver a stillborn child. What matter if the igle died now or later? Its spirit would live on in the Continuum. Wasn't that kinder?

"Thorne!" Emera looped, owning the sky. "Look at all the Dragons."

Dragon spirits rose from the river. Why so many?

Gaspotine the Dark approached Thorne. "Blood-drinker. Always you stir the Continuum."

"What do you mean?"

"The Dragon Council assembles." He pointed a claw toward the future where the five largest Dragon spirits hovered over the river. "They've summoned all Dragons."

Thorne couldn't imagine how she'd caused this. "Why?"

"To greet the Herald." He nodded at Emera who swooped over

the Silver River.

"Herald?"

Thunder boomed. Inky lightning cracked the sky, shooting black sparks. More Dragon spirits gathered along the river with newcomers floating above the first arrivers. All had auras of reddish silver and pointed their wings behind their heads.

Emera joined Thorne. "What's happening?" the Wanderling asked.

Before Thorne could say she'd no idea, Osterweis the Wanderer—who'd discovered the Continuum eons ago—lengthened his arms and coiled his insane spirit around Emera.

"The Herald has come," he announced. "Dragons gather to welcome her." His long gray hair and waist-length beard floated wildly about his head.

"What does this Herald foretell?" Anticipating the answer sent golden sparks crackling along Thorne's wings.

"Our Deliverer." Osterweis hugged Emera tighter. "When will he come?"

"Who?" Emera tried to peel Osterweis off her, but his misty form reattached at new spots.

"The Wanderer who will deliver us from the Niede, death's madness."

"My father?" Emera asked Thorne.

"I don't know." Whatever was happening had ramifications that Thorne didn't understand. They should return. She reached into her stomach. The igle twisted away as if suspecting Thorne intended to leave it behind. Before she could grasp it, a song distracted her. On the river, an anthem rose from the Dragon spirits, each with its own tone and pitch blending into harmonious melodies of earth, wind, water, fire.

"Dragon Song," Osterweis said.

The igle quieted. The music caressed Thorne's ears. She never wanted the song to end.

A lustrous Dragon spirit encircled Emera in his wings and said his name. One after another, Dragons clasped Emera, said their names, and bestowed some of their radiance.

Last, the Dragon Council embraced Emera, each leaving behind part of their silvery-red aura. By the time Erramon the Eldest, First Councilor and largest Dragon specter, gripped Emera, her spirit was the brightest in the Continuum. Staring at her stung Thorne's eyes.

"Welcome Herald," Erramon the Eldest said. "Long have we awaited your arrival."

Emera floated before the council. "I could stay forever."

That reminded Thorne to gaze into the river. "Your mother is panicking." Candlelight lit Thorne's room. How long had they listened to the mesmerizing Dragon Song?

"A little longer. How did you ever leave this wonderful place? I recognize every Dragon, remember every name. Why do they think I'm a herald? What's the Niede?"

"I'll explain later. We've stayed too long." When Thorne tried to touch Emera's mind, she hit a wall. Though Thorne tried to stay calm, her toes floated away. Not encouraging.

With ghostly fingers, the farseeing Osterweis clutched Emera. "She must stay." Holding Emera, he seemed less fragile; fewer wisps of him floated away.

Thorne sensed that the Song made it difficult to escape. If they lingered, they'd become like Osterweis. She couldn't keep desperation from her quavering voice. "Emera, look into the river."

"Mother's sobbing."

Thorne's fingers tingled as she cupped the igle's spirit. She'd soon be free of it. Strumgued would never know. But could she live with what she'd done?

While she hesitated, Emera took them back.

Thorne told herself that Emera had surprised her. For weeks afterward she debated returning to the Continuum. Now it was too late.

CHAPTER FIFTY-SEVEN

When the spring rains relented and melting snow cascaded down Ventamar Falls like tears, Thorne sent Raspberry-Frost to find the den of Nar the Insidious. She must transfer Nar's loyalty or after she died, Nar would return to Stonevar and kill everyone.

Eight days later, under a waxing Planter's Moon, the Fairy returned. Thorne sent word to Strumgued that she'd stay with her women. She hoped he'd think her lying in had come. Since her size made travel difficult, she doubted he'd suspect her intention to leave Stonevar.

By late afternoon the first day of their journey, she was certain they were being followed. Thorne, Glitter, and Emera waited on horseback behind a copse of birch trees. She suspected it might be Strumgued. But she wouldn't let him deter her, wouldn't tell him about her cramps, which had started as soon as she rode Wild-Eyes.

A single horse trotted toward them over the hard-packed dirt road. If their horses were quiet, maybe he wouldn't detect them. A foolish hope, since her husband was an expert tracker. Thorne recognized the rider's unbalanced seat before she identified the familiar voice.

"Hurry along, my beauty. We've lost sight of them." Even after years of riding, Zarra's buttocks bobbed on the saddle and her legs flopped about the horse's sides like ropes torn loose in a storm.

As the thief passed, Glitter asked, "Out for a ride?"

Zarra flinched, then grinned as she halted her black gelding. "Appears I lost my way."

Glitter smiled. "Depends on your destination."

Thorne should've known Zarra would follow. "You've no talent for staying put."

Zarra scratched her collarbone. "Turns out I itch when we're separated. Think you need me."

"I do." When Thorne urged Wild-Eyes onto the road, the igle squeezed her lower back. She could tolerate the discomfort, but couldn't risk delivering before finding Nar. "Do you know a farmer this far south?" she asked Zarra.

"What do you need?"

"A barn tonight. A horse and wagon tomorrow."

Glitter and Emera looked puzzled.

"Perhaps approaching Nar would be better done after the child comes," Glitter said.

Thorne couldn't say that there would be no "after."

"I've foreseen that the igl—child will wait until I've transferred Nar's loyalty to Emera." She lied, but Nella had foreseen Nar killing Emera in Stonevar's Great Hall, and nothing would stop Thorne from protecting Stonevar.

They spent the night in a dry barn. The next day Thorne bought a horse and wagon from the farmer and tied Wild-Eyes to the back. The warhorse shook her head, seeming offended. The women took turns at the wagon reins while Thorne stretched out in the wagon.

On the third day, they reached the bottom of the Caprine Mountains. Thorne had hoped to get closer to the den, but couldn't risk restarting the pains. They must wait here for Nar.

#

During the night, Spangle jerked fully awake. A shaft of moonlight cut the bed in half, separating her from Lott.

His callused hand stroked her shoulder. "What troubles you?"

She rolled into his arms, which smelled of earth. "I've a bad feeling about Glitter." Her sister and the others had been gone two days.

"An unpleasant dream?"

"A foreseeing." Since drinking Dragon blood, she had visions of herself or Glitter doing each other's chores. She didn't find this mysterious, assigning no importance to who fed the horses or shook fresh bedding. But this was different.

Lott smoothed her hair. "What did you see?"

"Nar's coils imprison Glitter. I felt him constricting and couldn't breathe." She'd never visited the Dragon Continuum but suspected this foreseeing, coming in the moments before sleep, was a glimpse inside.

"I doubt they found Nar so quickly." He caressed her cheek. "You're just worried."

This made sense. She pressed her palm against his chest, letting his hairs curl around her fingers. Exhausted from spring plowing, he fell back asleep, but Spangle could not. Her sister was in danger and so were the others. She must warn Thorne that Nar would betray them.

Spangle leapt from the bed, pulled on her tunic, then dug through a chest looking for trousers.

Lott sat up. "Where are you going?"

"To Glitter." From a small locked box, she retrieved a vial of Dragon blood and tucked it into her bodice, then picked up the sleeping Una, intending to take her to Bekka.

Lott groaned, clearly spent after the day's labor. "I'll saddle the horses."

If her arms hadn't held Una, Spangle would've embraced him. She almost believed her marriage could work.

CHAPTER FIFTY-EIGHT

Nar woke to Fairies tugging spider-silk ropes attached to his snout ring and pain ripping into his nostrils. He caught one of the tasty bites, but the rest flew out of reach.

"My Human summons Nar," a Fairy said. "Descend this rocky peak."

When Nar ignored this, the Fairies yanked harder, sending thorn-like stabs up his nose. Blood droplets spotted the cave floor. "Hurt. Hurt."

The Fairy landed between his eyes. "The Goddess of Stonevar summons Nar. Descend this rocky peak."

Though still sluggish, he remembered the white-haired Human who'd pierced his nose, severed his tail, and drove him from Stonevar. Why did Fairies help a Human?

When he moved, his empty stomach cramped his fifty-foot length. "Hunger. Hunger."

"Later."

No doubt the evil sprites would frighten game away until he complied. He uncoiled his emerald-flecked body, scarred from wresting this cave from a wole-bear.

As he followed the Fairies down the mountain, he complained about the ropes. The Fairies tittered and pulled them tighter. Hunger pains made him writhe, which yanked his snout ring, ripping his tender flesh. He vowed to crush the merciless pixies inside his coils.

When he reached the plain, a horse broke from a wagon. He lunged at it, capturing it in his coils. Ignoring the Human shouts and his burning nose, he squeezed the beast in a delightful death grip. The Human who'd banished him from Stonevar ordered the Fairies to give him slack enough to unhinge his jaws and swallow the horse headfirst. With his meal traveling down his throat, Nar looked around, flicking his tongue. The Humans had spread out. The one with crooked teeth stayed near the horses; the Wanderer near the Goddess; the last behind the wagon. All smelled tantalizingly of Dragon. Since leaving Stonevar, he craved Dragon eggs. The Goddess, who appeared to have recently swallowed a large meal herself, stimulated his appetite most. No Human would taste sweeter. He mustn't ignore the Wanderer, either; he'd always wanted to taste forbidden prey.

The Goddess raised her hand. "Nar will obey me."

He didn't like obeying. As she moved closer, he drew her into his eye.

"Still beautiful," the Goddess said.

A Fairy flew at his head, breaking his hold on Thorne.

"Caution everyone, or Nar will mesmerize you." The Goddess took the Wanderer's arm. "This is Emera. That's Glitter." She pointed to one behind the wagon. "Zarra calms the horses. These are my handmaidens. Do not harm them."

Undeterred, he tried to tempt Zarra with his eye. She pulled her hood down and unsheathed her sword. Remembering the farmer who'd stabbed him with a pitchfork when he was small, Nar retreated as far as the evil sprites allowed.

"We have a bargain, Nar. You owe me a service." The Goddess pointed at the Wanderling.

Nar turned his gaze on the willowy Wanderer. Her spirit jumped into his eye then back out, making him doubt he could enthrall her.

"Swear to obey Emera as you would me."

He flicked his tongue at Thorne. Having come, albeit reluctantly, when the Goddess summoned, all obligations were fulfilled. He'd done his service. He'd never swear anything again.

The horse slithering down his throat made his movements sluggish, but he was still quick enough to lash out with his tail and capture Glitter. Since he wasn't hungry his coils didn't instinctively crush her.

The Goddess unsheathed her sword. "Glitter, are you all right?"

"I can breathe."

"Release her, Nar."

Raspberry-Frost flew to Thorne's shoulder. "Nar says untie the ropes."

"If I do, he'll kill us all. Honor your oath."

Nar snorted and the Fairy translated, "Oath done."

Glitter screamed.

#

Thorne dropped Dracodurus, dashed to Nar, and pressed both palms against his emerald scales. Before he could crush her, she joined his mind and took his spirit into the Continuum.

In the swirling colors, blaring sounds, and unsettling odors, Nar's terrified gurgles battered Thorne's mind. She did nothing to soothe him, nor did she tell him how to shape the Continuum. Though his mind slid into madness, Thorne delayed separation until her sanity thinned to a thread.

In the Silver River, she saw Glitter and the others safe. Good, since she could tolerate Nar no longer and must disengage her mind from his. No doubt, when her spirit rejoined her body, she'd have the worst headache of her life.

But when Thorne attempted to release Nar, their minds remained linked. How long would she remain rational bound to a brainsick, panic-stricken serpent whose only distinct thoughts were of squeezing until entrails burst from his victims' gaping mouths?

CHAPTER FIFTY-NINE

As Nar's spirit twisted around Thorne, his brumous body separated into sections, which increased his terrified writhing. No matter where Thorne moved, Nar followed with fantasies of mutilation.

When Rustofona approached, Nar hissed and lunged at the Dragon. Rustofona clawed ineffectually at his vaporous form as he wound himself around her. "What madness have you brought?" Rustofona asked Thorne.

Nar's bedeviled terror made it difficult for Thorne to think clearly or to speak. "To save Stonevar."

"Slay him. The moment of his death will confine him."

"I cannot separate our minds. If I go back, he returns also."

Rustofona stretched her lizard-like head beyond Nar's coils; accordingly, the serpent swallowed her wings. "This one must die," the Dragon said.

While Rustofona occupied Nar, Thorne looked into the river and saw Spangle and Lott. Why had they come? Spangle stood between Thorne's body and the others, preventing Zarra from killing Nar. Spangle never could get it right.

"I'll ask Thorne." Emera climbed into the wagon.

"You can visit the Continuum?" Zarra sounded surprised.

"Thorne showed me."

Zarra braced hands on hips. "Showed you!"

"Only recently. I'll return in a moment." Inside the Continuum, Emera's spirit ascended from the river. Dragons also appeared, apparently to see Emera.

Rustofona bowed. "The Herald returns."

Nar leapt at Emera and squeezed. She ignored him. When he

271

swallowed her headfirst, she burst through his foggy length. That drove Nar into a writhing mass of panic.

"Tell Zarra to kill him," Thorne told Emera. "When Nar dies, our minds will separate." Her arms thinned as Nar's crazy thoughts weakened her.

"Are you certain killing Nar will free you?" Emera asked.

Rustofona answered, "Thorne must release him." She enclosed Emera protectively inside her wings, inciting Nar into a new burst of demented frenzy.

Thorne couldn't block Nar's insanity much longer. "Please Emera, go now."

The Wanderling dove into her stream and disappeared. Nar tried to follow but Emera's current flung him back.

Rustofona stared at Thorne's stomach. "Lay your egg before you're egg bound."

"I would if I could."

"A fat pig greases the way," Rustofona advised.

"Thanks for the suggestion." She hadn't expected birthing advice from a Dragon.

Nar wrapped himself around both Thorne and Rustofona. His bothersome behavior grew more irritating. His thoughts were jumbled glimpses of bloody, crushed flesh so mangled Thorne couldn't recognize what creature it had once been.

In the river, the Dragon Guards carried her body away from Nar. With nine ax swings apiece, Zarra and Lott chopped off the serpent's head. In the Continuum, Nar's spirit writhed wildly. He rolled into a contorted ball.

"The Niede demands he return to his dead flesh," Rustofona said.

Thorne's call to rejoin her own body jolted her. She tried to concentrate on moving her flesh-and-blood finger but failed. She dove into her current, but the river was bottomless. No matter how hard she swam the real world got no closer. Nar anchored her here. Like a caged Dragon she flapped her wings, flew in every direction searching for an escape, but every flight returned her to Nar's clutch.

Wisps of her wings and fingertips floated away. Unable to block Nar's ghoulish thoughts of crushing victims, she screamed. As insanity's tendrils slithered into her mind, she clutched at Rustofona, but her arms passed through the Dragon's smoky neck.

Emera shouted, "I can't touch your mind! Lower your guard!"

"Nar's madness will enter." Thorne wrapped her arms around her head. "Strumgued. I need Strumgued." When she reached for Emera, the Wanderling was gone.

Though the murky river, she watched them load her body onto the wagon and travel toward Stonevar. Then the figures blurred until the river seemed to flow with milk. Had she died?

Unable to see her friends, her last hope, she rolled into a ball.

#

"You want me to drink Dragon blood?" Strumgued asked Emera as he wiped sweat from his brow. When he'd discovered Thorne had left Stonevar, he and a dozen Dwarf warriors had ridden without stopping. After seeing Thorne in the wagon, he bade his warriors walk their winded horses to a stream. Her condition would only confuse them, and he was confused enough for all of them.

Thorne appeared uninjured. He didn't believe in spells, but what other explanation?

"We must hurry." Emera motioned for him to get in the wagon.

He looked at the women. The twins and the thief stood beside the wagon, all uncharacteristically quiet for females. Lott appeared as mystified as Strumgued.

The Wanderling held out a vial. "Thorne's spirit needs help returning to her flesh."

"How did her spirit separate from her body?"

"I'll touch your mind, take you to Thorne, then help you both come back. Now—please."

He wasn't skilled at reading Humans, but they appeared worried.

Emera put the vial of Dragon blood in his hand. "Drink. Then lie in the wagon beside Thorne."

The vial was warm. He inspected the ruby liquid, knowing the folly of going unarmed into unfamiliar territory. Thorne was no ordinary woman. Had Dragon blood made her so? Would it change him also? He didn't want that, being exactly the right height and having perfect hair color.

Emera gripped his shoulder. "For your child's sake, trust me."

Before he could talk himself out of it, he uncorked the vial and drank. The blood oozed into his stomach where it swirled into an eddy then came back up, making him gag.

"Don't throw up. Hurry, get in the wagon."

He wasn't accustomed either to cramps or being ordered about. Swallowing repeatedly, he lay beside Thorne.

Emera squeezed between them. "Clasp hands."

Something pushed against his mind, then he was drowning. Few things frightened him, but since Dwarfs didn't float, having his head underwater terrified. He held his breath, while flailing his arms and legs. When sense returned, he discovered he needn't breathe in this dazzling darkness, which was filled with light above and below. Where was he?

Where was the Wanderling, and where was his wife?

The liquid surrounding him was silver, streaked with gold, denser than water. Looking down he saw himself in the wagon with Thorne and Emera.

Garbled sounds came from overhead. Thorne's foggy form floated above the surface. Though she was rolled into ball, he made out her tormented face, eyes protruding, mouth gaping. Her wings didn't surprise him; only confirmed that she'd drunk Dragon blood.

He made little sense of the jumbled shapes and colors surrounding Thorne until the smoky form of Nar the Insidious wound himself around her. Strumgued tried to reach Thorne but hardly stirred the liquid. To his relief, Thorne seemed unhurt by the snake's constriction.

This must be some kind of Wanderer world. He recalled the legend: Wanderers traveled the globe seeking the doorway to Time's Continuum. Could such a place really exist? Unlikely. Wherever this was, he needed to get Thorne and leave.

A winged Emera now floated beside Thorne, mouth moving. He concentrated on blocking extraneous noise.

"I've lost Strumgued," Emera said.

That startled him. Evidently he wasn't supposed to be imprisoned in this thick liquid. Strumgued shouted, but Emera didn't hear. He moved his arms and legs in what he thought were swimming motions, gaining nothing. No wonder. His hands and limbs were transparent.

Thorne lifted her head. Her hair stuck out, giving her a halo of shimmering strands. "What did you do?"

"Spangle had Rustofona's blood. I gave it to him. Thought he'd need it to enter the Continuum."

He'd drunk blood from a she-Dragon. No wonder he sickened.

"I don't know what Dragon blood will do to him." Thorne spoke deliberately as if each word required effort. "Search the Continuum."

Emera flew off. The snake followed. Thorne unrolled slowly. To Strumgued, she looked frail, half her normal size. Bits of mist floated away as if she were dissolving. That couldn't be good.

If Thorne could lose mist, could he gain bulk? He concentrated on drawing in substance. Nothing happened.

Thorne had lost the top half of her wings. Not much time. He reached toward her. His arm stretched but without reaching the surface. He pushed his chest into his arm, lengthening his reach. A finger broke the surface. He pulled mist from his right leg through his reed-thin trunk into his arm. His hand emerged. He transferred the mist from his other leg, pushing his forearm above the silver liquid. He flexed his fingers and made a fist.

Thorne screamed, presumedly at his arm. He opened his hand. Her wispy fingers closed around his. He pulled her to him, enfolding her so she'd lose no more of herself.

That's how Emera found them.

#

Thorne opened her eyes in the wagon bed, with the Wanderling holding one of her hands and Strumgued the other, even as he vomited blood over the side of the wagon. Spangle passed him a flask to rinse his mouth.

"I hope that's all of it." Strumgued's face twisted like a black cloud in a storm. "I want none of that vileness left inside me."

After Thorne and Strumgued had recovered, the women prepared to stay the night, and the Dwarf warriors gathered firewood, leaving Thorne and Strumgued alone.

Pressing his palm to her stomach, he said through clenched teeth, "I cannot permit you from my sight."

As if sensing its father was near, the baby quieted or perhaps visiting the Continuum had tired it. Whichever, Thorne had no cramps.

"I had concerns to attend to." She breathed deep, treasuring the feeling. The Continuum would never be as easy for her as it was for Emera.

"I saw the monster Zarra and Lott killed. Let us hope that future concerns keep you at Stonevar."

When she didn't answer, his tired eyes, gleaming with anger and worry, narrowed. "You've no care for your health or my child within. If I must spend every moment with you until the child's birth then I will do so."

Thorne believed him. "I'll not leave again." Based on the intensity of her irregular pains, she'd be fortunate to make it home without delivering. "Thank you for . . ." She hated being indebted to him, for calling his name in the Continuum.

Strumgued grunted.

The next morning a cold spring rain drenched them, depriving Thorne of seeing the countryside for the last time. Instead she watched the Dragon Guards and Lott: the way they shifted on their horses, the way their faces moved when they talked or laughed. She observed Strumgued: his easy manner with his warriors, the way his stallion readily obeyed his commands.

For those two wet, bumpy days in the wagon, the pains stopped, and she was able to just be.

After they arrived at Stonevar, Strumgued escorted Thorne to the castle door with a promise—more of a warning—to join her soon. She kept her stride deliberate, not wanting Strumgued to know that her labor pains—the worst cramps of her life—now came at regular intervals. As it clawed its way out, the igle would bestow a slow death, giving her only hours to make sure her followers were solidly bonded to Stonevar and each other.

Everyone quieted when she entered, not even a baby cried. Having worked in the fields until dark, the men were still eating their meal. Through the haze of her contractions, they appeared gray, barely distinguishable from one another. She sensed their moods—puzzled, concerned, disapproving of her leaving so near the time of her lying-in. After she died, they'd call her reckless. She tried to smile, but a stabbing back pain pursed her mouth. If this were false labor, then she'd be in bad shape when the real thing began.

At the end of the table, the tallest of the gray people, Gil the Blacksmith, stood. She hugged him, smelled his sweaty charcoal scent, said his name, bade him speak so he'd stop being gray. Gil's wife, Velta approached. Thorne removed the giant porcupine quills holding up Velta's hair and stroked her deep black locks, smelled her scent of birch bark, said Velta's name, listened to her.

She listened to all the gray people and hugged them. If they stiffened, she held them until they relaxed, until they weren't gray, and she recognized them.

Scatt held out an infant. She didn't know it. The thick air made each breath feel as if she breathed through a narrow reed. Had she been so unmindful that she'd forgotten a child? A cramp twisted her pelvis, and she pressed her lips tight to smother a cry.

Bekka's smile lit up her face. "His name is Tope. Kora delivered while you were gone."

That was a relief. She'd wondered if she'd left part of her mind in the Continuum.

"Bless him, Goddess," Scatt said.

Thorne pressed her fingertips to the infant's forehead. "Tope, you will have strength and health, and live with honor into old age. You will climb trees better than your da."

The crowd laughed. She gave the baby back to Scatt.

She felt stronger until the next pain struck, then she leaned on the table, waiting for it to pass. "Each of you is vital to making Stonevar thrive. I apologize for neglecting you while tending the Dragon whelp. Those who guard Hellestorm are my handmaidens. They are dear to me but no dearer than all of you.

"The Dwarfs are our allies." She was grateful now that she'd never spoken of the Dwarfs as enemies. "They pay a premium for our trade goods. Their presence will discourage invaders until the Dragon matures."

The soldier-farmers grumbled.

"Dwarfs think they're better than us." Scatt passed the baby to Kora. "But none of them climb trees worth a copper."

Thorne laughed with the others. "You are great warriors but we are too few." The men were also middle-aged, having married after ending their careers as mercenaries.

Lott looked thoughtful. Edz nodded, though the others appeared unconvinced.

"To show my gratitude for all you've sacrificed for Stonevar, I'm deeding each family land. Lott will assign sections."

Everyone cheered.

Thorne gritted her teeth behind a smile until a pain passed. "For Stonevar to be a true city, we must form guilds." She waited for the mumbles to subside. "The Guildlord has appointed Spangle Guildhead of Stonevar."

That brought amazed gasps.

"Together we can meet any challenge. Because we embrace new ways, we will succeed when others fail."

When the next pain struck her lower back, a startled grunt escaped before she could suppress it. "Stonevar must always have a goddess, so if need be, Emera will stand in my stead." They seemed to take this for her lying in, not her death, and didn't object.

"Emera is young, so Nella will act as Magister." She motioned for Nella to step forward.

Nella bowed to Thorne then to the crowd.

"A woman?" Edz said with more puzzlement than anger, rubbing his whisker-covered scar.

Disapproving mutters became irate grumbles.

"Thorne's advice brings prosperity," Lott said.

She appreciated his support. Though she dreaded saying this, she knew Brutte would've smiled. "I am the Goddess of Stonevar and this is my decree." With the force of blacksmith's tongs, a contraction squeezed her lower back, buckling her knees.

Willow-Bender swept Thorne into her arms and up the stairs.

CHAPTER SIXTY

The Continuum continued to buzz with news of the Herald. Many Dragons left only to hunt. The prophecy said a Wanderer would come to announce the Deliverer. Gaspotine wasn't so certain Emera was the Herald; after all she was female, half Wanderer, and hadn't announced anyone. Maybe she was a false oracle.

On Emera's second visit, Gaspotine was even less convinced, especially after Thorne left behind that annoying snake. Nar remained by the Silver River, writhing and whining. When Rustofona wasn't watching Hellestorm, she pretended to lay an egg. Nar pounced on the vaporous orb. His writhing became more frenzied and his thoughts more crazed, which delighted Rustofona. Afterward she returned to observing Hellestorm, which eased her Niede.

Gaspotine still hoped discovering more of his progeny would mitigate his own suffering. He refused to accept that none lived. He swam far into his past to a fondly remembered mating with Maehitabelle the Merciless. That battle had so excited Maehitabelle that she'd nearly drowned him in a river. The memory made him shudder with gratification. Subsequently, others mated Maehitabelle, and she hatched Rendeius the Terrible.

When Gaspotine couldn't make out Rendeius's claws in the past where the waters were murky like old memories, he swam closer to the present and discovered Rendeius missing a toe. At one time he might've been proud to father such a vicious Dragon—if he'd thought about it, which seemed unlikely.

Many admired Rendeius for his fierce cruelty. How could the son of Maehitabelle the Merciless and Gaspotine the Dark be otherwise?

Gaspotine knew little of Rendeius, since the Terrible seldom lingered in the Continuum, preferring the physical pleasures of the corporeal world. With a familiar yearning, Gaspotine watched Rendeius hunt. His son's slim shape and broad wingspan let him manage a vast territory. Even so he ignored areas until Humans moved in and constructed their caves of wood. After twenty or so years he'd exhale down their smoke holes, exploding their dwellings to feast on those who fled. Discovering Rendeius was a bizarre kind of farmer, when Dragons disdained Humans for farming, gave Gaspotine more to think about.

He proceeded upstream, stopping when the Terrible attacked another red Dragon. After a daylong battle, Rendeius broke his opponent's neck, then watched the other Dragon suffer until it died. Even Gaspotine the Dark, brutal while he breathed, would've killed the red Dragon before five dawns broke.

He swam on, stopping when Rendeius injured a she-Dragon in a fierce mating. Rendeius claimed breaking her wing was accidental. From what Gaspotine observed, after she rejected Rendeius, he forced her submission by snapping her wing. A quick copulation preceded her drawn-out death. A damaged wing sentenced her to a flightless life. Rather than endure that shame, she starved herself to death.

Gaspotine would've spread this delicious gossip about another Dragon, but smashing a wing reflected badly on his son. Killing a breeding female broke Dragon law; a more serious violation than swallowing the Dwarf Mother with Dragon-Fating, which had doomed Gaspotine. He wanted to pretend Rendeius wasn't his spawn. Was this unpleasant sensation what Humans called shame?

While Gaspotine wrestled with unfamiliar feelings, Rendeius entered the Continuum in the form of a scarlet tornado. The Terrible joined Tallasha the Resplendent on the bank. He licked her throat in courting. Tallasha rubbed his tail with hers, encouraging him.

"I will come for your first mating," Rendeius said.

Why go to Elysia with she-Dragons on the mainland? Gaspotine shrugged. Desire obeyed no logic. What compelled Rendeius no other might understand, least of all Rendeius. Mating with Tallasha required a lair on Elysia to rest after a long flight and copulating. Dragons abhorred sleeping outside, wanting stone cozying them.

Not surprisingly, Vainglorian the Red bellowed. "Draw back

from Tallasha."

Tallasha lowered her snout and eyed Vainglorian. "You never court me."

Vainglorian pulled back as if surprised. Apparently, the Red hadn't seen the need. When he thinned to squeeze between the two, Rendeius bit a chunk from Vainglorian's throat. They tangled into a roiling cloud, scattering fragments of haze. Their battling became a contest of ripping away vapor faster than their spirits could reform. Tallasha's eyes distended with delight as the roaring combatants attracted a crowd.

"Dragon code forbids fighting in the Continuum!" Erramon the Eldest bellowed.

As Vainglorian separated from his rival, Rendeius rent the Red's wing. The crowd gasped. Tallasha folded her wings protectively.

Vainglorian bear-hugged Rendeius, hardening his spirit into ice, imprisoning the Terrible. Gaspotine had never seen such skill at controlling vapor and never suspected Vainglorian had this gift. The Red's jaws widened until he swallowed the squirming Rendeius. Then Vainglorian slowly excreted him in a tight log.

Tallasha laughed. The others joined in. Even Erramon guffawed. Gaspotine had never witnessed a greater insult.

"I will kill you." Rendeius shot into the air.

Vainglorian wiggled his back end. "I will piss on your head first."

CHAPTER SIXTY-ONE

Thorne's next contraction squeezed as powerfully as Nar constricted. She slumped against Strumgued sitting beside her on the bed. He wiped her face with a cool cloth.

She wanted to fight but had no defense for an attack from within.

"Time for you to leave," Fehera told Strumgued.

"Let him stay." Thorne clutched his arm. He gave her strength.

"Lie back, so I can check you." Fehera lifted Thorne's gown. "The child's head is large."

No surprise. Her belly was twice the size of most women's.

"Sitting will encourage birth." The healer motioned for Thorne to rise.

Thorne doubted the igle needed encouragement. With her husband's help, she sat on the edge of the bed. The igle pressed against her back, and she suppressed a groan. Only death would end this.

Raspberry-Frost flew in the window and landed on her belly. "My Human messes."

Water mixed with blood dribbled down Thorne's legs. Fehera assured her the baby would come soon. Thorne didn't believe her. The healer helped Thorne change her gown while Strumgued watched from a stool in a shadowy corner, tapping his foot, his gaze never leaving Thorne.

Time slowed. The pain-free intervals shortened until the contractions never ended. Her friends came and went. When sweat soaked her bedding, someone changed it. When darkness fell, someone lit candles.

The igle moved lower, stretching her thin. The contractions made her shudder. She hadn't known the pain would drag on until she'd welcome death. Still, instead of complaining, she must endure.

Past midnight, Strumgued and Fehera slumbered. Raspberry-Frost flew away. Thorne abided alone until the Fairy returned to her pillow.

"My Human, I bring relief."

Bright light illuminated the room. Thorne didn't have strength to look for the source. A moment later, surrounded by a white aura, Mother hovered over Thorne's bed, her long golden hair flowing about her shoulders, wearing a silver gossamer gown. Somehow Raspberry-Frost had brought Mother back from the dead. After visiting the Continuum, Thorne found this possible, even reasonable.

Mother, looking younger than Thorne remembered, kneaded Thorne's swollen belly, murmuring soothingly like wind sweeping currents through long grasses. When the pain persisted, Mother kissed Thorne's dry lips, leaving behind the taste of cherries, sending Thorne into the blissful state between sleep and wake where she floated above her body.

From this vantage point, the mirror behind Mother reflected a Fairy twice Raspberry-Frost's size. Thorne couldn't explain that. A small voice whispered that spirits don't have reflections, certainly not one resembling a Fairy. Thorne didn't care. The igle had quieted. The contractions had stopped. The small voice whispered that stopping them was dangerous. Thorne didn't care about that either; instead, she welcomed each pain-free moment.

Fehera's shouts roused Strumgued. "Thorne has stopped breathing!"

Thorne wanted to tell everyone that she was all right but couldn't speak. The healer begged Thorne to push. Impossible with her body so far away.

One after another, the Dragon Guards kissed her forehead and left with sad faces and drooping shoulders. Then the soldier-farmers and their wives shuffled past. The men hunched, seeming uncomfortable in her sleeping chamber. She wanted to welcome them, but her lips wouldn't move.

Zarra rubbed Thorne's shoulder and asked Emera to see if Thorne's spirit was in the Continuum. Emera returned shaking her head. The thief wailed and kissed Thorne. Thorne had never seen

Zarra kiss anyone, even a baby.

Thorne wanted to reassure everyone that she wouldn't go to the Continuum even if she were dying. She didn't want to spend eternity tormented by the Niede. Better darkness and peace.

Quist and Raspberry-Frost perched on the antlers over the hearth. Neither seemed concerned.

Everyone left but Strumgued. He stroked her neck before drawing his knife and scraping the beard from under his chin. Who has died, she wanted to ask. He scraped so hard that his blood dotted the white gown stretching over her stomach. Was he mourning her? She wasn't dead.

He placed his right fist over his heart, then extended an arm saluting her. Moisture slid down his pale cheeks. She didn't want to watch but couldn't look away.

The igle kicked, making her stomach jerk. Strumgued's eyes widened. Thorne felt nothing. He positioned the knife over her belly. Screeching, Quist swooped from the antlers and clawed his knife hand.

Raspberry-Frost dove at his eyes. "Cease cutting my Human!"

"Stupid creatures! I can save the nursling." Strumgued struck the Fairy.

Thorne wanted to help Raspberry-Frost but couldn't move. Was her Fairy mortally wounded?

Ignoring Quist's claws, Strumgued pressed the blade against her abdomen, which resembled a pod ready to burst.

"Stop!" Thorne screamed soundlessly. When she tried to grab the knife, only her wedding ring finger twitched. The serpent's single ruby eye glistened. Strumgued's knife clanged against the stone floor.

He tasted Thorne's mouth. "Cursed Fairies. Meddling vermin. Treacherous insects."

Strumgued shook Thorne's shoulders. Air hissed between her swollen lips. Her mind cleared. Mother couldn't have come. Raspberry-Frost had brought the Fairy Queen. What elixir tainted the Fairy Queen's kiss?

The cramps returned—harder, deeper. She wanted her stupor back. Maybe if she kept her eyes closed.

Thorne hadn't thought her contractions could hurt worse until Strumgued pushed on her swollen belly. She tried to shove his hands away, but her fingers were reeds against stone.

"Wake from this Fairy spell and push!" Strumgued ordered.

She screamed. As the pain peaked, she focused on the bloody gash over his eyebrow. She wished Raspberry-Frost had hit his eye.

"Leave me alone." She tugged the serpent ring from her swollen finger and threw it across the room. "I hate you."

"Hate, but push." At the height of the next pain, he pressed even harder.

She screamed until she'd no more breath. After the contraction waned, she begged him to let her rest. "A moment, please."

"Rest and die." His hands pressed with the force of a Giant. "Push so our nursling will live."

"Daisy will live?" Not possible. Her sister had died long ago. The tortuous squeezing—Nar would've been kinder—resumed.

"The Fairies drugged you," Strumgued bellowed. "If our nursling dies, I'll destroy every hawthorn bush and uproot every thorn tree on Elysia!"

Fehera threw open the door. "Why are you shouting?"

"Help me, woman."

Fehera stared at Thorne. "She's alive?"

"Raspberry-Frost." Thorne pointed at the floor.

"The vicious insect nearly took out my eye." Strumgued pushed again.

Thorne groaned. "Find my Fairy."

Instead Fehera examined Thorne. Countless pushes later, Bekka entered with a candle, and Thorne motioned at the floor where Raspberry-Frost had fallen. Bekka smiled as she returned the serpent ring to Thorne's finger. Thorne lacked strength to remove it. Where was her Fairy?

"Sit her on the birthing chair," Fehera said.

Strumgued half-lifted, half-dragged Thorne there. "Now push."

Bekka lit more candles.

"What time is it?" Thorne asked.

Strumgued wiped sweat from her forehead with his callused hand. "Near midnight."

"How many days?"

"Two." Fehera wiped Thorne's dry lips with a damp cloth.

"Battle is easier," Thorne told Strumgued between contractions. Croaking a dry laugh, she slid a finger under Strumgued's scraped chin. "A Dwarf Lord in love with a Human."

"You continually misunderstand me." He grabbed her jaw, forcing her to gaze straight into his eyes. "Push!"

"Aye, Lord Husband." She tried to laugh but it turned into a groan.

Strumgued's hands returned to her mountainous stomach. "At the next pain, push hard."

"There's no end or beginning."

"Then I'll tell you." After the briefest moment, he said, "Now!"

With a boulder-cracking scream, Thorne delivered the child into Fehera's hands.

"A girl." The healer cut the cord and passed the baby to Bekka for washing.

The pain stopped. Thorne pushed Strumgued's hands away, hoping no one would touch her for a long time. Fehera shattered that hope by pressing on her stomach to deliver the afterbirth.

As Thorne leaned against Strumgued, an eardrum-bursting bellow came from outside.

"What's that?" Thorne asked.

Bekka peered over the balcony. "Hellee's in the bailey looking for you."

"I must comfort him." Thorne tried to rise, but fell back on the birthing chair.

"If you persist," Strumgued said. "I'll see to him."

Nothing agreeable would come from that, so Thorne let her husband help her back to bed. He motioned for Bekka to bring him the blanket-wrapped newborn, then held her out for Thorne to see.

"Our daughter." He couldn't look more pleased.

Joyfully, Bekka described the baby as if Thorne was blind. "Beautiful golden-red hair like Cayeseed. A tiny round nose. Skin white as swan feathers."

Thorne pulled back the blanket. The newborn lacked the downy lanugo hair that covered Dwarf newborns. Strumgued would be disappointed. Good. "Show me her back."

"Smooth," Bekka murmured.

Thorne looked away, not wanting to become attached. Like Daisy, this child would die.

"Lie still." Fehera packed Thorne with bandages. "I must stop the bleeding."

When Quist flew close, Strumgued passed the baby to Bekka and batted at the Fairy-Dragon. "Get away."

Quist landed on Thorne's head, gripped her hair, and roared in a high pitch. Another time, Thorne would've smiled at Quist protecting her, instead she grabbed a bedpost and sat up. "Where's Raspberry-Frost?"

"Not here. Lie still or you'll bleed again."

Thorne hoped that meant Raspberry-Frost was well enough to fly. While Thorne tried to calm Quist, Magda scurried in and took the infant from Bekka. "The others are anxious to see her."

"Take her." Thorne didn't want to watch the baby die.

Twittering, Quist followed Magda and the child out.

Strumgued's frown cut deep grooves from his round nose to his mouth. "I don't like this. Return the child."

"Magda will bring her back." Fehera scowled at Strumgued. "Stop upsetting Thorne. She must rest."

Strumgued growled.

The room faded to black. Thorne remembered nothing more.

CHAPTER SIXTY-TWO

"**O**nly an unnatural mother sends her child away." Strumgued folded his arms over his chest.

Thorne sat up, setting every part of her aching. She dropped back on her pillow, rubbing her full breasts. "I must nurse. Stop scowling and have someone bring me your child." Pebbles seemed to fill her breasts, but at least her milk had come in, giving her hope that her baby wouldn't die after all.

Strumgued opened the door and yelled for Magda.

"Where's Quist?" Thorne wanted him to find Raspberry-Frost. She intended to see firsthand that her Fairy was unharmed.

"With the child. The mindless mosquito seems besotted with her."

Thorne tugged at her milk-wet bodice. "What delays Magda?"

After a few moments, Fehera entered. "We cannot find Magda."

Strumgued rushed out.

Thorne sat up but queasiness made her regret it. Moving beyond the chamber pot would be impossible. She didn't resist when Fehera insisted she lie down.

Pounding footsteps announced Strumgued's return. He pulled Magda after him. His clenched jaw and narrowed eyes increased the nausea rising in Thorne's throat. Willow-Bender followed, face grim.

"Tell him to let me go," Magda told Thorne, her pale face tear streaked. "He twisted my arm."

"Be grateful I didn't kill you." Strumgued thrust her from him. "I found her at the bailey gate."

"Where's the baby?" Thorne asked.

Magda crossed her arms. "You told me to take the

abomination."

"My child's no abomination." Strumgued's tone held a warning.

"Devil's spawn." Magda spat.

Strumgued slapped Magda, thumping her backward to the floor. He stood over her, hand raised.

"Please don't strike her again." Would he kill her foster mother? "Magda. My infant?"

"Malwood."

Thorne smothered a groan. All manner of wild beasts hunted there.

Strumgued yanked Magda to her feet and ordered Willow-Bender to saddle horses, strapping Magda to one if need be. Willow-Bender looked to Thorne.

"Find my baby," Thorne said through her constricted throat, though she feared they'd find only tiny remains.

After Strumgued left, she stumbled to the balcony and watched her husband gallop for the forest with a half-dozen riders. She leaned against the stone railing and closed her eyes, picturing Raspberry-Frost's silky wings, its sharp teeth, white head tuft, and the port-wine stain marking its pointed face. "Raspberry-Frost, your Human calls!" She yelled until she was hoarse.

When something nipped her earlobe, Thorne yelped.

"Howling Human. Hush."

"My Fairy." Relief poured through Thorne.

"My Human, you called." The Fairy perched on the railing.

"Where's my baby?"

"Humans cast her away." Raspberry-Frost sharpened her foot claws on the stone rail.

She didn't have time for this. "A mistake. I want her."

Raspberry-Frost tittered. "Foolish Human. Fairy Queen claims her."

On wobbling legs, Thorne pushed off the balcony, ignoring the blood pooling between her feet. "Take me to the Fairy Queen."

"No purpose." Raspberry-Frost hovered near Thorne's chest where milk leaked through her shift.

"Without food the baby will die." The room spun unevenly.

The next thing Thorne knew was Quist pulling her hair while she lay on the bed. Someone must have carried her there. With an arm weighing twenty stones, she tried to brush the Fairy-Dragon away, but missed. Thorne groaned. Her breasts ached; even the touch of her nightgown against them was unbearable.

The setting sun cast the only light. Where was Strumgued? She was alone save for Quist yanking her hair. "Cease before I pull off your wings."

Normally threats sent timid Quist to the corner of the room, but today he bit her nose.

"What is it, Quist?"

The Fairy-Dragon stuck his tongue in her ear. "Baby." Quist turned golden, then flew to the door where his color shimmered between gold and white.

Fully awake now, Thorne bit her lip and stood. Though her torso felt like one large bruise, she took a step. The room turned in opposite directions. She waited for her head to steady before taking another step. Quist tugged her hair.

"I'm coming."

She lurched to the door and nudged it open. Warmth continued trickling down her inner thigh. Not much, she told herself, though her blood's silvery scent smelled strong. Quist flew down the stairs. She leaned against the wall to navigate the stone steps. At the bottom, the Great Hall was dim. The hearth fire showed only small bundles along the walls, children sleeping. Presumably the adults searched for her missing child.

Five paces from the door, Thorne stumbled and fell. She crawled the rest of the way, then used a gnarled walking stick to pull herself upright. Although sweat soaked her shift, she shivered.

She snagged a cloak and opened the unbarred door far enough to squeeze through. Leaning on the walking stick, she limped into the bailey. The night air raised bumps on her skin, but did nothing to cool her fever. She whistled for Wild-Eyes, and for once the warhorse separated from the herd. She used the fence to climb onto the mare then rode bareback through the open bailey gate. On her left, the searcher's torches cast points of light along Malwood's border.

Clutching the warhorse's mane, Thorne swayed. Quist yanked her hair.

"Ow, stop," she said, though the pain prevented her from fainting.

Although the horse's gait sent knife-sharp pains stabbing up her trunk, she urged Wild-Eyes faster. As she followed Quist, a storm cloud moved off the rising moon. Its dull light cast undulating shadows over the hedgerow below Hellee's cavern. On reaching the thicket, Thorne tumbled from the horse, knocking the wind from her. Once the cold, wet grass soothed her burning forehead, she didn't want to move.

Quist's chirp roused her enough to try.

The moon pressed against her when she tried to rise. The warhorse lowered her head, and Thorne grabbed the halter, letting Wild-Eyes pull her upright. Wet warmth streamed between her legs. The moon grew heavier as she stumbled after Quist.

After a few shaky steps, she fell and with the moon weighing her down, couldn't rise. The Fairy-Dragon swooped, flying along the thicket before returning. Thorne suspected she might be dying. She didn't notice cold any more but felt terribly tired. She'd close her eyes for just a moment.

Quist bit her nose so hard she thought he'd gnaw it off. Apparently, she wasn't dead enough to ignore. She couldn't lift her heavy arm to brush him away. With effort, she rolled on her stomach. The moon had returned to its proper place. Advancing with numb toes and weak arms, she followed moonlight along the thicket.

Finally Quist darted into the brambles, only an arm's length ahead. Might as well be a league; she could barely move. She had an excuse—she was dying. Could a goddess die? She smiled at her jest.

Atop the hawthorn hedge, a dozen yellow Fairy eyes shone eerily in the moonlight, watching her. Why?

The Fairy-Dragon scratched at a pile of leaves. Was Daisy here? When Thorne reached for the leaves, the Fairies dove at her, biting her face, clawing her arms. Quist chirped angrily. Thorne pulled the cape over her head.

She scooped leaves until she uncovered a Fairy net around blue cloth. She pulled the bundle toward her, ignoring the Fairies tugging at her cloak, and opened the blanket. In the dim light, the infant's tiny face was ashen, her body cold.

"No." Thorne held the child close, transferring her body heat. She couldn't bear another baby dying in her arms. If only Strumgued was here. He'd broken the spell of the Fairy Queen's kiss. He could help Daisy.

Although Thorne's head was heavy, her mind seemed airy as

milkweed seed. She must save her sister. She blew into the baby's mouth and nose, but the child didn't breathe.

When a Fairy crawled under the cloak, she struck it.

Raspberry-Frost dodged. "My Human."

Thorne's smile cracked her dry lips. She shrugged off the cloak. The Fairies no longer attacked but perched on the hawthorn hedge watching.

Her Fairy hovered over the baby. "Suckling sleeps."

She opened the blanket for Raspberry-Frost to see. "She's dead."

Raspberry-Frost landed on the infant's chest. "Open mouth."

Thorne parted the baby's lips. The Fairy didn't fan her wings over the infant's nose and mouth as Thorne expected, but bit its own arm. A drop of yellow Fairy blood dripped into the newborn's mouth. Raspberry-Frost then offered its arm to Thorne who licked a yellow drop tasting of sour apples.

She stroked the child's cold cheek. The baby's whimper made Thorne's heart jump. With the last of her strength, she opened her nightgown and pressed the child to her breast. Milk overflowed, coating the tiny lips. The infant suckled, weakly at first, then stronger. This time, Daisy wouldn't starve.

Thorne, shivering on the damp ground, curled around the baby. The only warm place was between her thighs. Not even Dragon blood could save her from bleeding to death. She kissed the baby's head, feeling unexpectedly free. She could rest. This time, she hadn't failed Daisy. Why did people fear death? Death was easy. Living was hard.

As darkness shrouded her, a wole-wolf howled.

CHAPTER SIXTY-THREE

"**D**eath hungers," Quist said, wiggling his tongue inside Hellee's hearing slit.

Outside the cavern, a wole-wolf howled and another answered.

Hellee smelled the blood of First Mother and thrashed his tail. She was nearby, outside in the night. He didn't mind darkness and open air, but his Mothers preferred light and shelter. Their skin was soft, easily ripped by claw or tooth.

"What is it, Hellee?" This Mother scratched his neck. He called her Earth Mother because she smelled of plants.

He growled to show danger.

"Very nice."

This Mother thought he played a game. He galloped into the tunnel leading outside.

"Hellee!" she shouted. "A storm's coming."

He didn't like storms, especially ones with lightning. Nevertheless, he ran to the edge of the ledge where he sniffed again. First Mother was close. Still, going further would upset this Mother.

She caught up. "What possesses you?" She tapped on his front leg, signaling he should follow. "Go back."

He stretched his neck but couldn't see First Mother; she must be outside the hedge.

The wole-wolves howled.

This Mother surveyed the plain. "Night has a violet cast since I ate Rustofona's eye. I see the shimmering heat of wole-wolves running over the plain." She tapped his leg again. "The pack is hunting. Get inside."

If he smelled First Mother's blood so must they. Did he fear the pack? He hung his head. Dragons should fear nothing. When bad men threatened Little Mother and took First Mother, he hid. But he was bigger now.

A scout yipped. The pack answered. Hellee bellowed a warning, but the pack advanced. He must find First Mother before them.

When he stepped over the ledge, Earth Mother tugged his tail. "Please Hellee, stay." She was slight, only up to his shoulder.

Yesterday Raspberry-Frost bade him help First Mother, and he'd left the mountain. The Mothers yelled and put ropes around his neck, leading him back. Usually, the Mothers were kind, feeding him, never leaving him alone. He wanted to please them. Nevertheless, he plunged into the darkness, half crawling, half sliding down the mountain.

"Stop!" this Mother yelled.

At the bottom, he galloped five Dragon lengths to the thicket. Lightning jagged the sky. He flinched but scurried along the hedge, sniffing as he went. The wole-wolves were closer to First Mother than he. He ran faster.

A dragon-length from her, the wole-wolves stopped, gold eyes glowing, snarling and snapping with jaws strong enough to break a cow's leg. Still her Dragon scent would warrant caution.

Hellee wanted to roar a challenge but needed all his air to run. When the moon peeked through the storm clouds, he saw First Mother lying motionless. The largest wole-wolf lunged at her. One bite would kill her.

Hellee wouldn't make it in time. Though his leg muscles ached, he lengthened his stride, flapped his immature wings, and gulped air.

The largest wole-wolf yelped and jumped back. A streak of Fairy light followed its shaking head.

Hellee leapt at the rear of the pack and bit one's haunches. It stunk of dirt and rotten meat, pleasing odors which excited him. He tossed the beast over his head, tasting blood and trapping dirty fur in his teeth. He roared a challenge. The wole-wolf pack scattered. He clamped his jaws on a muscled gut, snapping the spine and silencing its growls.

He'd almost reached First Mother when two wole-wolves leapt at his head. With a claw he shredded one's pelt. The other bit through his lower lip. Hellee shook his head, ripping his skin as he tossed the beast into the thicket of finger-length barbs. The howling animal's struggle to escape the hedge only poked more thorns into its flesh.

Hellee lunged at the wole-wolf separating him from First Mother. Only starving wole-wolves would dare attack even a young Dragon, but the blood dripping from Hellee's bottom lip seemed to provoke them.

If they attacked together, could they bring him down? Kill him?

Never. He was a Dragon.

For endless moments the wole-wolves watched him. Then one sprang—not at him but at First Mother. Flapping his wings, Hellee jumped, raking the beast with front claws, spilling its insides over her. Hellee cracked bones and tore skin.

The other wole-wolves slunk away.

Hellee lay down beside First Mother, licking offal from her. She curled around something smelling of Human, Dwarf, and Dragon—something new.

As rain fell, he sheltered her under his wing.

CHAPTER SIXTY-FOUR

A wole-wolf howl woke Thorne, but she blacked out before she could move or hide. The second time, Hellestorm's rough, sulfurous-scented tongue woke her, but she couldn't open her heavy eyelids.

Later, Strumgued's shouting woke her. "Cease your noise, baneful beast! Get back!"

Hellee rumbled a warning. Quist twittered. Though Thorne blinked, she couldn't bring the moon into focus. Spots swelled across the broken orb until everything went black.

When Thorne again clawed her way to consciousness, her arms were empty. "Where's Daisy?" She must save her sister. Mother had childbed fever and couldn't nurse. Da couldn't afford a wet nurse.

Someone smelling of fish lifted her. Willow-Bender. Glitter and Spangle bathed, dressed, and covered her with furs. Thorne smiled weakly when Hellee licked her face. Nearby a campfire crackled. She threw off the hot covers, but someone put them back.

When she next opened her eyes, it was still dark. Her forehead was cool, her tongue dry as ashes. Turning her head hurt. moving her body hurt worse. Even breathing hurt. Strumgued sat staring into the campfire. Cursing under his breath, he patted windblown sparks on his leather jerkin.

She sniffed. The air carried no scent of her child. The ground seemed to fall away beneath her as it had when Daisy died. Then she'd fallen into a hole, where she didn't have to feel. Now she clung to the edge, resisting that comforting trap. Saving her own child had rescued her from the pit where she'd cowered like a frightened vole, and she didn't want to go back. "Baby?" she croaked.

Strumgued hurried to her. "Our nursling is safe. How feel you?"

On the brink but above ground. "Thirsty."

From his belt he removed a flask and bit away the cork stopper. Expecting ale but tasting water, she noticed fires circling them. "Who's out there?"

"Your Dragon Guards and more." Strumgued joined her on the furs and pressed his lips to her forehead. Not a kiss, only testing for fever. "They will die and bless their good fortune to repay you. Devoted as Dwarfs are they."

For the first time, she was glad she couldn't cry, knowing her tears would flow like Ventamar Falls. The debt was hers. To avert burying her face in Strumgued's chest, she changed the subject. "I named the baby Rosamund."

Strumgued grunted but seemed pleased. "In your fever, you called for Daisy."

Inexplicably, she felt comfortable telling Strumgued how her newborn sister died in her arms. He pressed his palm against her heart. That made her choke up again. Pressure built behind her eyes. Enough painful memories. "Where's Rosamund?"

"Humph." Strumgued gazed into the crackling flames. "So now you're glad of her?"

A child making her happy would take getting used to. Feeling unpleasantly vulnerable, she whispered, "Yes." Embarrassed, she tried to rise but fell back, weak as when her infected arm nearly killed her in Gaspotine's lair. "I want to see her. Where is she?"

A vein, normally concealed by his beard, throbbed in his short neck. "Dyadzan Castle."

"I must feed her." She touched her breasts. They were soft, her milk gone. Her arms were thin. For a long moment, she couldn't breathe. "How long did I sleep?"

"Five days."

She squeezed her empty nipples, wanting to retreat into the familiar dark hole where losing a child couldn't hurt. She resisted. Who was nursing? She couldn't remember, but someone must feed Rosamund. "How can you be so heartless? Bring her before she starves."

"She has a Dwarf wet nurse." He looked away as if unaccustomed to discussing female business.

Her breathing eased, but not enough. "Send for her. I must hold her."

"You're weak." He set his jaw in a familiar way that infuriated Thorne.

"Strong enough to hold a newborn." He wouldn't thwart her in this. When she reached for Dracodurus, her sword was gone. Fervid also. Otherwise, she would've threatened something lethal.

His eyes gleamed in the firelight. "She's safer away from Humans."

"Strumgued—"

"Do not raise your voice." His face turned the color of a bruised apple. "Twice you've been near death. Then my child disappeared. I've had enough."

Thorne hadn't seen him this disconcerted since Cayeseed died. She put her hand on his arm and said reasonably, "Rosamund's place is with me."

His eyes blazed. "Your motherly instincts are as mercurial as a cat with her first litter. A cat may raise or ignore them."

"You don't trust me with my own child?" She reached for the dagger in her boot, but felt only bare skin.

"I'll not tolerate neglect."

"Nor will I." Arms trembling, mid-section hurting like she'd been pummeled, she sat up, relying on force of will alone.

He crossed his arms. "I've seen what I've seen."

Though stars swirled around her, she resisted lying down, as stubborn as her husband. "You cannot keep her from me."

"I'll not risk my daughter."

"Cayeseed" lingered unsaid between them.

"You have no more feeling than stone!"

Strumgued smiled tightly. "Stone is not always as hard as it appears."

In the darkness, it seemed a boulder stopped snoring and unfolded into a Dragon. When Hellestorm the Great bounded toward Thorne, Strumgued sprang back. Thorne patted the ground. Hellee put his head beside her thigh, so she could scratch behind his brow bone.

Strumgued gripped his sword but left it sheathed. "Your beast saved you and Rosamund from a pack of wole-wolves."

"I remember howls but nothing more."

"They lay all around you, ripped to pieces." His tongue rubbed his upper teeth. "A mighty battle. Pity I missed it."

Quist nuzzled her neck.

Strumgued scowled. "That flying beetle near drove me to distraction while I hunted our nursling."

"Quist would've led you to Rosamund."

"So I suppose I owe it and that wyrm gratitude." He pointed at Hellee.

"You do."

Before he could reply, Fehera approached with her herb basket and immediately touched Thorne's forehead. "Your fever's broken."

More concerned about the castle than herself, Thorne pushed Fehera's hand away. She wasn't quite so dizzy now. "Is anyone defending Stonevar?"

"A few tend the animals. The rest camp in the field. They think staying in the castle without you brings bad luck." Fehera took a small pot from her basket and hung it over the fire. "I'll heat grouse broth for you."

"Something more than flavored water."

Fehera added bits of dried venison and turnip greens. In the gray light preceding dawn, Thorne ate the thin soup. Strumgued confirmed Fehera would stay with Thorne, saying he'd return after visiting Rosamund.

"You cannot mean to separate a mother from her child. That's not the Dwarf way." Thorne knew from Grandfather's book that Dwarfs were excellent parents.

"My daughter stays in Dyadzan Castle. My wife may grace my chamber."

Thorne took three deep breaths. "Will you always have your way?"

"Less often than you think." He bowed and strode into the dawn.

#

Thorne's journey to Dyadzan Castle in the back of a wagon seemed to take hours, and walking to Strumgued's chamber even longer. Each step jarred her bruised bones. But seeing Rosamund made her forget the pain. Ignoring the Dwarf nursemaid's objections, she unswaddled the sleeping infant, welcoming her child's cry. Seeing the plump folds on Rosamund's thighs lifted a world's weight from Thorne's shoulders.

In the ensuing weeks, she felt imprisoned in her husband's chamber. Though the guards let her pass, Strumgued's baby must stay. She rocked Rosamund in a willow rocker that Zarra had brought from Stonevar. Surprisingly, hours slipped by while she hummed and sang to the baby.

To anyone observing, she might seem happy, but Thorne hated this room—the many chests against the wall, the stumpy table, the small stools, the too-short bed. She hated knowing Dwarf guards watched her and hearing voices behind what must be secret doors. She couldn't sleep here and returned to Stonevar at night.

Worse, multiple times each day, the Dwarf wet nurse reminded Thorne that she couldn't feed her own child. Strumgued probably selected this particular Dwarf because she was strict in their ways, already acting middle-aged. She was squat and neckless with a thick red braid down her back. Strands of coarse hair curled outward around her face, making her big head appear even larger.

Though she complained to Strumgued that Quist might hurt Rosamund, he let the Fairy-Dragon stay. Thorne was grateful. However, he didn't join Thorne at night in Stonevar or for eventide meals. The former she expected so soon after giving birth. The latter she couldn't explain.

When the baby had survived a fortnight, custom decreed her mother bless her. A typical mother's blessing for a daughter asked for beauty, good marriage, and healthy children.

Thorne touched the child's forehead. "May you never know oppression. May you make your own way. May friends always surround you."

The baby smiled as she slept in the rockerless cradle.

No matter how Strumgued interfered, she'd help Rosamund find her own path, do what made her happy, let her stretch her wings. Wings! Ignoring Rosamund's cries, she pulled off the baby's clothing and held a candle near Rosamund's shoulders. Nothing odd. Still uncertain, she traced the child's shoulders with her fingertips. Everything seemed Human.

An hour later, Strumgued bent over Rosamund's cradle, offering his finger for his daughter to hold. He rubbed Rosamund's tiny fingers with his thick thumb.

"The name Rosamund means guardian and protector," he said.

"I didn't know."

"That's sometimes the way of it. The name chooses the child."

"Do you think her handsome?" Rosamund had Dwarf features, looking nothing like Thorne.

He scratched under his jaw as if the golden stubble itched. "Her round nose and full lips are most attractive. No downy fuzz covers her skin. And her head is small."

"It felt large to me." Thorne rubbed the small bump on her abdomen.

He seemed to force his full lips into a thin smile. "If she's not too tall and grows a proper chin tuft, she'll find a good mate."

Thorne scowled. "No spouse. And I hope she doesn't have a beard."

Strumgued laughed. Thorne liked the sound.

"Are you happy she's a girl?" Thorne knew the answer but wanted to maintain his good spirits.

His smile vanished. "Rosamund has enslaved me as did her mother."

"Perhaps Rosamund and I should return to Stonevar. You could spend nights with us there." By now, her husband must miss sharing her bed.

"All who enter Stonevar fall under the spell of its Goddess." Strumgued pulled Thorne against him. He cupped the back of her neck and his thumb stroked her throat. "Rosamund will live as a Dwarf."

CHAPTER SIXTY-FIVE

"Do you want to know what will happen if I don't join Hellestorm on Elysia?" Solanie asked Gaspotine.

"No. But I can see that you won't leave me alone until I do." Gaspotine embarked on a long swim into the future. Hundreds, thousands, tens of thousands of years. The farther he traveled, the more determined he became to know the end. After many generations, Dragon-kind would become as dull as beasts.

Catulicide caused this. Rather than risk their whelps shaming them, she-Dragons destroyed the unconforming—the clever, the curious, the cordial. Male Dragons knew nothing of this. If any suspected, they ignored it. What could they do when they didn't recognize their own whelps?

Together Hellestorm and Solanie would force change, which no Dragon wanted but would save Dragon-kind.

Disguised as a scarlet stratus cloud, Gaspotine considered what to do. Helping Solanie meant enduring more scorn. If he didn't help, Dragon-kind would degenerate into animals. In the end, he had no choice.

As autumn drew closer, Solanie called for Gaspotine until he re-formed from the cloud.

"What do you want?" Gaspotine didn't bother hiding his annoyance.

"I must leave for Elysia. Tell me how."

"If you do this, Dragons will shun you in the Continuum for all eternity."

"I know." She held her head higher.

"Hellestorm is still a whelp and may reject his destiny."

"I don't believe that."

"Bull Dragons have no paternal instincts." Gaspotine slammed a fisted claw into the riverbank. "He'll crush your eggs and eat them."

"He'll be unlike other Dragons. You saw that in his current."

"His stream has an undragonish number of branches. He'll make disastrous choices."

"He's Dragon-kind's only hope."

Gaspotine bellowed, spraying hot air. Solanie jumped back. He roared until his neck dissolved into steam, but Solanie didn't run away.

He deliberately took a long time mending himself, hoping she'd reconsider, then finally said, "When the wind blows hardest from the west, you must fly." He explained navigation using the sun, star tracking, and the circular paths of ocean wind. He remembered his own long flights with pleasure, even those that cramped his wings.

"How can I travel by night?"

He understood her concern. To fly long distances, Dragons rode air thermals, which formed only over land in daylight. "The wyrwind blows hard five days. Depart from the mountaintop where the wyrwind leaves shore. Follow its curve across the ocean. If it falters when you're at sea, you'll not reach land."

Her large eyes brightened.

He'd never seen a whelp more anxious to learn. "There are layers of wind. Some slow. The fastest blow high where the air thins."

"But I have five days."

Her earnestness made him want to lie. "Sometimes as few as three."

"Will that be enough?"

"For an experienced flier. Build your strength. Practice riding heaven's roads for a day and night." Her slight frame let her fly young. Would it give her endurance?

"I can do this." Solanie spoke with dragonish confidence. "When do I leave?"

"On a moonless night, the wyrwind will rise."

CHAPTER SIXTY-SIX

Nella nagged until Thorne agreed to talk with Magda, though Thorne would rather have skinned a live wole-lion. Nevertheless she carried a blanket to the dark corner in the Great Hall where Magda had huddled the past month and put it around her shoulders. "Magda."

The middle-aged woman didn't lift her head. "I almost killed your baby."

Thorne hadn't expected lucidity, and her tone was unforgiving. "Rosamund's all right."

"My mind wasn't working." Magda's eyes cleared, confusion melting like snow thawing on Ventamar Mountain. "I miss Brutte."

Mentioning Brutte softened Thorne, and she sat on the floor beside Magda. "Sometimes I pretend he's milking the cow and will come in complaining its teats are too small."

One side of Magda's mouth turned up. "He hated milking. Said a man should pull on two teats, not four."

Thorne smiled. "He was a great mentor to me. He must have been an astounding soldier."

"I never liked him soldiering." Magda drew the blanket tighter. The hearth fire never heated this shadowy corner. Had Magda chosen it to punish herself? "When my son was small, I minded less. But after he left with his pa, I was alone. Then Brutte came home crippled."

"That must have been terrible."

"I was glad. He wouldn't leave me anymore. With you I had a daughter. Made me happy like before my son died."

Like hot metal plunged into a blacksmith's water pail, Thorne's

304

anger cooled. "I don't know what would have happened if you two hadn't taken me in."

Magda smoothed Thorne's hair. "I've something to tell you."

With plenty of problems filling her haversack, Thorne didn't think she wanted to know.

"I don't care for Bekka."

She hadn't expected that. "Everyone likes Bekka. You convinced Brutte to let her come."

"To spite him. She's always nice. I can't abide it. If I grump at her, I feel guilty. I miss Olga."

Thorne tried not to laugh. Lott's sharp-tongued first wife got on well with Magda. "I hadn't thought a sunny disposition would aggravate you."

"I can't yell at a cripple."

"Does she do wrong?"

"No. Another vexation. At the Honey Lodge, the guests teased and joked with me. I miss them."

Clearly Magda was homesick, but Seahaven had nothing for her. Her friends were here, and Bludwelt had killed his father, her employer.

Magda smoothed her apron. "This is Brutte's fault. He picked people who get along too well."

Thorne covered her smile with a hand. "That is a problem."

"Can I see the baby?"

Before answering, Thorne checked if anyone listened. All were busy: sweeping the Great Hall, cleaning ashes from the hearth, scouring trestle tables with scrub brushes made from wood splits. Barefooted children dashed in and out the open door, ignoring maternal admonishments to stay inside or out. Few knew Strumgued didn't trust Thorne with Rosamund. She preferred it that way.

"Rosamund must remain in the Dwarf stronghold." Even whispering those words hurt.

Magda's face paled. "He won't let you bring her home?"

"No. I'm a visitor in my daughter's life."

"My fault."

Thorne squeezed Magda's cold hand. "Mine first for rejecting Strumgued's child." She put her head on Magda's lap. "I love you."

"And I you, Lass." Magda took a comb from her tunic pocket and pulled it through Thorne's hair. When they lived in Seahaven,

Magda had done this. Thorne could never be the daughter Magda wanted, so she allowed it.

Magda combed out a snarl. "Emera told me Brutte attacked the Dwarf Lord."

Thorne cringed. "So Strumgued claims."

"She said the Dwarf only defended himself." Magda avoided Strumgued's name.

Though Thorne believed her husband, not blaming him for Brutte's death proved more difficult than pulling pricker burrs from fleece.

"Brutte wanted to die fighting." Magda's comb raked Thorne's scalp.

"Ow. Knowing that doesn't comfort me."

"He had a warrior's mind. To make men fight, captains claim that battle brings honor. Reward comes after death." Magda yanked Thorne's hair. "Rat feathers!"

Thorne took the comb away. "Brutte taught that leaders must sometimes deceive." She didn't enjoy it, but her goddess image had helped Stonevar, as Brutte predicted.

"At least he passed before apoplexy afflicted him like his pa. Brutte didn't fear much—only sickness." Her lip quivered.

Thorne held Magda while the older woman cried. Magda seemed to have accepted Brutte's death and stopped blaming Strumgued. After forgiving Magda, Thorne felt better, knowing Brutte would want that. But could she forgive her husband?

After making sure Magda ate the midday meal, Thorne rode to Hellee's cavern, her first visit since giving birth.

Inside Bekka said, "Watch this. Fly, Aeron. Fly!"

Year-old Aeron opened his alabaster bat-like wings, twice the length of his arms. He galloped around the cavern, flapping them.

Bekka clapped, but Thorne's stomach lurched as if she'd missed a step. Look what she'd done to him by making Lily drink Dragon blood.

Watching the toddler made Thorne miss Rosamund. By now the Dwarf nursemaid would've swaddled Rosamund tight. Thorne hid the old swaddling in her pack, but the nursemaid always brought more. When Thorne returned, she'd unwrap Rosamund under the nursemaid's disapproving glare, letting the infant wave her arms and kick freely.

Bekka nudged Thorne. "He's advanced for only a year. Walks steadily and speaks short sentences. From Dragon blood?"

"Seems likely."

Bekka picked up a pair of leather gloves to mend. "Has it changed Rosamund?"

"Her eyes." Rosamund's eyes had elongated diamond-shaped pupils like a Dragon's. Each day Thorne checked for wing joints. The baby had thick, dwarfish shoulders, but no abnormalities. Why did Aeron have wings, but not Rosamund? Was it because Lily drank Dragon blood while pregnant? Or did Rosamund's Dwarf paternity prevent it?

Before Thorne could say more, Aeron ran to Bekka. He extended his hand toward Thorne. "Rock." He held a shiny black stone in slender hands like Lily's.

"Very nice. I see why you like it." Thorne pulled her sister's child into her lap and kissed his white hair.

Aeron smiled, then jumped down to crawl onto Hellee's neck. Unlike his mother, the child appeared fearless. The young Dragon remained motionless until Aeron was seated, then swung his head back and forth, making the boy squeal happily. Hellee's stomach rumbled. Zarra was overdue with his meal.

"He's handsome like his father," Bekka said.

"Unfortunate." Thorne hated admitting any resemblance. "What shall we tell him about Anders?"

"Only that his father was a sailor."

Thorne stroked Dracodurus's hilt. "I should've killed him before he touched Lily."

Bekka pricked her finger on the sewing needle. "Ow." She wiped blood from a glove. "If you'd killed him before, then Aeron wouldn't have been born."

"All right. I should've killed Anders afterwards."

"It's not right to harm Aeron's father." Bekka sucked on her wounded finger. "If you see him, remember that."

Thorne smiled. "I'm forgetful." Someday she'd meet Anders again. She felt it in her bones.

Bekka jumped up. "Where's Aeron?"

"He was here a moment ago." But he wasn't in the cavern now.

Outside, Aeron shrieked. Thorne had left the door open to let in fresh air. She grabbed her bow and dashed toward the tunnel. Bekka followed. Before they reached the Dragon Ledge, Aeron cried out again, sounding farther away. Had the toddler fallen?

Hellee galloped past them. Outside, a wole-hawk screeched, struggling to stay aloft with the kicking child in his claws. Flapping his immature wings, Hellee extended his neck and leapt, but the wole-hawk was too high. The Dragon's legs buckled when he landed, and he roared frustration.

Bekka threw a rock and missed, before dashing down the steps.

Thorne nocked an arrow and let go, refusing to worry about Aeron surviving the fall. The arrow wobbled in the wind. Before noting a miss, she shot another that whizzed past. She loosed a third—too low. The bird was now beyond range of even her dragonish strength. Nevertheless she shot again. This one landed short. As she knew it would.

The ledge seemed to dissolve beneath Thorne. Lily's child would feed wole-hawk chicks. Whenever she let herself care, disaster followed.

Below her, Bekka scurried across the plain in her unbalanced gait, yelling and gesturing at the sky. Thorne had never seen her move so fast.

From the direction of Malwood, Zarra yowled, racing toward them, dragging the carcass of a young deer behind her black gelding. For once Zarra's seat was solid. Her arrow flew true, hitting the wole-hawk in the thigh.

The bird continued as if the arrow had caught only feathers, then began to lose altitude. Much too high, the wole-hawk dropped Aeron. Zarra yelled to speed her horse.

Bekka shouted, "Fly, Aeron. Fly."

His baby wings couldn't possibly support him. But Aeron extended his wings and slowed his fall. Was it enough?

Screaming, the toddler slammed the ground.

Thorne hurried down the mountainside, leapt onto Wild-Eyes, and sped over the grassland, slowing only to pull Bekka behind her. By the time they reached Aeron, the child was quiet. Dead?

He lay on his stomach, eyes closed. His wings were bruised bright scarlet and angled to the side. Broken or dislocated.

Zarra knelt beside him. "He's alive."

Both Aeron's legs were twisted like curly willow.

When Bekka reached for him, Thorne said, "Don't touch him.

His spine might be broken."

Bekka sobbed. Hellee whined and licked Aeron's face.

"Get Fehera," Thorne told Zarra. Would Aeron die before she could know him?

CHAPTER SIXTY-SEVEN

The healer knelt beside Aeron to examine him. "Keep Hellee back. A small head bump. He hit feet first. You heard him scream on the ground?"

"For a moment," Thorne said.

"His spine feels whole."

Bekka clasped her hands as if praying. "His wings?"

"Ripped from their sockets."

Thorne cringed. That must've hurt.

Bekka's voice trembled. "Can you put them back?"

"I'll try. I'm glad he's unconscious." Fehera moved each wing until something popped. "Help me wind strips around his chest to hold them still."

"His legs?" Thorne asked.

"Multiple breaks. An adult would be crippled, but he's young. If we keep him swaddled, he may heal straight."

Biting her lip, Thorne fetched Rosamund's swaddling from her pack. Would the child be lame? She'd failed Lily again. Thorne resisted retreating into that dark hole inside herself.

After Fehera swaddled Aeron, she passed him to Zarra, who sat atop her horse to carry him home. Hellee resisted returning to his cavern until Thorne took him back.

Aeron was alive, but would he walk again?

#

Thorne kept watch on the door. Strumgued would be furious if he saw Raspberry-Frost perched on Rosamund's cradle. At the very least, he'd ban Fairies from Dyadzan Castle, and at worst he'd destroy their hive.

"My Human must know her legend."

"What legend?" she asked absently.

Raspberry-Frost's next words caught Thorne's full attention.

"Fae divined these words;

> Upon her chin a skylord's kiss.
> A captive fairy she'll dismiss.
> We will know her when she comes.
>
> With Fairy glamour to deceive.
> A Dragon's eye to Fae she'll cede.
> We will aid her when she comes.
>
> A giant serpent she shall kill.
> And save Fae from an icy spill.
> We will heed her when she comes."

Raspberry-Frost grinned, showing pointed teeth.

Thorne smiled. "So I was prophesied."

"Without doubt."

"Brutte once told me that a foolish man gathers his blunders, then declares them his destiny."

The Fairy scratched its narrow nose as if puzzled.

"Any more verses?"

Raspberry-Frost puffed out its furry chest and said;

> "A Dwarf Lord marches overland.
> His bravery will win her hand.
> We will know him when he comes."

Thorne inhaled sharply. "So Strumgued was foretold also. Any more?"

"No."

"Because you make up prophesies after they happen?"

The Fairy flew to Thorne's shoulder and nipped her ear. "Foolish Human."

Thorne rubbed its bird-like toes. "You believe Strumgued must stay, though he hates Fairies."

Raspberry-Frost waved its arms. "Human words bewilder Fae. Dwarf Lord wends a worthy way."

Thorne hadn't expected this championing of Strumgued.

When someone knocked at the door, Thorne motioned Raspberry-Frost away. After the Fairy left through the window, she opened the door.

Zarra handed her a cloth-protected plate. "Magda sent it."

Thorne uncovered honey cakes.

"Fehera said to tell you that Aeron is awake," Zarra said. "She gave him willow-bark tea for the pain." Zarra lifted the waxed leather lid on the largest, most worn chest in Strumgued's chamber.

"Those are Strumgued's." Thorne sputtered crumbs. "What are you doing?"

"Seeing what's inside."

Until now, Thorne had no curiosity about the chests, though having four personal trunks was unusual. "Strumgued may arrive any moment."

"Only old armor."

Thorne peeked inside, recognizing Strumgued's breastplate. Zarra was already opening the next one, a flat-lidded, four-legged panel chest ornately carved with horses.

Zarra held up a red velvet jerkin edged with elaborate gold braid. "Fancy. Didn't realize Strumgued was a pretty boy."

"He has official duties." Since he dressed like his Dwarf warriors, she'd never seen him wear anything like this. What occasion would require it?

Zarra dug further. "More clothes."

"What do you hope to find?" Seeing Zarra paw through Strumgued's things tightened Thorne's gut.

"I'll know when I see it." She moved to the next. "Whoa, my beauty. What's this?"

Thorne hurried to the third chest, which was simple, though finely made with dovetailed joints and a curved, leather lid.

Zarra unwrapped oilcloth from a helmet, which glistened in the candlelight. "Fine work. Too small for Strumgued." Next Zarra lifted out finely made chain mail. "Light, but would deflect a sword thrust." She gave Thorne a meaningful glance. "Too long for a Dwarf." Last she unwrapped a shield inlaid with a Dragon likeness.

Thorne held up a hand. "Don't say it."

"Why hasn't he given these to you?"

A shiver rose up Thorne's spine. "They're not for me. Put them back."

Zarra moved to the next chest.

"Don't open it." Thorne sat on the lid.

Zarra's eyes gleamed as if Thorne's resistance made her more interested. "What do you think's inside?"

"Nothing important."

Zarra inspected the trunk. "Legs. Not for travel. Did Strumgued tell you not to look?"

"He said nothing, and I didn't ask." He only focused on Rosamund.

"He must've known you'd open them." Zarra cocked her head. "You can't sit there forever."

"We have no right!" Her voice must have been louder than she intended, because Sir-Sir scurried from a dark corner, jumped onto the chest, and nipped Thorne's finger.

"Ow!" Thorne stood. "He never liked me." She sucked her wound as Sir-Sir hissed then bruxed—ground his teeth.

Zarra whistled, and Sir-Sir jumped onto her shoulder. "He thought you'd attack me." She lifted the polished oak lid and removed a dugout box carved with a resting Dragon—not a Dwarf emblem. Thorne snatched it. The thief seemed about to object until she lifted out a shimmering purple cloth.

"What's this?" Zarra said.

"Wabjeb." Grandfather had brought Mother a small piece.

"Never heard of it. Looks high-priced."

"Made from purple lacewing butterfly cocoons. They inhabit only one island. I wonder how Strumgued got it?"

Zarra pulled out more cloth. "Uncommonly white. Feel how soft." She removed gold braid from a bag. "Expensive."

"I don't want to see anything else."

"Why didn't Strumgued give these to you?"

Thorne inspected the stone floor. "They're not for me."

"They're for you, all right. What made him change his mind?"

"I don't care to speculate." But some part of her did care.

"He worships you." Zarra opened the small chest before Thorne could stop her. "Look at this." Zarra held up a diamond, ruby, and emerald necklace that would hang to Thorne's waist. "This would cost a kingdom."

She didn't want to see more. With the necklace replaced, she put the small chest back, and slammed the larger chest lid, waking Rosamund.

"Sweet thing." Zarra picked up the baby. "I'll be off so you can eat with Strumgued."

She didn't need to go. Strumgued no longer joined Thorne for the eventide meal, but she was too embarrassed to admit it. After Zarra left, Thorne stared at the last two chests. Though she cared nothing about fancy garments or jewels, they seemed to represent something she'd lost.

CHAPTER SIXTY-EIGHT

Gaspotine watched Rendeius the Terrible in his lair, hoping to see some of the traits that Solanie evidenced, qualities that might strengthen Dragon-kind.

Rendeius stomped between piles of rubble. "I will have Tallasha the Resplendent."

Gaspotine didn't doubt him. Rendeius had more obsessive determination than most Dragons. All had a compulsion to return metal and crystals to their source, so swords and armor, anvils and gold, diamonds and rubies littered their caverns. However, Rendeius seemed to have a stronger drive than most. Common sandstone and river boulders cluttered his cave.

Rendeius kicked a pile of bones. "I'll take Hellestorm the Great's cavern."

Gaspotine shot from the Silver River, scattering clouds. Could he let his son kill his grandson? Undragonish concern sent him spiraling, and he crashed on blue grass, flattening his malleable form. Erramon rolled his eyes, then looked away.

The Dark scurried behind a tree twisting at impossible angles. Interfering in a territory challenge would break Dragon Code, which no bloodless had ever done. His infamy would soar to unimaginable heights.

But Rustofona would be inconsolable if Hellestorm died. Worse, she'd go mad. Wanting her company was aberrant, but facing eternity without her was worse. His form started to melt.

With concentration, he thickened himself and glanced about, as if someone might detect his thoughts, grateful for the first time that few living Dragons paid heed to the bloodless. Except for himself and Rustofona, the bloodless ignored each other.

By the time Solanie returned from viewing Hellestorm's future, Gaspotine had recovered himself.

"The future has changed," Solanie said. "Rendeius's current swallows Hellestorm's. What does that mean?"

Rustofona pulled her head from Hellestorm's present. "What did you say?" Instead of waiting for an answer, she swam into the future and returned quickly. "I see Human undertows, eddies, and whirlpools in Rendeius's stream. They will try to protect Hellestorm but fail. The Terrible will kill my son."

Only death would deter Rendeius, and Gaspotine didn't want his son to die. A whelp raised by Humans was unlikely to survive. Better prepare Rustofona. "We can do nothing." Fog gushed from his chest; he grabbed for it but failed to gather it back.

"What about me?" Solanie swam to her future.

Rustofona's rolled tail reflected her fear. "The Humans must save him."

Gaspotine snorted. "They cannot defeat Rendeius."

"Hellestorm must survive."

"That's motherly delusion, not Dragon sense."

Her eyes threw black sparks. "Dragon sense means no sense at all."

"Silence." Was this undragonish attitude the price of sanity?

"I'll have Vainglorian kill Rendeius."

"Vainglorian thinks no further than his next nap," Gaspotine observed. "He's battled no one in a century."

"He's clever."

"After he slays Rendeius, he'll kill the Humans. Without them, Hellestorm will starve."

Solanie sped toward them. "If Hellestorm dies so will I."

Rustofona's head swayed. "I must warn Thorne."

"How?" Gaspotine scratched his snout, shredding his nostrils. Oh, how he missed rubbing his hide against a jagged rock.

Solanie's eyes widened. "I'll tell the Fairy Queen."

Gaspotine shook his head. "Too late. Rendeius is on his way."

#

Screeching, Raspberry-Frost flew into Thorne's chamber.

The Fairy's high-pitched shriek was like none Thorne had ever heard, and she stopped moving her clean clothes from basket to chest. "What's wrong, my Fairy?"

Raspberry-Frost circled Thorne's head, then ripped the sweater hanging from a wall hook. Thorne didn't want Magda upset by Fairy damage and would have to repair the garment before her foster mother noticed.

Raspberry-Frost unraveled the red yarn and tied it around her arm. "Rendeius the Terrible draws near."

"Who's Rendeius?" Thorne doubted she'd like the answer.

Raspberry-Frost clawed the air. "A Dragon most diabolical."

"Why come to Elysia?" The island couldn't support more than three Dragons.

The Fairy hugged herself. "To entwine with Tallasha."

"Why so worried? Tallasha's lair is a long way from Stonevar. He'll leave after mating season ends." Less than a week, hopefully. Thorne resumed the simple task of storing her clothes, which soothed her. Very little did nowadays.

The Fairy tugged at a button on Thorne's shirt, then chewed thread until the button came off. Thorne held out her hand, and the Fairy returned it. Thorne had never seen Raspberry-Frost so destructive. Fairies had no concept of ownership, but they normally took things when no one was around.

"The Terrible will challenge the Great."

"Other Dragons are supposed to respect Hellee's territory." Thorne threw the basket across her chamber, flinging garments over bed and floor. "Why don't Dragons obey their own laws?"

"None forbid dueling for Hellestorm's den."

"Hellee's only a baby." Rosamund was now a plump three-month-old.

"An easy victory." Raspberry-Frost yanked a single hair from Thorne's head.

"Ow. What are you doing?"

The Fairy nipped Thorne's ear. Clearly Raspberry-Frost was upset about Rendeius, but why hurt Thorne. In a flash of inspiration, she understood. "You believe Rendeius will kill me."

The Fairy hummed.

Thorne gave Raspberry-Frost the button. "Don't let Magda see it."

#

Rosamund fussed in Thorne's arms, wanting to nurse, but Thorne had sent the Dwarf nursemaid away. Strumgued had only one foot in his chamber before she announced, "A Dragon will challenge Hellee."

The Dwarf snickered. "'Twill be a short battle."

"Don't laugh!" She hugged Rosamund so tight the infant wailed. "He'll kill us all."

Strumgued set his foot on a bootjack and yanked off his boot with a pop. "How do know?" He didn't look at her, but his mouth tightened.

"Raspberry-Frost."

"A Fairy," he said scornfully. "I won't lose a single night's rest over what a Fairy says." As he removed the other boot, she saw shadows under his eyes.

Thorne scurried around the new four-poster bed, built long enough to hold her. "Below my balcony, the fire vines bud. When they bloom, Rendeius the Terrible will come to mate Tallasha and will challenge Hellee for his lair."

"Good."

Was he faking bravado? No. He wanted to battle an adult Dragon and restore his clan's honor.

She wanted to throw something at him but reined in her temper. "I need your help to save Hellee."

When Strumgued kissed the baby's forehead, Rosamund calmed. "Why should I?"

"Hellee saved Rosamund's life. And mine."

"Letting him live is reward enough." Strumgued moved to the water stand and scrubbed his face with soapy palms.

As Thorne tried for another argument, Rosamund's wails brought the nursemaid who set food on the table. After giving Thorne a disparaging glance, she took the baby away.

Strumgued dried his hands. "Join me at the table."

Thorne dropped onto a chair, only vaguely aware that this was their first meal together since Rosamund's birth. Though the odor of roast pork unsettled her stomach, she smiled as if pleased. What would convince Strumgued? "This time the Fairies are on our side." They were on Hellestorm's, which was close enough. Nevertheless she'd a premonition that if Rendeius killed Hellee, the Fairies would transfer their loyalty to the Terrible. But talk of Fairies would never convince her husband.

While Thorne tried to think of more reasons, Strumgued grunted approval of the meal.

"Regain your honor by killing Rendeius." That's what he wanted.

A storm raged over Strumgued's face, trenching his forehead, clouding his complexion. She immediately regretted reminding him of his ancestral humiliation. Her husband was like Da, even more stubborn when angered.

Heedless, she continued. "There's no honor letting a whelp die."

His eyes narrowed, but he seemed to listen.

She carved the pork, knowing this wifely task would please him. "You can revenge your clan by killing a red Dragon." Blood bubbled where she'd cut her thumb.

"Let me see." He wiped the blood away. "Not deep." Absently he licked her blood from his finger. The skin exposed by the V of shirt flushed, then his face. Now his eyes softened when he looked at her.

"How can we save Hellestorm?" Thorne asked gently.

He tugged at his shirt as if tasting her blood warmed him. "You won't like it."

"Will it save Hellee's life?"

"It will." He pushed beans around his plate as if reluctant to explain. "Block the cavern entrance with boulders."

"He'll be trapped."

Strumgued gnawed meat from a bone and chewed as he said, "After the invader's dead, we'll clear the stone."

"If we die—" She touched his bare arm and felt a tingle. Strumgued had Dragon-Fating, because he intended to help Hellee. Something she believed impossible. His musky odor now gave her shivers. She liked the feel of the thick hair covering his arm. She licked her finger, tasting his sweat. "If we die, what will happen?"

With an oily finger, he ruffled his mustache. "Best we live."

#

When the fire vine bloomed, the Dwarfs blasted the mountainside, crashing boulders onto the Dragon Ledge, exploding the wooden door, showering dust. Thorne coughed and covered her ears as thundering booms echoed inside the cavern. Hellee whimpered and scrambled behind her.

After the noise stopped and the dust settled, sunlight squeezed through narrow cracks in the barrier. Above them, light filtered through less than half the ceiling openings. Only a horde of Dwarf miners could move this much stone.

Thorne's heart pounded unevenly. What if Strumgued changed his mind? Too late now.

Four Dragon lengths from the tunnel entrance, Thorne, Bekka, and Zarra waited silently by a cold hearth, as if they might miss Rendeius's arrival if anyone made a sound. Bekka scratched under Hellee's chin, Thorne under his tail, Zarra along his back, keeping him quiet.

They'd removed all fire from the chamber anticipating Rendeius igniting his breath to burn them alive. Also when excited or frightened or grumpy, Hellee might forgot his training and exhale on the flames to create a fireball.

They waited for what seemed like days. But in hours Rendeius roared and clawed at the stone barrier. Everyone froze as boulders tumbled from the pile and crashed inside the tunnel.

Bekka covered Hellee's ear slits. "Will he get in?"

"I don't know," Thorne said.

The barricade shook. With Sir-Sir chittering on her shoulder, Zarra drew her sword.

Rendeius's forked tongue snaked between the stones, smelling or tasting or whatever Dragons did. Zarra nicked the questing tongue. It withdrew. Rendeius resumed digging. Rocks fell away, leaving a large hole at the top. The Terrible stuck his snout through the opening and roared.

Hellee howled and rushed at Rendeius. Thorne and Bekka grabbed Hellee about the neck. He threw them off and climbed the rocks.

Zarra stabbed Rendeius's nose, forcing him back. More rocks crashed outside. Rendeius would soon get his head through. When that happened, he'd kill Hellee.

Thorne tugged on the whelp's tail. "Come away!"

Hellee, a wild look in his eyes, snapped at her. She jumped aside. "Get me a rope!"

Zarra helped Thorne loop it around the whelp's chest. The three women pulled, moving him only a foot. A large boulder fell away, opening the top half of the entrance. Thorne and Zarra tied the rope ends around their waists and towed Hellee back. He bit the rope in two, and the women landed on their backsides.

Rendeius nosed through the hole.

#

Hellestorm was doomed. Gaspotine swam to stay in the present, watching Rendeius glide over the ocean. The next few centuries with Rustofona promised to be unpleasant.

The Magnificent wailed and looked up from her son's current. "The Dwarfs have trapped Hellestorm inside the mountain."

That surprised Gaspotine. "To destroy him?"

"Why else? Thorne stayed with him."

"Her mating with the Dwarf Lord must have gone badly." Dwarfs were great fighters, but he knew nothing of their mating. Perhaps like wole-lions, they rejected disagreeable females. Thorne was most disagreeable.

Rustofona stuck her nose into the Silver River. "Would Thorne remain calm if trapped?"

"Maybe the threat comes from outside."

She stared with one swelling eye. "What do you mean?"

"Rendeius."

As she shoved past Gaspotine to jump into Rendeius's stream, she clipped Gaspotine's wing. "I see only water below him. How close is he?"

"Less than a day." Gaspotine retrieved his wing.

A short distance later, Rendeius landed on the Dragon Ledge and dug at the boulders.

Gaspotine had to admit Dwarfs were clever. "Perhaps the rock slide protects Hellestorm."

Rustofona's tail rolled up. "Rendeius will get in." Some of her mist scattered as she rushed to Vainglorian's spirit reclining on shore. "Rendeius means to kill Hellestorm," she told him.

Vainglorian shrugged, evidently failing to realize the significance.

Gaspotine couldn't spend eternity with Rustofona moaning over Hellestorm. "Rendeius wants a lair on Elysia to copulate with Tallasha."

Vainglorian bellowed and bounded into his current, vanishing from the Continuum. Gaspotine and Rustofona returned to watching Rendeius dig at the boulders.

"He'll clear the rocks before Vainglorian reaches Stonevar," Rustofona said.

#

Rendeius screeched and yanked back his head as a second avalanche roared down the mountainside. Dust showered Thorne. Coughing, she covered her eyes and nose with her arm. Blackness engulfed the cavern.

After the rocks stopped crashing, Bekka asked. "What happened?"

Thorne brushed dust off her black Dragon leathers. "Strumgued must've ordered another rock slide. Larger than the first." Usually she welcomed stone enclosing her, but now she wanted to escape the tomb-like cavern, where metallic rock dust filled every breath.

Bekka sneezed. "Is Rendeius dead?"

"I can't hear him." Her dragonish hearing would detect his breathing if he were still on the Dragon Ledge.

Zarra's voice cut the dark silence. "I doubt he'll claw through that."

With a rustle of skirts, Bekka opened the hidden door by the fireplace and withdrew a torch.

Thorne followed. "Time we return to the castle." When Hellee rushed after her, she rubbed his snout. "Bekka will stay with you."

Thorne tried to untie the rope about her waist but the knot wouldn't loosen. She wound the rest around her. No time to cut it now.

Zarra passed Thorne the end of the rope hanging from her waist. "So we don't get separated."

"I won't get lost." Thorne had a dragonish sense of direction and could read Dwarf markings.

"We'll move faster," Zarra took the torch from Bekka, "if I don't have to check if you're still behind me."

Zarra set Sir-Sir on the floor and dashed after him, pulling Thorne along. Hellee's whimpers accompanied Bekka's comforting song.

After a somber trip through mountain tunnels, Thorne and Zarra emerged in Thorne's chamber and without stopping to catch a breath rushed onto the balcony. The boulders blocking the entrance to Redilik Cavern took up half the Dragon Ledge. Thorne couldn't believe the amount of rock. Digging Hellestorm out might take years—if they survived. She scanned the sky for Rendeius.

"Malwood," Zarra whispered.

Rendeius flew over the forest then approached Stonevar. Between the barns, the Dwarfs had concealed a ballista, a giant crossbow.

Strumgued shouted, "Fire!"

The first harpoon missed. The Dragon ripped off the stable roof with a loud cracking of wood. The horses squealed and kicked their stalls.

Rendeius dove again. The Dwarfs' second harpoon grazed the Dragon's chest. Roaring, he dropped the roof on the ballista, which wobbled but remained upright. Then he dove at the horses.

"Wild-Eyes." Thorne couldn't stand losing another horse. She snagged a metal chamber pot, climbed onto the stone banister and beat the pot against the rock wall. "Get away!"

"Come down!" Zarra urged.

In two wing flaps, the Dragon snatched up Thorne. Zarra grabbed for the rope dangling from Thorne's waist but missed.

As Rendeius folded his legs, the claw holding Thorne tightened. Those tips, white from sharpening, could eviscerate her in an instant. She struggled for breath, unsure her Dragon leathers would shield her.

When the Dragon rose higher, she hugged his leg. His red scales were smooth bumps against her cheek. Strumgued shouted something she couldn't hear. Beside him, amid the rubble, the ballista stood ready with a third harpoon.

"Shoot!" Thorne shouted. Strumgued shook his head. Didn't he know she was dead already?

Rendeius circled the bailey as if considering his next assault. The soldier farmers and Dragon Guards brandished spears. Zarra shot arrows from the balcony, but they didn't penetrate Rendeius's hide.

From the south came a roar—Vainglorian the Red.

Bellowing, Rendeius winged toward him. They met over the river, where they circled each other. Thorne's mouth went dry. A Dragon battle would surely kill her. She tied the loose end of the rope around Rendeius's leg so if he opened his claw, she wouldn't fall.

In the bailey, Willow-Bender pounded her drums. If the Giantess hoped to confuse Rendeius, he didn't seem to notice.

Maybe Willow-Bender hoped to give Stonevar's defenders the courage to withstand a double Dragon assault.

The Terrible snapped at Vainglorian's throat, forcing the older Dragon back. Rendeius bared his claws, dropping Thorne, leaving her dangling from the rope.

Vainglorian chomped his opponent's tail. Rendeius twisted to claw Vainglorian, slamming Thorne against the other Dragon. Her leathers didn't prevent bruising. Unable to avoid crashing into one Dragon or the other, she raised her feet, but could brace herself less than half the time.

When the Dragons separated, she twirled in the air until Rendeius retracted his leg. Aching from the beating, she climbed over his toes onto his foreleg. She retied the rope higher, focusing on surviving from one moment to the next.

Balancing on Rendeius's lower leg, halfway between the firmament and earth, she should be terrified, but without hope of surviving, the thrill of flying banished fear. Rendeius's pungent male odor intoxicated her. When he dove for Vainglorian, her heart swelled with a dragonish desire to fight.

Rendeius, the sleeker of the two, bit Vainglorian behind his head. Thorne nestled tight against Rendeius. Vainglorian screeched as he folded his wings, spearing lower before catching an air current that sent him soaring above them.

Suddenly, Rendeius plummeted, howling, and twisting. Evidently, the older Dragon rode his back. Thorne clung to the rope as the ground rushed toward her. Before they crashed, Rendeius threw Vainglorian off, regaining altitude, shrieking blood lust.

As Vainglorian struggled to right himself, his breathing roughened. Clearly, he tired. Rendeius flew at Vainglorian and savaged the heavier Dragon's wing with his rear claws. Vainglorian tipped sideways. Rendeius gripped Vainglorian's torn skin, tearing it from the bone as Vainglorian plummeted.

Thorne fumbled at the rope, desperate to free herself before the Dragons hit ground. She yanked the dagger from her boot but cutting the thick rope in time was impossible.

Vainglorian crashed on his side, uprooting the young fruit trees by the river. As Rendeius touched down, Thorne worked her knife tip under the heavy knot and jumped. The hard landing dropped her to her knees, but she pushed off and dashed for Stonevar.

Raspberry-Frost landed on Thorne's shoulder. "Help Vainglorian."

Thorne looked back. The Terrible clawed dirt as he circled Vainglorian, watching for an opening. Vainglorian bared his teeth and roared, inviting Rendeius's approach.

Thorne stumbled over tangled grasses. "Why?"

"He came to stop Rendeius."

Stonevar was close now. The Dwarfs rolled the creaking ballista from the bailey. Stopping Rendeius wouldn't be enough reason for Strumgued. Wasn't enough for her either, but she trusted her Fairy.

Thorne waved arms and shouted, "Shoot Rendeius."

Strumgued released the bolt. The harpoon nicked Rendeius's bony crown. The Dwarfs cheered.

The Terrible dove and grasped the giant crossbow with his rear claws. Everyone scattered as the ballista crashed on its side. Rendeius roared and returned to Vainglorian.

On the ground, Vainglorian flapped his useless wing, spattering Dragon blood. His bellowing weakened, as if he'd given up. Would he let Rendeius kill him without a fight?

"Fetch me fire!" Thorne shouted at the crowd gathering outside the bailey, and Edz did.

Rendeius dove, claws open, teeth bared. Thorne dashed to Vainglorian's head and threw the torch as high as she could.

When Vainglorian roared, his breath exploded. The fiery stream engulfed Rendeius's head. The air filled with the stink of scorched flesh. The Terrible screeched and back-flapped. Burnt skin curled around his eyes and inside his mouth, exposing the pink flesh underneath.

The older Dragon grabbed the tip of Rendeius's tail and jerked the Terrible back to earth. Rendeius flailed blindly, snapping his burnt and bloody jaws. His wild twisting severed his tail tip. He leapt skyward, spraying blood, and landed by the top of the waterfall.

Thorne rushed to the Dwarfs, who had righted the ballista and aimed it at Vainglorian. The Red had crawled to the river. He looked as helpless as a Dragon the size of ten workhorses could.

"Stop," Thorne called.

Strumgued dashed to her, face flushed, breathing hard. "You hurt?"

She shook her head. His Dragon-Fating jolted her.

"I will kill this Dragon." Strumgued motioned for his Dwarf warriors to ready the harpoon.

"Vainglorian saved us from Rendeius," Thorne said hoarsely, catching her breath.

The Dwarfs turned a crank, ratcheting the harpoon back.

"Happenstance."

Raspberry-Frost landed on Thorne's shoulder. "Rendeius is blind. His mouth burned."

"Good," Strumgued said. "The wyrm will starve. So will the one by the river. Best kill it now."

"Please. We can help him."

"Is your brain addled?" Strumgued released her arm.

Thorne curled her fingers to resist touching him. "Vainglorian won't harm me or the Dragon Guards," she said, but wasn't so sure. A wounded Dragon might not respect the laws protecting those with Dragon-Fating. "Vainglorian didn't harm Emera when she pulled arrows from his nose. He trusts her." And Emera was the Herald, whatever that meant to Dragons.

Strumgued braced fists on hips. "A Wanderer and Dragon conspiring. Splendid." He rolled his eyes. "I'll feel safer henceforth."

She was unaccustomed to his sarcasm. "Please, my Lord."

"Must every day hold some struggle between us?"

"Trust me."

His face reddened, as if a battle raged within.

Did her choice of words compel him to grant her request? She bit her lip, not daring to ask.

His eyes glazed. "Do not make me a widower again."

#

Vainglorian bared his teeth but didn't raise his head. In the moments Thorne had taken to fetch Emera and Fehera, the Dragon appeared to have lost all will to resist. But that didn't mean he wouldn't kill them.

"Fehera will heal you," Emera told him.

While Emera chanted to soothe Vainglorian, Fehera cleaned the massive wound with honey water, then stitched his ripped wing and covered her handiwork with plasters of winterbloom tincture and aloe.

"Tell him he mustn't fly until it heals."

"How long?" Emera asked.

"At least a week."

Vainglorian rumbled and Raspberry-Frost translated, "The Skylord doesn't like that."

"No one does."

"Tell him we'll feed him." Thorne still didn't know why Raspberry-Frost wanted them to save Vainglorian. Maybe because any other Dragon would be a worse neighbor.

"Skylord objects to sleeping outside," Raspberry-Frost translated.

"We'll guard him." Reflexively, Thorne clasped Dracodurus.

The Red rumbled laughter.

"Humans amuse," Raspberry-Frost said.

"So it appears." Thorne gazed at the top of the Ventamar Falls. "Is Rendeius still up there?"

"Flown to Tallasha."

Evidently not even a severe burn cooled Dragon ardor. "He's blind."

"One eye sees."

Being half blind wouldn't improve his disposition. Someday, Thorne's gut told her, she'd encounter Rendeius the Terrible again.

CHAPTER SIXTY-NINE

An explosion overhead made Thorne snap her head back. Hellee whimpered. After three days, the Dwarfs had cleared rock from only a single light source in the ceiling, leaving the cavern dim. Thorne doubted they'd clear the main entrance before winter. Even so, she hoped they'd finished blasting for the day. She had something to ask Zarra.

"Will you be Hellee's Second Mother?"

Zarra, cross-legged on Hellee's cavern floor, raised an eyebrow before throwing the ivory dice. Hellee's cave was empty of furniture since he'd chewed up the tables and chairs teething. That left only reed mats to sit on.

The thief smiled. "Nine. I win."

Thorne picked up the dice. Why didn't Zarra answer? "You're uncommonly lucky today."

"Most days since I met you."

The hammering above resumed. Hellee picked up his oversized wooden dice with his tongue and tossed them.

"Two sixes," Thorne said. No surprise since that's all he rolled. He'd gnawed on the sides so sixes always came up.

Zarra grinned. "Impossible to teach a Dragon to play an honest game of hazards."

"Maybe we shouldn't. Rustofona says he won't become a proper Dragon."

"Seems dimwitted caring what a dead Dragon thinks." Zarra rubbed Hellee's yellow snout.

Thorne rolled Dogs, two ones. "We must teach him to protect himself from other Dragons."

328

Zarra growled at Hellee. "You must be vicious."

He huffed a laugh. Zarra crinkled her long nose at his breath, which smelled like rotten eggs.

"We must teach him empathy."

"Bekka's got that aplenty." Zarra added coppers to the pot and tossed a five.

"Someday he must join Dragon society in the Continuum." A day Thorne dreaded.

"Emera can take him," Zarra said resentfully. "She gets along with everyone."

Hellee rolled another pair of sixes and squealed happily while wagging his tail.

"Strumgued doesn't like Emera. Seems he disdains Wanderers."

"Dwarfs only like other Dwarfs." Zarra threw until another five came up. "I am lucky today."

"Dragons don't even like other Dragons. But Hellee must learn to tolerate everyone."

"You don't want much."

A boom shook the cavern, sending Hellee into Zarra's lap.

"Ow! Your claws." Zarra pushed him off. "You've ripped my trousers. I'm bleeding."

Hellee whimpered an apology. Zarra patted between his eyes. "Only a scratch."

Thorne inspected Hellee's claws. "We should cut them."

Zarra fetched a toolbox from the tunnel and dumped the contents on the floor. "A Dwarf left it behind."

Thorne hoped Zarra hadn't stolen it.

Zarra searched through the tools. "Ask Fehera to be Second Mother. I got enough problems."

"What problems?"

"Don't want to bother you." Zarra held up a two-handed cutter.

Thorne took a guess. "Does becoming more dragonish alarm you?"

Zarra shrugged.

"Then what?"

"Hold his front leg."

Hellee scampered away. Thorne followed and straddled his leg like she was shoeing a horse.

"There's this thing." Zarra contorted her mouth.

"Thing?"

Zarra clipped a talon. "When I took that new cobbler to meet Hellee, I wanted to throw him on the ground and . . . you know." She flushed.

Thorne couldn't remember seeing Zarra blush. With Thorne distracted, Hellee snatched his foot back and dashed into the hatching alcove.

"Never felt this way." Zarra lifted her shoulders, retracting her head like a turtle. "Almost wish Spangle hadn't brought him, or he was older, uglier."

"When the fire vines blooms, Dragons mate." Thorne called for Hellee, but he backed away until his tail pressed against the wall. "The cost of drinking Dragon blood."

"Lott was whistling in field today. Seems Spangle embraces her wifely duties."

"What about the other Dragon Guards?"

"Fehera sits in her herb hut burning dried fire vine leaves and sipping fire vine tea, which dulls desire. Nella and Bekka join her."

"Will you?"

"Nah. They babble about lost loves. Drills a hole in my mind. Seems to me that never loving is better than their misery. You suppose thinking about that wharf sludge, Hauk, made Willow-Bender hike up the mountain?"

"I hope not."

Zarra rubbed her thighs. "Is this gonna get worse?"

Thorne nodded. Every year, staying away from Bludwelt got harder.

"Then it's good Emera escapes to that Continuum place. She says it's deserted save for the dead. Seems to have befriended Gaspotine and Rustofona."

This surprised Thorne. She couldn't picture any good coming from Emera liking Gaspotine. While Thorne digested this, Hellee butted Zarra, demanding she rub his snout.

"Hellee loves you." Thorne grabbed the whelp's leg and held up his foot.

"He loves all his mothers. You most of all." Zarra clipped a second talon.

Hellee curled his front claw. Thorne tickled his leg to relax him, then pressed a chunk of wood under his talons to keep them accessible.

"Because of Rosamund, I cannot tend him as much."

"Bring her. Hellee loves babies. He's gentle with Aeron and Una."

"No."

Zarra glanced a question.

Heat climbed Thorne's neck. "Strumgued doesn't trust me to take her from Dyadzan."

Zarra whistled.

"You understand why I need you to become Hellee's Second Mother."

"Me?" Zarra said as if Thorne had asked for the first time. "What about Nella or Fehera or Bekka or any of the others?"

"None have your she-Dragon instincts."

Zarra's laugh had an uncomfortable undercurrent. "Meaning?"

When Thorne released Hellee's leg, he licked his foot. "You're the least sentimental."

"My heart's softer than you think."

"I never doubted. Still, only you can do this."

"Lizard crap. Nothing I do that the others can't."

"You can make him fierce but kind. Wild but warm-hearted. Unpredictable but dependable."

Zarra cocked her head. "That all?"

"Enough for this winter. We must help him become the great Dragon that destiny intends."

"Whew." Zarra wiped her forehead. "That lightens my burden."

"It may seem impossible."

"Will you take me to that Continuum place?"

"It's unnatural for Humans to go there." Thorne shivered. "Every time I struggle to get back. Wouldn't want to lose you."

Zarra jumped to her feet but not before Thorne noted her disappointment. "Time to go. Fehera's removing Vainglorian's bandages today."

Thorne must've misheard. "You want to leave Hellee alone?"

"A mother Dragon leaves her whelp when she hunts. And we should sharpen his claws, not cut them." Zarra moved through the door. "Hurry."

Apparently, Zarra had accepted; a good thing, because when the whelp stuck his head through the door and whined, Thorne would've returned. But Zarra pulled her along, though his whimpers followed them down the tunnel.

Thorne had no idea how Hellee would become Hellestorm the Great, but these next few years would either make or destroy him.

#

Across the river, Dwarf Warriors camped with two ballistae pointed at Vainglorian. Thorne hadn't tried to dissuade Strumgued, knowing it hopeless.

Bekka rocked Aeron in a cart by the bailey gate. "Who's with Hellestorm?"

Zarra chewed a straw. "He's alone."

"Oh dear. He must be quite upset." Bekka stopped rocking Aeron, who wailed an objection.

"Thorne says we should behave more like a mother Dragon."

"Oh dear. Oh dear." Bekka took a pie from a sack and gave it to Thorne. "Do you think he'll be all right?"

Thorne nodded, though remembering Hellee's whimpers still stung. "Send Aeron inside. We don't know what Vainglorian will do when Fehera removes the poultices."

Zarra, ever thoughtful of Bekka's crooked back, took the cart handle. "I'll take him." Growling like a bear, Zarra pushed.

The toddler clapped and laughed but didn't move his wings. Fehera said they were healed, but he wouldn't unfurl them. Thorne didn't know if she wanted him to. Would people accept him if he flew? She'd worry about that later. Whether Vainglorian would kill them was enough worry for one day.

While they waited for the other Dragon Guards, Thorne sent Raspberry-Frost to fetch Willow-Bender and pulled Spangle aside. "This new young man—"

"The cobbler?" Spangle gazed at Vainglorian whose chest rose then fell with a whoosh.

"Does he like Stonevar?"

"Well enough. Other than hoping he'll stay, what makes you ask?"

Glitter crept up behind them. "Zarra fancies him."

"Say nothing." Thorne glanced around, hoping Zarra hadn't returned. She hadn't. "Does he willingly take orders from you?"

"He's willing enough."

That was a relief. He'd set an example. Thorne shaded her eyes as she gazed at the mountain. No Willow-Bender. "Any other guildsmen showing interest in Stonevar?"

"Few. The Guildlord warns they won't find another position. So they must commit to us."

"What made the cobbler?"

"A woman rejected him."

Thorne forced a smile. "Must we wait for more broken hearts?"

Spangle's laugh had a sharp edge. "I'm no expert on hearts."

Glitter stared at Malwood. "A pity we cannot visit Seahaven again."

The name "Bludwelt" lingered unsaid between them. Despising him didn't discourage dragonish desire; on the contrary, the stronger the hatred, then the more powerful the lust. Knowing Bludwelt affected Glitter the same way made it worse.

Glitter's smile flashed small white teeth. "At least since Vainglorian's not eating, I don't have to shovel Dragon dung."

When all the Dragon Guards had gathered, they moved toward Vainglorian. The closer they came, the more Thorne fidgeted. To distract herself, she retied the lace securing her hair. If Vainglorian turned vicious, he'd kill them all. Thorne didn't know what might set him off. Approaching too close? The wrong noise? Why did Raspberry-Frost insist they tend him?

Thorne walked Nella behind Vainglorian, which would block her view when Emera took her position by Vainglorian's head.

"How fares Rosamund?" Nella asked.

"Better than if I nursed her." They walked around a broken peach sapling. Vainglorian's landing had destroyed half their young orchard.

"No one thinks that." Nella patted Thorne's arm.

"Strumgued does." She'd find a way to get Rosamund away from Dyadzan.

"He seems a devoted father."

"Perhaps it would be better if he was less so." Thorne pointed to where she wanted Nella to stand.

"Do you think Vainglorian will fuss when Fehera removes the poultices?"

"More likely he'll devour us." Thorne smiled, only half joking.

With Nella and others positioned around the Dragon, Thorne

escorted Emera to Vainglorian's head.

"Would you ask Raspberry-Frost about Silver-Frost?" Emera picked a path around a row of crushed cherry trees. "I fear the Fairy no longer likes me."

Thorne whistled for Raspberry-Frost. It flew over the Dragon to land on her shoulder.

"Where's Silver-Frost?" Thorne asked.

"In Nar's foul mouth," the Fairy answered.

"Dead." The Wanderling's lower lip quivered. "I'll carve Silver-Frost's initial by Brutte's."

That surprised Thorne. "Where?"

"On a stone beside the falls."

"Why?" She couldn't utter more than single words.

"When I want to play draughts with Brutte." Emera's voice caught. "I perch on the rock and trace the letter. It soothes me."

Thorne would visit Emera's rock, if she survived tending Vainglorian.

Thorne and Emera met Fehera by the Dragon's head, where his breathing came in rattles and snorts and occasional gurgles.

The Wanderling cocked her head. "He looks sad."

"A melancholy Dragon is beyond my skills." Fehera took a dull knife from her bag. "Tell him to spread his wounded wing."

Emera chanted in a monotone with intonations that came naturally. The Dragon Guards hummed a soothing Fairy tune, which they'd practiced all week with Raspberry-Frost.

After ten minutes of Emera's coaxing, Vainglorian extended his wounded wing halfway. With one eye, he watched Fehera pull off plasters. The majority of the stitches were along the top edge where Rendeius had ripped skin from bone.

Thorne, alert for movement from the Dragon, watched Fehera inspect the patched wing. "Does it appear mended?"

"Yes. The stitches mostly held. His lethargy supports healing." Fehera climbed onto the wing where she ripped off poultices. "The center's healed."

Vainglorian stayed calm until an explosion boomed from Hellee's cavern. With a startled bird-like squawk, he extended his wings, flinging Fehera to the ground with a thump. Thorne dashed over and dragged her away. Fehera's eyes were open, but she was limp.

"Say something," Thorne begged.

"Air's . . . knocked from me."

The Dragon flapped hard, flinging plasters, knocking the others on their bottoms.

"Move back!" Thorne shouted.

The Dragon Guards retreated. Wing-wind tossed their hair as Vainglorian flapped harder.

"Look." Fehera pointed. "The wing's apex. The skin's tearing loose." Holding her side, the healer rushed to the Dragon. "Emera, stop him!"

The Wanderling dashed for Vainglorian's head. "Fold your wings! Fold your wings!"

The Dragon ignored her, rising on his back legs, preparing to launch.

Willow-Bender dashed past Thorne and seized Vainglorian's foreleg. He grunted and dropped. The Giantess twisted, putting him off-balance. He thudded to the ground on his side, appearing stunned. Willow-Bender lunged across his neck. Thorne did the same.

Across the river, the Dwarfs cheered. Thorne had no doubt they would compose songs about the Giantess who wrestled a Dragon. Zarra leapt onto the long neck beside Thorne. The others followed. Weak from hunger, inactivity, and depression, Vainglorian didn't struggle.

"Keep him still, so I can re-stitch the skin."

"You will obey." Emera's tone brooked no refusal.

Raspberry-Frost translated Vainglorian's rumblings. "He will."

After Fehera finished, Thorne asked, "Where's Bekka?" No one knew. She found the hunchback near the river where Vainglorian's wing-wind had thrown her.

Thorne fell to her knees beside the small woman, who even after drinking Dragon blood hadn't attained five feet in height. Her eyes were closed, her normally radiant face pale. Thorne reached out, but unable to endure losing her friend, couldn't touch her; instead she yelled for help.

Surprisingly interested, Raspberry-Frost flew around Bekka as Fehera pressed fingertips against Bekka's throat.

Glitter knelt beside them. "Alive?"

The healer nodded. "But weak."

Thorne took a relieved breath. "She'll be all right."

"Roll her over." Fehera examined Bekka. "Her spine's broken at least twice."

"Dragon blood will help her recover." Thorne's shaking voice belied her confident words.

"I must stabilize her spine before . . ." Fehera's voice caught, "she wakes up."

Glitter's eyes widened. "You don't think she will."

Brutte warned Thorne that she'd lose soldiers, but not Bekka.

"Fetch me a board to strap her to," Fehera said. "We must stop the swelling."

"How?" Thorne's chest pinched.

"Cold."

After Fehera strapped Bekka to the board, Willow-Bender carried Bekka to the river and submerged her to the neck. Thorne sent Spangle to Hellee, then joined the Giantess. The others followed.

After a few moments, Bekka's lips turned blue.

Fehera shivered in the water. "There's no reason for all of us to suffer."

"There's every reason," Glitter said.

The next night Bekka slept inside, the other Dragon Guards on the floor beside her. Thorne fingered the quilt covering Bekka's bed, recognizing diamond shapes from Aeron's baby blanket; triangles from Fehera's colorful skirts; scalenes of black and orange Dragon hide. Bekka had sewn them in a whirligig pattern. Superstition said whirligigs had the power to make obstacles become opportunities. Thorne wasn't superstitious, but if it helped Bekka, she'd believe anything.

Before sunrise on the third day, Bekka woke. "I'm on my back." With her crooked spine, she always lay on her side. "I don't hurt."

The Dragon Guards gathered around. Thorne lingered at the foot of the bed, working for each breath. Bekka couldn't feel her back. But she was alive.

Fehera took Bekka's hand. "Can you move your toes?"

Thorne yanked the quilt from Bekka's legs. Bekka moved toes and feet. Thorne collapsed on a padded rocker. The small seat fit Bekka but cramped Thorne. Dry sobs made Thorne bury her face in a fleece blanket smelling of Bekka, sweet like spring rain. When

Thorne looked up, the others had gathered closer. She was grateful no one watched her.

"Lie still." The healer adjusted the blankets. "Your spine's injured."

"What's wrong with Thorne?" Bekka asked.

Thorne waved a hand. "I'm . . . fine." She smiled weakly. "Just need to catch my breath." She pushed herself upright, looking for something to lean on. The two tables were against the wall; one holding Fehera's herbs, the other Bekka's sewing.

"I'm hurt badly?" Bekka asked.

Fehera sniffed. "Your spine's broken. I lined up your bones as best I could."

"You straightened my back." Bekka's smile squeezed Thorne's heart.

The healer put a hand on Bekka's thigh. "Can you tighten the muscles in your legs?"

"Yes." Bekka studied Fehera's face. "You don't think I'll walk."

"My dearest friend. I was certain you'd be paralyzed. I'm happy to be wrong. Dragon blood must've strengthened your spine."

"I'm thirsty." Bekka finished a cup and said, "I don't want to be more of a burden."

Willow-Bender tapped fingers over her heart. "I will carry you."

Bekka's smile made Thorne turn away. If only they could relive these past two days.

"You are all too kind." Bekka held Willow-Bender's thumb in her small hand. "What about Vainglorian?"

Zarra opened the balcony doors and leaned over the rails. "Gone."

"Strumgued will be pleased," Thorne said, delighted as well.

Raspberry-Frost flew past Zarra to Thorne. "My Queen will exult for Little Mother."

Thorne didn't understand. "What does the Fairy Queen know of Bekka?"

Raspberry-Frost winged for the balcony.

"Shut the doors!" Thorne shouted and Zarra did. "Block the fireplace!" Glitter flung a blanket over the opening.

The Fairy circled above Bekka's bed. "Free me."

Thorne moved between Raspberry-Frost and the balcony. For once, Raspberry-Frost was going to answer her questions. "Tell me."

337

"Queen views hereafter," Raspberry-Frost said.

Thorne's stomach cramped. She should've known. "Come with me."

The Fairy followed Thorne into her sleeping room.

"Did the Queen foresee Vainglorian hurting Bekka?"

"Little Mother will heal straight."

"Is the Fairy Queen certain?"

"Nothing is certain." Raspberry-Frost yanked Thorne's hair.

"Ow. Why did the Queen want to help Bekka?"

"Little Mother makes raspberry tart for Fae."

Thorne collapsed on a chair. Even the simplest action had unexpected ramifications with Fairies. She looked on the table where she'd put the jar containing Brutte's ashes. He'd be laughing now, shaking his finger, saying, "I told you so." Like Strumgued, he didn't trust Fairies.

And usually her Fairy ignored questions. Did Raspberry-Frost answer because Thorne asked the right questions or because the Fairy Queen wanted Thorne to know? "Did you lead me to Gaspotine's lair because eating his eye let the Fairy Queen enter the Continuum?"

"My Human wanted to live like a Dragon."

Thorne remembered. In Gaspotine's lair, she'd drunk Dragon blood as her Fairy demanded—a leap from a mountaintop, knowing she couldn't fly, uncertain she'd find ground beneath her. After Gaspotine died, Thorne gave his eye to the Fairies. It seemed little enough reward at the time, but now seemed huge.

Realization struck. "While I labored to deliver Rosamund, did the Fairy Queen foresee my death?" Thorne thought Mother had comforted her. But that couldn't be, since Mother had perished. Clearly, the Queen had disguised herself. In the mirror, Thorne had seen a Fairy's reflection. "Did the Fairy Queen's kiss make me appear dead to provoke Strumgued? Did the Queen know he would save me and Rosamund?"

"From death's abyss, Fae heard my Human call." Raspberry-Frost wrapped one of Thorne's white hairs around its arm, then unwound it. "My Human companions Dragon, Dwarf, and Giant. But only with Fae is my Human truly alliant."

"I'm grateful." She'd be dead many times over if they were enemies. Since Fairies commonly allied only with Dragons, Thorne considered herself complimented.

"Fairy Queen says Hellestorm the Great must live." Using its teeth, Raspberry-Frost cut a lock of Thorne's hair.

"What will Hellestorm do?"

Raspberry-Frost braided Thorne's cut tresses. "He will calm. He will conjoin. He will confound. He will cleave."

"You've said that before. But I don't know what you mean."

The Fairy tied the braid around its arm, which was the size of a tulip-stem.

A Fairy's friendship was complicated. Thorne didn't know whether to be grateful or terrified. "What else did the Queen say?"

Raspberry-Frost rubbed her cheek against Thorne's. "When Hellestorm meets Rendeius once more, only one Dragon will rise and roar."

CHAPTER SEVENTY

Raising Hellestorm the Great into an adult powerful enough to defeat Rendeius the Terrible would require all Thorne's strength. Mourning those she'd lost year after year enfeebled her. Each death—Brutte's, Lily's, Mother's, Daisy's—hollowed her heart, like burrowing shipworms weaken a hull. She must let the dead go.

She took the jar containing Brutte's ashes from the table in her room. "Help me find Emera's rock," Thorne told Raspberry-Frost.

Though the sun had only recently risen, the soldier-farmers were already in the orchard replanting fruit trees. Thorne waved as she passed, following a narrow path over a rise, then descending to the boulders beside the river. The closer the waterfall the heavier her step. She didn't know how to stop mourning those she loved.

Beside the river, Raspberry-Frost perched on a waist-high boulder, smoothed by rushing water. A crude "B" the size of Thorne's hand was carved into the stone. She set the jar atop the boulder then leaned against it, distrusting her shaking legs.

She stroked Brutte's knife strapped to her thigh. He'd warned, "Those who rush at life die young."

He knew better than to attack a Dwarf Lord. If he'd waited, let Strumgued see he was maimed, the Dwarf wouldn't have killed him. Strumgued and his warriors would have refused to fight a crippled foe. Brutte could've held off a Dwarf army. Did Brutte want to die?

She slapped the stone. "How dare you forsake me when I need you?"

Once Brutte advised, "When you cannot find an answer, turn over the hourglass of your mind, so the sand falls the other way."

She'd turned her mind over so many times she didn't know who she was or what she wanted. Though she tried to hold onto it, her anger drained away. Thorne picked up a stick and hollowed a deep cavity by the rock, away from the sandy beach, and set the jar inside.

Brutte had told her, "Bury my ashes deep, like warriors of long ago. Then tread boldly on my grave, so I feel your footfalls from below."

After refilling the hole, she stomped the dirt and marched until her legs ached before collapsing on top.

Raspberry-Frost snagged a cricket from the grass, bit off its head, and offered it to Thorne.

"No thank you. Maybe later."

With crackling bites, Raspberry-Frost devoured the insect. "My Human mistrusts death."

"A war rages within me day and night. I cannot let go of the dead."

"My Human fights the wind." Raspberry-Frost brushed bug remains from its furry chest.

Thorne held her knees and rocked. "I live behind a wall that no one sees."

"Do the dead dwell within or without?"

She stopped rocking. "What do you mean?"

"Walls neither safeguard nor hinder the dead." With a needle-sharp talon Raspberry-Frost traced Thorne's chin scar.

"The wall protects me." But carrying the weight burdened every moment of every day.

"Free those without breath so my Human can rest."

"I want to, but I'm afraid." Thorne had never said that out loud.

"Be free."

"Not so simple. The wall keeps away memories." Baby Daisy gazing trustingly at Rose. Mother pinning her wedding dress. Linking arms with Lily. Brutte laughing at her sword missing a tree branch.

Raspberry-Frost clawed Thorne's scarred chin.

"Ow." The memories stopped, and numbness set in. She let the wall crumble. It wasn't very strong, had done little to protect her. Nothing could. She must let the pain heal like any wound. "Why must people die?"

"Life is death."

"What does that mean?" Exhausted, she leaned against the boulder.

"Do the possible. Defer the impossible."

Thinking hurt. "I wanted the Dwarfs gone."

"Then fight."

"But Strumgued protects Stonevar. He stops Bludwelt from claiming me. He may disapprove, but he lets me do as I wish."

"Then accept."

"He made a bigger bed for me, but I won't sleep in the Dwarf stronghold. And he hasn't visited my room since I delivered Rosamund."

Raspberry-Frost cocked its head as if puzzled.

"I doubt it's from consideration."

With one eye closed, Raspberry-Frost inspected Thorne, offering no advice. With a finger, Thorne traced the "B" carved into the boulder, doubting even Brutte would offer guidance about her husband.

CHAPTER SEVENTY-ONE

Thorne hadn't seen Strumgued for a fortnight. Pride prevented her from inquiring about his whereabouts, but she used Rosamund as an excuse to sleep in his bed.

Strumgued, carrying a torch, opened his chamber door and grunted when he saw her. She raised the collar of her nightgown, hiding the scar from Bludwelt's sword.

The wet nurse nodded at Strumgued but continued feeding Rosamund.

From a wooden chest, he took a rectangular bundle. "I obtained this before Rosamund was born. It's of no use to me."

Thorne opened the heavy package and removed the parchment wrapping. A book. Tiny cracks, evidence of age, covered the ox-blood-colored leather binding. Etched on the cover was a rearing Dragon, claws bared, wings extended.

After reading the title page, she frowned. "Do you know what this book is about?"

"I cannot read Human writing."

"It's the story of a soldier who slays a Dragon to rescue a princess. They fall in love and marry."

Strumgued laughed.

"Thank you." She glanced at the chests containing the gifts Zarra had discovered. Why didn't he give those to her?

"I've something to show you. Will you accompany me?" This was not a request, though his voice was soft.

Thorne dressed, buckled on her sword, and slipped Fervid, the knife carved from Rustofona's rib, into her belt. Though Strumgued smiled, his eyes rebuked her for doubting his protection.

Carrying the torch, he exited through the threshold into the mountain. Thorne followed without asking their destination, sensing something momentous. The tunnel narrowed as they went deeper. The air dampened. Stone and ore scented the passageway. Strumgued said nothing until they reached a large chamber where a milky white substance coated everything. Cinched columns of various thicknesses intermingled with cones on the floor and ceiling. Someday these would meet to form columns.

Sounds of water dripping echoed in the moist, chalk-scented air. A blind albino lizard scuttled through white powder, leaving behind a wavy trail.

Strumgued slid the torch into a hollow in the wall before moving through the forest of white pillars. The alabaster walls faded into shadow, and Thorne couldn't judge the cavern's size. She passed a pillar and stifled a cry. Imprisoned in the stone column, the sightless eyes of a Dwarf stared back. White droplets trickled down his cheeks.

She hurried after Strumgued. Less than half the pillars contained faces and only a few complete figures, many with blurred features. Her husband stopped by a pool filled with what looked like thick cream. Drops fell from the ceiling, plopping on the surface, making ripples.

The closest pillar supported a half-done statue taller than the others. Wind-blown hair flowed around its lustrous ivory face. The figure's arm extended upward, holding a sword with the markings of Dracodurus. When she moved to touch it, Strumgued captured her hand.

"Who has done this?" she asked.

He bowed. "I carved this for my esteemed wife."

The air wheezed from her chest. Much of her upper body was revealed, but one shoulder and arm lay imprisoned inside stone. "The rock seems alive."

"This is an enchanted place."

He surprised her. She'd never thought pragmatic Strumgued prized anything imperceptible. "It appears white blood created these pillars. What do you call this rock?"

"Dripstone. Over time the statue will blur and must be refined. Only the most devoted carvers attempt them."

"Lovely."

Deep furrows cut his forehead. "For a time, you addled my

head."

Thorne's chest prickled, sensing a storm. "I prefer you addled."

He didn't smile. "I seized a Dragon's tail when I wed you. Now I must let go."

"Aren't you afraid of being eaten?" She hoped for laughter.

Instead, he scratched along his heavy jaw. "I blundered. Cayeseed died. Rosamund nearly so. Insisting we marry is the source of my misfortune."

A misfortune—for him? Before she thought of a scathing reply, he said, "I was wrong to force our alliance."

"You were wrong to force me to marry you, but the alliance has been profitable." And marriage had proved less monstrous than she feared.

"We cannot build a union upon a grave."

She didn't want to hear this. "What do you call this place?"

"The Cavern of Memories."

Intriguing. A few sculptures had fresh chip marks. "Are any others memorialized in rock still alive?"

He rummaged through a collection of chisels on a bench. "No. All are dead."

That seemed ominous. Did Strumgued consider her dead? "When did you begin?"

"What matter?" He selected a tool with a pointed tip.

Her mouth was dry as a salt lick. "Tell me."

"When you traveled to Seahaven without sending me word!" He quieted his voice. "I knew we'd never share an understanding." He rejected a slim adze for one with a heavier tip.

"I went to fetch Glitter." When he didn't respond, she asked, "Do you think I wanted to go?"

He stepped onto a box. After positioning the chisel where her statue's shoulder would be, he tapped with a hammer. A white chip clattered against the floor. "I know you hunger for him."

Heat climbed her neck. The last person she wanted to be near was Bludwelt. "My nature thrusts it upon me."

"What nature is that?" He tapped the chisel again and a section of dripstone banged the floor. He ran a thumb over the newly exposed curve.

"You once said we each have our secrets." She adjusted the gown's collar over her scar.

"Would yours be dragonish?"

"You discern too much." But she didn't mind him knowing, which surprised her.

"Some cannot accept the yoke of marriage. I am less welcome in your chamber than a winter wind. When you left for Seahaven, I saw that you had no respect for our union. When you confronted that giant snake, I knew you had no concern for our unborn."

"Accept my regrets."

"When you rejected Rosamund, I realized my mistake."

"I'm sorry."

He shook his head. "You have no trust in me."

"Nor you in me."

He set his jaw in that way she hated.

"I rejoiced in you, but you cannot reciprocate. I will dissolve our union if you agree."

She should be pleased, but his words chilled like a plunge in an icy lake. "I want title to Stonevar."

"I will cede it."

"I won't separate from Rosamund."

Strumgued crossed his arms. "Visit when you please. You needn't see me."

His past absences had troubled her more than she admitted. "For Rosamund's sake, I wouldn't mind seeing you now and then."

"Unnecessary." Behind him, the shadows lengthened against the white stone.

She had what she wanted—the upper hand. Yet nights alone held no appeal. When he slept beside her, he banished aloneness. Even his courtship no longer irritated. She twisted the wedding ring around her finger. Ending her marriage made her vulnerable to Bludwelt.

"You cannot rewrite the past." Thorne spoke louder than intended. "I fulfill my martial obligations, almost die birthing your child, then you discard me!" She drew Fervid and pressed it against his throat. Strumgued's eyes widened, but he didn't flinch. "You deceived me."

"I offer you freedom."

"Honor forsakes you. You force me to marry, then renege."

"I bestow what you desire. Dwarf custom requires both agree to divorce."

Thorne pressed the knife into his flesh. A drop of blood, with a rusty iron aroma, trickled down his neck. "That curly red-haired wench. You want someone like her, an obedient wife. Someone to fawn at your feet and fetch your ale."

Strumgued's mouth twisted. "No one accuses a Dwarf wife of submission."

She caught a drop of his blood and licked her finger, savoring the metallic taste. "You offered me your faithless heart if you betrayed or deceived me."

Strumgued's chest heaved as if he'd fought a great battle. "I will force myself upon you no longer."

"So you betray me instead."

His eyes narrowed. "Surely, you mock me."

"Surely, you must kiss my sword and swear allegiance to me, or bare your breast so I can cut out your disloyal heart."

He lifted an arm and lowered it, appearing at a loss, then stepped down from the box. With the back of his thick hand, he rubbed his mouth. "Present your sword."

She drew Dracodurus. Strumgued pressed his thick lips to the hilt.

With a snap, Thorne sheathed her sword. "As long as you don't interfere with me, we'll get along well enough."

His eyes glistened. "You mystify me."

"That's as it should be." As quick as a snake strike, she hooked her leg around his and dropped him to one knee.

He stared up in surprise. She placed her fist over her heart then extended her arm, saluting him.

Strumgued looked up at her. "You confound me."

After assisting him to his feet, she cut his palm and hers, and pressed them together. Ruby drops stained the white dust.

She felt a prickle as their blood mingled. "Say the words."

"You are blood of my blood." Strumgued tongued her bloody palm.

She licked his. "And you are blood of my blood."

He pressed her hand over his heart.

"I once believed that marriage would belittle me," Thorne said. "That I would become less, but I have become more."

Moisture filled Strumgued's eyes, and he squeezed them shut. "Your Fairy calls you 'My Human.'"

"Now you are my Dwarf."

A soft rumble started in the back of Strumgued's throat, building until his deep laughter reverberated through the Cavern of Memories. "You welcome the harness?"

"Your bullish shoulders, my Lord husband, will carry the bulk of the yoke."

CHAPTER SEVENTY-TWO

Bludwelt's pride took longer to heal than the side of his head where Thorne had struck him. At least no one in Seahaven laughed to his face or knew Thorne was pregnant when she bested him. By now she must've delivered the Dwarf's spawn. With that comforting thought, he crawled beneath silky bed sheets in the Magister's house. A hearth fire dispelled the autumn chill.

Hours later, unable to sleep, he'd relived every moment he'd spent with Thorne, dwelling longest on those in the Continuum. In the Silver River, he'd glimpsed his future, but hadn't understood its significance until now. He must protect himself.

Bludwelt jumped from the bed and sent Fexx for his clerk.

When the clerk arrived, Bludwelt told him what to write. The aged man quickly blanked his wrinkled face, but not before Bludwelt noticed. The clerk seemed anxious to leave. Bludwelt knew that by tomorrow, he'd tell anyone who'd listen. Even if he kept quiet, Bludwelt couldn't let anyone live with this knowledge.

The gnarl-knuckled clerk dusted the paper with fine sand to dry the ink. "Anything else, Magister?"

"Not now. Fexx will escort you home." Then Fexx would smother him.

After Fexx left with the clerk, Bludwelt examined the document. For all he knew, he could be holding it upside-down. His ignorance made him curse.

In the Silver River, he'd heard himself tell the clerk, "Dragon blood is not poison. Dragon blood heals the sick." No Dragon would survive after this became known.

He sealed the document in a chest to be opened upon his death.

349

While he lived, Dragon-kind would survive.

#

Under a waning moon, a thermal lifted Solanie the Resolute off the mountain. As it carried her higher, she circled before gliding downward, seeking another to carry her toward the coast. She opened her mouth, letting a breeze tickle her tongue.

Her journey took six days. To conserve her strength, she didn't hurry, taking time to rest and hunt. On a snowy peak by the seacoast, she slept. A shift in the wind woke her. As Gaspotine predicted, a wyrwind blew toward the ocean. She gulped down a half-eaten giant deer before leaping skyward into a moonless sky. She'd join Hellestorm on Elysia or die.

#

After Strumgued kissed her sword, Thorne couldn't sleep. Something was wrong. She walked by the river, breathing autumn crisp air. Lizards fled from her, leaving behind wavy lines in the sand visible to her dragonish eyes in the starlight.

When she reached Emera's rock, she placed her palms against it. "Brutte, I hope you approve of what I've done. Good rest."

Returning to the castle, she sensed disaster. She intended to check Magda first, but in the bailey, Glitter and Spangle exited their pink wagon, where they'd lived before Stonevar.

Glitter smiled. "We were going to find you. We have something to tell you."

"No need." Thorne didn't need to know the twins' secrets. She had plenty of her own and no time now.

"Come in." Spangle's eyes were sunken as if she needed sleep.

Thorne intuited she needed to listen. The wagon smelled like frankincense. Pale blue, pink, and purple silk covered the walls. The twins had taken most of their fragile furniture inside the castle, but there remained two narrow beds covered with tasseled quilts and brocade pillows. Glitter leaned against the cushions and patted the bed. Thorne shook her head.

Spangle cleared the other bed, raised the top, and removed a chest. "Gold we saved."

"You need it," Glitter told Thorne. "Now that Strumgued's

taken Rustofona's treasure."

Thorne shook her head. The twins had endured the unthinkable to secure their future. "Thank you, but I don't want it. I hope I never will." She avoided hardship by charging Strumgued inflated prices for their goods.

Thorne hugged them both. The feeling that something was wrong grew stronger. "I must check on Magda and Bekka."

Inside the castle, Magda slept peacefully. Thorne moved upstairs to Fehera and Bekka's sleeping room. Bekka's quilting frame stood in one corner beside Fehera's bags of dried herbs, which scented the room with lavender, sage and basil. Tonight the healer guarded Hellee. Was Thorne's unease for the whelp?

Still bedridden, Bekka motioned for Thorne to approach. "I feel better. Fehera says I can try walking tomorrow." She gazed at Aeron sleeping beside her. "Aeron stays close. I don't know if he's worried about me or afraid."

Until the hawk snatched him, he'd been a fearless toddler. Thorne kissed his pale forehead. "Raspberry-Frost says Aeron attracts birds. The wind binds them."

"What does that mean?" Bekka asked.

"The wole-hawk didn't intend to eat him. Still, until he's too big to lift, we should keep watch." She bade Bekka good night with a hand squeeze.

At the farthermost occupied room, she listened to Willow-Bender's snores. Thorne wouldn't risk another Giant Rampage even if that meant Stonevar never had a ship. Thorne pressed her cheek against the door. Willow-Bender had shared this room with Lily. Thorne whispered, "Good night, Lily."

Everything seemed fine, but she still felt as if something worse than a Giant Rampage threatened Stonevar.

She paused outside Nella and Emera's room and heard normal breathing. Last she pressed her ear against Zarra's door. No sound. Where had the thief gone?

"What you listening for?" Zarra stood behind her.

Thorne jumped. "Where were you?"

"Smelling the cobbler."

Thorne smothered a laugh. "What does he smell like?"

"Like leather and shoe black. Last night, I dreamt Dwarf cobblers chased me with tiny shoe hammers."

Thorne's smile slipped. "I'm feeling unsettled. Would you help Fehera guard Hellee?"

Zarra nodded.

When Thorne finally joined Strumgued, Rosamund slept in her cradle, and her husband snored softly. She found nothing amiss, but that didn't get rid of her sense that something threatened. She closed her eyes but took a long time to fall asleep.

Raspberry-Frost nipped Thorne's ear. "Wake, my Human."

Thorne jolted awake. She'd dreamt again of a man with white hair riding over Stonevar plain, a forewarning that someday Lord Bludwelt would rule Elysia. Was this dream connected with what troubled her?

The Fairy tugged Thorne's hair. In the moonless night, the room was dark, Raspberry-Frost a blurry glow on her pillow.

"What's wrong?"

"Solanie the Resolute comes."

Thorne's hand sought Strumgued's.

ABOUT THE AUTHOR

D. L. BURNETT grew up wanting to write books like those that made her fall in love with reading. She wrote this book from a love of Dragons, Fairies, and women who strive to control their own destinies. She hopes you enjoyed reading it. Currently, she's working on Book 3: FAIRY VERSUS DRAGON. She lives in Wisconsin with her family.

www.DLBurnett.com

www.ingramcontent.com/pod-product-compliance
Lightning Source LLC
Chambersburg PA
CBHW031426240626
47154CB00001B/217